110672300

37653001125288
Main Fiction: 1st floor
FIC GASKIN
Fiona

✓ III 4/95 – 8/95   28.7

CENTRAL ARKANSAS LIBRARY SYSTEM
MAIN LIBRARY
700 LOUISIANA
LITTLE ROCK, ARKANSAS 72201

FIONA

Books by Catherine Gaskin

FIONA

EDGE OF GLASS

THE FILE ON DEVLIN

THE TILSIT INHERITANCE

I KNOW MY LOVE

CORPORATION WIFE

BLAKE'S REACH

SARA DANE

DAUGHTER OF THE HOUSE

ALL ELSE IS FOLLY

DUST IN SUNLIGHT

WITH EVERY YEAR

THIS OTHER EDEN

FIONA

BY CATHERINE GASKIN

Doubleday & Company, Inc.

Garden City, New York

1970

Library of Congress Catalog Card Number 69–15173
Copyright © 1970 by Catherine Gaskin Cornberg
All Rights Reserved
Printed in the United States of America
First Edition

This book is for Sol,
who gave me the place for it

FIONA

Prologue

The Scots call it "the sight"; some think of it as a curse, to others it seems a kind of gift of grace. I have it, and in my own heart I hold it a curse—undeserved, perhaps, but there, like a birthmark, or a twisted body.

From the time I first knew of it, when I was nineteen, until now, at twenty-three, it has cost me my peace of mind, and three positions as a governess—positions hard to come by for the daughter of an impoverished Scottish clergyman. So that was why I tramped the hills above my father's little parish of Silkirk on the Ayrshire coast above Ballantrae in the late spring of 1833, unemployed, impelled by a restless energy, wondering what was to become of me, and what other crisis this unwanted gift of fate would bring to me.

I thought about it often now as I sat among the heather to rest on these long walks, watching the grey sea that swept down the North Channel from the Atlantic, past the top of Ireland and the Mull of Kintyre, watching the ebb of the tide and the shining miles of strand exposed, and then its slow return to the inlet of Silkirk. I kept telling myself that there would be a return from the ebb for me also. This could not be the end, here at Silkirk, with the journey hardly begun.

From the first two positions I had left with excellent references and there had been no problem about a new position—just a matter of answering advertisements and waiting. That was because the ability to see into the future was an uncertain thing, not to be called up at will, not to be conjured up for one's own good or gain—it was just a flash of a coming event, and a warning, with no reason behind it. It had not then brought me into trouble.

I had been governess to a small boy when the first sight had come —and it could, charitably, have been dismissed as sharp hearing, or a kind of animal instinct of things not being right. But it had saved a coach with my employers and their son, as well as myself, from plunging into a river from which the bridge had already been swept away by the rushing floodwaters of a cloudburst. The coachman had been pushing his team against the slashing rain, one lamp extinguished by water, racing to get home to a warm kitchen and his supper. Suddenly I had screamed for him to stop, had pounded like a madwoman against the carriage roof, striving to make him hear, and finally lowering the window and letting the rain pour in upon us all to reach around and somehow grasp his coat. We stopped in time; but the bridge had been at the other side of a sharp bend, and no one could have seen in that blackness that it was gone. They didn't believe, either, although to make it seem right, they said they did, that anyone could have heard the changed sound of the water as it crashed over the debris of the bridge. My employers were grateful to me, but they didn't talk about it, and I knew that from then on a sense of unease rested on them about me; but the coachman talked, and in the village the locals turned to look at me. There was something not quite right. I was an excellent teacher, my reference said, and good with children. But they sent their son to a preparatory school sooner than they had planned, and I think they knew a kind of relief when I was gone from their roof.

The next pupil had been a girl, Charlotte, a spoiled and pampered darling, saved by a sense of humor and a sweetness that no one, least of all myself, could resist. I was with her two years, mostly in the big house in Edinburgh, with summers spent at the family's lonely retreat among the hills and hidden lochs and islands of the far Highlands. Many of the family came to that distant summer house, cousins, in-laws, grandmothers. It was a young cousin, seventeen, called Bruce, who had got out the boat for the sail he made on their own private loch whenever the weather would permit. This day, I remember, seemed made in heaven—golden, calm, with soft clouds drifting before a barely perceptible breeze. Charlotte had waited impatiently, skipping from one foot to another, as Bruce readied that small craft moored at the dock. That was how I saw them from the windows of the drawing room. Charlotte's mother sat sewing and gossiping with Bruce's mother, her sister. I remember I suddenly cried out, "No—no, they mustn't go! Something is going to happen! There's going to be . . ." I stopped. I didn't know. I had the sight, but I saw imperfectly.

I remember also the sharpness of the tone that answered me. "Nonsense, Miss McIntyre! What can possibly happen? Bruce has been sailing all his life and on a day like this . . . They are quite safe. Calm yourself!"

But I didn't. I remember running from the room, and the slam of the front door behind me, and the rush down the slope of the path slippery with pine needles. I remember, too, with awful clarity, the raising of the sail, and the way the playful breeze took it, and the gaily painted little craft standing out from the jetty. I remember my cries and shouts, and the breeze blowing them back at me, and Charlotte's saucy wave, and the sun on her golden hair. The little waves lapped the shores, and the pines sighed above me, and it was a happy, lazy, gentle day for sailing.

It stayed that way for an hour, and stubbornly I sat on the jetty and waited until the little boat should round the bend of the island, set secret and mysterious, in the middle of the loch. I was there on the jetty when the squall came, as it does so often in the Highlands, rough rain and wind sweeping in suddenly. They found the capsized boat quite soon, but it was a week before the bodies of Charlotte and Bruce were found at distant parts along the shore.

Charlotte's mother wrote my reference, again an excellent one, but her face was turned away from me, as if she strove, in charity, not to let me see that in some way she held me responsible—as if my vision of tragedy had somehow caused it to happen. Her hands and voice were cold in parting as she said good-bye, and made herself wish me good fortune. I had brought, she seemed to say, no good fortune to that house.

From the third position I was dismissed without a reference, and, I suppose, in justice, I deserved none. I had done no wrong to the family, but I had behaved in a way that no respectable young woman ever should. But I have been compelled by that same force that had occurred on the other occasions—something so strong that I had had to act upon it. Something I could not explain, and which could not be proved. So I was back home in Silkirk, answering advertisements for GOVERNESSES WANTED, but getting no replies because that vital reference from my last employer could not be supplied. I walked, and waited, and fretted, and wondered why I had had the bad luck to be born as I was, with those terrifying flashes of the future, which threatened to destroy those they concerned, and perhaps me. Three times I had looked into the face of the future, and I hated the power of this awesome gift.

Chapter 1.

Suddenly the rain was not the fine drifting mist that had veiled the hillside all afternoon, blotting out the sweep of the higher mountains and the distant glimpse of the peak of The Merrick; now it was a torrent that came in sheets. I felt the weariness of tired limbs and wet skirts clinging about me, and the cottage was there, at hand—an almost ruinous cottage, the thatch ancient and the whitewash peeling, the little enclosed yard a pool of mud with steppingstones to the door, and a few hens crouching close to the wall for shelter. A thin smoke drifted from the chimney, and no dog barked to challenge my entry. It was a struggle to open and prop back in place the dead tree limbs that served to keep out the wandering mountain cattle. By the time I had done it, I expected the door to have opened, and the woman to be standing there. But it remained shut blankly, the rain beating against it.

It took a time too, even after my knock, for her to come, although I knew she must have watched me from the single tiny window. Finally the door opened grudgingly.

"Will you let me take shelter for a moment? I've a mile or two to walk before I'm home, and I've no thought to take a drenching." I said it confidently enough, because the tradition of hospitality among these people was as deep as their poverty. And she and I were not strangers to each other. On finer days when the cottage door had stood open and she had sat by it at her spinning, we had exchanged nods as I passed. Or rather she had returned my greeting with a long, vaguely hostile stare.

She said nothing now in return, just jerked her head to a stool before the smoky peat fire. But when I seated myself, and tried to shake a little of the wet off my cloak without spreading it about the room, she came to the fire herself and swung the black pot on its hook over the embers. Then she went back to her spinning wheel close to the window, and bent about her task again in the wan afternoon light. The rest of the room was dark, and it was cold, despite the fire. There was nothing much in it—a single table and a few stools, a row of blackened pots on the mantel, a pallet of straw on the hard-trodden earth floor, with a bundle of rags as bedcovers. I remembered that a few years ago, when I had sometimes walked this way, there had been a boy, her son, I supposed, who had tended the few sheep which provided the wool the woman spun and wove. There had been a barley patch and a few potatoes. The remains of a poor garden were still there, but there was no man about the place—it had the look of it. The boy would be grown and gone, gone to Glasgow probably in hope of work and wages, exchanging one poverty for another. The woman looked old, but she may not have been so old; need and hardship lay in every line of her face.

It was an embarrassment, then, to see her take down from the mantel a pewter caddy, and measure with careful hand, the tea into the earthenware pot. For her, tea would be an almost unthought-of luxury, something she permitted herself a few times a year.

I made a gesture of protest. "No . . . please, no . . ."

She made a clicking sound with her tongue, slightingly, as if to remind me that she knew the ways of those better off than herself. "Dinna ye be the minister's daughter?"

I nodded, shamed to think of the poverty that seemed to us to sit on the manse so heavily, and yet it was only the poverty of lacking new dresses and bonnets, and my father wanting books he could not buy. This woman seemed to put me in my place; I took the black brew in a tankard from her meekly. "Thank you, mistress."

She took no tea herself, but retreated again to the wheel, bent over it, her face turned away from me. For a time I felt uncomfortable sitting there while the silence grew thick between us. Even through the thatch I could hear the rain, and there was no excuse for going; I sipped the tea, not enjoying it, but knowing I had to drink it to the end. Hospitality had been offered, and must now be endured, no matter the cost. I only wished that her hostility had seemed less personal—more against the world than against me. But in her few glances in my direction it was me she saw, not merely someone from a more fortunate world. I waited, but still the rain came down, and there was no decent escape.

After a while though, I retreated to my own thoughts, those useless and wearisome companions of these last months; I seemed imprisoned in the black hopelessness of them, and was tired of their repetition. The questioning never yielded an answer. My father just said: "Wait— something will come." I hadn't his patience, and his belief. For me, waiting was hard.

There was a reason, more subtle and never spoken of, other than the need to unburden my father of my support, for having to leave the manse at Silkirk. I was now, at twenty-three, already regarded by some as an old maid, and I had three pretty young stepsisters coming along, the eldest, Mary, being courted by an eligible young man from Ayr. For some reason, since I had come home, the courtship hadn't been progressing very well. It wasn't to be believed, of course, that he found me more attractive than that Dresden doll, Mary. I wasn't the kind of woman that eligible young men paid much attention to—hair too red, and apt to be too wild, as was my tongue, at times. It was true I had had, until last autumn, a suitor of sorts, a rather solemn professor at Edinburgh University who wrote scholarly letters, but hadn't seemed able to make up his mind whether or not I would be a suitable wife for him. I know I was said by some to be too large, and certainly I towered over my stepmother and sisters. But my father said I had my mother's eyes, the tilt of her chin and head; that seemed for him to make up for any other deficiency. But it still was no reason for a young man like James Killian to listen to me with more attention than he gave to Mary, and to suggest that everyone should go walking on Saturdays when I said I was going alone. So now, on Saturdays when he was expected, I left the house before he arrived, and came back when he could be reckoned safely to have left. I was growing tired of my lonely meal of sandwiches eaten on the mountainside while my stepmother invented tales of my gay social life that took me elsewhere. I don't think James Killian believed those tales. Each time he asked about me, and each time more searchingly, as Flora, our all-purpose maid eagerly related to me from what she overheard. All of us knew it would be better if I could leave Silkirk, and leave James Killian to Mary.

I thought now longingly of that last position, governess to the three rough-and-tumble little sons of a Glasgow merchant. I had enjoyed it while it lasted, and the family had been good to me. It was cruel it had had to end, by my own doing, that day last autumn in Kelvingrove Gardens.

It had been such a fair day, a day suddenly given back from summer, a Sunday afternoon with the sun warm, and still there was the scent of damp, rotting leaves. The sun had brought out thousands to stroll in the gardens, for the most part a fashionable crowd, with the light striking the velvet bonnets and the tall silk hats. The man who had set up his little rough-hewn platform at the junction of several promenades didn't belong to the well-dressed crowd; his clothes were shabby and careless, his accent was working-class with the overlay of some learning upon it. I don't know how long he had been speaking to the crowd that had gathered about him when I came—there was no policeman in sight, but I supposed it was against the bylaws to hold meetings like this one in the park. But he was the kind who never would pay attention to bylaws. And what he had to say wasn't for the ears of the Glasgow tenement dwellers either, from whom he was probably sprung, and who could do nothing about his cause even if they had wanted to try, which was doubtful. His audience was here, among the prosperous who did the trading and the moneymaking, who built the ships and made the contracts. As I remember every detail of that afternoon, I remember that man's face—pale and thin, and burning fire-like with his passion.

"And will you not, my brothers, set them free? Will you not end this traffic in human misery—end this shame set upon a great nation like a running sore? Who can expect the blessing of serenity when men and women are still born into a lifetime of slavery, still branded and sold from one man to another like cattle . . ."

A speaker in a park can never expect to have it all his own way; inevitably there are the hecklers, and he knew to expect them. Men who build ships, who deal in trade of any kind, go pale at the thought of anything interfering with that trade; I think there were some there who simply cried out in anger because one of this kind had come to disturb their comfortable, well-fed Sunday afternoon.

"You are behind the times, friend. The slave trade was abolished long ago."

A pointing finger from the speaker on the platform. "*You're* behind the times! Don't you know that a pirate trade still plies from the

African shores to the Indies, with conditions worse now than ever before. And have you no pity for those who are already in bondage, born to it, condemned forever to it, the outright property of their masters, who have the power of punishment, even of life or death over them?"

"And haven't we," he was answered, "taken them from their own brothers who sold them into slavery? Taken them from the darkness of their ignorance and shown them the light of the Christian God?"

"Under the lash we have given them the Christian God. Who of them may not accept Him?"

"Don't the plantations feed and clothe them?"

"In rags, and feed them on what they can raise on the Christian Sunday in their own garden patch. *That's* how we feed and clothe them. Try it, my friend—try just one day working the cane under that sun and under a whip, and you will know what a damnation slavery is. You will rise up in your thousands and demand that Parliament pass the Emancipation Act—"

"And who will pay for it, my friend? Who will put the sugar in your tea—or shall we do without it?"

Another voice, "And who will pay the indemnities? Or shall we send our own to work the plantations?"

With horrible humor someone shouted back: "That would be a good way to get rid of a few undesirables from these shores—the over-breeding rats of the slums—"

Suddenly it seemed to involve them all, all of that once good-humored crowd that had paused to hear some madman rant on about a question that everyone knew he could not solve, and what's more, in its solution, would dig hard into the pocket of the taxpayer. The question of money had been raised against the question of the freedom of unknown, ignorant blacks. Money will always involve a Scotsman, one way or another. A dozen voices shouted at the speaker; some argued back and forth with each other. For the moment I didn't think about what was being said, slavery or not; I stared, fascinated, at that tired, strained face, a face with the look of hunger upon it, and eyes that seemed to consume him with their own fire. It seemed to sway and hover above that jostling mass of people, disembodied almost. I began to hear the rising menace in the low murmur of anger that had come to join the indignation and outrage. The sacredness of property had been questioned. The first, quick reaction seemed to be the urge to strike down the one who dared to question—except that

it was impossible that such a thing would happen on a Sunday afternoon in Kelvingrove Gardens. No, such a thing would never happen.

And yet it was then I felt it—or rather, I saw it. I saw it with the
most fearful intensity of any one thing I had yet experienced in my
whole life. This was not like the other times—this I *knew*. I saw a
crowd, I saw this man standing above them as he did now, shouting
at them with his passion-choked voice. I saw a sudden surge, and he
was pulled down. I saw blood, and the man lying still, and the blood
in pools upon the ground, the silent, terrible witness. I tell you, in
God's name, *I saw it*. And yet it did not happen. The man still stood
there, striving to make just one person among them understand and
feel what so stirred him. And what I saw was his danger—I saw his
death, and there was no power in me to stop me doing what I did
then.

I pushed my way through the people, some of them giving way
sheerly in surprise that it was a woman who thrust through them so
wildly. When I reached the little platform there was no choice about
what I must do. In a second I was up there beside him, almost pushing
him off, his surprise more than anything making him give way. All I
knew was his mortal danger, and I had to avert it.

"Listen . . ." My voice hardly reached the first rank of the crowd,
but the sight of a woman there beside him silenced some simply from
curiosity. "Listen . . . you must stop. You must stop this! Let him go;
—I say let him go his way. Or terrible things will happen . . ."

I was mad, of course. Even as I heard my own words I knew how
they must have sounded. The man didn't want me there beside him;
he didn't want any woman to fight his battles. "Miss," he said, "get
down! I thank you—but get down!" What he didn't know was that
he needed me. He hadn't seen the vision of the crowd and the blood
and his own still form. But suddenly I knew that even if he had seen
it he would not care. The man was born to die by whatever caused
him to live. And he lived now for the issue of slavery. He did not
want the presence of some hysterical woman to detract from his
martyrdom. Almost roughly he tried to push me from the platform; I
clung to his coat sleeve for a moment, unwilling. And then the focus
of the crowd changed to me. I heard the sounds of disapproval, the
words and catcalls "Shameless . . . Brazen . . ." I did this man no
good—no good at all. I was a wretched embarrassment to him, unwanted. It was then I felt the tug on my own arm.

It was a woman who touched me, a middle-aged woman whose

gentle face was puckered with disapproval. "Come down at once," she said, in a tone that was accustomed to being obeyed. "You do this unfortunate man no good—and you make a spectacle of yourself." Beside her stood a man, her husband, shaking his head, regretting that someone like me, who might have been a daughter to him, should so far forget herself, should do this inexplicably mad thing.

"You don't understand," I said. "Something terrible will happen if I don't stop it . . ."

But it was then I knew that the vision I had seen was not something that was certain to happen now; there was a time for it to happen, and a place. And if the time was not now, then there was nothing in all God's world I could do to stop it. It lay somewhere, waiting, in the future; it was in time to come. I was suddenly cold with shock and fear; I felt my body go limp, and meekly I stepped down and permitted myself to be escorted through the crowd by this unknown man and woman. The people parted before me, perhaps sensing that I was someone set apart, wanting nothing to do with my kind of madness. Afterward, I thought of the act of kindliness and courage performed by those two to take me from this place of spiritual hell. But I was not aware of it then, only of my own agony. I turned and looked once at the man on the platform; as we walked away down one of the paths toward the gates of the gardens he had begun to speak again, and once more the jeers and the heckling had begun. How did I tell him that one day he would face a crowd, and then he would lie still upon the ground in his own blood. I shook and trembled, and wished I did not have to bear the knowledge, but it was with me. I had seen it, and there was no way to wipe it out.

* * * * *

I remembered afterward that I had not thought to thank the man and woman who had delivered me back to the merchant's house. I did though, still haunted by the man in the park, manage to ask if they knew who he was. "Scobie, his name is," was the reply. "Thomas Scobie—a well-known radical. A rabble-rouser. He'll come to a bad end, I've no doubt."

I didn't have any doubt, either.

Of course it was inevitable that news of what was called my escapade should reach my employer. And of course it was embroidered until it seemed that I had stood there and harangued the crowd in a violent antislavery speech. I did not deny it; I probably was against slavery, except that it had always seemed a remote thing and beyond my power to change. What I could not do was to explain the real reason that had compelled me toward that platform; I could not bring myself to tell of the vision of destruction; better be branded wild and indecorous than as one who had that dreaded gift, "the sight." So I said nothing, and packed my bags, as asked to. There were tearful farewells with the little boys, but plainly it was unthinkable to keep me on.

I made one more effort for Thomas Scobie's sake. On the way to the inn where I would get the coach to Ayr at which place my father was to meet me with the trap, I stopped the cabbie.

"Would you know of a Thomas Scobie—a man who holds meetings—addresses crowds? He's antislavery . . ."

"I've heard the name. He's agin many things, that one."

"Would you know where he lives?"

"The Trongate, somewheres. Wouldna doubt if we went there we could ask, and find him. But it's nae place for someone like you to be going . . ."

"Go," I said. "We'll try."

We went, and I was regretting it from the moment we turned in among the warren of the tenements. The cab itself was a sensation among those high, swarming buildings, the narrow alleys between, the stench and dirt and noise. We inquired many times, and found the place where Thomas Scobie lived. "I'd go with you, miss," the driver said, "but I daren't leave the cab. There'd not be a piece of your luggage left, or even the cab itself if I trusted it to one o' these. Here, get away there, you rotten scum . . ."

I pushed through the teeming gutter urchins, shaking off their plucking hands, refusing their pleas for money. I walked up the six flights of stinking stairs to where they said Scobie lived. I knocked three times at the door that was pointed out, and there was no answer. It yielded, though, when I turned the knob.

That remembered face, white, strained, hungry, looked up from a table littered with papers; he frowned. "Dinna I tell you . . ." He stopped, and the frown grew deeper. "It's you! What the devil do *you* want? Haven't you done enough—you nearly caused a riot the other day. And no one would listen to me any more."

"I came because I couldn't leave without telling you . . ." He made a difficult audience. He just sat there, not offering me a chair, nor any encouragement. I stumbled through what I had to say; it sounded ridiculous, and at the end of it he gave a kind of snort of derision.

"You mean you came here to tell me *that*. A piece of foolishness like that!"

"I *had* to. My conscience wouldn't let me go without . . . You see, it's not the first time."

He pointed his pen at me. "Get out, woman. Do you think I've time to waste listening to this foolishness? All right—you've done your duty, and I suppose I should thank you, but you're wasting your time, *and* mine. I'll tell you, it takes no great prophet of the future to predict what will happen to me. Up and down the country men like me will die before the injustices of the people are righted. Slavery isn't the only issue that must be fought. In one place or another I *know* I'll die. Do you think the memory of Peterloo isn't in the hearts of all of us? Of course I'll die, and most likely by violence. It is something all of us know. *Now* will you leave me be . . ."

I went, and it had been a waste of time, just as he had said. He had not seen it exactly as I had, but he knew his chances, and he accepted them. Miserably I pushed my way through the children once more, and the crowd of women who had come to join them, some of them shrieking insults at the woman who visited the like of Thomas Scobie. The cabbie whipped up, and we charged through the crowd. At the public coach I had to give him an extra large tip because he complained so bitterly at the danger to his cab and horse in going into such a place. I couldn't blame him; I had only the consolation that I had done what I could. Thomas Scobie knew what was coming.

Back at Silkirk I attempted to tell only my father of what had happened. It was one of his rare failures in understanding; he turned his face from what I described as if it were a blasphemy. Only God knew the future, he said, and only the devil could have induced such madness in me. He told me to pray on it, and after that he never mentioned it. Some closeness that had been between us diminished then; my stepmother and sisters knew only that I had made a spectacle of myself, and been discharged; bewilderment and a kind of pitying worry settled on them. Clearly I had become a great liability to the family. Only my little half-brother, Duncan, the only child of my father's second marriage, the beloved pet of the household, didn't understand or care that I was in a kind of limbo. I delighted in him, played with him, taught him, and he was the only joy of those sombre days.

When I was not with Duncan, I walked the hills and chafed against the bonds of being a woman and unable to strike out for myself, at the bonds of convention and family. My father grieved for my impatience and my stepmother worried for my future—and the worry turned to hostility when James Killian, even knowing of the madness I had committed in Kelvingrove Gardens, took to speaking admiringly of me. "Shows great spirit, Miss Fiona," he kept saying. "Not many young ladies would have dared." After he said that for the third time, rather too warmly, I began to stay away from home on Saturdays.

I think I must have sighed then, as the weight of the whole thing pressed upon me too strongly. Suddenly the woman sitting by the window spoke.

"Ye've trouble for one sa young . . ."

I didn't bother to ask how she knew. The village knew everything.

"I have," I answered flatly. "Who hasn't?" I was selfish, and young, and I didn't stop to think that my troubles were trifling compared to what hers must be.

"Aye—precious few," she answered, but not rebuking me.

And then the silence fell again. It seemed that silence was the habit of years with this woman; she might almost have forgotten how to speak. But I had grown uncomfortable again, impatient for the rain to ease, so that I could, with decency, leave. But it still continued steadily, sheets of a wet curtain. It fell, hissing, into the low fire, and threatened its extinction.

"Yer mither used to walk this way too—I mind her, often, walking here among the hills."

"She did?" I couldn't remember. I wondered why this woman would break her silence to speak of such a thing, except to imply that my mother had had reasons also for unhappiness, for restlessness, that drove her from the house. But this couldn't have been so; there could have been no really deep troubles for a woman as loved as I knew my mother to have been; I had been brought up in the sounds of my father's adoring recollection of her, and once I heard him say, in a kind of agony, "Perhaps I loved her too well. Does God mean us to love a human creature in that way? Was it His judgment . . . ?" I had been too young to deny that doubt, and wouldn't have known how. In my father's eyes and memory she had been always young, always beautiful. They had been young together, and there had been hope, and promise for the future. William McIntyre had been a young minister to watch, and with a wife such as Elizabeth McIntyre, kind, tactful, good with the poor of the parish as well as the elders of the kirk, everyone knew that he soon would be leaving his country parish for a calling of wider importance. But Elizabeth McIntyre had died—a terrible death, and with her had died their second child, my brother. Ambition and concern for the future alike both left my father that day; he never moved on from his country manse, and he didn't care.

It had been many years before he had married again, and this time it was to the widow of a distant cousin of my mother. Her husband's death had been fairly recent, and she was utterly helpless in her new position. She had three daughters, and a tiny pension. My father had gone to Edinburgh to try to help her with some legal matters, to ease her burden, and had returned married to her. I didn't blame him; she was pretty still, with a delicate, winning air which called out the protector in a man. But I sensed almost at once that my father regretted the marriage, acknowledging, as time went by, that it might have been a hasty mistake, something undertaken out of a feeling of duty to my mother's family. I thought my stepmother, though pretty, was a rather stupid woman; or perhaps this opinion was only my jealousy finding another name, for my father never said a word against her. The marriage, though, had brought the great joy of this other son, Duncan, now six years old—a beautiful, intelligent, golden child whom the whole household worshiped, myself, I think, most of all. For this gift alone the marriage must have seemed worthwhile to William McIntyre.

"Ye've the look o' her."

I was wrenched back to this room and this woman. "Who?—Who have I the look of?"

"Yer mither—though she were more delicate-lookin'. Finer, ye might say."

Blunt she was, but at least it was something to be compared to my mother in any way.

"I mind her once, settin' where ye are now. It was rainin' that day, too." Some of the rigid self-control faded from that cracked voice, as if memories of happier times softened her. "I mind I had ma husband then, still. And ma own child was underfoot. Playing there by the fire, he was, and the golden head of him puttin' yer mither in mind o' her own wee bairn. She said she would bring him to play next time—though it were a long way for a wee lad's legs to carry him, and he had not yet got her fondness for climbing on the hills. But she brought him, as she said. A bit worn out, he were, fra' the walk, but it were like an adventure for him to be sa far fra' the village. He got a liking for ma own son, Keith. It were strange, a lady like yer mither t' come sa far t' sit in a humble place like this. For her sake I persuaded ma husband to make the journey to the kirk a few times, though he dinna approve much o' the minister. Too fancy-like, he thought him. She brought me wee things—home baked bread, and the jams she had put by in the season, and such things. A good woman—and it wasna her fault that the curse was upon her. She herself were fra' the Highlands, and they do say there be many there that have it so."

I swung on the stool to look at the woman. The spinning wheel had stopped, though she still bent over it, holding it, as if to call up from it the memories of things just as they had been then.

"The curse?" In Scotland that meant only the one thing, and the very sound of it filled me with fear. "You are wrong!" I cried at her. "There was no curse."

She lifted her head. "Is it nae a curse t' see the future? For that was what she saw. I will never forget the day or the hour—a day when it rained like this, and she sat before the fire with the two wee boys playin' about her feet. It was the last time she ever came, and ye dinna wonder I wasna at the door to welcome ye this day, for I never wanted kith nor kin o' hers across this threshold again. Bad luck is bad luck, I say, and the sight is bad luck to most."

I hadn't the strength to deny it now. "What happened?"

"I dinna ken. I was workin' here—probably here at the wheel, as I did most afternoons. Then at a sudden there was a cry fra' her, as if she had been hit. I turned an' looked at her, an' I never saw sich a look on the face o' mortal woman. Afeared, she was, an' stricken terrible. 'The child,' she called out. 'The wee child!' An' then on a sudden she were snatching up her boy, and dragging him away fra' ma son. I asked her what frighted her, and she wouldna say. She took him at once an' reached for her cloak, an' would ha' been gone on the instant if I hadna caught her by the arm an' held her. 'In God's name,' I said, 'wha' did ye see? Wha' did ye see that so frighted ye?'

"She pulled her bairn fra' the house, as if the plague ha' come on us asudden. 'Death!' was wha',' she answered me. 'Death! I saw a golden-haired little boy lying dead. It was . . .' I remember she moaned and cried. 'Dead he was. Your son was lying dead.'

"An' she broke fra' me, and took the bairn wi' her, runnin', an' me runnin' after her, followin' her a good way down the hillside, pleadin' wi' her, beggin' her ta say in wha' way it would come. But never a word she said, an' never again she came."

For a time I could say or do nothing, just sitting there frozen in a kind of agony of soul and body. At last I made myself stir and gather my cloak about me; it still rained, but that didn't matter. I had not been welcome here in the first place, and now we both knew why I could not stay.

At the door I said to her: "Was it soon after that it happened?"

She nodded. "I had waited wi' this terrible fear in ma heart, not darin' ta speak it ta ma husband, lest speakin' bring it to come about. I waited, and I watched ma bairn, an' wouldna let him fra' ma sight. But then one day I heard it—when the wind is right ye can hear the tollin' o' the kirk bell fra' here. An' then I knew it wasna ma son she had seen lying dead. I sent ma husband to find out what was the trouble. But before he were gone even I knew in some way that the wee bairn were dead. She had seen it, but she hadna been able t' believe it were her own son, and she hadna been able t' keep him fra' it."

I nodded, and she stood at the door and watched me make my way through the rain-sodden yard, and struggle again with the gate of logs. Of course I knew how my brother had come to die. My father would not speak of it, but in a village like ours, and from kitchen gossip, a child learns such things. My mother had been driving the little governess cart along the sea front, along the part where the thick, high wall protects the village from the waves of the winter storms. No one had ever noticed what caused the pony to shy, and to break from her control, but the racing, swaying cart had gone the length of the front, faster and faster, as if the animal had been maddened by the shrieks and cries of those who witnessed the wild dash, and by the man who had tried to grasp the bridle and had been thrown to the ground. My mother had clutched my brother, the reins gone from her hands; they say the cart hit the sea wall three times in that terrible run before it finally splintered, and the two were thrown from it. They were horribly injured; they say my brother lived only a few minutes after the blow on his head. But my mother survived for some hours, carried to the nearest cottage across the road. But she was conscious, and she lived long enough to look on the face of her own dead son, and perhaps to realise, in that final horror, which of those golden-haired children she had seen lying dead that day, as they had played together in the crofter's cottage on the hill.

But at the gate I suddenly stopped, and I don't know what made me do it. "And your son?" I called to her.

Even through the rain I saw her face darken. "What's it t' ye?"

"He's not here now?"

"Nae—he's gone. He's good an' safe. Gone to Canada."

"You've heard from him?"

"There's nae been time. A few months only he's been gone. I'll hear fra' him as soon as there's news o' a job t' be tellin' me. In a few weeks I'll be hearin' fra' him."

I said it. God, what made me say it—why didn't I keep my mouth closed on what I seemed to know? "You'll not hear from him."

Then a wild stream of curses fell upon me, curses in the ancient Gaelic tongue, fearful-sounding, and scarifying. I was grateful for my ignorance of what she was saying, and wishing I had left her in the same ignorance, wishing I had left her her peace for as long as she might have it.

I turned and stumbled down the hillside, slipping and sliding in the wet earth, through the heather and the cow pats, her cries growing fainter and fainter, but never quite lost to my hearing, because they went with me, and never ever afterward could be erased.

II

My clothes were sodden and mud-grimed by the time I reached the manse. I went round by the back through the stables to avoid the stares I would have encountered from the windows along the sea road; even in the distress I felt there was always the obligation to keep up my father's position in the village. And this way I stood a better chance of avoiding James Killian—though perhaps it would have been a good thing if he could have seen me then, wild and distraught, my wet hair streaked across my face, my clothes like a peasant's, a creature, almost, from another world. But the trap he hired each Saturday was gone from the stables.

I stood there thankfully in the shelter of the archway, trying to draw breath, struggling to gain a little composure before going into the house, planning my way up the back stairs, and how I would have Flora dry my clothes before the kitchen fire. I was deadly cold, and yet I could not bring myself to go in; how could I encounter any member of the family normally with the stream of that woman's unintelligible curses still swirling about me? And why had I said, against all knowledge and pity, that she never would hear from her son again? Well, I said it, and there was no taking it back. The worst of the afternoon was the knowledge that this terrible thing in me had had its seed in my mother; until now I could have believed in coincidence and chance, but no longer.

It was then, just as I was gathering myself up to make the final dash across the yard, that the kitchen door opened. Duncan's small, bright face looked out, scanning the yard. He seemed to have been waiting; his expression lit up as if patience had been rewarded. "Fiona!" And then, bareheaded in the rain, he was racing toward me.

I put out my arms to him, to the innocence and warmth, but this was a day that was to be blackened forever in my memory. As he came toward me, and as I leaned to embrace him, I had another vision of him—of this small, eager-faced child. But now he was fleeing from a building that burned furiously. Behind him I could see the flames, leaping high, lightening the darkness of the dreary evening. His expression seemed to change to terror, and a kind of madness. He was mortally afraid, and then, so was I. I didn't know at that moment whether I saw him dead or not, because the vision went no further. He was pursued, but not only by fire.

As he reached me I pulled back my arms that had meant to welcome him, and he cannoned into me.

"Fiona!" It was an expression of pained reproach. Never before had I treated him this way.

"Duncan, laddie . . . oh, Duncan!" The vision was gone, and though its horror remained he was there, safe, well, unafraid, beside me. I swept him into my arms as I had meant to, and prayed that my touch was not some kind of contamination to him, that contact with me would not mean the fulfillment of that dreadful sight that I had seen.

"I've been waiting," he said, the reproach melting, but he was still aggrieved.

"Waiting? For what?—you knew I would be back."

"Yes—yes. I knew. But I wanted to be the first to see you. To tell you the news."

"Is it Mr. Killian, Duncan? Has he spoken for Mary?" I felt a great sense of relief.

"Oh, *that*. No—not that! He's just been here all afternoon. They've been doing silly things like singing in the parlor. No—I wasn't waiting to tell you that. It's the letter. The letter that's come."

"What letter?" A kind of desperate hope sprang in me. Someone had offered me a position. I would soon be off their hands at Silkirk.

"A letter from a long way off—Mama says from the relations out in the West Indies. I didn't know about the West Indies, but Father has promised to show me in the atlas after supper."

"Yes?" I urged impatiently. "Yes—what about the letter? What did it say?"

"Well, it says for Mary to come. There's some little boy they want her to look after and teach. But of course Mama won't let her go. She says there's Mr. Killian to think of, and Mary mustn't go."

I knew at once what was to be. "So I'm to go in her place? That's it, isn't it?"

He wrapped his arms tightly about me, squeezing the wetness of the cloak to my body, heedless of the rain as we swayed a little out of the shelter of the arch.

"But Fiona, you won't go! You won't go, will you? They say it's a fearsome long way off, and when will I see you ever? Fiona, don't go! You'll stay here—won't you. I don't want you to go!"

But I knew if there was the least chance, I would go. I clung to Duncan, and the pain of the thought of going was a physical thing. But I would go, not mainly because it was a position to go to, a reason to leave Silkirk, though much farther and more irrevocably distant than I had ever been before. I would leave because I was now afraid of what my very presence would do to this precious child. It was possible, as perhaps my mother had done, that I carried some cursed seed of tragedy within me, innocently, but like some disease. If I were not here perhaps the vision of Duncan running terror-stricken, pursued, with the flames leaping behind him would never come to pass. Perhaps it was my presence that would bring these things, and my absence would deny them.

"We'll see, my pet," I said, stroking his wet hair, and trying to comfort him. "We'll see—the West Indies isn't so very far away." It was the other end of the earth, and if what they said of the fevers and the sicknesses were truth, I might never see Duncan again. But by that single fact I might spare him. So I would go.

III

"They say they are very rich."

"*Who* says, my dear?" my father asked patiently of my stepmother, trying to calm the excited nervousness behind the words.

"The family—the family, of course. One hears these things. Oh"—

a toss of her pretty head—"I *know* we are just the poor Scottish branch
and the London family only ever paid a courtesy call whenever they
happened to be in Edinburgh. But then they *did* very kindly invite
Mary for that lovely visit to London last year, so we know how well
they live. But the West Indian place was mentioned—wasn't it, Mary?
—and the London family have some interest in it . . . And even so—
aren't all West Indian planters rich? All that sugar . . . ?"

"On slave labor," my father said, but no one paid any attention
to him. I saw his glance go quickly to me, and away again; were we
both thinking of what I had tried to describe to him of that day in
Kelvingrove Gardens? But we would not talk about slavery here among
the family.

We were seated around the big table in the dining room, Duncan
had gone to bed, and the youngest of the little girls, Sarah. The supper
dishes had been cleared, and the door to the kitchen passage firmly
closed; the fire had been built up, and we were there, plainly, for
as long as it took to reach a decision. As far as I was concerned, the
decision was made. I knew clearly that in the minds of my stepmother
and Mary it also was made. Now it needed my father to go through
the motions. Emily, the middle girl, was there only because she was
of an age now to be included in family councils, not because she was
old enough to be sent in Mary's place. The fact that we, the children,
were consulted at all, was rare indeed; in every other family we knew
the father alone would have made the decision.

"Of course Mary may not go," my stepmother said. "Mr. Killian is
on the verge of a declaration, and if Mary were even to indicate that
she thought so little of him as to even consider leaving here, why he
would be offended to the point where he would be justified in giving
up any thought of making an offer."

"That is as may be," my father answered. "But why must Fiona go
in her place? Fiona was not the one asked for. Why not simply write
and say that Mary is about to announce her engagement, and that
will be that."

Why did I feel so grateful to him, so warmed. Just to know that
in all the difficulties I had brought on him, in the impossible position
in which I had placed myself, he still did not grab at this opportunity
to see me gone, and off his hands. Some of the closeness we had known
came back with those words. I wanted to grasp his hand, to let him
know that I would bless him forever for what he had said, but that

would have stiffened his attitude. It would have made him fight to keep me here.

"But it is a *marvelous* opportunity," I said. "I should *love* to go." I watched my stepmother's eyes light with pleasure and approval. "The Indies are so romantic, aren't they? Sunshine every day—and those exotic flowers and birds . . ." I was desperately reaching for whatever I could remember, leaving out the darker side—the illnesses, the miscegenations, the whispers of witchcraft, the strange tales that filtered back of the Creole families. Let my father not be reminded of all of this side of the picture.

"Of course, Fiona is *trained*," my stepmother went on. "They will be getting a real governess instead of Mary, who hardly could cope with a growing boy . . . Doubtless they have no notion that Fiona is free of her last position, or they would have asked for her. Perhaps it is just as *well* they don't know. The reason was awkward . . . And they do say they are rich," she repeated, as if that should finish the argument. "There would be many servants—"

"Slaves," my father corrected.

"Oh, you know very well that the house slaves are just like ordinary servants here! Fiona would be well looked after. And who knows . . ." She brightened still further. "They say young ladies are scarce out there. Fiona may make a good marriage. They say the planters are very rich . . ."

"Who says?" my father insisted. "I beg you, Dorothy, not to make these generalizations. *Who* says all these things?—and why should it be so desirable for Fiona to be married so far away from home?"

Her head came up. "As to that!—the farther from home the better! Fiona has *ruined* herself here. She has no chance of marriage at all. Out there—well, they'll just never hear of her escapade, and I *do* know they are rich, William McIntyre. At least, the Maxwells are rich, and that's all that counts." She pointed to the letter lying on the table. "If Fiona does not take her chance now, I think she will regret it for the rest of her life. There is not time to write and suggest that she come in Mary's place. We will, of course, inform the London Maxwells at once. But out there they need a governess at once. When Fiona arrives they will be so pleased to have her, a young lady from a good family, with training, that they won't ask any questions about how she came to be available. That is"—she looked pointedly at me—"unless she takes it into her head to harangue them on slavery. *Then* I should think her stay would be very short indeed."

"Dorothy—that is enough." On a very few occasions my father's authority was exerted, and he was obeyed. "It is for Fiona to decide. After all, what do we know of what she is going to? What do any of us know of the Maxwells except that they are reputed to be rich?"

My stepmother was sobered. "What do we know of anyone?" she asked, in truth. "We just have to trust. Andrew Maxwell, the boy's father, is getting on in years. It was a late marriage. He has heard through the London Maxwells that I have three daughters, and the oldest is of an age to go out and help to take care of the son, and to teach him. The salary is handsome—and Mary—Fiona, that is—is to be treated as one of the family, since she is so. A nice change, I would think, from dinner on a tray in the schoolroom."

Put that way, it sounded like a fairytale that governesses sometimes dream, and there was nothing in the letter that lay between us on the dining-room table to shatter the dream. I reached for it, and studied it yet again. The tone was polite, even appealing. *"My husband, you must know, is advancing in years, and I must help him a great deal with the business of the plantation. This leaves me less time than I would like to spend with our young son. It would be esteemed a great favor by my husband and myself if one of the Maxwell family could come to help with his teaching and training. We hear from our London cousins that your daughter, Mary, is of admirable temperament and suitable age . . ."*

There was more like it, and it sounded too good to be true. To begin with, women who wrote in a hand so thick and bold and black were not apt to be so polite. And there was the slightly foreign flavor to it, as if she had once been taught how to write polite English letters. And all the unspoken authority of a woman who was used to running things, who was used to being obeyed, and did not for a moment expect these poor Scottish relations to refuse her offer was to be seen in the arrogant pride and assurance of that elaborately penned signature: *Maria de Medina y Palma de Maxwell.*

I stared at it, fascinated, mistrusting the writer, somewhat afraid of her already, but knowing that I would do what she asked.

IV

I went almost before there was time for second thoughts. The London Maxwells were written to, as Maria Maxwell's letter had instructed, to advance the passage money. "Merchants—and something in banking in the City" was how my stepmother described them. She said only of me that I was free to go, whereas her own daughter was not, and how fortunate it was that I had already had some training in the charge of small boys. I was described fulsomely in terms that my stepmother had never used of me before; Andrew Maxwell was getting a paragon to take care of his son if the letter were to be believed. The reply came at once. The firm of Maxwell, Maxwell, Maxwell & Grimmond—which Maxwell it was we could never decide from the signature—were sure that Miss Fiona McIntyre would make an entirely satisfactory substitute for her stepsister, and the writer would be pleased if she would find it convenient to embark on the *Clyde Queen*, leaving shortly from Glasgow. Passage had already been secured. The shock came when the sailing date was mentioned. It was in ten days' time.

My stomach turned as I thought of the long voyage, and so little time to prepare, so little time to be sure that I was doing the right thing. But the surety came whenever I looked at Duncan. And I learned to shrug my shoulders; when was one ever sure what was the right thing? In that, at least, my stepmother had not been stupid.

So a trunk was brought from the attic and I packed my clothes; there was little among them suitable for the climate I was going to, but there was neither time nor money for new ones. On the last day Mary came to me with a pincushion she had made, and an embroidered ribbon fashioned into a bow for my heavy knot of hair. The gifts were offered without words, but with a look of thanks whose meaning I understood. I packed some books for this new young charge whose name I didn't even know, and tried to brush aside Duncan's tears and protests.

It was hard when the time finally came. My father had hired a carriage to take us all the way to Glasgow, and would come with me to see me aboard the *Clyde Queen*. Duncan clung to me then, and I tried to calm his sobs and howls of outrage; he had consulted the atlas, and he knew that the Indies were much farther away than London, which was the farthest his imagination yet reached. I was fighting my own tears when my father touched my arm.

"There's a woman there, Fiona—she had come and asked to speak to you." He seemed puzzled, but he was invariably courteous to anyone who came to make a request of him.

I turned, and there, standing by the arch of the yard, where I had seen my vision of Duncan on that terrible day, stood the woman from the crofter's cottage. Very slowly I released myself from Duncan's embrace, and went toward her, a sense of dread growing in me. I still heard those ancient curses that had followed me down the hillside.

She gave me no greeting, but her voice was low. What was said was to be between us only. "They say ye are goin'—they say ye are goin' a long way, and some never come back fra' those parts. So I thought I would come an' tell ye, so that ye would know."

"Know what?"

"Ma son, Keith—ye asked if I hadna heard fra' him, an' I said nae. I told ye he were in Canada, an' soon I would ha' news o' him. An' ye answered that I never would hear. Well, I came t' tell ye that ye were right. Ma son is dead. He never reached Canada. Some sickness on the ship, and he lies buried out there in the sea. So ye knew it, an' I have come t' tell ye that. Bad luck ye bring wi' yer cursed sight o' what is not yet known. So leave wi' that gift fra' me, and remember this lonely woman."

Then she turned, that gaunt figure wrapped in her ancient, ragged plaid, and started along the road that led from the village.

"Fiona—" my stepmother called, perhaps startled by what I knew was plainly upon my face. "Who was that woman?—extraordinary!"

I did not dare to look at Duncan. "Come, Father, it's getting late. The ship will not wait on the tide . . ." A hasty embrace, the quickest for Duncan, who clung hardest, and then I was in the carriage, and we were moving. I turned my face to the window, and my father, with understanding I sometimes did not give him enough credit for, asked no questions.

There was no real hurry, and we made the *Clyde Queen* three hours before the tide. As we cast off my father stood on the dock, his hat raised, and the freshening wind fanning his long, silvering hair. Although there were miles of the Clyde yet to come, and the Isle of Anan and Ailsa Craig and all the other islands standing off the coast, he was truly the last sight of Scotland for me. I passionately willed that with my going would go that threat to Duncan, that the end of Scotland would be the end of the curses and the visions that are legend among our history. Deliberately I turned my face toward the yet unfelt sun of the Indies, welcoming it, wanting it. I turned my face and my future toward a mansion called Landfall.

Chapter 2.

"It will be the first thing ye sight as the sun rises. Be ye here at dawn, before the clouds have cleared off Kronberg. We will be hove-to all night. I'll not risk rounding the Serpent Rocks after nightfall."

The quick tropic dusk had come down just as the outline of the island had appeared. There had been the call from the lookout, and the half-smile of pleasure which Captain Stewart had permitted himself at the exactitude of his navigation, and my wild rush to the bulwark. But the swiftness of the dark defeated me; the island was there, hilly, rolling, sweeping in the southern end to the sharp outline of the volcanic peak, Kronberg. The sea purpled suddenly as the light rushed away, and the island was gone—a dark land-mass that disappeared as the stars already blazed in the light-blue sky. It was too late even for Captain Stewart's glass to help me. The trade winds that had driven at our backs most of the way across the Atlantic had died, as they did at night.

"Do ye not smell the land?" he said. Yes, I smelled the land.

I smelled it too before dawn as I crept up the companion ladder and once more stationed myself at the bulwark. The light was rushing in as it had ebbed last night, a swift tide. The stars grew paler, the sea lightened; the coolness of dawn still lay on us, but my palms sweated slightly as they gripped the taffrail. My mind was crowded with the few things I had been able to gather to myself during the long weeks of the voyage, the snippets of information, the words half-said. The *Clyde Queen* was an island ship, delivering and taking on her cargo from all over the Indies. Any officer who had made the voyage a few times had already gathered the stories of the islands, heard the names of those who mattered, could embroider the histories and the legends. But it was the third mate, young Mr. McPherson, this only his fourth voyage, who had told me most about the Maxwells, and about Landfall, and that wasn't much. I had often walked until late at night on deck, savoring the coolness after the heat of the day, knowing I would not sleep well in the stuffiness of the cabin that had not seemed to have a whisper of fresh air since we had passed the Azores. Once or twice we had stood together by the rail, watching the stars swing with the gentle roll of the ship, and he had told me his little knowledge of the Indies, and had ventured a question or two about my own journey. After we had left the Clyde the thrust of the North Atlantic had produced the expected seasickness in the four passengers the *Clyde Queen* carried, a man and wife, and another woman, going, like myself, as governess, but to a family on Barbados. We were some days at sea before all four passengers were gathered about the captain's table, and the questions were asked. "I," I said, "am going to take care of a little boy on San Cristóbal. The family is kin to my mother."

"And which family is that?" Young Mr. McPherson blushed as he spoke. The third mate did not often speak in the presence of his captain, but he seemed eager to talk to me. I remember, though, the instant expression of grim dishumor that had crossed the captain's face, and he glanced sharply down the table at his officer.

"Maxwell," I said quickly. "Maxwell, of the Landfall plantation. Do you know of them?"

The captain answered for him, and silenced his third mate. I don't recall that Mr. McPherson ever spoke directly to me at table again.

"Aye, Miss McIntyre, the Maxwells are known. Anyone who knows San Cristóbal and the islands thereabouts knows of Andrew Maxwell."

And there was what had been said to me, in Mr. McPherson's low voice at the rail those few evenings when his watch had permitted him time to talk, or his captain's eye had not been upon him. When I had tried to question him, he had shrugged ruefully, and smiled. "I've been told, Miss McIntyre, that I'm not to discuss the Maxwells with you."

"Why ever not?"

"Because I found out—or was told, very bluntly—that the London firm of Maxwell are part-owners of this vessel, and one doesn't discuss one's employers."

"But one also can't be so rude as to refuse to answer a lady's natural questions, can one?"

He chuckled in the darkness. "No, Miss McIntyre, one couldna be *that* rude. I don't know much, mind you . . ."

"Maria Maxwell?" Why did she interest me, I wondered, more than her husband.

"A great beauty, they say. I've never seen her. Spanish—almost purely Spanish, although the island has been British for so long. The Dutch had it for a while in between the Spanish and the English. All these islands have a checkerboard history—prizes of war, and pieces of paper signed in Paris or Vienna. But a good many of the old Spanish aristocracy lingered, and are as clannish as we Scots. There are a good many Scots on the island, I know. Where the English settle, the Scots come to do the hard work. Andrew Maxwell is a big landowner, Miss McIntyre, but I wouldna doubt he worked hard enough in his time. It wasna given to him on a plate."

"He married late . . ."

"Aye . . ." A hesitation. "He married late." I was not so innocent I didn't know his embarrassment. He didn't mean me to suppose that Andrew Maxwell had been some crabbed bachelor.

It might have been two weeks later before we had our next conversation. Maria Maxwell, what little he knew of her, obviously fascinated him also. "They say she is magnificent—and almost runs the plantation singlehanded now. They say no woman has ever been able to control slaves the way she does. They say . . ."

"You are keeping Miss McIntyre from her rest, Mr. McPherson." It was Stewart's voice behind us; the rebuke was very clear. I was neither to be spoken to, nor was gossip to be related to me. It was the last time Mr. McPherson ever sought my company alone, or spoke to me privately. But I felt him watching me; often I felt his gaze on me as he stood his daytime watch on the poop deck. But that was all.

Now it was Captain Stewart who joined me at the bulwark. The first tip of the sun was appearing, and the island was abruptly bathed in an unearthly light, the water suddenly brilliant aquamarine, shading to sapphire where it ran to the shallows, the land mass itself purple, with the top of Kronberg still in mist, but the long ridges of its sides brightening to green as I watched. The coast stretched long and far out of sight, the bays indented, this north side rocky and wind-driven.

"Maxwell's kingdom." The captain's voice sounded more than usually acid and burred. "Everything stretching from Kronberg to the Serpent Rocks on this side is his, and much more on the other side of the mountain—no, you dinna see much of the cane fields this side —too wet and steep. But the house is there, on the ridge. There was a time when it was the first thing you saw of San Cristóbal—that and Kronberg and the Serpents. Landfall House, and well named. You can see it there, white, though the garden grows close. And I've no doubt Andrew Maxwell's glass is trained on us at this very moment. Old men don't sleep late."

I don't know what loosened his usually taciturn tongue; perhaps he forgot, in his memories of the many voyages at which he had made this landfall, his usual habit of discretion; perhaps he was moved to give me the information I had sought from McPherson. "It's never been a lucky place," he added suddenly. "I couldna pretend to know all its history, but it was built long before Andrew Maxwell was born. Been left to go derelict several times, I think—absentee owners. I did hear some tale that when it was being built there was some trouble between a female slave and her mistress—some white women are particularly savage with slaves, Miss McIntyre. It was said that before she was done to death, the slave put a curse upon the house. Well, I don't know why I repeat such things—the islands are full of fanciful stories of curses and spells and witchcraft. It follows wherever the African goes . . . And Andrew Maxwell has had his share of trouble."

Since I was to leave the *Clyde Queen* so soon, I risked his displeasure. "You don't seem to care for Andrew Maxwell, Captain Stewart."

"Ah." I had the feeling that if I had not been there he would have spat into the water below us. "It's not ma business, Miss McIntyre, to care or not to care for Andrew Maxwell. I have other things to think about. I neither care nor don't care for Negroes, either, but I have never touched the trade, in all my years sailing these seas. Men make fortunes from other men's backs, Miss McIntyre. That's legal and permissible, but a Christian doesn't have to admire it. Slaving's a dirty business, no matter which end of it you're on. Oh, I know, the transportation of slaves from Africa was supposed to have ended years ago, but the illegal cargoes have been making three times the money they did before it was forbidden, so it still goes on. Well, you'll see—and you'll probably accept what you must in the life you see lived here on these islands. *You* can do nothing to change it. Females do best to mind their own business, and especially where you're going. Good morning, Miss McIntyre. We should be docked by ten."

And then he turned from my side and bellowed an order to the brigade of hands who had appeared with brushes and buckets for the morning ritual of deck-cleaning. The captain ran a tight ship, and it would arrive in Santa Marta, San Cristóbal's harbor and main town, with its decks holystoned white, and every piece of brass gleaming.

And I would go below and pack my trunk, giving my last glance to that partly obscured white house on the ridge, not able to stand still any longer under the spyglass of an old man who woke early.

*   *   *   *   *

They had sent an elegant light carriage for me—shining black with yellow-spoked wheels and gold tassels on its cushions; its Negro driver was clad in white duck with yellow epaulets, a black tricornered hat bound with gold, and he wore a look of massive imperturbability; a young boy, dressed much as he was, but without the dignity of the hat, held the horses while he inquired at the gangplank for the lady to be taken to Landfall. No one of the household had come to welcome me; perhaps that was too much to expect. The big Negro was silent and unsmiling as he helped me to my seat, and strapped my trunk to the back of the carriage. Captain Stewart had bade me goodbye at the top of the gangplank. Without knowing why, now that the ties to the *Clyde Queen*, never strong or affectionate, were cut, I felt alone and almost afraid in the midst of all that bright bustle of the ships at anchor, the carrying of the bales and barrels, the singsong voices of the slaves speaking in their gulla language what they didn't care for the white man to know. There would be a sudden burst of laughter, and then nearly always the irate voice of an overseer checking it. There was movement and color and sound all about me; and most of all there was the brilliant sun, the sun that reached everywhere, hurting the eyes and blackening into shadow any place it could not reach; there was the splash of shocking colors in unexpected places, vines spilling over walls, colored cloths bound around the heads of the Negro women, the warehouses along the dockside painted in fading pinks and blues and greens. It was a cheerful chaos of movement and color and light, and yet even while the sweat ran off me as I waited, I felt the strange, cold undercurrent of fear. It might have been Captain Stewart's speculative eye still on me from the ship, or it could have been the frozen attitude of the driver, or one of the many, quick, but blank glances that went to me from the Negroes who passed the carriage, the sideways glance under heavy lids, that neither welcomed nor cheered me. Relief from it came at the last moment; the driver was gathering the reins into his hands, and reaching for the whip when there was a sudden clatter down the gangplank.

Under Captain Stewart's eye, Mr. McPherson ran toward the carriage. I felt his hand, moist as mine was; his brow was beaded in perspiration.

"Good luck, Miss McIntyre. Good luck at Landfall."

I pressed his hand. "Thank you . . . thank you very much."

"Perhaps . . . perhaps when the *Clyde Queen's* next in Santa Marta. Oh, well . . ." He shrugged.

I said something in reply, heaven knows what it was. But his act of defiance of his captain had served to raise my own spirits. I drew myself up straighter as the carriage slipped at a smart rate through the business section of the town, the warehouses and the streets arcaded against the sun and the rain; then we came to the big houses with the gardens enclosed by high walls, the shutters already closed against the sun, the tangle of blossoming vines cascading over wall and arched gateways. Down the lane between, and at the back of the houses, were the unpainted shacks, with sagging shutters and lifted off the ground on rotting wooden stumps. A breeze blew now in my face, and the sweat began to dry. We came to the outskirts of the town; the houses gave way completely to shacks, and then the start of the cane fields. There were long, rolling hills of tall cane, endlessly tossing and waving in the wind, so that the color changed as if one watched the shadows racing across a field of unripe corn. But this was gold that the planters set into the ground, and with the sun and the rain it grew gold for them. There were sometimes little clusters of wooden huts where dirt roads bisected; there were signposts which I realized pointed not to villages, but to plantations—Barrow's End, Montrose Hall, Mary's Fancy. Now what caught the eye were the greathouses themselves, always set upon the ridge of a hill to catch the breeze, and sometimes Spanish-looking bell towers outlined against the hard blue sky, the conical shape of the stone windmills that served the sugar factories. Kronberg, my own particular landmark, grew nearer, but it took a long time for us to reach the rather severe whitewashed archway and the signpost that said LANDFALL. The cane fields went on, then a group of palm-thatched shacks, and a faded sign that was lettered WINTERSLO.

At this junction was the stump of a crumbling stone pillar with the chiselled words SAN FRANCI. They were worn by time, almost obliterated, and hardly registered. More and more cane fields—the roof line of a house, very spare, against the dry side of the mountain. Then Kronberg was upon us; the carriage climbed a little about its base, a narrow road; the cane fields were behind us, an almost rank tropical growth had begun. Deep shadow, tall trees, huge thick vines like languorous snakes twined about them, strange, unknown flowers, and the flash of colored birds; we had come to the windward side of Kronberg, the side where the rain spilled down, too steep for cane, magnificent in its dark beauty.

And then there were tall stone pillars, and great iron gates and a tracery of iron archway set with a lantern, grander than anything I had ever seen. Suddenly the small boy who up to now had copied the silence and dignity of his senior could bear his solemnity no longer. He turned and there was the quick flash of an unexpectedly cheerful, prideful smile. He might be a slave, it told me, but he belonged to a rich master.

"This Landfall," he announced.

II

As the drive wound toward the house there were glimpses of the sea, the sapphire flash, the fleck of white curling over the rocks. The trees were tall, and within their shade the huge-leaved tropical plants; in the spaces between the sun was fierce to the eye, and the bright green grass grew, hot and brittle-looking, as if it were razor-edged, and would not be kind or cool to bare feet. Everything was immaculate, and yet I sensed that a year's neglect—even a month's, perhaps—would bring the vines rampaging, and the grass waist-high.

We swept up smartly before the high white stone house, the drive circling about an enormous, grey-trunked tree, perhaps the biggest I had ever seen. The driver checked the horses expertly; our arrival was accompanied by the clamor of dogs, who darted from around both sides of the house, and by the children, dark-skinned children in faded cotton who seemed to come from nowhere—they had not been there, and suddenly they were there, soundless, shy, keeping well back, ready to disappear once again, and yet with children's eagerness to witness what was going on. Half their attention was on me, and half directed toward the steps that led up to the house. They held themselves in readiness to go when someone should appear.

At first there was no one. Once the driver had shouted the dogs to silence, the quiet was painful, just the steady stir of the wind through the branches and vines. As if he knew the awkwardness, the driver took his time getting down and handing over the bridle to the boy. His slowness increased as he opened the door and let down the little folding step. For a moment he hesitated, as if he feared to offer his black hand to my white, as if his should not be the instrument of welcome to the house of Andrew Maxwell.

His action was halted by the boy. "Here is Master." He was not smiling now, and it was said almost in a whisper.

The house was surrounded on all sides with a deep, two-storied, veranda supported by vine-thickened pillars—later I learned to call it the gallery. Its depth matched the great height of the mahogany shutters that framed each of the many french doors—all of them standing open to the breeze. So intense was the shadow cast by the gallery that for a moment I had difficulty seeing past the glare of the white stone to the man who stood in the doorway opposite the steps. Then I took in the hugeness of the figure, the white clothes he wore, and the flamboyance of the red silk sash bound about his waist. We stared at each other for moments, my hand still extended toward the driver, but his was no longer there to help me alight. Then I saw the silver-topped cane in the hand of the white-clad figure, and the sure movement with which it was discarded—not thrown to the floor or leaned against the doorframe, but just simply put away from him, and received by another hand, a slave whose presence there he took for granted. I saw the effort to straighten the great height and bulk, the effort to pace the wide veranda with some youthfulness of movement. But as he stepped out into the sunlight, his hand went to the hot iron railing for support, and it was an aging, and possibly ailing man who came carefully toward me. He did not flinch at the burning kiss of that intricately wrought rail; the steps curved outward in a graceful sweep, and he held the rail all the way down to the end posts, which supported two great lamps like that above the gateway.

But the expected words of welcome were not the first which came as he started toward the carriage.

"Fergus—Goddammit, Fergus! Where is Fergus?"

The strength and power of the voice fought the wind, and seemed to echo back through the whole house; the dark-skinned children vanished, the dogs crept back to the shade, or toward the stables. No word was said to me. In the stillness of the moment I was suddenly aware of a quick flash of color, as a huge bird, scarlet and yellow plumaged, swept by with a harsh shrieking cry, like mocking laughter.

Now Andrew Maxwell addressed the driver, whose own stillness seemed part fear.

"Where is my son? Was he not on the dock?"

"Master Fergus not there, sir."

"Goddammit!" For a second I thought one of those giant hands might rise to strike the man. But the fist unclenched, and instead the hand went at last toward me.

"Miss Mary Maxwell—welcome to Landfall." The big, puffy lips parted in a smile that showed tobacco-stained teeth; but I had the odd sensation that the smile was genuine. I was not included in the general anger. "Forgive the seeming churlishness, Miss Mary. I had instructed my son to be on the dock to meet the *Clyde Queen*. You must think us a strange, unmannerly lot here at Landfall."

He could be charming; a pointed beard hid the fleshiness of chin and neck, and he had somehow the look of a rogue; but he could be a charming rogue. At last I was out of the carriage, and tall as I was for a woman, I still had to stare up at his face. I squinted against the glare; the sun burned and the sweat bathed my whole body again. It was no place for explanations, but I could not, even for a moment, assume Mary's identity.

"Thank you for your welcome. I hope I will be just as welcome when you know that I'm not Mary Maxwell, but her stepsister, Fiona McIntyre."

The thick lips tightened just a trifle, and the eyes narrowed. He looked at me closely, my face, and then a careful up and downward sweep that took in all of me. There was no subtlety in that look; it was as frank as anything I had ever been subjected to.

"I think," he said finally, "that we had better go inside." And then he took my arm; it was not a gentle touch, but rather as if he had taken me unto himself in place of the cane he had discarded; the pressure of his fingers on my arm hurt, and he meant them to, as if he tested me, and must make me know how much strength still remained to him. This way we climbed the stairs, his hand again on the rail, the other pressing, leaning, cruel. Having shown his own strength, he seemed to want to gauge mine, to find out how long it would be before I would pause, or try to shift the burden. I did neither. We continued on into the blessed shade of the gallery, across its checkered marble floor and then entered an inner gallery, as wide as the first, furnished along its whole length like an informal sitting room, and running, as the outer one seemed to, around the whole house. I felt the cooler air here, and the relief to the eyes. Then we passed through to the core of the house—a hall whose beautiful staircase split to branch in two directions, the open doorways to a great salon on one side, and to the dining room on the other. The pressure on my arm directed me toward the salon, much as the pull on a bridle. Compared to the glare outside, it was almost dark here. There was mahogany, floors and massive furniture, there was silver and paintings, and crystal chandeliers whose prisms tinkled gently together in the tropic breeze. Here, at the center of the house, with the breeze flowing straight through, untouched by the sun, it was as cool as a summer's day in Scotland. Again I felt the perspiration drying on me, and the strange chill of the tropics struck at me.

"Sit there." He indicated a chair in which I must sit upright, a chair for a tall man rather than a woman. He himself went to a sofa, big, heavy, red, whose sagging springs told me that it was his own special place. As he sat he clicked his fingers and a servant appeared—I reminded myself that I would have to get used to the idea that these people were slaves, not servants, with no choice to disobey, without the chance to leave to find some other work. This was their life—the beginning and end of it. At this moment the black faces seemed anonymous to me, featureless, indistinguishable, the carefully downcast eyes without identity or will. The plain cotton dress of the house slaves furthered this illusion that all were the same person, forever reappearing in a different role.

"This is Dougal," Andrew Maxwell said. "He oversees the house." A Scottish name; I wondered if they had their own private names, the names that came from Africa, or were they also lost in the generations of slavery. Perhaps I shivered a little at the thought, and Andrew Maxwell saw it.

"You'll take this little drink now," he said, as Dougal laid a tall glass on the table beside me, and another, together with a jug, beside his master. "I know what's on you—it's hot as hell, and yet you're cold. You're wearing the wrong clothes, of course. We'll have to see about that. But you must guard against the chill. Watch for it at night . . ."

I sipped and felt a fiery sweetness against my tongue and throat, and a burning within me. It was not unpleasant—too sweet perhaps, but pervasive; there was the scent of spices, cinnamon, and nutmeg.

"In Scotland, Mr. Maxwell, ladies rarely drink spirits. Especially ministers' daughters."

He slapped his hand against his bulging thigh as if challenged. "And here, miss, you will do as I say. And I say that a little rum to burn out the chill will do no hurt. I've lived in this climate all my life. I *know* how a white man survives. And so we'll have no namby-pamby notions about what ladies do or don't. *Here* they do!"

"Perhaps you're right," I answered coolly, "but that is surely something I'll have to discover for myself. *I* haven't lived here all my life, but I've been wet a thousand times up on the mountains in Scotland with no more when I got home than a cup of tea to take away the chill. Scotland makes hardy women, Mr. Maxwell. My blood isn't thin yet."

For some reason this defiance pleased him. He threw back his great head, and the chuckle of appreciation was rich and long. "Then you *are* no namby-pamby miss. Not a bit of it! No thin blood in you."

I looked down at my glass with mock demureness. "Don't you want to know, Mr. Maxwell, why I am here in place of my stepsister?"

He sighed. "I suppose so—but you suit me, I know that already. I was expecting a Miss Pink-and-Pretty, described to me by old Jeremy Maxwell when we wrote about someone coming out for the boy. I suppose she couldn't come, for some reason, and they sent you instead. That's it, isn't it. Well enough then. I would say we've done well in the exchange . . ."

"I *insist*, Mr. Maxwell, on presenting my qualifications. I am quite experienced as a governess. My references—"

"You insist, do you?" He laughed at me. "I can *see* your qualifications, Miss Fiona McIntyre. I like redheaded women, and all the better if they're big and shapely. You're a fine woman, Miss Fiona. The women used to be like you when they first came out to these islands—like my mother, a strong, handsome woman, and if her husband hadn't been killed, she would have borne him a dozen sons. But in a generation or two the blood thins out in more ways than one. I'm sick of looking at sallow Spanish complexions on women who haven't the strength to lift a child. The Spanish blood here, Miss Fiona, has run to seed . . ."

Was he drunk already, I wondered?—at this hour? I had smelled the rum from him as we had walked together, that and a strangely sweetish tobacco smell that seemed now to cling even to my own clothes. Did he always speak to women in this way? His gaze upon me was so frank that I wanted to turn away, or look down, but would not give way before him. He was complimenting me, flirting with me almost in a way that was shameless and highhanded, since I was almost as bound as his slaves. He said he liked women big and redheaded, and despised the thin blood and sallow skins of the Spanish. And yet he was married to a woman whose beauty was a legend even to those who had not seen her. And where was that woman?—and where was the child I had come to care for, and teach? Why did I sit here, near noon, drinking rum with a man with a lecherous eye and a rough tongue. The answer was as it had been all of my adult life; I had, at this moment, no other choice. You stay where you are when there is no other place to go.

"There wasn't time to write, you understand," I said. "It would have taken months for letters to be exchanged, and Mrs. Maxwell's need seemed urgent. Since I had had experience, and my sister none, we thought . . ."

He cut me off with a wave of the hand. "Oh, they wrote us about the other one—Miss Pink-and-Pretty. I didn't care for the sound of her. Too young. Too . . ." he weighed his word ". . . innocent. She might not have stood the test. I've a feeling you will. I would have chosen you—"

"Was anyone else doing the choosing, Mr. Maxwell? Is there someone else? And who are *they*?"

"They?—damn them! The London Maxwells, of course! Everything arranged through them. Poking and prying, and saying do this and do that. Just because they have a small interest in Landfall. Merchants, Miss Fiona—bankers and merchants, not men. Is there a percentage in it?—they'll take it. That's all they go by! One of their kind here at Landfall now. A Maxwell—one of the clever young men of the firm. Old Jeremy's youngest. But old enough to be a pryer and a snooper. He's got a game leg—hunting accident. Supposed to be a crack shot. But he's one of your cold-fish type. Shoots and rides because a man has to do those kind of things, not because he likes them. Careful with his drink and his talk. And what's worse, a reformer. Wants to change everything. Damn near to being a radical. I keep telling him he'll reform himself right out of his fortune if he's not careful. I'm so damn tired of hearing about Wilberforce and Wesley. Busybody, that's what he is . . . Wish he'd go home. Only been here this two week and I'm sick to death of him. Supposed to be recouperating after an illness . . .

he's in better health than most men will ever see. Excuse to be here, that's all. Busybody . . ."

"Mr. Maxwell—have a care. You say too much! You forget I'm a stranger, and governesses aren't supposed to gossip."

"A stranger?" He looked puzzled, confused, and abruptly, even in the dimness of that inner room, his age was more apparent. "Yes, a stranger, I suppose. Brought here. Brought here like Miss Pink-and-Pretty would have been. Forget the governess part . . . But a Maxwell, still. Your mother was a Maxwell. The Maxwell part counts. That's what counts . . ."

He took up his glass and drank, and for a time I had vanished for him, like the dark-skinned children he never saw, like the silent slaves whose presence one didn't acknowledge. He sat and brooded, an old man, massive, seeming ill, loaded with a life behind him and little ahead. I might almost be sorry for him, but no one could ever be sorry for Andrew Maxwell. I was forgotten; when he spoke it was as if it were for himself alone, a reassurance, a prop, a reminder. "You have to watch what is done to you." He was remembering something out of his own experience, something that his first remark about Mary Maxwell being brought to this place had evoked. "You have to fight for what should be yours, or they'll take it. They'll take it all . . ."

"Women don't often have the chance to fight, Mr. Maxwell." I recalled my presence to him; he saw me again with a start of recognition; his eyes alert again, and wary.

"Women have their own ways. What is it in the Bible about the little foxes and tender grapes? . . . come, you know the Bible! You're a minister's daughter, aren't you?"

I chose not to supply the words for him. "I take and remember what parts of the Bible I want to, Mr. Maxwell. I am not sure yet whether I'm a Martha or a Mary. Life is hard . . ." Why was I saying this to him, who would be expected to have little sympathy with the trials of governesses? "Life is hard, and a woman learns to take it as she finds it."

"Aye, and it's well you should know it," he answered, with no consolation for me. "Well that you should know it and act upon it. But women who suck the heart and spirit from a man . . . they're the devils who walk the earth. The dark devils . . ."

He drank again, deeply, and once again I also sipped the fiery drink, and he was right about it; it was strangely comforting. I felt the stiffness leave my body, the chill all gone. I waited for a time that seemed polite, but Andrew Maxwell appeared to have nothing more to say to me. He could, if he wished, exercise his prerogative to make talk or keep silent, but the drink had made me bolder.

"Mr. Maxwell—might I be shown my room? And when may I meet my charge?"

"Your charge?" He looked bewildered again, and then light broke on him. "You talk like a governess, Miss Fiona. You mean my son. No—no, you can't meet him yet. He's out with his mother. They ride together every morning. She is teaching him, you see, how to care for the plantation." The words tumbled together in a burr of anger and resentment.

"Teaching him to . . . ?" I leaned forward. "But he is only—how old, Mr. Maxwell?"

"Seven!" He almost shouted the word at me. "Seven years old, and his mother thinks it time he learned to take charge of the plantation. Speak to me now of little foxes . . ."

"Foxes?" It was strange how both of us froze at the sound of that voice, I, who had never heard it before, as well as the old man. He was gazing toward one of the doorways that led from the front galleries, and I saw his free hand tightly grasp the cane that had once again been placed beside him. For myself I had to turn.

"There are no foxes on San Cristóbal."

I rose to my feet. They stood there, as beautiful a pair as ever I had seen, this mother and her child. The woman was dark, with the classic, rich beauty of Spain in her face, in the dark magnificence of her eyes and hair, in the high cheekbones and the smooth complexion like warm ivory. She was not tall, but seemed so, in the perfection of her body, closely outlined by the dove-grey riding habit. In place of the high black hat that would have gone with the costume, she wore the broad-brimmed Cordoban knotted beneath her chin. There was style and grace and an arrogant sureness in every line of her. I knew that only this kind of woman could have penned the black, confident, aristocratic script of the letter which had come to Silkirk, and now that I saw her, I knew that every word of that letter had been a lie. This woman needed help from no one, least of all a governess from a Scottish country rectory.

At last she conceded to the ritual. She came toward me, peeling off her white cotton gloves, which were then thrown with her riding crop onto a table. "I expected to welcome Miss Mary Maxwell—but surely you cannot be she?"

She was quicker than her husband had been; I was not the one she had written for, not the one described. I was older, I had not Mary's air of gentle docility; at that instant I was glad Mary was not here. She could not have stood for a moment against this woman. But somehow I knew that Maria Maxwell would have preferred my stepsister.

I explained, as I had to her husband, the reason why I had come in place of Mary. "We wrote to the Maxwell firm in London, of course, as you instructed, and they assured us that my coming, since Mary was not able to, would be in order. I have their letter to you . . . I have had experience . . ." I stumbled over references and such things. Her detached gaze disconcerted me; she seemed determined that nothing should be made easy.

"The Maxwells—ah, yes, they would approve. It only needs their approval. Well, you are here . . ." The rest was left unsaid. Belatedly, almost as a gesture of contempt, her hand was extended. "Welcome to Landfall, Miss McIntyre." We touched for the minimal time that courtesy demanded. "We are surely fortunate, are we not, Andrew, to have the services of such an experienced lady. I had expected to welcome Mary Maxwell, of whom we had heard such good reports, but one is lucky under any circumstances to induce a Scottish lady of good family to come here . . . especially a Maxwell."

I at once felt old and big and awkward, and a poor substitute for the one expected. I murmured something in reply; all of it was false, and we all knew it. Whatever the reason, I was not welcome at Landfall by this woman.

And now she beckoned the child toward me. There was no doubt in her mind, as had existed with her husband, what role I was there to play. "And this is to be your charge. This is my son, Duncan, Miss McIntyre."

Her son, not our son. The boy came toward me confidently, though having waited until his mother had finished speaking. And what had been the mere outline of a golden-haired child against the greater brightness of the gallery, fresh-skinned and pink-cheeked, now assumed features and a personality. My hand, instead of going toward him, clutched at my skirt, as the perspiration of shock struck at me. I could hardly believe what I saw. I wondered if the strength of the rum had hit me as I rose, or the nostalgia for home and the familiar things had gathered force to deceive me. Before me seemed to stand my own Duncan, my little half-brother, the adored only son of my father. Of course there were some differences—slightly higher cheekbones and a more pointed chin which he took from his mother; but otherwise the

Maxwell blood had recreated this extraordinary replica of that other Duncan, growing up in the Scottish rectory. I glanced back to his father, this big man whose grey hair would once have been the same red-blond, whose beard and heavy jowls hid what once would have been a face like this one. The Scottish strain had won over the Spanish. It would not have troubled me—I would have been glad except for the terrible memory of a golden-haired child racing toward me from a burning building, racing in terror—and terror not only of fire. I had crossed an ocean and come to a strange life in order to place distance between myself and my own little Duncan. And now I was confronted by this other one, and the danger must still be faced. I remembered the words of the woman from the mountainside cottage. "Bad luck ye bring wi' yer cursed sight o' what is not yet known. So leave wi' that gift fra' me, and remember this lonely woman." I was remembering, and I was terrified.

The silence had become too much; I must move—must say something. The child stared at me with unabashed wonder, not used to having his advances spurned. Maria Maxwell's voice broke the spell.

"There is something wrong, Miss McIntyre?"

Desperately I ran my hand down my skirt to remove the sweat, and held it toward him. "No!—no, nothing wrong. It is just, Mrs. Maxwell, that your son so much resembles my half-brother. Extraordinary . . ."

She was not pleased. "Yes—visually the Maxwell strain is strong. But for the rest—"

I didn't hear what she said. I had gripped hands with this Duncan, and for a child it was a hold of astonishing strength and firmness. I could feel the muscles of my face relax, and I must have smiled, because he suddenly smiled. The kind of radiance and beauty that had blessed my little half-brother's face was there, the winning grace, the eager pleasure.

"I'm glad you've come," he said, the only real welcome I had had at Landfall. "We'll be doing all kinds of things together, won't we?"

It was childish and normal. I put the terror and shock from me. If I had to come just to be here for this child to run to, then this was reason enough. "Yes, we're going to do all kinds of things. We'll teach each other things . . ."

I had one friend at Landfall, and he was a seven-year-old child.

*　*　*　*　*

It wasn't until I was upstairs, sponging myself all over with lemon-scented water, that I remembered when Andrew Maxwell had struggled down the stairs to the carriage, the name of the son he had called for, the one he had cursed for not being on the dock to meet me had been Fergus, not Duncan. I remembered, too, the words of the third mate of the *Clyde Queen*. "He married late. . . ."

* * * * *

I lunched alone with Duncan, in an upstairs corner room that was to be our schoolroom. It was like no schoolroom I had ever known before; two sets of french doors opened to the upper gallery in two directions—one to the mountain, the other view through the garden, beautiful, slightly mysterious with its winding paths and unfamiliar plants, vines smothered with blossoms which were almost unreal in their size, gave tantalizing glimpses of the sea; there was the sound of the waves against the Serpent Rocks, always diffused and broken by the wind that occasionally grew to the strength of gusts. Duncan talked— mostly I listened. He was accustomed to being listened to, as had the Duncan at Silkirk. He talked of his pony, Ginger, and the coves along the two shores of Landfall—the wild Atlantic side, the dead-calm bays of the lee shore. He talked of the sea creatures he saw there; he pointed out the tiny lizards that ran freely through the house, and we laughed at their curious *geko-geko* cry. They caught the insects, he explained, and he watched me closely, testing me like his father to make sure that I showed no fear of them. Often in his talk there was mention of Fergus, but I did not ask him about Fergus. Children have a way of knowing which question is meant to lead them on. He warned me, in a way his father would have, of the sun that could make you ill if you went out in it hatless; he talked of the rains that came sweeping suddenly and drenched you right through, and were gone within minutes, leaving the earth steaming. But such soakings didn't trouble him; always there were fresh, dry clothes, and the comforting black hands, and all was effortless. He didn't have to ask for anything; it was there, like the thin, black woman, Juanita, who came to lead him away.

"The siesta," he pronounced to me. "Everyone rests now."

Even for me, even for a governess there were the hours of the siesta, because no one else in the house stirred. But I noticed, as I walked the gallery from the schoolroom to my bedroom, that the gardeners still worked, the sun blazing upon their ragged straw hats. In my room a

woman waited, impatient with my seemingly aimless lingering, to close
the louvered shutters against the light. She said her name was Charity,
and she was to look after me; I could have laughed, but she wouldn't
have understood why. My stepmother had been right about my having
things that no governess dreams of. I rather liked the look of this
woman, plump, young enough still, her skin a pleasant, shining brown.
She didn't avert her eyes from mine quite as swiftly as most of the
other house slaves had done, and her head did not go down automatically when I appeared. She had been unpacking my trunk, and she
went back to the task, clucking in a forthright way over the heavy
clothes she brought out.

"What kind of place this, mistress—where you wear such things?"
She touched them with slightly disdainful fingers, and they did look
ugly and rather sad in this white, lofty room, with its mahogany
dressers and wardrobe, with the large bed dressed with a white spotted
Swiss muslin canopy and fine linen sheets. No room for a governess
this one, and no place for my old grey alpaca and plaid shawl.

"Very cold," I answered. "Not like this at all. There is much snow
where I come from."

Her expert hands loosened the strings of my stays. "I hear about this
snow thing, mistress, but I no believe it. No thing like that happen
here." We were standing before the oval pier mirror, and I saw her
dark eyes examining me closely as I stood there in my loose shift with
its low neck—a summer one, the lightest I owned. There was something
in the look that reminded me of the way Andrew Maxwell had ex-
amined me, almost a summing-up.

"You damn fine woman," she pronounced at last. "You got fine
breasts and hips, like the men want. It pity you wear such ugly
clothes." And then as my own hand had gone automatically to take
the pins from my hair, her own had brushed them aside, as if even
this slight task must be too much for any white woman. My hair came
down, the whole, full length of it, past my waist, and I heard her give
a little gasp; her fingers ran through it slowly, finally crushing its thickness. "It like fire and silk," she said, in a hushed voice.

I turned away and went toward the bed, unable to answer her. In
Scotland such things are rarely said, not with that implication of sen-
suality. I had never lain down to sleep in the afternoon in my life before, but now it seemed my senses craved the dimness, the impression
of coolness. The linen sheets and soft mattress received me as if I had
known them always. I heard the soft shuffling of Charity's bare feet

for a few moments longer, then stillness. I sensed her near me, and opened my eyes. She was standing quite close, gazing down at me. Even in that plump and pleasant face there was a knowledge of hardness and pain. Again her eyes assessed me. "Yes, mistress—it good thing you come to Landfall. A woman like you. Maybe you ease the trouble of this house." Then the slap-slap of her feet on the polished floor, and the repeated whisper as the door closed. "Like fire and silk . . ."

*　*　*　*　*

Perhaps it was the voices which woke me, or just the sense that the heat of the day was passing. I lay still in the dimness, unused to the surroundings, feeling the strange wideness of the bed after the narrow bunk of those weeks of the sea passage. And then the voices, not close to me, not the singsong of the slaves. I recognized Andrew Maxwell's tones, the rumble and the burr, rising suddenly, as if he could not long contain himself.

"Damn you, Fergus!—I told you . . . !"

I rose and went barefooted to the shuttered doors, and swung them wide. The afternoon sun was low enough to have begun to probe the depth of the gallery. I went to the railing, not bothering to conceal myself, just driven by curiosity about this Fergus who had failed to meet me at the dock that morning. I possessed no light wrapper, and in the warmth of the afternoon it had not occurred to me to reach for my plaid. I stood beside one of the great pillars of the house, which dripped with a vine whose flowers were enormous golden cups. The sun caressed my bare neck and arms, but did not bite as it would have done at noon. The full languor and beauty of the waning tropic afternoon was on Landfall, and the effects of sleep were heavy on me, making me careless.

I leaned far over the rail to see them. Andrew Maxwell stood on the lowest step as if he had followed his son down to emphasize what he was saying. There were no slaves in sight, though probably they listened, just as I did.

". . . you think I am too old now to be obeyed?—that you know everything? I still give orders here. I am still obeyed!"

The other man, face screened by the wide straw hat he wore, was mounted on a good chestnut horse. He sat it well, and held its impatient movement with ease and sureness. "And I tell *you*, Father, that while there are more important things to attend to, I'll leave the meeting and escorting of little Scottish governesses to those who have the time. And God knows, if there were a dozen of me working at Winterslo there still wouldn't be time for fripperies. Can't you ever get the notion into your head that a man can *change?* And if you've still any notion to force me into something I don't want, then, my father, you had best put it from your mind. The woman I—"

I must have leaned too far, absorbed, unabashedly listening and craning to see this man. First he looked up, his talk suddenly checked; then the old man turned slowly, his neck bending upward stiffly.

At once the hat of the young man came off; he was his father's son, as Duncan was. He was as Duncan would one day be. I was suddenly aware of the size of him on the horse, the red-blond hair, the fair skin that had somehow accommodated itself to the sun and was deeply browned. Even at this distance I was aware of the blueness of his eyes, like Duncan's, but these with sun wrinkles about the corners. He was beautiful, in the way a man can be, and never more beautiful than as I saw him that afternoon, before I knew him, before I loved him.

And then it came. The sudden awareness of something wrong, the chill of the soul that was no part of this tropic warmth. Why did I seem to see, back there, deep in the shade of the giant cottonwood tree that guarded the house, the shadow of another horseman?—this all black, and vague, without form, but charged with a terrible threat? It was like seeing this young man mirrored back there, a double-image, but the dark side of the mirror. One instant only, and it was gone. An illusion perhaps, a shred of my uneasy dreams. But the shape had seemed to me like the horseman of violence.

The illusion was fully gone as I heard the raw, licentious chuckle that broke from the old man's lips; I was made aware of myself—of my hair, tumbled from sleep, falling about me, of the loose, low-necked shift, of my whole abandonment to the sun and the languor, and my rooted fascination with the young man below me.

"There's your little Scottish governess, Fergus. It's a pity you chose not to obey me and be at dockside this morning." The laugh that followed was wild, and I turned and fled back to the shadow of the room.

And as I went I saw her, Maria Maxwell. She stood in the doorway of what must be her own room, for all the bedrooms opened onto the common gallery. She, too, must have been wakened by the voices. Her wrapper was of the finest lawn, and laced with red ribbon; her feet were in tiny red satin slippers. She was smiling oddly, and I saw the contempt in her smile. She said no word, and there was no reproach.

There was no need; I knew what I looked like, disheveled, loose, frowzy —a woman with no sense of decency. She made me feel like some bawd —and I was an eavesdropper as well. I felt my face burn with shame, and I could stand her gaze no longer. I crashed the shutters closed behind me, and fell onto the bed, weeping the first of the tears I was to weep at Landfall.

III

I did lessons with Duncan until it was time for his supper and bed. It seemed strange to begin work again almost at twilight, but the dusk came early, and the hours of the siesta made it necessary to divide the day in this way.

He was a strange child—oddly precocious in some matters, shockingly ignorant in others. He knew some of the history of Spain. Cortes and the conquistadors were his heroes, rather than Columbus. He knew the life of the plantation, and he was conscious of money in a way my own half-brother never would be. He knew about the West Indies, about London, Bristol, and Liverpool, and nothing else. "They sent the slave ships from Bristol and Liverpool to the Gold Coast," was his explanation. "Then they didn't let anyone take slaves from Africa any more, and everyone thought that was the end. But the slaves kept coming. They always do."

There was a kind of cruel indifference in the way he said it; slaves were not people, just objects. That was what he had been taught, and he had never heard any other opinion. For the beginning I would have to let it go; you did not change a child in an hour, and I still must find my way at Landfall. We did arithmetic and a little Latin; he was intelligent, but opposed to anything that did not bear directly on the business of the estate.

"Won't you have to count your barrels of sugar?" I asked. "And calculate how much they will earn on the London market?"

"Yes, but I won't be doing it in Latin."

I applied the chalk firmly to the blackboard. "Nevertheless, we will learn Latin. Do you want to look like an ignorant fool when you visit your Maxwell cousins, and go into London society?"

The Maxwell pride was touched. "No," he said. "No—I never want to be a fool."

"Then learn," I said. "The Scots have made their way only by fighting, working, and learning. In Scotland a scholar is an honored man."

He wasn't quite sure whether to believe me. His world was quite secure. "My father—Fergus—I don't think they're scholars, Miss Fiona, but I don't think . . ." But he did think. "My cousin, Alister, I suppose he knows a lot. I suppose he knows Latin and all those things." He was suddenly aware of a wider world. I had challenged him, and the soft little child's mouth was set. "We will learn then, even if it's Greek."

"Greek you'll not get from me, my laddie. I'm only a woman, after all. But before I leave you'll at least know there's such a place as Greece."

He looked astonished. "Why, will you be going, then? I thought if you had come all this way, you would be staying forever."

"Nothing lasts forever, lad," I said. "You'll grow up . . ." But I really meant that already I saw in Maria Maxwell's attitude that my time here was limited. One day would come the clash that could never be forgiven. As if aware that it might come soon, I hurried him on. "Now, let's move along. Time is going."

He bent over his slate, but in a moment or two his head was up again, the puzzled, winning, utterly irresistible look upon his face that my own little Duncan had often worn. "You know, Miss Fiona . . ."

"What . . . ?"

"You're quicker than all the other ladies I know." His brow wrinkled. "I don't know what it is. You talk so quickly . . . and move . . ." With a cheeky gesture his fingers walked across the slate. "One, two, three, four. Quick—quick!"

"Impudence!" And yet I couldn't help laughing. "Well, then, we'll make the best of it while it lasts. A few weeks of the siesta, and I'll hardly be able to move across the room."

"No, not you," he said, and he bent once again to copy the Latin declension. Before it was finished, the lean, saturnine Juanita, the slave who had taken him to his siesta, entered with a tray of food. It was set for one only.

"Mistress Fiona to eat downstairs with the master and mistress," was her curt explanation. At least that part of Maria Maxwell's letter had been the truth.

While Duncan ate I began to read to him from a history of Scotland that had come with me in my trunk. It was time he had other heroes besides the gold-seeking Spaniards.

* * * * *

I wore my best summer gown that evening, the one reserved in Scotland for the very occasional garden party I had attended, the summer church festival. Charity clucked with disappointment as the dress was put on. It was a pale green sprigged muslin, fine enough in Silkirk, but looking terribly old-fashioned, limp, and prim here. Why did the constant crying of the cicadas, the scent of the jasmine, the soft warmth of the night induce such discontent? Why did I long, passionately, for the first time in my life, to be beautiful, to wear the plumage of the peacock?

"Why you wear that silly dress right to the neck, mistress? Why you not show yourself off—fine woman like you?"

But still she piled my hair up, her fingers handling it with pleasure and skill; the candles were set in hurricane glasses to protect them from the breeze; in their gentle light I thought I looked better than I had ever done before. But I had to stop Charity placing a camellia above my ear.

"Governesses don't wear flowers, Charity."

She snorted. "You damn fine woman waste yourself." I laid down the camellia with some regret; there were just a few times when I felt life wasn't quite fair.

* * * * *

I thought I was the first downstairs; the candles in the chandelier were lighted in the hall, through the open doors to the dining room I caught a glimpse of the long table and the gleam of silver and crystal. But no one moved there, and no voices came from the salon. From the back of the house I could hear the sounds of the kitchen, the chatter of the kitchen slaves, the occasionally sharp command from Dougal. Strange how the openness of these West Indian houses distorted sound —brought close what was distant, while the breeze carried away that which was near. Perhaps that was why Maria Maxwell did not hear my approach. The cicadas thundered their nighttime chorus, the air was filled with the fragrance of the flowers that spilled everywhere, from heaped bowls on polished tables, from the perfumed garden itself. I felt that same mad discontent swell in me. It made me long—for what? For what?

I experienced a sharp upsurge of this unfamiliar state of being when finally I did look upon Maria Maxwell. I paused in the open doors of the salon, and she was there. At the far end of this great room stood a chimney and an elaborate carved marble mantel—this same feature appeared in balance in the dining room, surely an immigrant architect's nostalgia for the centerpiece of the great drawing rooms of European houses, for this climate could have had no need of such things. Above it was a large mirror, framed in scrolled silver-gilt. On the mantel were the only two candles that were yet lighted in that vast room. Just that one pool of light, and what I saw in it made me draw in my breath, and something as close to real envy as I had ever known shot through me.

The fact or the thought of jewels had never entered my consciousness before—perhaps because I had never seen any such as these, just the garnet brooches and gold chains of my employers' wives. I had never imagined such as I saw now. Maria Maxwell's back was to me, and in that mirror I saw the unforgettable fire of diamonds about her throat, the great green glow of a huge emerald star in her hair, the long green cataract of the emeralds hanging from her ears. She studied her own image intently, perhaps as fascinated as I was, and then she raised both hands to her face, fingers spread on her cheeks and the mirror seemed to explode into a thousand colors as the candlelight flashed back the burning torches of sapphire and ruby. The beveled mirror edge caught the leaping colors also, and for a moment Maria Maxwell stood there ringed with the fire that lived within the depths of those stones. I was transfixed. I felt as if I had unwittingly stepped into some other time, some other place, that in a moment wigged footmen would bring candelabra, and there would be laughter, and music and other such bedecked women in some fairytale palace in a world dreamed by a child.

The dream, like the vision in the mirror, was shattered by the hoarse, growling voice from the dark place where the red sofa stood.

"Maria!—can't we have any damned light in here? Here's Miss Fiona, and she can't see her way across the room."

She turned. "It *is* dark. How careless of me."

She faced me fully now. There were no jewels. There was no play of fire about her. Her throat and ears and hands were bare. There was no glowing warmth of emerald in her dark hair, just the perfect symmetry of her perfect body outlined by the close fit of the emerald silk gown she wore, its low bodice revealing her upthrust breasts. The only glow was the ivory sheen of her skin.

A clap of her hands, and Dougal was there, and lamps were springing to life.

I blinked stupidly as the familiar objects were revealed. It was all as it had been at noon, when Andrew and I had sat here. But what had I seen in the mirror? Was it a chance and freak reflection of the color of the gown in the beveled edges of mirror and silver frame. Was it . . . Did the spirit of some woman who had once inhabited this house come sometimes back to peer wistfully through Maria's eyes at the reflection of what no longer existed? Did Maria herself long to see her own reflection decked in such jewels, and had I caught an instant's manifestation of that longing? Was the discontent I had experienced not all born in my own soul, but communicated through some unwanted bond with this woman? Had this been what Maria *wanted* to see in the mirror?

I thrust my fright and bewilderment from me as best I might, and stumbled toward the nearest chair. Maria gave me a tight smile, a smile that seemed to take in the limp, prim gown, my awkward movements, the lack of social ease. Andrew Maxwell acknowledged my presence with a wave of his glass; he made no motion to rise, just looked at me with a vague indifference, as if the spark of lewdness that had leapt in him at the sight of me in my dishevelment that afternoon had died.

"Miss McIntyre, may I introduce your kinsman, Alister Maxwell?"

I hadn't seen him; I had had no notion of his presence there either. He was leaning against the doorway that led to the outer gallery, as if he must catch the breath of the night, as if this inner room bound and confined him too closely. I thought it extraordinary that three people had been in this room as I entered, and each had been alone, in silence and, except Maria, in darkness.

He came forward at once, and took my hand, as if glad of the release from his solitary state. He was not what I had expected. The limp was there, yes—as Andrew had said. What else had I imagined?—the reformer dressed in sober blacks, the horseman and expert shot watered down to some pallid stick with the Maxwell blond hair gone pale and sleeked down by the weight of piety? What I saw was a gentleman of fashion, tall, slender, immaculately dressed and tailored, though there was nothing of the dandy about him—just the impeccable fastidiousness of the silk shirt and waistcoat, the fine leather of the closely fitting boot, the cut of the buff-colored coat. The drawing room seemed his place, not the dreary meeting halls of the reform leaders. I could not imagine that immaculate coat ever spattered by rotten vegetables, nor that hand raised to quote the Bible to curse another.

"Miss McIntyre, I'm delighted to meet you. I remember meeting your mother once on a visit to Edinburgh as a child. The family always considered her a great beauty, I do recall."

In that case, I thought, I was probably a sorry disappointment. Well, what did it matter? I was grateful for his presence, for his smile, a rather grave smile; I began to feel that I would like him. He certainly didn't make me feel like a disappointment, and—this was unexpectedly welcome—he didn't look like a Maxwell, either. At least he was not blond and handsome in their fashion. Dark, rather sharp features, thick eyebrows, a long face. In a moment of wicked relief that here was not yet another of the blond beauties, I thought it was just as well he had not been born a woman. That face, in a woman, would have resembled a rather intelligent, thoughtful, elegant horse.

"Some wine, Miss McIntyre?" Maria Maxwell gestured toward the decanters. I saw that she had no glass herself, so I declined. And then I wished I had had the courage to take it because it might have helped me through the pause that followed. I was still shaken by the sight in the mirror. With half my mind still upon it, I must have seemed raw and ill-at-ease. But then who would not have been? This room had contained three people, and the atmosphere that hung on it was that of some violent quarrel, though no word had been spoken. Or perhaps it was that whatever quarrel existed at Landfall was of such long duration that it had settled upon the place, like fungus growing steadily on the walls. I remembered then Captain Stewart's comment . . . "It has never been a lucky place . . ."

Movement and pretense of ease were made by Alister Maxwell, and I blessed him for it. There are some men gifted with manners, with concern, and he seemed to be one of them. He drew a chair toward mine, and sat down.

"I'm in Scotland far too seldom these days, Miss McIntyre, and the Maxwell cousins are so numerous . . . It has been shameful on my part that I have never been to pay my respects to Cousin Dorothy—and your good father, of course. It's a remote parish, is it not . . . ?"

I lost myself for a moment in telling him—the sea, the hills behind, the summer visitors, the long winters. He knew it all, of course; he had been in Scotland enough times to know. But at least there was talk to relieve the deadly silence between Andrew Maxwell and his wife.

"Your stepsister, Mary, came to visit an aunt in London a little time ago. I remember her well. A pretty little girl . . ." He sounded as if he knew what we all acknowledged about Mary—she was as pretty as a doll, and in time grew just as boring.

Abruptly Andrew Maxwell's glass was raised, thrust out toward us. "Ah—Miss Pink-and-Pretty. Come now, Maxwell—you remember her better than that. At least your father does, from his letters. She was being looked over. Not good enough for a London Maxwell—but all right to send out here. Good enough for my son—"

"Andrew—"

Maria Maxwell's voice was a whisper, but he turned quickly in her direction, and her look had the same power over him as it did me. He was silenced; but he signaled to have his glass refilled once more. Now, because politeness demanded it, Alister Maxwell gave his attention to Maria. There was some discussion about a horse that had gone lame, how it should be treated, what had caused it. I did not feel left out; Alister had helped me over my first difficulty, and I expected no more of him. I felt free now to let my eyes wander about the room, since Andrew was disinclined to talk. I saw more things than I had seen at noon, when he had commanded all my attention. It was as richly furnished as I remembered, but rather heavy in feeling. There was much plush and heavy gold-tipped frames on age-darkened pictures of people in stiff dress that I imagined might have been of the Spanish court. The piece that drew the attention, after the white marble mantel, was the huge cabinet, reaching almost to the ceiling, with long glass doors two thirds of its length, and drawers beneath. It could have come from some palace in Spain; magnificently carved, with thin, elongated figures of what I imagined to be the twelve apostles forming the divisions between the glass doors, and surmounted in pediment fashion by a host of child angels. The whole was topped over the center doors by a carved cross which looked as if it had once been broken off, and replaced slightly askew. It gave the massive cabinet the look of being about to fall forward. It was a gloomy piece, but its contents were of a different order. It contained books, as one might have expected, but one whole shelf was given over to a collection of dolls. Maria and Alister were still talking horses, and I felt free to rise and go to it. They were not ordinary books, nor ordinary dolls. Each volume was bound in vellum, the titles inscribed in faded manuscript in an ancient style. The dolls, though, riveted my attention. Exquisitely dressed, all of them, they seemed to represent the regional dress of different parts of Spain—among them even the Moorish dress of Andalusia, and one with the wide panniered skirts and tight curls of the Valásquez portraits. The wax faces were fashioned with great artistry, not blank and staring, but with the expressions of real people. They seemed old; some of the fabrics were starting to rot; they each had their appointed place, the rag bodies held to a wooden rack, I would not have dared to touch them, but instinctively my hand went up toward the glass as I leaned to get a better view.

"It is locked, Miss McIntyre." Maria had been watching me, for all her apparent interest in the subject of the horses. "I dare not allow the hands of any of the slaves upon those things—even Duncan might be tempted. They are very old, and very precious. The manuscripts, some of them, are illuminated, and one or two are believed to have come from the library of the sainted Phillip the Second . . ."

"I must persuade you, some day, Cousin Maria," Alister said, "to allow me to look at them. In a very humble fashion I am also a collector of books."

She swept the statement away. "And the dolls—they were made especially for the Infanta Catalina, and given to a cousin of my great-great-grandmother, who had been a lady-in-waiting . . ."

A roar of derisive laughter came from Andrew. "And a lot of good they do you, that pile of junk. My wife's only dowry—that cabinet and its contents, and I am tired to death of the sainted Phillip and his books moldering away with mildew there, and those stupid dolls. No wonder the Infanta got rid of them—if they ever belonged to an Infanta. Probably gave them to the washerwoman."

"*Hombre!* Despicable liar—!"

Dougal's soft voice. "Dinna, mistress."

In an awful parody of normalcy, Alister took Maria's arm as they moved through the hall to the dining room. Andrew was helped to his feet by Dougal. He leaned heavily on his cane as he started, and was about to reach for the arm of the slave for support. Then he remembered me. His head jerked around, and a strange light came to his face, as if he were recalling something of long ago. The ugliness of his ill-humor with his wife disappeared.

"Come, my dear. It's a long time since I've had the pleasure of escorting a real woman to dinner . . ." But his hand did not take my arm. Instead I felt his own arm about my waist, his weight heavy and dragging. "You must forgive an old man his infirmities." But I felt no infirmity in the way he clutched my waist behind his wife's back, nor the press of his fingers into my flesh.

* * * * *

IV

Dinner was a little better. The wine that was served to all of us seemed to stimulate Maria Maxwell; she talked—though exclusively to Alister, demanding gossip of London, of fashion, of the theatre. The controlled face grew animated; she flirted harmlessly with the practised ease of a born beauty. Her mouth pulled down at the corners in an enchantingly provocative pout. "We are so dull here—of course my husband does not permit us to entertain at Landfall. But when one goes into society—only little parties, little race meetings. No real *ton*—is that not the word, Alister?"

He smiled indulgently. "The exact one, Cousin Maria. But I would dispute your contention of dullness. Life is dull in most places—it isn't all one long party. People work in London just as they do everywhere else. *I* work—I go to my offices every day, and sit over my dull accounts—"

She cut him short. "But nevertheless, I would like to go to London. Since those wretched Bonapartes ruined Spain, there is no place to go but England."

"That isn't what I hear from you, Maria," Andrew said, stuffing his mouth with bread. "All I hear is those two years you spent in Madrid and your noble relations. How grand everything was—how high class. Apparently the Bonapartes didn't ruin *them*."

She shrugged. "The aristocracy survived even the Bonapartes. But they kept to themselves. Life was not . . . gay. Some fortunes were ruined. You do not have the French and the English fighting across a country for all those years without life being affected. No—if I had my choice it is to London I would go now. But my husband will not be budged—"

"No—and well you know it, Maria." The undercurrent of anger seemed always present in Andrew Maxwell's voice. "And you know yourself you're talking a lot of nonsense. If I said tomorrow that you must pay a long visit to London—that you must take Duncan to see the sights and give him an idea of how life is lived elsewhere, you know you wouldn't leave. After all"—and now his tone became sneering—"who would run the place? Who would see that we were not being cheated? Who would see that the slaves were kept properly in order?

Not *this* old man—not this poor wretch who was only fit to build up Landfall, but not to . . ."

She replied with swift cruelty. "You are quite right, my dear husband. Who would do all these things?" Now she looked at Alister. "You see, I also have my dull accounts to attend to." She gave a little sigh and a shrug. "And London is so far away. No—it is better to stay. One must be content . . ."

"Content!" The voice was harsh and low, and came from the darkness of the gallery beyond the dining room. We had heard no noise of his horse, so he must have walked from the stables. No slave had come to announce his arrival. He stepped into the light, Fergus Maxwell, big, handsome, carelessly dressed in the shirt he had worn that afternoon, neck loose, even a rip in one sleeve. His hair was tumbled and untidy. I might almost have thought him drunk, if the voice and the stance had not been so firm, so sure.

"My dear Maria . . ." He advanced a little into the room toward her. "What is this about contentment? *You* will never be content until you own the whole island. My father, for once, is quite right. You will never leave Landfall for London. After all, the money's at Landfall, isn't it? And in London there is only all this nonsensical talk of emancipation."

She chose to ignore his words. "Good evening, Fergus. I did not expect the pleasure of your company for dinner, but, of course, do sit down . . ." She snapped her fingers, but it was unnecessary. A place was already being laid, and three slaves waited by the big silver serving dishes until Fergus should be ready for them. He went to the sideboard and poured himself wine. He was about to put the glass to his lips, and then he paused.

"Thank you for your welcome, Maria. And my father. It is always good to know that one is welcome in one's home." He raised his glass to them.

"Sit down and stop making a fool of yourself," Andrew Maxwell growled.

He seemed not to hear his father's words, nor to see the chair held for him by Dougal. Instead, he walked down the long table to me.

"And this, of course, is the little Scottish governess. Not quite what we were led to expect. But welcome to Landfall. My name is Fergus Maxwell. Everyone seems to have forgotten to introduce us. Fiona McIntyre, isn't it? Well, it's a nice change from having another Maxwell—"

"And what's wrong with being a Maxwell?" I said. I heard my own voice, and it sounded tart and sour, like a governess's. I had spoken like that because I hated his mockery, because I feared to reveal the kind of strange warmth the sight of him gave me. His manners were atrocious; he seemed to want to hurt each person in that room, and perhaps all beyond it. And yet I couldn't dismiss it as mere bad manners; in that marvelously handsome man whose grace should have won him friends effortlessly, there was an air of defensiveness. The blue eyes, with their sun-wrinkles radiating from them, were wary. I could remember seeing dogs and horses like that—some that had been treated harshly and never again would respond to a friendly overture, and yet whose pride would never permit them to grovel or beg a favor, no matter how badly needed. He could have been twenty-six years old, and for a man of that age, the son of his father, he looked tired and confused and reckless, as if he didn't know what to do next, nor did he much care. Like a child he wanted to provoke and annoy, and yet the adult knew all the play acting was nonsense. He was too young to have begun to despair. This was what I felt about Fergus Maxwell, and I wished with all my heart that our first meeting might have been more private, without the eyes and attention of the whole room, white, and black slave, upon us.

And then I added, more softly, perhaps with the hope that my words would not reach the others, perhaps with the thought that I could erase the image of the acid-tongued governess, "One accepts what one is, Mr. Maxwell. I hope I have not suffered from being my mother's daughter."

It took him a very long time to reply. I thought I saw a flicker of regret in his expression; but Fergus Maxwell would not be accustomed to a polite apology. He looked at me carefully, and the appraising stare was like his father's; I was forcefully reminded of Charity's words as she had gazed at me as I had undressed. "I would say you had not suffered from that cause at all, Miss Fiona. No—not suffered in the least."

He gave a little bow, the best he could do, I thought. And then he went to his place at the table. The talk flowed on as before, and as before, it was only between Maria Maxwell and Alister. Sometimes a sardonic, derisive comment came from Andrew, but his son said nothing. He said nothing at all while the dishes were passed around, and the wine continued to be poured. But I saw how often, almost an involuntary action, his eyes went to Maria; it made me almost sick to see it, that look of mingled longing and hate. He seemed unable to help himself and I—I was no better, since I could not myself turn my eyes from him. He said nothing at all until Maria rose to indicate that the meal was ended. I knew that I would not be expected to sit with her in the drawing room, and the men probably would sit over port. I said my good-nights quietly.

As Maria reached the door Fergus, only half-risen from his seat, called loudly to her.

"I suppose it's all right if I stay the night? The roof of my room at Winterslo is leaking like a bucket full of holes, and my well-trained servants have managed to get my bed stuck nicely in the doorway. I thought I might take shelter with you until we either take the door down, or cut the bed in half. I suppose that would be the solution, since a bachelor needs only half a bed—"

I wished that something, just once, would have shaken her coolness. "There is always a bed for my husband's son at Landfall. Gentlemen—good-night."

I followed her, my steps dragging. As I passed Alister Maxwell, I looked at him fully, frankly appealing to him for some support, some sense of normalcy in this house full of mockery and contempt and tension. I sought light in my bewilderment and confusion. As if I had spoken my need he answered at once. "Let me fetch your candle, Miss Fiona."

Andrew said sharply, "There's half a dozen housemen to do those kind of things, Alister. Pass the port—"

His way of disregarding Andrew was not so pointed as Fergus's had been; he simply indicated without rudeness that he would do what he wanted to do. He even took my arm as we went to the long table in the hall where the candles in their glasses were lined up. With a wave of his hand as practised as Maria's he dismissed the slave who had lighted one at our approach. He came only to the foot of the staircase with me. I stood on the first step, and we were poised there in full view of both the drawing room and the dining room. Andrew Maxwell and his son had both turned to watch us, and Maria had resumed her stance before the mirror, but this time facing the door. Alister and I were a little tableau motionless for their gaze.

I forgot decorum and the newness of our acquaintance in my desperation. I spoke very softly, and I hoped to the watchers it appeared to be the conventional phrases of thanks and leave-taking.

"For God's sake—*who* is Fergus Maxwell? I was told there was only one son. And his father married late. Was there another marriage—a first wife?"

"No first wife. But Fergus Maxwell is the son of one of the island's celebrated scandals."

We could say no more. Charity had appeared at the head of the staircase, waiting. I took the candle from Alister Maxwell's hand and turned and started up in obedience to the unspoken command that had seemed to come from each one of those who watched us.

V

The tropic night is not a silent one; the cicadas sing, the lizards give out their strange cry, sometimes the rustling of bat wings is heard, and distantly the surf pounds against the Serpent Rocks. But the wind dies, only to rise again with the strengthening of the sun in the morning. So the night was hot and airless, the fine linen sheets damp beneath my body, the pillow wet with the sweat of my neck. A dozen times that night I felt that I must chop off the weight and length of my hair; later I learned to braid it.

So wearily, with little sleep to help me, I got up when the first light began to penetrate the downslanted louvers; I seemed unsteady on my feet as I threw back the shutters, and saw the beginning of that most precious of times on a West Indian island, the beginning of the day. I walked out to the edge of the gallery; everything was calm about me, no wind stirred, no leaf moved. The distant sea was the pale, pale blue it is only before sunrise; I heard the first crow of a cock. I knew that the time of peace would be of short duration. But it still was the time of enchantment; everything at that moment looked as if it were freshly born. It was as if I were there, at the beginning of all things, at the beginning of time, of creation itself. My father would have recognized this moment; it was all unspoiled, unsullied, innocent.

I went to one of the low cane chairs that stood about the gallery, feeling sure that no one else of the household would be astir at this time. I was filled with a sense of futility, almost despair. I felt I would not stay long at Landfall; everything was against it. Even though a kind of vision had brought me here, I began to recognize that I might see what should be done, what role I should play, and yet be prevented from playing it, I had not been able to do anything for that young man, Thomas Scobie, who had spoken to the crowd in Kelvingrove

Gardens; he would go on to whatever his fate was, quite regardless of my warning. I had a terrible presentiment that all here at Landfall were headed for destruction. There was already a kind of moral rot, but their ruin would be total. It would come in some physical form. But what could I, a stranger, an outsider, ignorant of every single factor of their lives and histories, do about it? Perhaps I was merely sent to witness the destruction, powerless to prevent it, knowing my impotence beforehand. Perhaps I was to share in the destruction. These are the thoughts that gather after a sleepless night.

"You too are awake early." I hardly recognized his voice; it was different, hushed, weary. Perhaps his night had been like mine; perhaps the vast quantities of rum did not bring sleep; I remembered what Captain Stewart had said about old men not sleeping late. Andrew Maxwell stood at the corner of the gallery; perhaps he had been looking at me for some time. But now it didn't matter about my nightgown, and the plaid thrown loosely about me, my bare feet; it didn't matter about the tangled and sweat-soaked hair. There was none of the posture of the lascivious man who had gazed up at me from below yesterday, the one who had squeezed my waist last night. This was just a tired old man, subdued in the aftermath of an uneasy night. He wore a long silk robe, rumpled, frayed about the sleeves and neck, and his feet, like mine, were bare.

"One usually does not sleep well in strange places the first night. And then, I am not used to the tropics . . ."

"None of us gets used to the tropics," he replied. "Our bodies aren't made for it, even if we're born here." He went to the railing as I had done, just standing, watching the light grow, the outline of the coast appear, the clouds begin to lift off Kronberg.

"The best time of the day," he said. "Always has been—just these bare few minutes—fresh, still. Now—and late at night. I used to walk late at night, when I was able. I used to swim early in the mornings. At night the stars are so close even an old man can dream of reaching to touch them. And the sky is blue, not black . . . you will get to know these things, Miss Fiona. But I doubt you'll ever get used to them. There are too many contrasts—the violence of the rain at night, and then this stillness in the morning. I love to hear the rain pounding on the roof at night—do you know that? I love this peace at dawn. And then the heat of the day comes, and you long for the dark again."

He came and slumped into a chair near mine. "Well, what do you think of Landfall?"

"What can I think of it? It's a fine house, Mr. Maxwell. A very grand house—but I haven't seen anything else, have I?"

"Don't be a fool, girl! Landfall isn't just the house. What do you think of *us*? Landfall is a house anyone can admire—anyone who comes here does. But *we* make it. I want to know what you think of us."

I faced him quickly. "It isn't fair to ask such questions of me—and I don't intend to try to answer. What do I know about you?"

But he pressed. "What do you think of my son, Fergus?"

"He is a handsome, bad-mannered young man. That's all I know about him. I didn't even know he existed . . ."

"Well, did you think it was something my wife would write in a letter to invite a Miss Pink-and-Pretty out here? Would she say that a sometime member of our household was her husband's illegitimate son? Well—would she write such a letter to the wife of a Scottish preacher?"

"It would have been more honest to do so." I was growing angry. "Perhaps my father would have looked more kindly upon such an admission than upon its concealment. What did you expect me to do, Mr. Maxwell? Throw up my hands and weep? Pack my trunks? Governesses don't enjoy the luxury of such displays. And don't you think my father has tried to help many a girl in our village 'in trouble' as they say. He's a human being . . . a good, kindly man." And then I added, I don't know why, except that it seemed suddenly important to remind myself of the fact, to hold it to me as a defense against what I saw here. "He loved my mother. He knows what it is to love."

"It's strange he didn't know about Fergus. Perhaps he did, but he didn't talk about it. It might have made you decide against a good position—"

"He didn't *want* me to leave Scotland. I didn't have to come."

"The London Maxwells knew about Fergus," he persisted.

"We never see the London Maxwells. Only the time Mary went . . ."

"Ah, yes, Miss Pink-and-Pretty. Well, old Jeremy wouldn't have told her. Ears too delicate."

I gathered the plaid about me and started to rise. "I think there's no point in our continuing to talk now, Mr. Maxwell. I will say things I would rather not—should better not—say. I don't like to hear my stepsister referred to as Miss Pink-and-Pretty. There's a deal more to her than that. I can hardly instruct you in manners, but you need instruction as badly as your son."

He waved his hand. "Hush, hush, girl! Yes, I go too far, I know. You will have to try to forgive my crudities. I've not had anyone worth practising manners on for some time—not really ever. I could like you, girl. For that I'll try to mind my tongue. So sit easy and enjoy what's left to us of the time before the bell."

It seemed churlish to reject his offer of peace, and besides, I was awash in a sea of ignorance. If he was in a mood to talk, before there was too much rum in him, it might help me.

"You've wondered about Fergus, of course."

"Of course," I answered.

"Well, better hear it from me than some mumbled half-truths from Charity, and snippets from our Cousin Maxwell. He'll only have what was told at secondhand, in any case. After all, Fergus is my son. I'm the one who knows."

I saw his fingers flex and unflex on the arms of the cane chair; it was almost as if he were counting back the years, ticking them off to arrive at the time when the story had begun. It mattered what was important to him, and it did not begin with Fergus.

"I said you reminded me of my mother. She was your type of woman—a fine, handsome, strong woman, with more strength in her soul even than in her body. As I said, she would have borne a dozen like me, if my father hadn't been killed. He had brought her out here as a bride, and they were carving a small estate out of uncleared land—land no one had bothered with before—they were building Winterslo. It was fierce, hard work. He had very little capital, and that meant fewer slaves than he needed for the work. He couldn't afford a white overseer, and so he mostly acted as his own driver—that's the man who moves the slaves in line through the cane fields. They have to be kept moving, you know—and often the whip is needed. All of them are lazy rascals. It happened then as it happens still. The black man rose up with his machete against his master; they say my father died with one stroke. Well, the slave was flogged to death—or hanged. I don't know—my mother refused to speak about it."

Suddenly his tone changed to impatience. "Oh, don't look like that, girl! Men die violent deaths. It has always been that way. Slaves are a tricky business. Never trust a slave. They will steal your food and your secrets, and if they can, your life. Better to flog and be sure, than trust and be dead. Don't try to make them grateful to you for favors.

They have long memories—their memories go back to Africa, and there is no forgetting. Just be warned."

I took what he said, and knew I could not protest. I had known what I was coming to. Had I expected it to be pretty? Hadn't I known that humans in bondage forced the making of rules, and that life on a plantation would be lived according to them? I might as well have expected to walk and see innocence among the stews of Glasgow, as expect to find slaves happy in their plight here in the islands of the sun.

"What did she do, your mother?"

"She went on. She was that kind. She had more courage than six men. With Winterslo half-built, she made a few rooms habitable for us both, and no slave slept within the house at night. She learned how to handle a pistol, and she carried it with her, as well as a whip. She carried me with her also into the fields, holding me before her on the saddle, and when I was old enough I rode my own pony. But I suppose I was hardly ever beyond her sight until I proved I could take care of myself. She taught me what I know of books—mostly it was accounts that mattered. There was no money for such luxuries as a governess. It was a hard life we both knew, Miss Fiona—acre by acre slowly cleared, a room at a time completed at Winterslo. She had to learn it all, and then teach it to me."

"Did she every think of remarrying? White women must have . . . ?"

"Perhaps she had some romantic fancy that no man she ever met came up to my father. Perhaps she was too engrossed in the plantation, too busy, to affect the idle airs that might have made her attractive to other men. You age quickly in a life as hard as hers. It's even possible, Miss Fiona, that she frightened men off. They don't like to know that a woman can do a job better than they can. She would have made a difficult wife for any man who didn't measure up to her standards. Who would expect such a woman to sit idle in the drawing room of some plantation greathouse? In any case, for whatever reason, that was how it was. She didn't marry again."

"And you didn't marry?"

He shrugged. "I hardly had time to notice. Oh, let us not be delicate about it. Of course there were women. Where there are slaves there are always women to be had. And there were others—others I came across in Santa Marta—quadroons, octoroons—women who never expect to marry a white man, but don't want a black one, either. As long as you have a few gifts for them . . . well, I was no saint. I was a young man, and I took what I needed. My mother didn't expect otherwise. She just ignored it, as all white women do out here."

"Then what?—Fergus had a white mother." He was talking now, and nothing would stop him. I could ask him anything, and the answers would come tumbling from memory, perhaps from nostalgia. He needed to speak it again.

"I must have been thirty-six—yes, I must have been all of that. Can you imagine that I fell in love for the first time? She was white—of course she was white. And she was seventeen years old—a child almost. I met her at a ball in Santa Marta. I wasn't considered eligible, you know, but bachelors were always invited. She was the most beautiful thing I had ever seen—and no one since then to touch her. She was soft, and yet like porcelain—great green eyes shining. Enough to drive a man out of his mind. I remember I knocked a man unconscious out in the garden so that I could have his dance with her. And I made her—I *made* her—promise to come riding with me the next day. I half expected her not to appear, but she did. Of course there was a groom with her, but he was a slave, and he did what he was told. We met often after that—an old ruined greathouse in the hills. She would have been whipped and locked up if her parents had known."

He added, "It was the first time I had been in love. I didn't pay attention to the rules. I didn't even know them."

He sighed; it was the sound of a man who has almost begun to regret the looking-back, the pain, the confrontation of old memories best left dormant. "I wondered why she kept putting off the time when I would go and speak to her father. I wanted to marry her. God knows, I was probably the least eligible, in terms of material goods, of any man on the island, but no man could have loved her more. Then she told me—in the end she told me. She was engaged to marry the heir to one of the richest and highest-born names in England—let's not talk of the name, Miss Fiona. You would know it, but it no longer matters. He had come out on a visit to one of the family planta-tions on San Cristóbal, and had merely seen her. He hardly knew her at all—she was still in the schoolroom. But connoisseurs as well as rough men like myself know something unique when they see it. She was spoken for, and she was to be married by her eighteenth birthday."

He gave a harsh, wild laugh, that seemed too loud for the stillness that yet surrounded us. "But it was too late, you see. Those meetings at the greathouse, and the slave who was too frightened of me to speak to her parents. I was mad for her, and she was only seventeen. Yes,

I suppose you'd say I had seduced her, but I'll swear to this day that she loved me, and it seemed no willful violation, but just the only thing that could have happened between two people who felt as we did.

"Then suddenly she stopped coming. I went to her parents' house, and no one would admit me. I inquired after the slave who had always ridden with her. He was dead, Miss Fiona—he was dead. Never trust a slave.

"No one saw her in Santa Marta, and there were rumors that she was ill with fever. Her noble fiancé was expected back at any time. I was frantic, and yet I couldn't get in to her. Short of shouting her name in the streets of Santa Marta, there was no way I could force her parents to see me. It went this way for several months. Oh, yes, I got a note—one of those little schoolgirl notes dictated by a mother with that rubbish about my attentions being unwelcome. I didn't believe a word of it. I even heard she had been shipped off the island, back to England. And then there was the day the man she was to marry arrived. It was some months before he was expected, I remember. No letter to announce him—nothing. Just his arrival, and his natural demand to see his future bride. They tried to stop him—they told him, I think, she had a contagious fever. They had hoped, you see, to have it all over before he came, but he came too soon. He persisted—perhaps he loved her, too, as much as one could without knowing her. Well, he saw her finally, and he saw that she was carrying another man's child. He said nothing to her, I'm told—no words of love or reproach. He put his hands about her throat, and choked out of her the name of the child's father. And then he turned his back on her and left. An hour later, in the presence of several witnesses, he swore to kill me.

"He did it, of course, in the proper English fashion. He sent his seconds, and I rounded up a couple of real friends I had, and we met as arranged. I shot him through the heart. And my poor little girl—my little love—gave premature birth to my son, and died. I never saw her before she died."

His voice now was a hoarse whisper. "Perhaps I never would have seen my son, but the slave entrusted with getting rid of him—drowning him, probably, or throwing him where he would never be found—preferred the risk of telling me that he had been born, and still lived. I went to the house that night and demanded him. They made very little trouble over giving him over to me—who wanted such a child? But how much better if they had given me his mother."

After all these years the pain was still there, the sense of loss, of being cheated. "So I brought him back to Winterslo, more dead than alive—a tiny, half-breathing, seven-month infant. I gave him to my mother, and she took him. She saved his life—found a wet nurse for him, constant watching, keeping him warm, keeping him cool. He was strong, for all that he had come too soon. But he survived those first weeks, and I had my son. What I wanted was the mother."

It had been the beginning of the hurt in Fergus, of course, the child there at Winterslo instead of the mother, the child brought up by an aging woman. There would have been little softness in Fergus Maxwell's childhood.

"There was an inquiry, naturally," Andrew went on. "Dueling is illegal, but a man has the right to defend himself. There was a fuss in England, but the courts here didn't touch me. But it was the beginning of isolation at Winterslo. We had never had much time or money for social life, but after that we went nowhere and were asked nowhere. And I didn't care to go, either. I turned my back on the whole island, and I gave everything I had to making them regret that the mother of my child hadn't been permitted to marry me."

"But Landfall . . . ?"

"I'd been watching Landfall—coveting it, probably. Some of the best sugar land on the whole island. What was wrong was an absentee landlord—and a series of mishaps and unlucky chances ever since the house had been built. The best overseer you can get isn't enough to counteract the absentee owner—you have to be there yourself and know what you're doing. I knew the state it was in—it adjoins the Winterslo lands, though Winterslo doesn't produce half the crop by the acre. I knew the Landfall overseer was drunk half the time, and I made it my business to come over here regularly—drink with him, though never half as much as he did. I saw to it that he always had a good supply of rum, and I made up from my own store what he took from the Landfall barrels. Within two years Landfall was showing so little profit that it was ready for anyone who would take it. So that was when I went to London—to the Maxwells. I mortgaged Winterslo for everything it was worth, and with it went my own record of working it up to that point. They lent me the money, and kept themselves an interest in the place, and I came back here, and Landfall was mine. It was mine—under a staggering load of debt, but it was mine.

"That was the only time I ever left the island—and I didn't stay a week in London. Give it to the Maxwells—old Jeremy didn't keep me hanging about for an answer. While I was there I used another name. Because of the man I'd killed—his family was very powerful . . .

"One other thing I did, though. Mostly for my mother's sake, but partly for my own, I traveled up north, far into the Highlands, to the village that both she and my father had come from. I did not say who I was, contacted none of the families. I just looked, and climbed those mountains, and knew a different kind of rain than I'd ever known before. I saw how they lived. And then I began to understand what made them as they were—that streak most Scots have in them. Stubborn, independent, prideful, damned obstinate, and able to take what life hands to them. I came back knowing better who and what I was . . .

"The rest was hard work, and the refurbishing of this house. My mother was against ever coming here; she wanted no part of it. It was half in ruins, and she would have let it go. But it was first the garden that caught me—it had been planted more than a hundred years before that, when the house was first started. I cleared the vines and the undergrowth, and the pattern of the garden came to life. I learned about plants, because there were some plants here I had never seen before. I sent to London for books—how Santa Marta would have laughed if they'd known that rough, uncouth Andrew Maxwell was sitting up of night over botany books. And then the house began to fascinate me, as the center of this garden. I set some men to work on it—it was half-unroofed, but its interior had been built of mahogany, and the termites don't take hold in that too easily. My mother opposed it all the way, and probably she was right. I was in no hurry, but room by room it was restored, and I began to pick up furniture, and bits and pieces. And the stories got about Santa Marta, and everyone thought that one day I would break out of my cocoon, and Landfall would be a great place for visiting and parties. Perhaps they were nearly right. I didn't realize it until the place was finished, until the gardens were restored to what they once had been, that probably at the back of my mind I had been preparing a home that the parents of the girl I had loved so much would have been proud to see her mistress of. And when it was done I closed the gates; those eager to see it never were invited. My mother was dead; Fergus and I lived here alone —that is, until eight years ago."

"And Winterslo?"

"That belongs to Fergus now." His voice rasped on the words. "It was good enough for my mother and me. He complains, but it is *his* turn to work to get what he can from that land now. It doesn't yield like Landfall, but a man can live from it. An estate can't be cut up, Miss Fiona—that's how you make peasants of landowners. There can be only one heir to Landfall."

"And that will be Duncan."

"That one will be Duncan."

From the back of the house, somewhere, a bell began to toll. It was a mournful sound on the morning air, like a lament, slow, reluctant. Andrew Maxwell began to heave himself out of his chair. He was without his cane, and the movement was painful.

"That's the bell to get the slaves into the fields. They do a few hours work before breakfast is brought to them. Charity will be bringing your water up. It's time to get ready. We work early here, before the heat of the day." Then, as if it were all part of the same thought, he added, "Teach him well, Miss Fiona—if you can, teach him quickly, and teach him some Scottish good sense. There could be troubles coming for us here all over the Indies, and he's very young yet."

Very slowly he left me, bare feet shuffling more heavily than the slaves, his hand occasionally going to the wall to support himself. I sat for a while longer, pondering what I had been told, listening to the sounds of Landfall coming to life. Mostly I was thinking of Fergus, the child that Andrew Maxwell's conscience had saved from death, who had been willed to life by the care of an aging grandmother, the child gradually learning these things about himself in the isolation of Winterslo, and thereafter hating the world for what it had not given him. Was that the darkness I had seen behind him yesterday like a second rider in the shadows of the great cottonwood?—the black bitterness, the dark past? There were things at Landfall I did not understand, perhaps never would. Did they come from the past, like the vision of the jewel-bedecked woman I had seen last night?—were they the future? Did they exist in this time now? I could not tell. The solid walls about me seemed to breathe of things to come—or were they past? My weary mind could not accept it all; I shook myself as if to wake from a sleep of many years. My very limbs felt old as I gathered myself up and began to make my way back to my room. I turned the corner of the gallery dreamily, hardly distinguishing the figure who leaned back against one of the pillars, the red-blond head crushed back into a tangle of honeysuckle, perched on the railing itself, one foot touching the floor for balance, the other drawn up, his knee clasped by both hands.

"As he said, Miss Fiona, the best time of the day—almost gone now."

Now he turned his face fully toward me. "I should be back there at Winterslo now, beginning the day with my hands in the fields. But I was remembering too—just as he was." The tone was gentle, without mockery. I just stood rooted, staring at him; the face was strangely naked, vulnerable. He would not quip with me as he had done last night. He must have listened to the whole recital, the story retold.

"I'm glad you know it all, now," he said. "And best it came from my father. You know, you look at him now—gross, half the time drunk, smoking that rotten weed, that Indian hemp, and it's hard to believe he could have loved so romantically—with that kind of delicacy and absolute loyalty—and such a creature as he describes. Could it have lasted, I wonder, if she had lived? But for him she lives forever—just as she was. But as he said, he wanted her, and he got me. I was remembering . . . I was remembering Winterslo, and my grandmother. I was remembering being young here at Landfall without her. I hated it—this grand big house, and just the two of us. You heard how it was. He prepared this house for a woman who was already dead. A house made ready for a ghost—a bride who never came. No carriages came driving up, no champagne was drunk under those chandeliers. There were just the two of us, staring at each other down that long table. Is it any wonder we hated each other?"

"Hate . . ." I said slowly, shaking my head trying to say clearly what I meant, but the words were leaden on my tongue. "It was here before you—it goes on."

"I know." He put his other foot to the floor and straightened. "We met it here, and it goes on. What can one do?" Then his tone changed. "But he said one thing to remember. Duncan!—try with Duncan. He needs it. None of us can give him what he needs. Perhaps you can. Good-bye, Miss Fiona. I don't come often to Landfall. I don't know when I'll see you again."

I almost put my hand toward him. "Perhaps . . . No, it is nothing."

He may not have heard; in a way I hoped he hadn't. Did I want to be even more vulnerable? He was almost at the corner of the gallery when he turned and looked back. He didn't even smile as he said it.

"You know, you're really quite beautiful when you're not all tidied up."

Chapter 3.

Slowly, with a care that I had never practised before, I began to find my way at Landfall. The first day set the pattern of the day-to-day happenings; the times of rising and going to bed, the times of meals and lessons with Duncan. But that was only the outward rhythm, the set time pieces by which any household runs. There were a thousand things I did not know about Landfall, but the key lay in the people who inhabited it, and there never was again a session so frank and open as I had that first morning with Andrew Maxwell.

It was true that I still woke when the first light fell across the louvers; before sunrise the cocks crowed but now the sound signified something more to me than the break of day. After the first day, after my first walk beyond the house itself, following the paths that led through the garden, I found the slave quarters. I did not inspect them closely; hostile dark eyes told me that these wretched places were private, and that no stranger was welcome. They invited no scrutiny; least of all they invited pity. I left the dank and crumbling huts almost as abruptly as I had come upon them—they were closer to the greathouse than one thought, but in the tropics, the eternal cloak of greenery hides many things. But I knew now that as soon as the cocks crowed, those quarters, still in darkness, were astir, the black forms stumbling forth from sleep so as to be ready for the bell that called them to the fields. I learned to dread the toll of that bell. Always, just after it sounded,

Charity would appear with my scented water, and I would wash and dress. But I never did it without thinking of my little labors that lay ahead, and of those who went to the field under the sun and the plaited bull-thong lash of the driver.

Almost every morning, after I woke, I heard the barefooted shuffle of Andrew Maxwell on the gallery as he paced; sometimes there was that awful sweet smell of the hemp, as I now knew it to be. But not again did I open the shutters and go to the railing to watch the swiftly passing moments of the dawn. The first morning had been an accidental meeting; now it would seem to be an attempt toward intimacy, and I would not give Maria Maxwell cause ever again to view my dishevelment with her contemptuous amusement, the suggestion in her glance that I offered myself regularly to the gaze of a man clad only in a nightshift. I had only the weapon of dignity against Maria Maxwell; I could not afford to blunt it.

Breakfast was in the schoolroom with Duncan—an early breakfast. As Andrew had said, work began early here against the heat of the day, the dead part of the afternoon that no white person seemed to be able to go through without seeking the relief of the darkened bedroom, the uneasy doze. It seemed a strange breakfast to me—fruit, papaya, mango, bananas, the juice of oranges, little bread rolls and butter already soft even though it was stored in the cool cellars of the house. Always a few blossoms lay on the tray as it came—hibiscus, frangipani, a sprig of bougainvillea. It was as if all white people must begin their day with the offerings of the Indies, the fruit and the flowers. The meal was made gay by the visits of what Duncan called the sugar-stealer, the bananaquit, a tiny, sparrow-like thing, black with a yellow belly who came boldly to take the sugar from the bowl, and to peck at the bananas as we peeled them. And always, at the vines, the humming-birds danced on the air with the myriad stirrings of their wings, seeking the sweetness buried in the blossoms, seeming to stand still before one's eyes so fast was the movements of their wings. And there were the others, particularly the glossy black grackle who came fearlessly to the gallery to wait for the crumbs that Duncan spread. I had to stop Duncan crumbling whole rolls for them, knowing that whatever was not eaten from our breakfast tray would go into Charity's pocket on the way downstairs. I was still too Scottish to see the birds, although Duncan's playfellows, fed before the people. I was beginning to find the Scottish habits of economy and diligence more than a little difficult to make sense of to Duncan. There was food, plenty of it, and always someone else to do the work. What other kind of life was there? Why should he be put to the trouble of finding out about it, of practising its ways? He was intelligent, willful, more given to talking than to learning. It was hard to be stern with him; he was too much like my half-brother; in the waves of homesickness and nostalgia that would sweep over me, all I saw was the face of that other child, the face of my father, also. In the midst of all the exotic comforts of Landfall I found myself sometimes longing for the chill of the Scottish manse, and the cold wind that drove in on that other side of the Atlantic.

Our lessons were interrupted midmorning when Maria Maxwell came to call her son to her side to accompany her for her ride through the plantation. He would go quickly for his riding boots and hat, and a miniature riding crop to match his mother's, his very eagerness a part of the dismay I felt at the task of trying to change what was born in him. When they went, my time was my own. On my first day, feeling that the hours of idleness were not justified, I asked Maria Maxwell if there was something I could do for her during this time.

"I know a little about accounts," I said, faltering under her amusement at the offer. "And I can do a little plain sewing . . ."

She almost laughed. "Really, you must not trouble yourself, Miss McIntyre. There are those who already attend to such things. And besides . . . the accounts of a plantation are hardly simple arithmetic." Her tone quite clearly implied that that was all I might be trusted with.

She swept from the room in her dove-grey habit and Cordoban hat, Duncan running beside her, his face upturned with admiration and the desire to please and interest her. They rode away, and often I watched them from the gallery—she on a grey horse, with white mane and tail, which she sat superbly, Duncan on a blond-red pony, a frisky, difficult animal, almost too much for a child to manage. But he permitted himself no sign of doubt or fear; if his mother expected him to ride Ginger, he would ride him.

"She could kill them both one day." I spun round at the sound of Andrew's voice. "She will egg the boy on to something that's beyond him, and they both will come to grief." It was difficult, when Andrew knew I was freed from the schoolroom at this time, to avoid him. "She won't even take a groom with her. It isn't right. No white woman should go alone . . ."

Usually by this time of the morning he carried his glass of rum with him, or a slave was at hand to place it where it was wanted. It must have been a deprivation for him, in those first days I was there, for him to leave it behind, to bestir himself to take me through the gardens of Landfall, naming the trees and plants for me—sometimes stumbling over them, annoyed when his memory betrayed him. The marvelous flamboyant trees were in bloom, but he dismissed them as common stuff, preferring the scarlet upthrust of the magnificent African tulip tree. The names were magic: Showers of Gold, Chinaberry, Pride of Burma, Cordia, the Geranium tree, the great Lignum Vitae, the heaviest wood in the world. "I could make a fortune by selling a few of those trees to shipbuilders," Andrew remarked. There were sweet-sop trees, West Indian almond and pomegranate. There was the Immortelle. "Poison," Andrew said. "There are a lot of poisonous trees in the tropics. The natives use the leaves and seeds to stun fish. And the oleanders—watch for them. Even something cooked over the wood of oleander is poisoned." He showed me the precious cacao trees, always planted under the shade of the pinkish-flowered "Madre de Cacao." There were the pink and yellow pouis, the Jacaranda, and even the rare Napoleon's Button. "It's only seeded once in twenty years," Andrew growled at it. "A botanist's curiosity." Cup of Gold, Alamander, Petrea—strangely like lilac—twined themselves wherever they would find space. "We are in the rainy season," Andrew said. "They like it—the heat and the wet. There will be less wind from now on. Hurricane weather is still. November will see us through it. The cane grows and ripens now, and in January we will start to harvest. Don't be deceived by this garden, girl. The heart of Landfall is those cane fields out there . . ."

He took me for a cursory tour of the sugar factory, where the cane was fed into huge pressing machines, and the juice extracted. He showed me the vats where the juice was boiled up, the scum taken off, the boiling process being ever refined until the rum or sugar or molasses was ready. "Landfall's rum is good," Andrew said. "Good soil . . ."

He chuckled grimly as he pointed to the huge ax that hung on the wall of the factory. "That's for any slave who's foolish enough to fall asleep feeding the cane into the rollers. The only way to save them then is to cut off the arm—some do. We work long hours when the harvest is coming in . . ."

It seemed a grim place, imbued with the weariness and sweat of those who had toiled here, curiously ramshackle by comparison to the rest of Landfall. Andrew didn't seem to notice. He pointed out to me the paths of the garden that led to the wild coves of the Serpent Rocks, and those that led over to the lee shore, where, he said, I would find the bays like glass.

"I don't go down to those places any more," he said. "It's too much to climb back. I could always take a horse, I suppose, and go over to the lee shore—but I don't swim any more. I used to be a strong swimmer. Good enough, even for the Serpents. I don't want to flop about like a jellyfish over there in those warm bays, and remember what it was like when I could breast the surf of the Serpents. And the heat of the day is too much. I don't care for it at other times. I've never liked shadows in the water—can be sharks or barracuda. I like the sun now in the water; I need the warmth. At one time I didn't care. That is why an old man takes a young woman to his bed—he hopes for warmth . . ."

In those first days I saw nothing more of Fergus, and in a way I was glad. He disconcerted me as even Maria Maxwell could not, and I had enough strange and new things to learn without trying to fathom Fergus, his silences, the light that just might be contempt for himself that came and went in his eyes. And yet I kept watching for him; I know I did. When we sat at lessons, and I heard the sound of a horse on the gravel paving before the house, it needed as much discipline as I possessed to sit still in my chair and not to go to the railing to see if it was he who had come. But I would hear the voices, and it was always Alister; no visitors ever came to Landfall. Duncan talked often of Fergus; he seemed to have a deep attachment to his half-brother, strange in that they were so far apart in age, and Fergus saw him so seldom. But Duncan had a child's sure knowledge of those who liked him. Perhaps out of his loneliness he was striving to establish a cama-raderie, an identification with another male creature, someone not worn out and disinterested like his father.

"Can you ride, Miss Fiona?"

"A little—but I've no habit. Why?" I thought of the old walking boots and the serge skirt that would have to serve me. I had grown out of the habit that had been one of the extravagances of my teen-age years, and now Mary wore it.

"Because I want to ride over to Winterslo and see Fergus."

"You may do nothing without asking your Mama first."

"Well, then, I shall ask her. She lets me do anything I want."

He didn't tell me that the request had been refused, but I knew it was, because for a day he sulked, and went petulantly to fetch his hat and riding crop when his mother came for him the next morning.

It was Alister who was my prop in those first days; the one figure of normalcy in that household. Without him I don't know how I could have endured those dinners, when Maria Maxwell blazed in the full brilliance of her beauty and talked and laughed and flirted with a falsity that was like ice in the heart. Without Alister there I imagine the meals might have gone forward in silence, and that I might have readily blown out the candles at my end of the table and simply have vanished. But Alister talked to me as if I existed; as if I were a person, and not just a figure—a governess. He was tactful beyond belief; there were amusing stories dragged up from his childhood when the Prince Regent had been at the height of his follies. "My father's bank never lent money to the Prince. He preferred to forgo the Baronetcy and save his money." He spoke of how twice he had seen the young Princess Victoria driving in Hyde Park, the very young lady who would be Queen. "Not exactly a beauty, but sweet-looking," he said. "I would wish for more spirit—but they say her mother, the Duchess, permits her no liberty. Poor child . . ."

He was the first I had ever heard to express pity for someone who would be a monarch; somehow it made me feel that he saw greater equality in women than most men did.

Judiciously he urged Maria to talk—especially when she had had enough wine she might bring forth one of the old island stories. Who had married who, and why, and why this estate or that had been lost or won. There were stories of week-long card games from which men had emerged beggars, or had climbed nearly to the top just by the winning of some hundreds of acres of cane fields or a consignment of slaves. But there were never stories of the slaves themselves; there seemed an unspoken agreement among whites that the evil and danger they lived with must not be spoken of too openly, as if the fears that possessed one must somehow be held down. There were no stories, even when no slave was present to listen, of such things as had happened to Andrew Maxwell's father; there were no tales told of the night that certain greathouses that I saw outlined on the ridges in ruins had been burned. And yet there was always the sense of looking over one's shoulder.

There were the times, also, a little further gone in wine, when Maria boasted of her ancestry giving, without words, her opinion of the lowliness of the Maxwells. "The Medinas are grandees of Spain," she said. "The San Francisco holding is an original land grant from Isabella and Ferdinand." San Francisco was her family's estate.

"San Francisco is three acres and a chicken run," Andrew said, taking his wine with relish.

She flashed him a look that would silence any man. "San Francisco was once half the island of San Cristóbal. Stolen—stolen by the English."

"Your men were too weak to hold it, my dear. The Spanish blood gone to seed. They'd been in the Indies too long without ever accepting them as their home. They lived as exiles, without ever embracing what was theirs, clinging to a worn-out tradition. What was it about those card parties . . . wasn't that how San Francisco went . . . a hundred acres here, fifty there . . ."

Her eyes flashed pure hatred. "Sometimes a generation comes where there is not weakness . . . someone who knows how to win back . . ."

He wasn't paying attention. "What a pity Columbus was an Italian," he rambled on. "Or we should never hear the end of this Spanish business."

"But the Spanish had the wisdom to put up the money for Columbus's voyages," Alister put in quickly, dampening the spark that flared. "The Genovese bankers didn't have the vision of Isabella. Thoughts like that serve to keep bankers humble." He bowed his head in mock penitence. Maria was a little appeased, and I marveled again at his adroitness.

But Alister was busy in other ways than just that of enlivening the evening meal. He seemed to come and go a lot, riding to Santa Marta on business he never talked about. Whatever it was, it was business that seemed to disturb Maria. Often she would refer to these journeys —teasingly asking him what the gossip of the town was, as if she hoped to find out just where he had been. And he was always ready with some story for her, a morsel picked up at Lawrence's club, or on the gallery of the Royal. He wasn't quite successful in giving the impression that he spent his whole time at those two hotbeds of island gossip, but he made a good try. And there often was a little present for Maria from Santa Marta's best shop, Rodriguiz—a fan, a gossamer length of silk for a stole, the latest London magazines, which, naturally, were months out of date. But I knew he did these things not because he had time to spend in Rodriguiz, but because he wished Maria to think he did. I don't suppose any of us were deceived; Alister Maxwell had never wasted time in his life.

But when Alister rode it was not only to Santa Marta. "I need the exercise," was all he ever said about it. But quite early in the mornings, and in the late afternoons when the shadows had begun to gather I would see him go off along the paths and bridle trails that led from

Landfall. Sometimes he would take food with him, and stay away the whole day. Maria never got much return to her questionings about how he spent those days. "I just ride—I look at the estates. Sometimes I find a cove and bathe. That's what the doctors told me to come here for . . ." He added, with a wry touch of humor, "People are beginning to get used to seeing me riding in all kinds of odd places—that madman from London who doesn't know enough to stay in out of the sun. Sometimes I fear I trespass, but no one seems to mind. Sometimes I'm invited into one of the greathouses for a drink. I don't know whether it's need for company, or sheer curiosity, but the ladies of San Cristóbal love to talk . . ."

"*Them*—gossips, all of them," Maria pronounced. "They just want to find out what goes on at Landfall. No one comes here, so they must make a mystery of it. They have all the time to just sit and gossip. An idle lot . . ."

"Your mother, Donna Isabella, is not among that number, then," Alister said, obviously amused by her vehemence. "I thought the other day it was high time I paid my respects to Donna Isabella, so I rode over to San Francisco—mind you, I've passed it many a time, but I didn't think it an advantageous hour . . ."

"You *went* to San Francisco!" Maria looked startled. "You should have told me. I would have sent a message. I would have taken you there myself . . ."

Again Alister's wry smile that said nothing. "It might have been just as well if you had. I never did meet your good lady mother. She's very adept with a musket—or rifle—or whatever firing piece she had. I didn't wait to find out. She judged the range to a nicety—not to hit but just to warn, I imagine."

Maria's cheeks flushed. "A thousand pardons, Alister. She would never have done such a thing if she had known it was you. But they are three women alone there at San Francisco, she and my sisters. There are very few slaves, and none worth the having . . . She lives in the past, sometimes, my mother. As if there were still things to protect there. She is old—her mind wanders a little."

Alister shrugged. "Her aim doesn't. But no matter—I had no business calling without prior notice. I hope you will convey my apologies . . ."

Andrew laughed loudly at the story. "She's still a fire-eating old bitch. A dab hand with a gun and a whip and her tongue, that one."

And then, too, there were the mornings when Maria was out with Duncan that I heard Alister's voice coming from the office where the estate business was managed, a sectioned portion of the inner gallery at the back of the house, a room lined with ledgers and journals. Some, which Andrew himself showed me proudly, were the ledgers of Winterslo, kept by his mother. The place was the workroom of a young, nondescript man, Fellowes by name, who seemed on a perpetual seesaw of hate and fear toward his mistress. Maria went there every afternoon after the siesta; sometimes their voices, his low and, I thought, abject, hers reaching a shrillness not heard in the salon, would rise to us in the schoolroom. Often I heard him called a fool and an idiot; his stooped figure over the ledgers was another symbol for me of Landfall. He seemed to work irrational hours—sometimes absent, sometimes burning the lamp late into the night; but never was he invited to the table, or to a glass of wine. And yet, like a dog's, his gaze would follow his mistress with a kind of hopeless adoration; she knew it, of course, and received it with her own kind of tantalizing contempt. Fellowes seemed to me one of the typical tragedies of the Indies—the young Englishman without money who comes in hope of a fortune, comes much too late, and is doomed to the two-room house with the tiny veranda not too far from the slave quarters, who eats his meals alone in the room next to the kitchen, and whom no white woman will marry because, unless he has luck with cards, and entré to the clubs, he will stay in that tiny house, on one estate or another, for all of his life. His life is likely to be short in the Indies. There are no companions but the flask of rum, and one of the lighter-colored slaves.

What interested me was Alister's apparent right to enter the estate office at any time, whether Fellowes was present or not, and open up the books. He did this most often when Fellowes was away—during the siesta, or at the time when Fellowes went to check stores and equipment, or into Santa Marta to give the orders for the plantation's needs. I found that Alister took to the siesta no more readily than I—and sometimes, in the walk I took after lunch, before I would give in to the temptation of that darkened bedroom, I would pass on the outer gallery, and he would be there, seated at the desk. Sometimes he heard my footsteps, and turned from the books to nod toward me; sometimes he was too intent and I passed unnoticed. There were the times, also, when Maria herself broke the sacred custom and stayed with him after lunch in the office. But at those times her voice was not the one she used to Fellowes—I heard it soft and slow, explaining, laughing off some item of expenditure, almost cajoling. I would go to my room, and later there would be her footsteps on the stairs, and much later, Alister's.

I had begun to notice that on the evenings after these sessions in the office she took more than usual trouble to be charming to him. And all the time Andrew Maxwell did nothing, said nothing. He asked no questions about the management of Landfall, did not turn even a page of the current ledgers. Will and energy was gone from him; he seemed to drift, simply to wait upon the arrival of each new day.

There are some things that governesses learn, and I thought I had learned them all—to hold my tongue, to bide my time, like Andrew, just to wait. In theory I knew them all; at Landfall I transgressed the rules. It is a risk which leads to victory and a certain ascendancy, or to being sent home. In those early days, I didn't really care if I were sent away from Landfall; I didn't care except for Duncan.

Perhaps it was because the evenings seemed exceptionally warm. "—hurricane weather," Andrew pronounced as he slumped into his chair for the evening meal. The dimity dress, my best, had been handed over to Charity to be washed, and had come back a limp survivor, and I had by now gone through the second best summer dress—one never needs more than two "best" summer dresses in Scotland. And so that evening I suffered through a meal of curried meat in a dress tight to the neck of wool. I could feel the perspiration standing on my forehead, once or twice I wiped it from my eyes. The wine kept coming, and out of desperation I drank it, and it made me all the hotter. I listened to Maria flirt with Alister, and I hadn't the spirit to try to salvage any of the conversation for myself. At the end I could stand no more. As Maria rose, I came to my feet with a speed that took the slave, who had been waiting to draw back my chair, by surprise. It slid across the polished floor, and crashed against the wall. I had not meant such violence, but there it was; it always happened that way with me.

"Mrs. Maxwell . . ." Andrew's apathy was broken by my tone. "Mr. Maxwell, I would like to talk to you both . . ."

Instantly Alister rose. "Permit me—I'll leave you alone."

"No!"

With a jerk of her head Maria had signaled Dougal to remove all the slaves. They went silently; at least they were beyond our sight, but one knew that they waited in the hall, listening, they stood within the shadows of the shutters in the hall. They knew how to wait silently and to listen. They were beyond our sight, but we knew they were there.

Maria resumed her seat; the calmness of her movement made mine seem exaggerated and absurd. "Please do not leave, Alister. As a member of the family, I am sure there is nothing that Miss McIntyre has to say that may not be heard by you."

"It's just that . . ." I was lost and foolish; how stupid to make a scene at dinner just because one was hot, when a few words to Maria any morning would probably have achieved the same result. But still I was conscious of her face-saving concern before the men.

"Very well, then—I'm sorry it has to be before Alister, because it is of such small importance. It is simply that I need to have my quarter's salary advanced. I need it at once."

Maria's eyebrows shot up. "Indeed? I wonder why? Are you not catered for at Landfall? Is there some complaint? If you have been neglected in any way, you may be sure Charity shall be punished . . ."

I threw back my head and laughed—a laugh I would not have believed of myself; was it true that the wine and the tropics and the heat did something to one's head? I heard this stranger laugh.

"What is the use of punishing Charity for what she cannot help? Look at me—just look at me!" I tugged at the high neck of my gown. "I'm dying," I said. "I'm stifling. I came out here at two weeks' notice with clothes suited to a Scottish winter, and no money for others. I must have some dresses—some cotton. I'll make them myself—even if the result will hardly do credit to Landfall and its standards. Or perhaps—" and now I overreached myself, looking directly at Andrew. "Perhaps you would rather I came down in my shift."

It was the end; of course it was the end. I would leave Landfall tomorrow. I had opened my mouth wide, and said the first thing that came. I had done myself in, and perhaps I was not sorry. Perhaps it would be no bad thing to be leaving Landfall.

"God's blood!" The shout came from Andrew. "Girl, are you such a fool you couldn't have spoken before this? I mentioned it to you— when did I mention it to you?—about wearing lighter clothes." He pointed at me. "I've meant to speak of it—every day I've meant to speak of it, and I keep forgetting. Another week in things like that you've got on and you could be dead. Cotton—Lord, girl, you must have clean cotton every day in this climate. Maria, why have you not done something about it? She should have silks, too. You're supposed to pretty yourself up. Silks—ah, yes, that's it. Silks—light as a firefly. Blue silk and green silk, for your eyes, girl—and orange silk, for your hair . . ."

He was drunk, of course. I stared at him, stunned, my hands gripping the table because of the weakness in my knees. Suddenly he was on his feet, his chair sliding back just as mine had done, and there was a great running stain of wine on the lace frill of his shirt. He was beside me, grabbing my arm painfully. I was reminded, through all the chaos of this scene, of the way he had held me in the first moments of our encounter.

Now I was hustled from the dining room; I heard a kind of hiss of protest from Maria, but she seemed as bewildered as I. As one would have expected, the doors of the dining room opened as Andrew dragged me toward them. No need to guess that the slaves had heard every word of what had been said.

"Up here—up here." Andrew was hauling himself up the stairs, leaning heavily on me for support. When we reached the landing and turned, I saw that Maria and Alister had come to the foot of the stairs, and were staring up at us. For once the coolness of the woman seemed to have deserted her. Her eyes burned with fury.

"Andrew—what are you about? Have you taken leave of your senses?" The English so perfect, the strength of her passion so Spanish.

"Oh, for pity's sake, woman, be quiet! I am still master at Landfall, aren't I?"

We had reached the tall presses where the household linen was stored. I would not have thought that Andrew carried keys to such places, but the habit of ownership had not yet completely died in him. He went to the end press, fumbling terribly with a ring of keys, trying many before he found the right one, as if he had not used them for a long time. While he did this I saw that Maria and Alister had come to the landing of the staircase, holding back, but ready, as if they expected that Andrew might do himself or me some harm.

Now the doors of the press were flung wide. Rolls of cloth lay folded neatly on the shelves, plain cottons, printed cottons, Swiss muslins—cloths for a lady, these; nothing here for the household slaves. But there, to the side, lay the silks, bolts of them, it seemed, glowing with richness and texture in the dimness of the evening. Andrew's hands reached for them with the wildness of a drunken man; they tumbled on the floor, all about us, spilling like some rainbow fountain, a mad glory of color and sensuous delight. One he clutched and draped about my shoulders. "There's silk for you, girl! There's silk for you. More than one woman could ever wear. Here—take your pick. It was bought by Landfall. It belongs to Landfall!"

I had only the strength to make the token gesture. I picked up and refolded one of the rolls, hurriedly, not well, but at least it was done. I placed it back on the shelf.

"It belongs to the woman for whom it was bought. No other."

Then I turned and left him. I did not go to my room—the rooms at Landfall are too accessible. Instead I found my way back along to the stairs and to the landing where Maria and Alister stood. I brushed past them without a word. My shoes clattered on the stairs. The slaves parted automatically as I reached the hall below. As I stumbled toward the door and the steps to the garden I heard Andrew's bellow, loud and pained, shocked into a kind of sobriety.

"Girl—I'm sorry. Come back. Come back . . ."

When I paid no heed he must himself have hurried to the top gallery overlooking the darkness of the garden. He could not see me as I ran along the first path that presented itself. But he knew I was out there, and he was startled that an apology from him had not brought me instantly to heel. His voice strained above the chorus of the cicadas as he called into the darkness.

"Girl—come back! I'm sorry. God damn it—*I'm sorry!*"

II

Alister found me perched on a rock above a path that led down to one of the coves of the Serpent Rocks. I don't know how I had come so far, but suddenly I had been there, the pounding of the surf in my ears, the curl of the white water tumbling dangerously below me. It seemed the end of a journey; I could go no farther, and all the Atlantic stretched before me, reaching away to home and familiar things. It was here, with the thunder of the surf at odds with the calm brilliance of the tropic night and the stars, that I clutched my knees with my arms, and put my face down and wept my tears into the wretched wool dress. I wept, and the sound of the surf drowned my tears, and the scurrying noises of the lizards and land crabs, and the thousand things that inhabit the tropical undergrowth. I wept, and forgot to be afraid of those scurrying creatures about me; it seemed easy to weep at Landfall, I who had shed so few tears in my life. And when the tears were done, there was just the sitting, and the dumb misery. I hated Andrew Maxwell for the crudity of what he had done—I hated myself for having been part of it, for having allowed it to begin. I hated all of Landfall, and that really didn't matter because I would be leaving tomorrow. No, it did matter. Hate is a corroding thing, and I would forever look back on this night with shame.

Alister was almost beside me, and because of the crash of the surf I did not hear him come. "Fiona . . . ?" I could see the blur of his face, and my shame was thicker than ever. But I was glad it was he who had come—that they had not sent a slave to fetch me back ignominiously.

"I've been searching for you," he said. "They were going to send out slaves, but I thought that might . . ." He didn't quite know how to say it. "I thought you might be frightened."

"It was good of you." I made myself turn back to face him, made myself say what had to be said and get it over with. "I've been such a fool. I'm ashamed of myself. It was a dreadful scene—"

"Enough of that, now." He scrambled up on the rock beside me and established himself there, knees drawn up as mine were, as if it were the most natural thing for a fashionably clad man to be settling down in this hot thicket above the cove to talk with a stupid, weeping governess. "You've nothing to reproach yourself with. It was natural. I'm ashamed of myself, indeed, that I didn't stop that fool, Andrew Maxwell. To have placed you in that position . . . unforgivable. But between that stuff he smokes and the rum, I sometimes wonder if he's sane. But it was also unforgivable of me to have let it happen."

I felt my hands clench tighter about my knees. "But I was so wrong to choose that time. I should have spoken to Mrs. Maxwell privately. It was just so hot . . . and the curry. But that's no excuse. I should have more control."

"And Mrs. Maxwell should have seen your need the second you arrived at Landfall. In fact my partners should have known that in London, and made an appropriate allowance. It was shaming for you to have to speak of it at all. I should have done something myself, but a man hesitates to butt into women's affairs, and I had hoped that Maria might have already started someone to work on things for you. Poor Fiona . . . one gets desperate, doesn't one? Is it the heat?— hurricane weather, as Andrew says. Or is it just Landfall?"

"Well, I'll know soon enough, because of course now I must leave Landfall. I'll leave tomorrow. There must be some place in Santa Marta I can stay, and I suppose there's *some* employment I can take until I have enough money for the fare back home. Perhaps you could . . . you must know some people in Santa Marta . . . ?"

His hand was upon me. "You cannot leave Landfall. You *must* not."
I had never heard that urbane voice so intense.

I shrugged. "What choice is there? How can I stay? Mrs. Maxwell
will see that I'm well gone by midday."

"Maria will do no such thing. It will not be permitted. It *is* not
permitted. Don't you think that has already been decided? Do you
think we said nothing to each other back there? You will stay."

"It doesn't much matter whether or not I am *permitted* to stay. I
cannot stay. I have been embarrassed, and have made a fool of myself.
I have my own pride, you know. What is left for me but to go?" I
turned to him; his face was grave, intent, brows drawn together with
concern, all revealed to me in the brilliance of the night, and the light
thrown upward by the crashing surf. "It is an impossible situation."

"Nothing is impossible if you have the will to survive it. You are
needed at Landfall."

"Nonsense!—no one needs me."

"Duncan needs you."

In spite of the warmth did he feel my shiver?—how could he know,
how could he have touched on my spot of secret vulnerability? He
could not even guess of that moment under the arch of the stable-yard
at Silkirk, the vision I had sought to flee only to be confronted again
by it here. I saw Duncan again, and I was cold, despite the warmth
and the wool dress.

He knew what my silence tokened. "If you go, who is there at
Landfall to help Duncan? Knowing what he needs, how can you go?"

There was nothing to reply. He did not know the exact reason why
I would stay; he knew only that I would.

I felt my hand grasped as he pulled me to my feet. "Come now, we
must go back. You would be less than I think you are if you do not
go back—and stay."

I let him lead me along the twisting path back to the gardens and
the house; he led my footsteps now where before they had found their
own way; I was weak and exhausted and unresistant. And when we
came in sight of the house there were no slaves to mark our coming.
Alister still led me, my hair slipped from its knot, my body and dress
soaked with sweat, up the stairs to the gallery. Only one light burned
there. Beyond it, on the inner gallery, almost lost in the darkness,
Andrew Maxwell sat. He said no word, but his head bowed slightly
as we passed. If this were an apology, it was as much as I would get.
In the hall one of the row of candles was lighted. Alister lighted an-

other from it, and held it high as he helped me up the stairs. As we approached my room the door opened and Charity stood there.

"Come, mistress . . . you need rest."

And for the first time I knew the experience of falling into the skillful, ministering arms of a black woman.

III

My exhaustion lasted beyond the first light, beyond the crow of the cock. It lasted even beyond the ring of the plantation bell, because I did not hear it that morning. I didn't hear the shuffling of Andrew Maxwell's bare feet on the gallery; what I woke to was the pounding of his fist on the shutters. "Wake up, girl—wake up! We've got to be stirring early. Have to get to Santa Marta before the heat. Get up . . ."

Charity was there with the water, and she opened the shutters a half inch to hiss at her master, "Mistress getting up. You go about yor business."

And only a raucous laugh greeted her impudence.

There were no lessons with Duncan that morning. Before we had finished breakfast I heard the sound of the carriage on the drive; Andrew stood before us, immaculate in his white clothes, resplendent in a fresh red silk sash, his beard trimmed and combed, his hair scented.

"Come now," he said, "no time to dawdle." And instantly he was frowning. "Where's the thing I told them to have ready for you this morning. You can't go into Santa Marta in *that*." I was wearing a flannelette blouse, thin, shrunken from washing, tight under the arms, and seeming ready to break its buttons. "*Charity* . . . God damn you, Charity! I'll have you flogged within an inch—"

"Here, master, here." Her dignity under provocation was impressive. "Jus' finished. Things not made in five minutes. But ready, like you say." She held a garment in her hand, held it toward me. It was a blouse of exquisite *broderie Anglaise* as light as a puff of wind, frilled, shirred, tucked. There was no way to know how many women had sat up all night over its creation while I had slept.

"There, girl, go and put it on. And let's get on our way. It's getting hot already."

As I went with Charity I heard Duncan's argument begin. "But I'm coming, too, aren't I, Papa?"

"No—no, son. This is a woman's day. We have things to get for Miss Fiona."

"But, Papa, I want to come. Just once, can't I come with *you?*"

In the walk to my room I measured the long pause. Then Andrew's voice, muffled, as if he choked a little. "Son . . ." Another long hesitation. "No, there's no reason why she should have you *all* the time. Go—go and get your hat. Go—and hurry up."

IV

It was a day such as I had never known in my life before. Chaos, excitement, talk, argument, and the final exhaustion—all this combined with the fierce heat of the busy town as the sun moved higher, where one welcomed the breeze that sometimes blew up the streets from the waterfront, and the deep shade of the arched galleries that protected the pavements from the sun and the swift, passing showers. Alister had ridden with us in the carriage into Santa Marta, but he had little to say during the journey, and went his own way as soon as we reached the town.

"What's the matter, Alister? Are you afraid of women's things?—don't like to be seen buying with a woman?"

Alister smiled lazily. "Indeed I'm not. But I'm too much of a politician to get involved in choices. No, let Miss Fiona have her own enjoyment. Too many cooks, you know, Cousin Andrew . . . Shall we meet at the Royal for some lunch?"

But whatever Alister thought, I wasn't having too much my own way. We drove on to Rodriguiz when we had set Alister down at Lawrences'. Andrew simply stood in the doorway, blinking after the glare outside, and thumped his stick. At once the manager and a clerk were at his side.

"Ah, so good to see you here, Mr. Maxwell. You don't often venture from Landfall these days. Rodriguiz isn't often honored by your presence, though we *do* see Mr. Alister Maxwell . . ."

Andrew ignored the courtesies. "Enough of the talk, Alvarez. We've things to do. First some chairs, man. Do you expect me to stand about in this heat? This is my kinswoman, Miss McIntyre. We'll have something to drink, if you please. And see that there's something worth the drinking in mine . . ."

"Of course, Mr. Maxwell—at once, sir." Alvarez clapped his hands agitatedly. "Oh, and—er, welcome to San Cristóbal, Miss McIntyre. I *did* hear that a relation had arrived at Landfall . . ."

Andrew dropped into a cane chair and thumped his stick in earnest. "Alvarez, I said enough of the talking! We need things, and we've not got all day. Now my kinswoman, Miss Fiona, didn't have time to prepare for her journey here, and arrived without proper clothes for this climate. She needs everything—*everything*, you understand. Now start—and bring the drink!"

Alvarez, with a shop manager's acumen, knew what my station at Landfall was, and that governesses did not dress to compete with their employers. So with quick Spanish gestures assistants were summoned, drinks laid before us, Duncan was greeted and inquiries made for the health of Mrs. Maxwell, and with clicks of his long snapping fingers the appropriate rolls of cloth were indicated and brought for inspection. They were what one would have expected, the sensible things, the dull cottons, the serviceable linens, the hard-wearing carefully chosen fabrics of my calling. Andrew rejected them all without consulting me. "God's blood, man, she's not a nun! Look at her!" He jabbed his stick violently at the magentas and dark greens and several rolls of cloth went tumbling to the ground. Duncan burst into a child's hysterical giggle.

"And what are *you* laughing at, damn you?" Andrew snapped, already out of patience. "I only brought you on condition you didn't make a nuisance of yourself. Do you want to see Miss Fiona dressed in *those* drabs!"

"No—they're ugly." His face screwed up in distaste; he wriggled off the chair and solemnly walked the length of the counter, Alvarez and an assistant now following him with intense seriousness. "I like that—and that—and that. And that thing there—the one like the inside of a shell . . ."

It was beyond my imaginings, the old man and the child together picking the daintily printed cottons, the sprigged and dotted muslins, the fine lawns and batistes. It could have been a trousseau for a bride and was completely incongruous for my position at Landfall.

While Alvarez was directing one of the assistants up on a ladder to pull down yet another roll of cloth, I leaned close to Andrew and whispered, "Mr. Maxwell, I *can't* allow it. It's preposterous! Who ever saw a governess tricked out in things like these? I'd have to work ten years to pay for them. Have you forgotten who I am? Are you trying to turn me into some kind of peacock?"

"And what if I am?" He shouted the words at me, and I fell back in my chair in shock. "And who said anything about payment?" His third glass of rum was on the counter beside him; he was almost sulky, the way Duncan sometimes was when he was thwarted in some desire. "Can't a man have some pleasure in his life? I don't like looking at drabs . . ." He broke off, looking up sharply at a thin, elderly man with a stylishly waxed beard and moustache who had approached, and was bowing to me. "Well, Rodriguiz," Andrew said grumpily, "still overpricing everything, I see."

"Ah, Mr. Maxwell, still with your little joke. Miss McIntyre, welcome to our establishment. And as for our prices, Mr. Maxwell, you know well that quality has never been cheap. Value for money, always, as your good lady wife knows through her dealings here over the years."

"You talk too much, Rodriguiz. Well—I suppose it's business." Andrew waved his stick to indicate the whole shop. "You're carrying some pretty fancy lines. There must be some who are still spending, despite all this talk of emancipation. We'll all be paupers then . . ."

"You're doing some spending yourself, Mr. Maxwell. You can't believe much in emancipation. And yes, there's still money on San Cristóbal, praise be. We've been trading for two hundred years on rum and sugar, and I don't believe it will all come to an end tomorrow."

"We've traded out of those black skins," Andrew said, pointing at a young Negro woman who was dusting counters, and carrying glasses used by other customers to the back of the shop. "When that stops—when they've the right to turn their backs on us except for pay, then we're all finished."

Rodriguiz bowed again, a faint, unbelieving smile trying to stretch his thin lips. "Then may that day be far off, both for Rodriguiz and for Landfall." He turned to me, cutting off the discussion. "Any assistance you need, Miss McIntyre, I am entirely at your disposal." And then he sauntered to one of the many arched doorways that gave onto the street, hands behind his back, bowing and nodding to almost every white person who passed, a man as dependent as any on all the black ones whose presence he didn't even seem to see.

I turned back from my study of him because Andrew once more was violently rejecting something which a young woman was offering. She was a handsome, haughty young thing, in her early twenties I guessed, with a skin that was almost white, and hair that was a lustrous and straight black. Because of her skin color—an octoroon, I thought—she qualified to wait on white customers, and might have been used by Rodriguiz to tempt his male customers to purchases they wouldn't have thought of making. Rodriguiz seemed that kind.

But now Andrew was waving his stick in violent rejection of what she was offering us—an array of corsets, all ribboned and embroidered. "No, she doesn't want any of that kind of thing. Doesn't need 'em. For God's sake, *look* at her, woman. You want to bundle her into those stupid things, so she'll have the vapors."

"I *am* looking, Mr. Maxwell," the girl replied, with a cheeky toss of her head. "I can't imagine Miss McIntyre wearing an evening gown without something of this kind . . ."

Andrew saw the picture at once, perhaps remembered his wife in the evenings, her high-pointed breasts thrust up by the lightly boned bodices. "Yes—yes, I understand. Well, go ahead . . ."

"It will be necessary to try them, sir. . . ." Andrew was still grumbling over the waste of time as I was escorted upstairs by the young woman to one of the fitting rooms that opened onto the upper gallery of Rodriguiz. No customers sat up here; the louver doors were open for air, and a large screen protected the modesty of the customers should one of the assistants happen to pass.

The girl knew as well as Alvarez what my position was at Landfall; except for color, I had fewer advantages than she as far as money was concerned. She dealt with me with a kind of realistic arrogance that acknowledged both her position and mine.

"A lucky one, you," she said, as she tried the first of the corsets. "Mr. Maxwell's in a buying mood." She nodded toward me in the mirror. "Well, at least you've got something to put into a corset . . . You should see some of the ones that come here expecting us to make them sprout bosoms by magic. Mr. Maxwell, he'd appreciate that kind of thing. Lucky for you Mrs. Maxwell didn't come. Lucky for me, too. She looks at the cost of everything three times, and expects her discount, and then there's no commission for me."

"I can't discuss my employers," I said, an angry flush mounting in my face. And yet I was helpless before the girl's insouciant humor. We were both dealing with the whim of an old man, and she wasn't unfriendly. She just knew who I was, and what I counted for.

"No, wiser you don't," she answered, and laughed with a flash of marvelous teeth against the café-au-lait skin. "You play it well, Miss McIntyre. No talk—no trouble." She frowned critically into the mirror. "Look, I've something that will suit you better than this even. Might as well have the most. Wait—I won't be long. Shall I send something to drink up here?"

"No . . ." She was gone swiftly, with a rustle of skirts, a young beauty helplessly trapped in her color, and making the most of what there was. I guessed that Rodriguiz wasn't her only source of commission.

She took longer than she had promised, and I sat on a cane chair behind the screen, and closed my eyes for relief from the excitement and chaos of the last hour, the varying emotions, the shock of knowing that here I was treated as some kind of upper servant to whom an aging employer had taken a fancy and to whom everything in the shop was available. I had an uneasy feeling that they half-believed that I was Andrew Maxwell's mistress; I was grateful for the first time that Maria was a beauty, and therefore the idea less likely.

The door opened softly, and the young black woman who had been dusting downstairs was suddenly before me, a tall glass of lime juice on a tray. "Miss Charlotte, who wait on you, she say bring drink. And gentleman downstairs, he send this note."

"Gentleman—you mean, Mr. Maxwell?"

I sipped the drink, and she shrugged, her expression blank and vacant, as if, like most of her kind, she took refuge behind feigned ignorance. "I don't know name—he just put it on tray as I come upstairs. . . . He ask if only one lady up here."

I reached for the note, puzzled. It was written on a Rodriguiz sales slip, as if it had been scribbled at the counter in a great hurry. There was no signature, just an indecipherable jumble of initials. I read it and knew at once that it was not meant for me.

"Savannah Trader stands off S.F. tomorrow night."

I refolded the note and laid it back on the tray. Before I could explain to the girl that there had been a mistake, the door was flung open violently, with no preliminary knock. Rodriguiz himself burst in, his face under the waxed beard and moustache was tight with fury. He took no notice of my state of half-undress, as if there was something of far greater importance to him that simply blanked out what I looked like.

"A thousand pardons, Miss McIntyre. I'm afraid you've been bothered by this stupid girl here, who has instructions never to approach any customers. Stupid, all of them." Almost as a reflex he gave her a blow across the face that sent her reeling back, and seemed to leave an imprint even on that dark skin.

"Really, Mr. Rodriguiz!" I protested. I was playing now at an instinctive game of holding him off. Something was much more wrong than the fact that a slave had come into my presence without permission. "The girl was simply bringing me a drink which apparently Miss Charlotte had instructed her to bring. There can be no harm, surely . . ."

"The note," he said, his hand reaching to snatch it from the tray. I was quicker. I held the slip of paper there, and smiled innocently.

"Why?—is this some message from Mr. Maxwell? He must be growing impatient. As a matter of fact, I didn't notice it, and the girl didn't say anything." I lifted it and started to unfold it.

"You have not read it?" Rodriguiz demanded. He was desperately striving for his composure, the urbane air he affected.

I smiled again, looking vague and blinking, as if I couldn't imagine what the fuss might be about. "Why no—I only just had time to sip the drink, which was most welcome—it grows very hot doesn't it, Mr. Rodriguiz, in the town toward midday. Was the note not for me, then? In that case, you must certainly take it to whomever it was intended for." I relinquished my hold, smiling, and then as if remembering that I was sitting there in a corset and shift, made a movement to throw my blouse about my shoulders. All the time I looked beyond Rodriguiz to the black girl who had brought the drink and the note. We both knew I had lied; I wasn't sure why I had done it myself, except that I had the feeling that I now knew something that I or any other outsider was not supposed to know. I could see the face of the black girl melt in a kind of relief. It would not be she, either, who told that I had read the note; she was already in enough trouble for having brought it to me without permission.

Rodriguiz was bowing, his expression relaxed somewhat, but I wasn't absolutely sure he believed me.

"A mistake," he said. "Simply a customer who believed it was some other lady upstairs." He warmed to his explanation. "Rodriguiz is something of a hub for town business, you understand. Many people make appointments to meet here, or discuss business that has nothing to do with us. Of course we don't mind—" He spread his hands. "The more people come into the shop, the more goods I sell. Forgive the intrusion, Miss McIntyre. You are most gracious. And, yes, I believe you are quite right. Mr. Maxwell does seem to be growing impatient. I'll send Miss Charlotte up at once." He bowed himself out, and I was left sipping the drink and thinking about what had happened. I was startled again by the sudden appearance of the black girl, who had come along the outside gallery, and paused fleetingly in the doorway.

"Psst!" She was dark as a shadow against the glare outside. "No mistake. The man ask if there is lady upstairs. I say only one. He give me the note to take. I didn't know it not for you. Good thing you say Mr. Rodriguiz you not read it. I get more beating. He beat if I do something—he beat if I not do it. You good to keep your mouth shut—"

She suddenly vanished from the doorway on silent feet, as if her ears, keener than mine, had heard Miss Charlotte's step. The young woman bustled in, her arms piled with more corsets.

"I'm sorry," she said. She was panting, as if she had run up the stairs, and her own stays were far too tightly laced. "Mr. Maxwell is putting on a turn down there. Hurry . . . hurry . . . He wants everything done in five minutes . . ."

"You've become busy down there then?" I said. "There are a lot of customers?"

She snorted. "Here, slip this on. I think it's the kind for you." Then as she laced me she answered my question. "Busy?—we haven't had such a quiet day for weeks. Mr. Maxwell is still the only customer on the drapery side. My commissions are going to be small enough today. Over next door—the provision side, is packed with men, buying whatever they buy—bolts, screws, flour. Nothing in that for me. The little boy's gone over there, and he keeps bringing his papa things he wants to buy, but Mr. Maxwell, he isn't moving from his chair. . . ."

Her chatter continued as we raced through the business of selecting what we thought was best. But my mind wasn't on the business and I let her make the final selection. If Andrew Maxwell and Duncan were still the only customers in the drapery side, then whoever had sent the note had assumed that it could only have been Maria Maxwell upstairs. The note had been meant for her, and somehow Rodriguiz had found out the mistake and come running, ready to cover both for Maria and whomever had sent it. I worried the question as I dressed again quickly. I was sweating, but not because of the heat, as I ran down the stairs again to Andrew.

His humor, as Miss Charlotte had warned me, had suffered a reverse. Before he had been jovial in his rudeness, but now he had tired of the whole thing. He had bought Duncan a model ship, and a silver studded harness for his pony that was an absurd luxury for a child. He had visibly wearied, and I saw that a whole jug of rum now stood beside him. I was told to give the size of shoes and riding boots I needed, and a selection of bonnets was to be sent with the rest of the purchases. I was not permitted time now to try any.

"Just send a lot," Andrew ordered. "What we don't like we'll send back. And have the whole lot waiting at the Royal by the time we have finished lunch. See that it's there, Alvarez. I won't wait."

"But, of course, Mr. Maxwell."

Andrew began to heave himself from the chair. "There's just one other thing," I said.

Irritably, "Well, what is it?"

"Oatmeal," I said.

Alvarez clasped his hands together as if the thought were ecstasy. "Oatmeal—but of course. If you would just step next door into the provisions department . . . there are many things that might interest you, Mr. Maxwell. New delicacies we are importing all the time, as well as, of course, the general rations for the slaves . . ."

But Andrew was staring at me in wonder. "God's blood, girl, what in the world do you want oatmeal for? Is this some foolish cosmetic fad? Leave your complexion alone—it's white enough for any man's taste."

"It isn't a cosmetic I'm thinking of, Mr. Maxwell. It's Duncan's breakfast. Have you ever heard of a Scot growing up without oatmeal for his breakfast?"

Momentarily his good humor returned. "Oatmeal? Of course—oatmeal! Don't know if it's ever been cooked at Landfall. My mother must have cooked it last when Fergus was young. Yes—oatmeal. The child needs it!"

"I don't want it," Duncan wailed. "I don't like the sound of it."

"Alvarez—send oatmeal." Andrew struggled to his feet, aided by Alvarez and an assistant. Rodriguiz had not reappeared. "And you," he said to Duncan, "will do as you are told. You will mind what Miss Fiona says, and you will have oatmeal for breakfast."

Alvarez helped Andrew into the carriage, and me, with considerably less deference. I glanced back as we drove off, and Alvarez was standing in the sun watching us, wiping the perspiration from his forehead, with the desperate air of a man who doesn't know whether to smile for the business he has done, or shake his fist for the insults he has endured. I felt almost the same way about the treasures that had tumbled into my lap that morning, and knew the growing conviction that some price, not money, would be exacted for them.

*   *   *   *   *

Alister was waiting dutifully at the Royal for us, and we lunched on the upstairs gallery, which gave directly onto the town square and the whole line of the waterfront, with the vessels riding at anchor, some of the bigger ones out in the harbor, others moored to the piers themselves, taking in and discharging cargo. The gallery of the Royal was as near to a club as anything I had ever experienced; everyone knew everyone else. There were few women, and I felt the many glances, and in some cases, the frank stares directed at me. Andrew grumpily returned a few greetings and didn't encourage anyone to linger by our table; there was one exception though—a grizzled man, older than Andrew, a retired sea captain who was now a ships chandler in Santa Marta. Malcolm Gordon was his name, and his knowledge of Andrew seemed to run far into the past. They had that sort of unwordy acceptance of each other. He was invited to join us.

"Well, ye've turned a head or two, Miss McIntyre," was his greeting to me. "A young and handsome female new in Santa Marta has all us old coots fidgeting in our chairs. Dinna have much else to do these days. This middle of the day lot—we're all past much less but looking. 'Tis in the evening the young ones come, and then no ladies will be here."

"If you've a notion, Gordon, you're talking to a lady—and you're right about that—then keep a decent tongue in your head. Or I'll be telling you to find your own table," Andrew said.

"Aye, Maxwell—pleasant as always. And right, too. I forget how to talk to ladies these days."

Andrew ordered lunch without consulting any of us, and a jug of rum. "Quit the cackle, Gordon, and stick to what you know. What's in the harbor? How's business? Is anyone making any money?"

"Aye, money's still being made, and everyone looking for a good harvest. There's lots o' talk about this emancipation business, but most think it's only talk." He made a sweeping gesture at the harbor. "Well, look for yourself, man! Look at that line of craft—does it look like there's business? Busy as any time I've known. Bigger ships coming in too. There's the *Lady Beatrice* loading these two days by tender and full to the decks—she'll go with this evening's tide. This is the fifth time this year the *Josephine* has been in. She and the Yankee ship out there, *Savannah Trader* will go with the morning tide . . ."

I spent my lunch hour absently attending to the conversation, keeping Duncan in order, but staring mostly at a graceful vessel that rode well out from the piers in the deep water. She would leave with the morning's tide, Captain Gordon said. But the scrawled note had said she would stand off—where?—tomorrow night S.F. If the note had been intended for Maria then I knew. Tomorrow night the *Savannah Trader* would stand off San Francisco. Why? There was no answer in the faces about me. Rodriguiz knew, but Andrew did not; I would have been ready to swear that he did not.

V

The spirit of gaiety and adventure was gone, and we drove back to Landfall in a mood of irritability that bordered on depression. All Andrew's store of strength had been used; he had eaten a huge lunch unwisely in that heat, and drank heavily, but I thought it was not merely the discomfort of the meal and the drink that showed, but actual pain; for the first time, as I covertly studied his face as we jounced over the island's roads, I saw the pallor of grey beneath the weather-beaten and burned skin. Often he shifted his bulk uncomfortably; beside me, Duncan had lost interest in the model ship and had fallen asleep, leaning heavily against me; once he opened his eyes as we hit a particularly deep rut. Then his hand stole into mine as if seeking some comfort he could not ask for; I kept it there, our palms moist against each other. I sat upright, supporting Duncan's weight, looking out the window at the endless cane fields that seemed to blur before my eyes. It was very hot; the fine *broiderie Anglaise* was crushed and rumpled, and it stuck to my back wetly where I leaned against the leather cushions. The journey back seemed longer than I remembered. I stiffened my body against the desire to slump, to succumb to the weariness. Then finally I turned to the two other occupants of the carriage. Alister, who had taken the sunny side, had tilted his hat to relieve the glare on his eyes; under the shadow cast by the brim, I found his eyes fixed on me, intent, thoughtful, speculative. Quickly I looked from him to Andrew. His gaze, too, was rooted on me and Duncan, the crumpled mass of we two together; for a moment his lips twitched, but there was no way to tell if it had been the beginning of a smile or a grimace of pain. I turned back to the cane fields, and Duncan's head fell forward against my breast. I held him there, letting him sleep on in this attitude of babyhood again, letting him dream his dream until this seemingly interminable journey should be over.

The only thing that marked any stage of the journey was the sight of a solitary horseman at a point on the road where we had passed the junctions that led to any of the plantations except Landfall, San Francisco, and Winterslo. The man put his hand to his hat in the barest gesture of recognizing a fellow traveler on a lonely road. He said nothing. Andrew gave no sign of recognition at all; he stared at him with glazed eyes, as if he were no more important than a thousand men he might have seen on the streets of Santa Marta. But strangers did not come this way. Only the three isolated plantations lay beyond.

It was then I began to wonder if Maria had received her message after all.

* * * * *

It was long past the hour of siesta when we reached Landfall, but gratefully I obeyed Andrew's orders to retire until dinner. There was no sign of Maria. Duncan's voice echoed plaintively through the rooms as he called for her to come and see his silver harness. But she was not there to answer, and his lip drooped. He was taken by Juanita, and I heard his voice, petulant and complaining, as his sweat-soaked clothes were removed and he was prepared for his rest. Another thing I heard as Andrew pulled himself up the stairs on Dougal's arm. It was a whisper of pain, as if he did not mean to give it utterance, but it escaped him. "God damn her—oh, God damn that she-devil." And then, "Dougal, bring my medicine. The strong one."

* * * * *

I slept heavily, and it was Charity who shook me awake. "Come now, mistress. It late already."

I bathed in the midst of what should have been the happy chaos of the day's purchases. Charity purred with pleasure over the things, and I wondered at her—she in her coarse cotton, her wiry hair bound in the white handkerchief, fingering with unfeigned delight what she could herself never possess, relishing them in a kind of triumph.

"You sure set that ole man on his ear, mistress. Now you be fine— like her. Now I be proud when you go downstairs. The mistress not the only one now . . ." The plump brown face beamed with satisfaction. "Here, you put on one o' des new corset . . ."

Then she brought out the green dimity dress, freshly laundered, limper than ever. But it had changed. In place of the high neck with the little tight collar, the whole top had been cut away almost as far back as the shoulders. It was cut very low, and a trimming of ruffled lace gave a bare sense of decency.

"Charity, what has happened? I didn't tell you to do this." But she had it over my head, and my protest was muffled.

"It wear out," she answered, with half truth. "When it washed it all come apart. Best we could do with it."

I was angry, wondering by whose orders this had been done, feeling the outrage of being manipulated by an old man's spite against his wife. "And the lace. Where did the lace come from?"

"The mistress give it." Yes, I thought, as she must have been forced by Andrew to "give" the *broiderie Anglaise* last night. Then I turned back to the mirror and saw my reflection. It could have been that I had never seen myself before. The cleverly cut corset gave all the advantages it had been intended to; the low cut of the dress was almost indecent to my eyes unused to the sight of myself this way. Charity's quick hands were already at work on my hair.

"Charity, I can't wear this! It's—it's shameful!"

"It's all you got to wear," she answered cheerfully. My hair was going higher, pulled and twisted and puffed. What was nearly a lady of fashion looked back at me. "You got something to fill a bodice like that, you wear it," she added fiercely, tugging at my hair. "What you afraid of? You white, mistress—you beautiful to a white man. Everything here to take. You put your hand out for nothin', you get nothin'. So you wear yor pretty dress and you put out yor hand. 'Cause you get nothin' settin' like a mouse . . ."

*   *   *   *   *

But it was like a mouse I crept downstairs, hoping to be the first in the salon, hoping to find the seat farthest from the light and the gaze of the others. I thought I had done it; I was halfway across the room before Andrew spoke. He was seated as if he also wanted to avoid the light, away at the far end of the room, near the open doors and the smell of the garden.

"Splendid!" he said. His voice sounded oddly weak. "Come sit here by me, girl. It's been a hard day." And then when I came to the chair he had indicated, he nodded slowly, with satisfaction, almost like Charity's. His look was quite without the half-leer that I had expected; it was dispassionate, detached. The pupils of his eyes were dilated. He did not seem drunk, but the customary glass was close at hand.

He said a strange thing then. "We will have company now. Now Fergus will come."

I accepted the drink he offered, because I had to have courage to face the others. And I sat silently there in the growing darkness with him, experiencing almost a sense of comradeship, and yet wondering why he had said that now Fergus would come.

Chapter 4.

The next morning, as soon as Maria had taken Duncan for the usual ride, he quivering with excitement over using the new harness, I walked with a purpose for the first time toward the coves that lay on the lee shore, past the Serpent Rocks. I wasn't sure where I was going, or how I would know if I ever reached the place, but I was going to find a bay belonging to the plantation of San Francisco where a ship might lie. I followed the paths that Andrew had indicated; they grew wilder and more overgrown as I went. I could not use Kronberg now as my guide because the sight of it was lost by the trees crowding here. I did not want to take the road that led out of Landfall, the one where the signposts pointed to Winterslo and San Francisco. That might have been, in the end, the easier way. But I had no excuse to be there on that hot dusty road by myself, among the cane fields; I would not risk skirting the greathouse of San Francisco itself. I had too vivid a memory of Alister's description of a sharp-eyed old woman with a gun who sat on the gallery and did not welcome strangers. So I went on in the heat in the direction Andrew had indicated, and the jungle-like growth gave way to drier, more scrubby land, and Kronberg once again appeared. I did not know whose land this was, or if it had ever been thought worth cultivating. I emerged at a kind of a headland that seemed to form the last of the Serpents, and there, below me, was the first of the coves.

It was unexpected; I had only Andrew's description and it had not prepared me for the sheer perfection of the place. Suddenly from the headland I looked down on the dazzle of almost white sand, lined with sea grapes and almond trees; the sapphire shallows were like glass, wavelets, a bare inch high, lapped the shore. Few strong tides would ever touch this place; a line of sea debris marked their farthest reach— pieces of wood, seaweed, coconut shells. There were tracks across the sand, the webbed feetmarks of birds, long trailing lines that could have been made by crabs. But it seemed to me then that no human foot had ever touched this virgin sand. It was enchantment—it was primitive, lost paradise. Huge-mouthed pelicans swooped for fish, gulls cried, overhead a hawk hovered, waiting, watching, the "John Crow" scavenger bird of the islands. For a few minutes I stood still, entranced, given over to the magic of it, to the peace in the midst of its teeming life of bird and fish and lizard and lowly ant. I, who had lived by the sea all my life, for the first time knew the feeling that it would have been a heady intoxication to tear off my clothes and plunge my body into that warmly receiving water. I knew why Andrew did not come this way any more. It was a place of innocence, and youth and strength —all lost to him now.

After a while I remembered why I had come. I had to plow across the sand, and then climb to the next small headland—another cove, much as the one I had left, and the water more inviting as the sun grew hotter. Yet another scramble, this time making my way around comparatively level rocks; another cove and there at the far end, a massive headland, and something—at this distance I could not see very clearly through the scrub that overgrew it—the semblance of some buildings.

My breath was laboring, and I was tired by the time I gained the top of the headland, and the first signs of the buildings. Here, under the sprawl of vine and thorny scrub springing from pockets of wind-blown soil, I could see the traces of level, man-made floors. But I didn't go on at once, because from here, also, for the first time I glimpsed two houses. They were set back, on the slopes above cane fields, the farther one hardly visible, the nearer one so massive that even at this far distance I could feel its overwhelming presence. It could only be San Francisco, and that dusty white speck set on a far ridge, several bays over, would be Winterslo.

The headland where I stood narrowed to a long spit of land that hooked around its bay like a long, protective boom. Beneath the scraggle of the pervasive growth I could just discern the outline of what must once have been the ramparts of a fort-like building. And everything about me declared that this had once been the outpost of the first protection of Santa Marta harbor. Any ship approaching from the east would have had to round the Serpents and fall into line of the guns that must have been mounted here, and those from the south and west could not make the harbor without being seen and the signal sent. San Cristóbal had been a way-station on the treasure route from Central America to Spain. This warren of crumbling lava-rock beneath my feet had served its purpose to guard and protect, and the mansion on the hill behind had been part of the great Spanish presence in these islands—shrunken and all but gone.

Like the grandeur of Spain, this too had gone. Sea grapes grew in roofless rooms, vines smothered the crumbled walls, walls that were so covered with lichen they were nearly indiscernible from the sea rock itself. Lizards scurried from my path as I scrambled over the broken walls, birds started up before me, shrieking. I saw places where iron had fallen—gates, window bars, even huge cannon, and were now mere rust stains on the white sand. I stared down into rooms deep in the ground that must once have been dungeons. I felt the impress of the Spaniards here, striving to hold the land against the many invaders; even under that burning sun it was gloomy, with the indefinable stench of decay, almost the smell of things that had happened here, men dying, or being put to death, and the rampant vegetation taking it all back, remorseless, unstoppable. I did not like the place, but before I left it I believed I had found what I had come seeking.

There was one room that would once have faced upon the beach itself, but now was almost screened by the sea grapes. It was the first floor of what had been a taller building; the higher walls were nearly gone, but the stone floor which formed the roof of the lower room was still sound. Nothing marked it from the rest except that through the sea grapes I caught the glimmer of new metal, and when I had pushed my way through, instead of the open, gaping doorways that had greeted me everywhere, here was a stout, good wooden door, with new heavy hinges and locks; high up in the wall was a single air hole, and there, too, the bars had been renewed, not the rusted stumps I had seen elsewhere. There was no sound from within—no movement. But everywhere here in the sand I could see the footprints; there were those who wore boots, and those, as always, who were barefooted. I looked back at the perfect calm of the bay, the hooking headland that guarded it, the narrow passage with no ripples to mark hidden rocks, and I thought that if the *Savannah Trader* had a rendezvous here, there was no place more fitting. It was the first time I had a premonition of danger, and I turned and scrambled across those perilously rotting walls, over the farthest ramparts, and slithered, panting, back into the bay by which I had approached the fortifications. When I had gained my breath I took the first path that led back in the direction of Landfall and the Serpents. I no longer had the time to scramble from cove to cove, nor would I now, after what I had seen, expose myself at each headland to a possible watcher on the gallery of the San Francisco greathouse. I felt I must now be on San Francisco land; tracks led through fields of thin cane, weeds growing almost as high as the cane itself, the scrub starting to invade. But there were no slaves at work in the fields here; I saw no one. I kept heading toward Landfall at a stumbling run, and I was near exhaustion by the time the welcome shade of the great trees came, and then the cleared paths and the cultivated gardens. I went around past the stable-yard, up the back way, hoping that Maria would not be in the office. Juanita saw me from the kitchen, but I was past, and round the bend of the back stairs before she could do more than come to the doorway to get a better look. Duncan was halfway through his lunch in the schoolroom, his mouth drooping because he had been left alone.

"I went for a walk and got lost," I said, as I gulped a glass of water. It wasn't right to be making explanations to a pupil, but Juanita would ask him when she took him to his siesta.

"You've been over on the bays on the other side," he said.

"How do you know?"

"Sand," he answered. "The Serpent bays are all rocks. Your clothes are full of sand."

I sighed, and nodded, knowing that soon every slave in the household, and Maria also, would know that I had sand in my clothes.

* * * * *

But it was Andrew who brought it up at dinner that evening. "So you got over to the lee shore, did you?"

"I hardly meant to go so far—I was curious, after what you had told me. But I got lost on the way back . . ."

"Should have asked for a horse," he grunted. "Don't go wandering about in the heat. The sun is more deadly than you know, Miss Fiona. But the bays . . . what did you think?"

I sighed, and made myself remember only the first of them, recalling the enchantment, the peace, the beauty. "I think it was the first round the point from the Serpents," I answered dreamily. "It was so beautiful I couldn't believe it. I just sat there under the trees. I kept very quiet, and watched the birds . . ."

"It was a long walk," Maria observed, with her usual cool civility.

"Not for a Scottish governess," I answered forcing a smile. "In Scotland most families expect governesses to walk with their charges at least two hours every day. It's called 'hardening them up' or 'getting plenty of fresh air.' Most times it's just cold, wet air, Mrs. Maxwell. Yes, I'm used to walking . . . I've done it all my life. It's natural to me now. Just as the siesta is here."

"Next time take a horse," Andrew said. "The heat can be a killer, girl. And don't ride alone. You don't know what you can run into. I'll send for Fergus—"

"Fergus has his own concerns," Maria observed. "As he keeps saying, Winterslo is very demanding of his time."

"I don't want to cause any inconvenience," I mumbled, feeling my face blaze. "It's much easier to just go down to the Serpent side . . ."

"Much easier," Maria agreed.

Alister broke in with his cool drawl. "I'll be delighted to escort you any time you wish to ride, Miss Fiona." And then with a quizzical look at Maria, "But we will remember not to intrude on Donna Isabella's peace."

Now Maria's eyes flashed. "Forgive me for my seeming neglect of your entertainment, Alister. A visit to San Francisco must certainly be arranged. Any time . . . but I, like Fergus, have my duties . . ."

"Oh, enough!" Andrew said impatiently. "San Francisco isn't worth a visit. That old witch over there and the scarecrow daughters aren't worth any man's time . . ."

I sighed and leaned back in my chair, away from the light of the candles. Andrew was showing his drink, and the smell of the sweet tobacco was all about the room; it was the usual night at Landfall.

*　*　*　*　*

But it was not quite the usual night. Sleep had never come easily at Landfall; the tropical night is not a peaceful one, and now, as the days grew hotter and the air stiller, the heat stayed trapped even within those high, shaded rooms. But this night I waited, not for sleep, but for some sound that might tell me that indeed it was San Francisco bay to which the *Savannah Trader* would come, and that it was Maria who would go to unlock that strong new door in the ruins of the fortifications.

But one does not go through the whole night without sleep; many times I slipped into an uneasy doze and woke with a start. But what did I listen for?—what did I expect to hear? I didn't know; and I should also have known that it wasn't my concern.

But after these weeks I knew now the approach of dawn long before the first cries of the cocks. By then I could stand my sweat-soaked bed no longer. It was still dark when I went out on the gallery. My bare feet made no sound; in the darkness there is the instinct to walk on tiptoe. I kept close to the railing to avoid the chairs scattered about. The scents of the jasmine and honeysuckle were strong. As I passed Andrew's room I heard the sound of his heavy snoring; had this been one of his times for "the strong medicine" as he called it, or had the heavy rum drinking of the night before carried him long past the time of his usual waking? I went round to the back of the house, the side of the stables and the way to the lee shore. What did I wait for? I didn't know. But I leaned against one of the pillars, half-seated on the railing, as Fergus had been. The dark blue started to drain from the night sky, and the paler, predawn color came to replace it. A little while longer and that mystical moment of the dawn in the tropics would be upon us. I closed my eyes, and for a few seconds the whole still universe about me seemed to hold its breath.

In that time I almost missed her. With nerves raw and taut, perhaps I sensed her, rather than heard any sound. She moved with the lightness of a cat from the deep shadows of the trees across the open space of the driveway to the back steps of the house. I pressed back against the pillar and I had only those few seconds to be sure that a figure actually moved there. A slim young boy she looked like, in tight black Spanish trousers and jacket. The brim of the Cordoban hat kept her face completely hidden until that one brief moment when she looked up. No one but Maria had those perfect, chiseled cheekbones, that long sweep of neck, that particular set of the head upon the shoulders.

Did she check for a second, as if she saw me?—or was it my own sudden intake of breath? But noiselessly she moved on and up the steps, and was lost on the gallery below me.

I remained frozen there, pressed against the pillar. And then abruptly I woke to my own situation. Already Maria would be making her way into the house and toward the stairs. In a kind of agony of deliberately slow movement I felt my way back along the railing; turned the corner, heard once more Andrew's snores. The jasmine and honeysuckle crushed wetly between my groping fingers, giving off their strong perfume. I blessed the change in the light in these last minutes; I could now see the outlines of the chairs, and, more important, the half-open door to my own room. I was there at last, gasping, shutting it with shaking fingers and not daring to push home the bolts lest the sound be heard by Maria. Inside it was still dark. I caught my toe in the edge of the woven grass matting, and almost fell. The bed received me like a haven. I turned my face into the pillows, and spread my arms as though at the end of a night of restless dreams. And with every nerve I listened; there, on the other side of the landing, in the second of cessation between Andrew's snores, I heard what I had waited for, the faintest click of a door opening and closing. Either she had not seen me in that one brief upward glance, or she knew that I must already have abandoned my post. Maria would never betray herself by making a scene.

The beating of my heart slowed at last. Then the sleep that my outraged nerves and brain demanded fell upon me; I woke to Charity's hand on my shoulder, and the bright sun streaming in at the slatted louvers.

"You sleep like you was dead, mistress."

II

If, indeed, Fergus had been bidden by Andrew to come to Landfall, he, as he had done on the day of my arrival about the command to come to the dockside, chose not to obey. I did not hear any more from Andrew about Fergus coming; I just knew, without reason, that I wanted him to come. After the expedition to Santa Marta a quietness settled on the household, but for me there was no serenity in it. It was like the stillness of a cease-fire; we were quiet, but not at peace. The days passed, and Maria gave no hint that she knew that I had seen her return to Landfall in that dawn; she was civil to me when she encountered me, but most of the time she seemed not to notice me. I never made up my mind whether this was a genuine preoccupation with other things, or a studied insult. For her, I almost was not there. Alister continued his comings and goings, either riding the roads around the estate, or making the day-long trip into Santa Marta; he also continued his sessions in the estate office, alone or with Maria or Fellowes. His good manners preserved a pretense of normalcy at dinner each evening. A few times, quietly, beyond Maria's hearing, he complimented me on my appearance; I would smile and thank him, knowing it was simply part of his effort to make me happy at Landfall, but what he said didn't bring the glow of pleasure it had been meant to do. I knew what I wanted, and it was to hear those words from Fergus; but he did not come. So I grew bored now with the endless trying on of the new dresses made by the Landfall seamstress from the materials that had come in such quantities from Rodriguiz. I stopped protesting about the low necks of the gowns for the evening. I accepted anything and everything because none of it was part of me. I would leave them all behind when I left Landfall.

Andrew seemed less evident than before. Not often now was there a return to the vigor of some of our first exchanges; less often did I hear him pace the gallery in the moments before the sunrise. "Master not well," was all that Charity would answer to my inquiries. I could not ask Maria about her husband; this was one of the many things not said between us.

Despite her shrug and laugh, though, I asked, and received permission to go into the kitchen to instruct in the making of oatmeal. At first Duncan refused it, and then I began to mix a little honey with it as it was served, and he accepted it. Andrew, often at a loss for something to say to a child so removed in years from him, would tweak his ear in passing, "Having your oatmeal, eh, boy? That's good—that's good!" and would shuffle on, not waiting for an answer.

I saw him roused, though, to attention one day as he sat on the outer gallery. Duncan had just returned from his morning ride with his mother, and we waited for the call to lunch in the schoolroom. Duncan was hopping from one square of black and white marble to another, chanting softly to himself, "Fulodden—Cuflodden—Glencoe . . ."

Andrew stirred, as if some lost-past memory had returned to him. "Flodden—Culloden," he corrected automatically. "You're learning about your people at last, laddie. I know all those names—the way my mother taught them to me. You come from a strong, hardy people, boy, and never you forget it. When I'm gone, you've to remember, always, that you're a Maxwell."

During lunch Duncan stared at me apprehensively, stammering a little over the question, apprehensive, wondering.

"Do you think Papa is going to die? I heard Juanita say to Flora that he—"

"We are all going to die, Duncan, some day. Never listen to gossip."

"But *soon*," he persisted. "They think he will die soon."

"Your papa is getting old, Duncan, even though you are still young." I had learned the folly of telling half-truths to children, the cruelty of it, the way they always found you out and held it against you.

"But if he died, you'll stay here, won't you?"

"When your papa dies—and that could be a long time from now— you will still have your mama."

"But *you?*"

"I might be old then myself. I might want to go back to Scotland."

He scowled. "I *hate* Scotland. I hate oatmeal, too!"

I walked every morning while Duncan rode with his mother, deter- mined, somehow, to keep the lassitude of the tropics at bay. There was the sense of a struggle between me and the elements; if I softened or gave in, I would be lost. I clung to old habits with a kind of despera- tion, and Andrew kept telling me not to walk in the sun. But some- times I was drenched in the sudden rain, too, and watched the steam rise from the baked earth, and I thought of the workers in the cane fields, endlessly moved forward under the lash of the driver, soaked six times a day at this time of year, and drying off under the pitiless sun. I saw them, and more often heard them singing in the fields when I walked, and they were the saddest songs I ever heard, sadder even than the ballads of Scotland, because they were without hope.

Sometimes, though not often, I walked through the slave quarters, empty during the day because fieldhands were away, and noisy only with the sounds of the children. The very young ones were friendly, curious, still smiling when they saw me; the older ones, already set to tasks about the house and garden, depending on their ability, had begun to display the sullen indifference of their parents. They would look at me with blank, impassive gazes, dropping their lids over dark eyes, and it was impossible to do more than offer the morning greeting. This would be answered with the tipping of the ragged straw hat, and some slurred response, which could have meant anything. Those children lucky enough to have shown some aptitude were put to work in the house; they were the envy of their brothers and sisters who were doomed to the endless hoeing and cutting in the cane fields, the endless sun, the endless fear of the lash. Not that the house slaves were exempt from the lash, but they were quicker and cleverer, and knew how to conceal their failings. In the fields the weaker dropped behind the line of workers, and the punishment was inevitable.

"Mind you," Alister once said to me, "Maria runs a good plantation. It's probable that the slaves are better off under her than they were under Andrew. But that is because she knows their value. When Andrew began, you could always buy more slaves from Africa when yours had been worked to death. It was legal. Now you have to go round the law, buy them from the illicit traders, or breed them. Maria, you've noticed, is very careful of her slaves who are with child—gives them privileges that encourage them to become mothers, to keep their children to full term. She excuses them field work for the last months, and for the first month after the birth. I suppose to most of them here, bearing a child must be like a great long gift of rest. Other plantations I've seen . . . well, pregnancy is a curse as well as a burden. Many children are lost. The mothers risk their own lives to get rid of the child . . . There's no marriage, of course. Just the offspring of one of the few joys they know . . ."

There was something still rudimentary and essentially Scottish in Alister which showed through the politeness and London veneer at times. We were talking now on a subject that few men of his background would discuss with an unmarried woman, and he did it without embarrassment or fuss. Oddly, we had grown to be friends, and I thought with a little dismay of the time when he would leave Landfall.

"But the children here at Landfall?—do they all stay?"

"They are Maria's by law. They are hers to do with as she wishes."

"To sell them?"

He answered reluctantly. "To sell them. To keep them. Whatever suits the economics of the plantation."

"It's monstrous! It's wrong! *You* can't believe—"

"I didn't say what I believed, Fiona." It was a mild reproach. "What I'm telling you *is*. But it is all coming to an end. It will all soon be finished. Wilberforce is old, but his movement is far stronger than one old man. Parliament will finally pass its act—this year, next—some time soon. Emancipation will come to the British colonies. There will be no more holding, or buying or selling of slaves. No man will own another man, body and soul. Slavery will be dead."

"And Landfall?"

"Landfall will die too. No plantation owner can afford to *pay* these people to grow sugar cane, now that the British monopoly is dead. Year by year money has to be poured back into the plantations. They do not sustain themselves, even if they pay nothing for the labor. They must meet the price of sugar on the world market. Without slaves, they cannot do it. No—Landfall and all its kind will die."

"Are you sorry?"

"Sorry?—no. Why should I be? My grandfather made a fortune from sugar on estates all over the Indies—a piece here, a piece there, never giving himself the trouble of managing any of them himself, but never financing absentee ownership. The man to whom he lent money had always to be here, watching the cane grow, seeing that the rum and sugar and molasses got onto the first ships available. No Maxwell ever dealt with an overseer. Yes, he made a fortune. I'm not going to deny that fortune or its origin in slavery. But everything comes to an end in its time."

"And the time is soon?"

"I think the time is very soon. There will be no more Landfalls built—except in the American South. When the slaves are free they will try to cultivate their own little patch, will try to buy the few acres from their former masters. And their masters, lacking every other means to get money, will sell it to them acre by acre. The whole system will crumble. No one knows what will happen to the price of sugar then. All I know, Fiona, is that all this is finished. It is finished."

"They don't act as if it is finished. Santa Marta—Rodriguiz. No one seems afraid."

"Because they do not believe that the stroke of midnight is at hand." It was high noon when Alister said this to me; we had paced a garden walk together, and finally sat on the bench beneath the great cotton-wood that faced the house. I looked to its white, dazzling splendor, the dark, cool inner recesses, the distant figure of Andrew on the inner gallery with his rum. It did not seem possible that it was all over. Alister recognized the disbelief in my face.

"Because they can't accept that emancipation is more than a bad dream to disturb their slumbers. They can't believe that a British parliament will set out to kill them, but it will. The moral movement is there, in England, and the profit is going out of sugar. When the two forces combine in sufficient strength, there will be the end of slavery, and the end of Landfall."

"You don't seem disturbed. You—the Maxwells stand to lose a great deal? Or do I presume?"

"Presume as you wish, Fiona. We have had our time, and our profit. Can we press more blood from these black skins? Can we take more from a man than his life and his soul? I—I for one, will see the end of the whole business without regret."

And then, abruptly, without excuse or farewell, he left me. I remember the tall, elegant figure, marred by his limp, pacing off along the path away from the house. I did not know why he was here, except to preside over a death. I looked back at the house, at the old man there, and thought of the young child riding out with his mother, riding out into a way of life that he thought would last forever. And I was charged, in whatever way I could, with preparing him for the knowledge that it would not be. Alister had charged me with this task without actually speaking the words; Andrew also had said it, when, on that first morning at Landfall, he had told me to teach him well. Andrew might close his eyes to it, in every way he could, but he knew, as well as Alister did, that the end was coming.

But I knew what Duncan saw each morning, the row of black, sweating bodies moving ever forward, the rhythm never to be broken, the sting of the lash to give them strength and energy. The task laid upon me seemed more urgent and nearly impossible.

A few times I took again the long walk to the first of the coves beyond the Serpents, on the lee shore; it was, as before, languid, utterly beguiling, with only the glare of the sun on the white powder sand to strike the eyes. Sometimes I took off my boots, hitched up my skirts, and joyously walked the shallows of that blue-green bay; then I would sit hunched beneath the shade of the sea grapes, watching the birds, and pondering what was happening at Landfall. Most often I thought of Maria; I thought of the note that had come to Rodriguiz, of that slender figure passing in the shadows before dawn into the house. What was I to make of it? Was it an assignation which was none of my business? I could not imagine the fastidious Maria making a rendez-vous in the humid cellar behind that locked door in San Francisco bay. But then, what did I know of the passions of a woman like Maria? The exterior was a careful mask; would I do any good to rip part of it away to expose worse? And what right had I? My first duty was Duncan—to preserve, to protect, to arm him. For this reason I never spoke of what I had seen and witnessed to the only person I could have spoken to, Alister. I believed he would be no part of it; one does not prematurely topple the structure that one knows is bound to crash. I clung to the thought that I was here for some purpose, something to do with Duncan. For this reason I had to survive and endure, and I would.

More often, on the morning walks, I went to the Atlantic side—the side that faced on the Serpents. I went, perhaps because it was closer to the house, perhaps homesick for that wild surge that reminded me a little of the pound of the waves against the seawall at Silkirk. Here, in the wild, wave-dashed cove below the rock where I had sat with Alister on the night of my humiliation, I seemed to hear more clearly the voices of home. Here I was not lulled by the tropical languor, this was not the lotus-land of the dead-calm sea. Here the final strength of the long Atlantic rollers tumbled into rocky pools, and my feet felt the sharp sting of the cuts inflicted by their roughness. I tasted the salt spray on my lips, the dash of salt to cut through the soggy-sweet veneer that lay on everything at Landfall. I learned to love the endless swell and crash of the waves, the backward suck and once again the swell. I learned to observe the minute things of the sea that inhabited these sun-warmed pools, the tiny fish, the myriad life that swarmed and teemed; I grew used to the sight of the hairy leeches clinging to their rocks, and I even found a pool that was the home of a small octopus. Once, as I pried and poked with a stick I saw the slow, waving tentacles rise—baby tentacles, yet full of menace. Like the cove on the other side of the Serpents, the San Francisco cove where the crumbling fortifications held their own sense of horror, I learned to stay away from this pool also.

It was to this Atlantic cove I came after I heard the news of Thomas Scobie. I walked onto the outer gallery one day after Duncan had left with Maria, and Alister was seated in a chair near the steps. In his hands he held a letter—that was not unusual. Many letters came to Alister, following him faithfully across the sea as if he were someone that the correspondents could not let go of, even for a brief time. But now he was not reading, just staring ahead at the massed green foliage of the garden, a look of abstraction and doubt on his face that seemed wholly foreign.

"Alister?" I made no attempt to phrase my inquiry discreetly; we had passed that stage with each other. "Alister—is there something wrong?"

He turned to me slowly, and he was frowning, as if he didn't know how to answer the question. "Wrong—no, nothing more wrong than is ever wrong."

I took a chair beside him. "And what does that mean?"

He touched the letter. "A friend, Peter Jenkins—he was fighting a by-election near Bristol. Of course the emancipation issue was a big one—Bristol grew rich from the slave trade when it was legal and there are plenty of pirate ships that bring slaves over still owned by the Bristol men. Well, it wasn't a pretty fight, and my friend lost. Oh, we expected to lose, but one must fight these battles regardless of the chances. But that wasn't the tragedy. One of his helpers, someone who went around the villages speaking for him, was killed. It was a mob killing—stoned and kicked to death, and no one to hold responsible for it. No one to bring to justice." He looked down at the letter again. "He was a Scot. Thomas Scobie by name. From Glasgow. No education or money—he wasn't well known in the movement. But he puts the rest of us to shame by giving his life for it."

There was cold misery in my heart. I wanted to shriek, to cry out that I had known, and I had told him. But I also had known that he would go on to whatever was determined for him, the end that I had already seen. But I could not tell Alister. It was past, and the warning had been useless, as I knew it would, and by malevolent chance the knowledge had followed me all the way to this place and this hour. I wished I had never known what happened to Thomas Scobie. I wished I had never heard his name again. But I had; I had been meant to know about Thomas Scobie. One does not escape.

But I said something. Thomas Scobie had at least the right to the memorial of having his name spoken. "I once heard Thomas Scobie speak," I said. "By chance—in Glasgow. He was the kind who would be . . ." I hesitated. "A martyr."

Alister nodded, as if the coincidence didn't seem strange to him. He tapped the letter with impatient fingers. "I'll be leaving Landfall soon, Fiona. I can't sit here much longer, going over accounts, trying to find the ways, large or petty, that Maria is cheating. I've had enough of endless arguments about slaves and food allowances, and how many yards of cotton the women need each year. There's too much work waiting in England. What's wrong at Landfall is only a tiny part of what's wrong everywhere. And there are men dying to put right what's wrong, and I'm sitting here. Well, a month will see me gone."

"You'll go back into the family business?"

He sighed. "Yes—I have to. One needs money to fight battles. One needs influence, and that's all that money is—all it's worth."

I gave a half-laugh to try to cover my dismay that he would be gone so soon, and I would be alone here, facing Maria. "You'll have other responsibilities, I'm thinking, Alister. You'll not remain a bachelor forever."

He shrugged. "You know, one can stay a bachelor too long, looking for the right woman. And then suddenly you find no one will have you—that is, no one you want. I haven't seen my chances when they've come, and I don't know them until they're gone. I'm a very plain man, Fiona, and, with women, sometimes a shy man. I've always been apprehensive of great beauties—they demand so much, as if beauty was all they needed to give. What I want to do in life needs a certain kind of woman. She would have to be someone who knew what I was about, and believed in it. Someone who would understand neglect, and long hours, and sometimes a boring social life cultivating people who don't interest her for what they may do to help. Your little misses of seventeen bore *me*, and the ones who might know better also know what they could be getting into."

"Getting into—?"

"When I go back to England I'm going into politics. Not just with money this time, but with my own person. If other men can stand on platforms and face hostile crowds, so can I. I'm going to stand for Parliament whenever there's a chance, and I'll get there, if it takes me ten years. And I'll do it on my own terms, without compromise."

I shook my head. "Then you'll have women clamoring for your attentions. A member of Parliament—a position of honor. What woman wouldn't be delighted—"

"There aren't many who'd be delighted by what I'd be going to Parliament for. I'm going to be one of those damned reformers Andrew's always cursing at. Oh, emancipation will have come by then, I've no doubt of that, but there are more things than you can think of that need changing. We have to clear the children out of the factories and lower the working hours—we have to get the poor decently housed. We have to do something—if, God help us, anything can ever be done for that wretched country—about the Irish question. These are the things that concern me. Oh, I know I sound like a prig, a pompous prig, at that. But I can't help it. I've come to the time of my life where I either have to fight or I'll lose whatever soul I've still got. So you see a wife, Fiona . . . well, women don't like having a perpetual fight on their hands. They don't like seeing the money their children should inherit going on nameless brats in the mill towns and the mines. But that is how it will be."

I looked down at my hands clenched tightly together in my lap. "You make me ashamed, Alister. I've never thought to do such things in my whole life. I'm a minister's daughter, and yet I don't seem to have taken in the first part of what it means to love and to work for something not immediately touching one . . . Yes, I'm ashamed."

"Women haven't the weapons of men," he reminded me. "They sustain, and comfort and succor. But as for loving . . . you have the gift. It shines from you . . ."

He rose abruptly, and the last words were almost lost in the scraping of his chair on the marble floor. Perhaps he hadn't meant me to hear them. "I must go and answer this. There's a vessel leaving Santa Marta for London tomorrow . . ." He left me, and I wished he had stayed, because he left me with only the thought of Thomas Scobie for company.

So I took my hat, and went out into the sun, taking one of the paths that led to the Atlantic coves. But Thomas Scobie marched there beside me, that pale face and the eyes of a man in fever. He was with me still as I found my boulder down in the first cove, just clear of the dash of the high-flung spray. I crouched there, knees drawn up, under the shade of the big hat, my boots and stockings beside me, my bare feet drying quickly in the sun, the salt caking on them. I had plucked at a hibiscus as I came through the garden; I don't know why, except that they were there in their thousands for the taking. I saw it, already wilting in my hand, and I let it go. The wind carried it backward, but the next wave reached the pool where it had fallen, and it was sucked away, and gone. It was the only tribute I could offer to Thomas Scobie —that and my memory of him.

I sat on, careless of the time slipping away from me, knowing only the sun and the crashing rhythm of the waves. And it was here that Fergus came upon me. I was glad it was not as Andrew had planned; I was wild and wind-blown, clad in a high-necked, long-sleeved cotton blouse and an old skirt I still wore on these morning walks. I was just what I was—no silk-decked lady seated in a candlelit salon; I was plain Fiona McIntyre, Scottish governess. I didn't have to try to be anything else.

I simply looked up, and he was there, barefooted himself, boots thrust under his arm, swinging across the rock pools toward me, the quickness of his stride telling me how hard his feet were, how used to the bite of the rock and the tiny shells, the sting of the salt.

"Well . . ." he said.

"Well . . . ?" I questioned. It was neutral ground. Neither had the advantage; neither owned the sea nor the scene, the grandeur, the splendor.

"May I sit with you?" he said.

I moved my boots and stockings to make room on the rock, and the ghost of Thomas Scobie rode out on that Atlantic wind to give way to this most living man. Fergus sprang up beside me, sitting closer than I had thought he would, not looking at me, but out across the cove to the Serpents. The sea is a great equalizer; if we had been back at Landfall I would have been nervous, flustered. Here the tension was all in the crash of the waves, not between us.

"I see," I said, "that someone once taught you manners—taught you to ask for things politely. I was afraid, perhaps, you were just like your father."

He laughed. "You see through him, don't you? He's mostly humbug—especially with women. All that rudeness—it's just a show. He has to cover up, because he's getting old now, and he feels he's losing his power. But you're right, of course. Someone did teach me manners—the same woman who taught him. It's a pity neither of us remembers those lessons better. My grandmother was a little like you. A bit of a stickler for the right thing—not necessarily the proper thing. Just the right thing. The plain Scottish virtues. I'm sorry I seemed to laugh at them. In my way I'm as bad as my father. All humbug. But I hope you can teach a few of these things to young Duncan. God knows, he'll have need of them."

"I do my best," I said quietly. They all demanded this thing of me, as if all else were helpless, as if some evil threatened Duncan that they already knew of other than that he would see great change and must be prepared to meet it. What none of them knew was what I had seen of this child in that brief, terrible vision on the other side of the world. "But I have no power—governesses don't. And little influence. And far too little time. Duncan is a strong-willed boy, and he has been terribly indulged."

Fergus leaned in closer to hear me over the sound of the waves. "Indulged . . . yes, I know. Fought over. Spoiled . . . But perhaps not yet beyond redemption. A pity you didn't come sooner."

"His mother . . ." I said.

"His mother—yes, there's his mother." It was answered with a kind of bitter finality. "There's no way around that woman. She is stronger than six men. Yes, I suppose all the plain Scottish virtues— even if you had had him from birth—would have small chance against that diabolical Spanish greed, that obsession to get back the things of the past. Oh, yes, I'm sure you've heard her boast. But in part she's right. San Francisco *was* an original land grant from Isabella and Ferdinand, and it was almost half the island of San Cristóbal. The Medinas are grandees of Spain. Probably these were poor country cousins, but there's a nut of truth in all her talk. No one would care if that was the end of it. But she pours all that rubbish into Duncan's ears, when all need or use for it is gone. The Spanish side is better dead in him, but Spanish pride doesn't permit of such things."

"Scottish pride is a wee bit stiff-necked, too," I reminded him. "But you might do your share if you really are concerned for him. He admires you . . . he talks of you constantly."

"My father won't let me near him—nor will Maria. No—Duncan won't learn from me. Better he shouldn't. There's too much you don't know about Landfall, Miss Fiona."

I didn't want to drive him away, and yet I had to risk further; it had come to me that these moments were incredibly precious. We had come so suddenly together; we were talking as if no barrier of space or ignorance had ever stood between us. It was hard now for me to credit that there had been a time when I had not known Fergus. Somehow the whole world had changed since he had pulled himself up on the rock beside me. We were two people, not strangers. We were a man and a woman; the elaborate ritual of formality was dispensed with. There had been no intermediate stage, no drawing room play, no polite invitations to walk, to fetch wine, to turn the pages on a music stand. We would never have any of these things. A whole chapter in the book had been skipped and neither of us missed it. The story went on.

I said, "What was it like at Landfall in the early days—when you were a child? You began to tell me that morning . . ."

"There wasn't much. All of the things that are good were there at Winterslo. It was my grandmother, really. She was the soul of the place. She was a Bible-reading Christian who still could defend her husband's tolerance of slavery, who forgave her son *his* bastard son, and brought that grandchild up with love and dignity. She was rigid and stern, but she believed in the commandment of love. She was just there, like a tall tree for me to cling to. My father clung to her too. She ruled us both, but there was no cruelty in her. I remember how completely she disapproved of my father attempting the rebuilding of Landfall—grandeur was no part of her ambitions, and, in any case, she knew that we were destined to be no ordinary plantation family—giving parties and going to parties. You know she died before Landfall was ready, and I remember . . . well, I remember it was just as if my shelter from a hurricane had suddenly been taken away. My father knew only two things—he was just as he is with Duncan today. A shower of presents, and utter neglect. I came to the stage, I remember, when I would have gone back gladly to the nightly Bible-readings of my grandmother in preference to the things he showered on me. It was his time I needed, not his presents. And it was like that with the plantation, too—the times when he worked all day in the fields, and half the night over the books, and the times when he almost forgot that Landfall existed. These . . . these where the times when he was occupied with some woman." He suddenly gestured to dismiss any idea I might have formed. "Oh, make no mistake—none were brought to Landfall. I knew only what I learned from the slaves. They know everything. I never knew who the women were—perhaps quadroons or octoroons. There may even have been a white woman or two in Santa Marta whose family was poor enough to let her think of marrying Andrew Maxwell. But nothing came of any of it, and he never let things get completely out of hand. Landfall prospered, in spite of slaves being expensive and hard to come by. Before he was ill—before Maria and that rotten weed she gave him to smoke— that, and the rum—he was a clever manager. I think he made a lot of money. He didn't tell me such things, and I wasn't allowed any part in the management. Then he gave me Winterslo, and they are the same hard, infertile acres that my grandfather worked, though every crop that comes from them they grow poorer and meaner."

"I'd like to see Winterslo."

"You wouldn't like it," he said quickly. "It isn't Landfall."

"I would like to see it." Then I halted. I didn't know who else lived at Winterslo. I kept blundering and stumbling between one piece of ignorance and another. "Well, perhaps . . ."

He turned swiftly. "All right then. Come. Come tomorrow. Can you ride?"

"I'm not a horsewoman like Mrs. Maxwell. Something gentle and old."

"I'll come for you tomorrow—when Duncan has gone with Maria. Come to the stable yard."

He went back across the rocks to the path that led to Landfall. He didn't wait for me; didn't ask my company. He just went. He had dispensed with so much, and yet some of the lacks were painful. I was reminded of what Alister had said about a woman having to stand neglect. Beyond the reach of the waters, I put on my stockings and boots, and climbed up toward the path. The sun was unbearably hot, and I was weary and my senses drained. My head ached fiercely; I was conscious of a terrible loneliness in his absence.

III

I went to the stable yard the next morning as soon as Duncan and Maria had left. I was nervous, hoping I would not be too early, hoping not to have to wait about while the slaves stared at me, yet afraid to waste a moment of the few hours that were mine to be with Fergus. I remember I even worried, as I ran to change into my old skirt, that Fergus would choose this time again to assert his independence, and simply not appear. But he was there, waiting, none of the arrogance of the usual manner apparent; and I—I was like a schoolgirl, shy, tongue-tied.

Maria's particular groom was there also, holding, though that didn't seem necessary, an old mare who wore a sidesaddle. This was the slave, Samuel, the massive silent man, wooly hair going grey at the temples, whom Andrew ordered to accompany Maria and Duncan each morning, and whom, just as firmly, Maria usually ordered to stay behind. He was said to be devoted to her; I had heard Maria herself boast, "That man—he will die for me." But this morning, for some reason, he seemed pleased to be a party to a meeting that Maria knew nothing about.

"Ready then?" Fergus said. "I thought women always kept a man waiting."

"*That* can't have been among the list of Scottish virtues your grandmother admired." I looked at the mare; her head drooped, and she stood perfectly still in the sun. "You were making sure, weren't you? I think even I can manage this one." I felt the gentle strength of Samuel's hands as he helped me from the mounting block to the saddle. I looked down into the black face upturned to mine, and for once the eyes did not shift away, the confrontation was not evaded. "Mistress be all right on old Rosa. Jus' try her firs'. Nes time, perhaps something better . . ." For some reason he seemed to wish me well, and when I smiled my thanks an answering smile came, not the mechanical response that he was bound to make.

I had to urge Rosa forward. Fergus on his chestnut moved off from the stable yard and along one of the back trails that led away from the house. There was not room for us to ride abreast, so we were silent as we went through the deep shade, sometimes ducking under vines as the way grew rougher. We took a fork in the trail that I had not ever noticed on my own wanderings. The vegetation was wild and rampant on either side, but the single trail was well-marked, as if used frequently, by a horse and rider. It was a track actually carved into the side of Kronberg, but much higher up than the carriage road that led to Landfall.

"I've never been here before," I called ahead to Fergus.

"It's the quickest way to Winterslo. This part gets the most rain—a real rain forest, isn't it? Never been cultivated. You couldn't clear it. Once we're round this next corner, though, it's like the desert again. Kronberg takes all the rain on the weather side. There's nothing left for the lee slope. That's where Winterslo is."

It was, as he said, a sudden and startling change. The breeze fell off, the trees grew scattered, and we were in sight of the lee shore of the island. From this height we could look down on the sparkling green of Landfall's wide acres of cane. There was the greathouse I had seen from the headlands of the coves, the hook bay where the fortifications were. And then, farther along, and higher up toward Kronberg's slope, was the dusty white house I had taken to be Winterslo. We had started to descend, and rode now abreast, on a dusty track between cane fields. The cane wasn't as tall as that on the Landfall fields, nor the ground as well tended.

"I don't have enough slaves to work it properly," Fergus said. "Most of this is ratoon cane. It means you just let it come back from its own roots for a third and fourth year instead of replanting every second year. Doesn't yield such a good crop—each year the cane is smaller. Each year I replant a few acres, but it's never enough. I do what I can, but the place needs money and more labor. My father neglected this land after my grandmother died—said the soil wasn't worth the effort when Landfall produced much better." He pulled his hat more firmly over his eyes. "But I'm supposed to work it somehow, and make it pay. It's an inheritance, he keeps telling me—something my grandfather and he toiled over. Somehow that is supposed to inspire me."

We were descending now a much gentler slope between the cane fields; the road was deeply rutted with ancient wheel marks. I could see no slaves working in the fields. In this same stretch at Landfall there would have been several gangs, the air would have been full of their voices, the oddly melancholy songs they sang that made the rhythm of their movements among the cane. Here was silence, not the sound of birds, even.

Then suddenly, involuntarily, I checked Rosa. I looked from side to side among the cane, but could see nothing. But something had caused me to stop. In the midst of the fierce heat of the sun, there was a coldness here; I couldn't repress the shiver that went through me. I turned back to Fergus to find him staring at me strangely, a puzzled and somehow shocked expression on his face.

"What is it, Fiona?"

"Nothing—nothing at all."

"But you stopped!—you look . . . strange."

I tried to shrug and smile. "I don't know why. I thought there was someone here. It's ridiculous, I know—but I suddenly felt cold."

He edged his horse close to mine, our legs rubbing as the horses came together. "You feel it? You know?"

"Know?" I wished we might move on. "What is there to know?"

He knew that I hated the place; he urged the horses forward again before he answered. "It was just about that place, my father tells me, that my grandfather was murdered. There, just out of sight of the house. It was about the first thing I can remember, being brought here and being told about it. My grandmother didn't like him doing it, and he defended himself to her by saying that I had to be impressed early never to trust a slave—if possible, never even to turn your back on one." He paused, and then added, "Well, it's something that comes to you. You get used to learning to live with the feeling. I suppose every white person is afraid most of the time, even if we do forget about it. It's always there, somewhere at the back of your mind. But we try to put it away from us, or we'd go insane—or never go to sleep. Most, I think, sleep with pistols beside their beds—there, that's Winterslo."

We had turned from the cart track onto what must be the dirt road that joined the Landfall road farther down. We approached it from the side, but I had been right when I had recognized it from the headland, this straggle of buildings. There was an avenue of sorts, almost as rutted as the cart tracks, lined with thin casuarina trees, planted long ago with Scottish carefulness as a windbreak, rather than for their beauty. The sugar mill was close to the house, loosely joined by a line of stables and outbuildings. The house itself was smallish, symmetrical, only the necessary gallery around it to distinguish it from the sort of foursquare house that fairly prosperous farmers in Scotland built. There was no striving for presence or grandeur here; it was simply the house that a hard-working Scot had built for his wife and child, and then had murdered at a spot on the ridge above it, out of sight. I said nothing; there was nothing I might say about Winterslo that Fergus would not have called humbug. As we came nearer the shabbiness became more evident. There was no garden to speak of—just the bare place in front of the house partially shaded by a few clumps of mampoo trees which leaned away from the wind. The earth seemed dry and cracked; hens scratched about without enthusiasm. Where the windows would have been in a Scottish house were the french doors—the heavy hurricane shutters hung on the outside, the louvered inner ones for closing at night. All of them sagged and leaned, needing paint. Fergus had to shout before a slave came from the direction of the stables to take our horses. He did not come at a run as those at Landfall would have, but shuffled forward, in dirty white clothes, with a kind of lazy indifference that told me he had little fear of his master.

"Damn you, Daniel, can't you move yourself once in a while?"

The man shrugged. "I no hear master come." It told me something I had wondered about, as I was bound to. Fergus obviously did not use a whip—or very seldom. The man led the horses away, chanting something to himself; there was no backward look. He had no fear of later reprisal. Fergus had forgotten about him; he took my arm with all the solicitous politeness that Alister might have used as he led me up the few steps to the gallery—not here the wrought-iron rail, the curving stairs of Landfall. The gallery was furnished with a few sagging cane chairs. But he led me farther into the dimness of what was the main living room and staircase hall at Winterslo.

It was dusty, even dirty. Balls of fluff raced across the floor at our advance; dust lay on everything, save on one end of a big mahogany table—one good enough to have graced Landfall. Everything else was cane—chairs whose supports were crisscrossed with cobwebs, a few small tables. There was an elaborate sewing table whose silk had rotted almost to nothing; there was one age-spotted mirror. In places the heel of my boot seemed to crunch into the rotting wood of the floor.

"Welcome to Winterslo." Fergus said it with no conscious irony; he was used to the place. He clapped his hands. "Hannah—Hannah! Where the devil are you?"

It took some time for the woman to come from the back premises; the kitchen would be out there, separate from the main house. She was thin, laconic, middle-aged.

"You call, master?"

"You know damn well I call. Bring us some lime juice, with rum for me."

She shrugged. "No limes, master."

"Then *something*—and try to be quick!"

Fergus shook his head, as if knowing he was being made a fool of. "It's no use. I have no hand with them. They do as they like. Well, here it is. Sit down."

"Am I not to see the rest of it. Upstairs? I haven't much time, you know. Duncan comes back and I am expected to be there."

"Upstairs?—upstairs is what you'd expect. Worse than this. Leaking roof. Spiders. Termites in the stairs and floors. Well—I invited you to Winterslo. You can't see the kitchen. You'd probably be sick. Well, then —come upstairs. It will certainly take Hannah her own good time to bring two drinks."

I followed him up the stairs—not a grand staircase like Landfall's, but the narrow, wallhung one of a Scottish house. The railing was dusty under my hand, and the sweat made the dust stick. A corridor at the top divided the bedrooms. Six, there were, I think.

"My grandfather hoped for many children, I suppose. This house would have done for a time."

He led me from room to room, flinging open the doors, showing the rooms empty except for a chest or a wardrobe, too plain to be moved to Landfall. He came to the end room, the corner room with two long windows that opened on different aspects. "This is where I sleep now. It used to be my grandmother's room."

It was barren, unswept. Whatever embarrassment I might have feared, there was none here. If Fergus had a mistress, if he had had many mistresses in the past, none were here at Winterslo. The four-poster bed was roughly made. Two worn silver-backed brushes lay on a bureau which had one drawer missing; a clothes press with an open door swinging on one hinge revealed a jumble of clothes. There was a kind of awful bleakness about it that had nothing to do with poverty. No one cared. No woman lived here—a flower or two would have helped, a picture on the wall, even one of the shells that lay strewn on the beaches. But there was nothing. I could make no comment; I just went to the window that gave the view of the sea. Unlike Landfall, Winterslo did not possess the luxury of an upper gallery, so the sun blazed directly through the open shutters. Even with the breeze that moved between the two windows it was very warm. The shutters reached down to the floor, and a little railing stretched across each window.

"Don't lean on it," Fergus cautioned. "Everything is rotten with termites. The whole place needs to be gutted. Perhaps," he added and I felt that he wasn't joking, "perhaps there will be a revolt some day, and the slaves will oblige by burning it down."

I turned back to him. "Do you expect a revolt?"

He shrugged. "They threaten at times, like hurricanes. Sometimes they strike—mostly not. But they are part of what we live with, like the pistol by the bed."

Instinctively my eyes went to the table by the bedside. Its dust was undisturbed, but it had a drawer with a keyhole. He knew what I was looking for, and he nodded. "No slave sleeps in this house at night. I bring one of the dogs in. It can't be helped. It is the way we grow up out here."

"Alister says that . . ."

He cut me short. "I'm not interested in what Alister says. He's full of what London thinks the West Indies are all about, but he doesn't know the reality. He's read the books, but he's never known how it feels to see the cane flattened by a hurricane. He will spout Wilberforce at you, but he doesn't know how much better off these people are than they were in Africa. They were slaves there, too. One tribe selling another tribe, and it's a damn shame the trade was ever stopped. We're dying out here for need of slaves, and in Africa they're eating one another. No—don't talk to me about Alister. The man's a pompous ass!"

As if he were afraid of my rebuttal he turned swiftly and started from the room. "We'll go down. It's damned hot up here in the middle of the day—and even Hannah must have produced something to drink by now."

I took another swift look about before I left, impressing the cheerless quality of this room upon my memory; I knew that I would think often of Fergus here. One other thing I noted. From the window that faced toward the shoreline, the ridge that ran between these lands and San Francisco's was too high to permit a view of the hooking bay below the greathouse; a vessel riding there would be seen by no one except those at San Francisco itself.

There was a sickly sweet drink waiting for us below on a table on the gallery, and Hannah had added rum to both. "She doesn't know any different," Fergus said. "I can't teach her—haven't the patience. She doesn't want to be taught. She likes things the way they are. When I want to frighten her I threaten her with bringing a wife to Winterslo —there's a lash still hanging in the kitchen from my grandmother's time. But she only laughs at me. She doesn't expect a white woman at Winterslo very soon. She isn't so stupid, either. What woman would want to come here . . ."

I didn't know what to say; I just stared out to sea, and sipped and was strangely glad of the rum to ease my nervousness. But if I had any more I might talk, and I might say things that should not be said. I wanted to lean over and touch this man's arm; I wanted to feel his hand rest on mine. We were as different as two people could be—he rough and prickly, of no intellect and little education, holding views on slavery I found hard now to accept. I saw no books in this house, and I had lived all my life with books. But he had a curious sensitivity; he seemed to know what was in people's minds, and when one was past the brusqueness, he was a gentle man. No slave at Winterslo feared the lash. He attracted children as well as women—I knew Duncan's devotion to him even though the two rarely saw each other. He was a man who could appreciate the wild grandeur of the Serpent coves, and went there alone just for the beauty of it; and yet I knew the stories of his often having been involved in brawls in drinking places in Santa Marta. But one would forgive him that when one knew the cheerless state of Winterslo, and the grudging, tension-laden welcome he received at Landfall. He was a man disinherited, and yet he did not hate the child who was the cause of it.

My thoughts grew dangerous. I was suddenly swept with a desire to have him myself; it is a terrible thing when this happens in a woman. In these awful moments I knew that my desire was as strong as any man's could ever have been. It was not supposed to happen, but it did. I could make no move, and I was choking on my own need. There is an awful knowledge that comes to one at such times. All at once I understood why people acted in the madness of passion—why lives were swept away, ruined; I understood now the meetings between Andrew and Fergus's mother, the girl of only seventeen in the deserted great-house in the hills. I understood why Fergus had been born—but now it was the difference between merely knowing and understanding. I had not believed before in this flood of need and longing; now every nerve in me stretched and strained toward him. If he had made the least move in my direction I would have clutched at him, and my soul would never again know freedom. Was I to call this love?—it was absurd. How could I love what I didn't know? The trouble was that I hadn't experienced the sickness of love before; I hadn't known its irrational power.

My hand was shaking as I put down the glass, half-full still.

"I must go." How had I managed to say it?

He looked at me fully in the face. "Do you want to go?"

Did he know, as he seemed to know so many other things; I thought I could not bear it if he knew my torment now, and yet, if he never were to know, what a waste it was, what a lack of honesty. If he knew, would he hold the knowledge like some weapon? I had put myself at his mercy—but then he was not an ungenerous man.

"It isn't what *I* want, is it? I have to be back at Landfall. I'm not paid to . . . Well, I must go." The cane chair creaked violently as I pulled myself out of it, and I held it a moment for support.

"I know . . . I know."

It seemed an interminable time until the horses were brought around, and all that time we said nothing, just stood by the steps, waiting. But something in Fergus's expression warned the slave who brought the horses, because I saw the grin, that had seemed to be habitual, suddenly wiped away. He too said nothing as they both helped me mount. We rode off down the dusty avenue; a quick glance back, and Winterslo was less inspiring even than before I had seen inside it. And yet I wanted back there; I yearned toward it, and dreaded the return to Landfall.

At that same place, just over the rise on the way to the Kronberg forest, Fergus checked his horse. He looked back at me.

"Fiona—how did you know? How did you know it was here?"

I shook my head, refusing to meet his gaze. "I just had a feeling . . . How was I to know?" I appealed to him.

"All right." With that strange knowingness of his, he did not press me further, did not seek to probe the sore point of my existence. He urged his horse forward, speaking back to me over his shoulder. "I think of it myself each time I pass here. But you *knew*. I would never have known where it happened if I hadn't been told. There's the difference, you see . . ."

He knew about me, I thought, and yet he did not shrink from the knowledge, nor fear it. He accepted something in me that he did not understand, but he demanded no explanation. We went on, and did not speak again until the trail cut into the slope of the mountain joined the fork that led to Landfall.

"You can leave me here. I know the way now."

"You don't want me to come?"

"It's probably better if you don't."

He nodded, half-turned his horse, then checked again. "If you know the way back, then you also know the way to Winterslo."

"Yes—I know it."

"Perhaps you'll come."

"Perhaps."

He hesitated. "Just tell Samuel . . . he's a friend. He'll see you have a horse."

"It isn't usual," I reminded him. "A woman to come visiting alone . . ." How mean and pitiful the words sounded; I was ashamed.

"Not to a bachelor's house . . . ?" He had said it for me. "Not to the house of a man like me?" He edged the chestnut back closer, and leaned in the saddle toward me.

"You do care, Fiona? Do you care about what's the usual thing and what isn't? Or should I say the proper thing?" Now he leaned so that his face almost touched mine, but both hands stayed on the reins. "Fiona, you're not like other women—we both know that. I have the feeling—I know—you've seen things that other people have not seen. Somewhere, in some place, you've been in a kind of hell. Each of us has our own. Most of us never admit they exist. But you and I—we know they do. There's at least that much honesty. So if you come on this trail again, you will know what you're doing. And if I see you come up the avenue at Winterslo again I will know that you have admitted that you don't give a damn about what is the usual thing. You know the way—and I will look to see you coming."

I held Rosa, and watched him until the green tangle had absorbed the form of the horse and rider. Then I moved Rosa forward, back to Landfall. I had never known anything like this wildness of joy, and at the same time the fear of committal. I was coming to recognize that no love that carried this burden and this reward could ever be a peaceful one.

IV

I made myself wait. I told myself that I must wait at least three days —five days—not so much that pride had to be satisfied, but that I could not trust my own senses because of the tumult within me. Everything that was reasonable told me that to love Fergus Maxwell was folly—to think of marriage to him was madness, even if he had wanted it. But marriage—I was going too far. Good sense would tell anyone that for the woman who married Fergus Maxwell there would be no future; if Landfall had no future, then even less so did Winterslo. But the coldness of this reasoning shamed me, and the heat of my own passion hardly let it have expression. In all my moments, the best and the worst, I could only think that to marry with Fergus Maxwell would be both pain and pleasure; pain I already had—would I not also reach for the pleasure—try for it? And then I called myself a fool. All he had asked of me was to come again to Winterslo. This was not the fashion in which a man courted a woman he thought to marry. He had said: "Do you care, Fiona—do you care for what is the usual thing?" Was this an oblique invitation to take his bed but not his name? And I was just mad enough to do it.

So I made myself wait. In a kind of agony I made myself wait. And finally he came.

He did all the correct things. I heard the argument that raged between the connecting bedrooms of Andrew and Maria when his note came very early one morning asking permission to come that evening to dine. He also, it seemed, asked if Duncan might be permitted to come downstairs to dine with them, as it was so long since he had seen him. "Goddammit, he's still my son!" I heard the angry bull-voice announce. "And Duncan is his kin . . ." And Maria's tones, rising too shrilly, dropping into Spanish when her emotion became too intense. But Duncan himself won.

"I am to dine downstairs," he said to me as breakfast was brought in.

"Then mind you be credit to Miss Fiona," Charity said, determinedly shouldering Juanita out of the way as they served dishes.

I seemed to be in a fever all day. I did not take my usual morning walk when Duncan left with his mother; the hours of the siesta were sleepless. I deliberately stayed indoors, not wanting to bear the stigmata of the sun in freckles and reddened skin. He had seen me at my worst, in the sun-baked cove and in the dust of the cane fields. Now let him see me as Andrew had thought to contrive it—cool, silk-clad, a creature of the salon. But in the end I was afraid. I dressed early, and did not let Charity fuss too much with my hair; the dress was the simplest that the seamstress had fashioned, though still with the low-cut neckline that seemed to be her forte.

I crept downstairs and sat on the inner gallery, far in the shadows. But Fergus was early, too, and it was here he found me. He was as well-dressed as his household could contrive, the shirt ironed, though none too well, the jacket of indifferent cut, dusted and sponged. He had left his horse in the stable yard, and came walking quietly in the dusk. The slaves were just beginning to light the candles in the salon and dining room. He came up the front steps unheralded, blinking a little in the light that came from the hall; but before he moved on, he looked carefully up and down the length of the inner gallery.

"Fiona?"

I stirred slightly, and he came toward me, his step quick now.

"You didn't come!" It was an accusation, a cry of wounded pride, of disbelief.

"Must I come every day? I have other things . . ."

He leaned down, gripping the arms of my chair so that his face was very close to mine, intense, passionate, so startlingly like Duncan's when he was disturbed.

"I would have you come every day, I waited." Again it was a reproach. "And what other things have you to do? Is it Alister? Does that fool take your time? If I knew . . ."

And then he straightened, and stepped back, and the look of reproach changed to a puzzled frown. "You're different! Why are you all tricked out like that? Who gave you that dress? Why are you wearing it?—is it for Alister to ogle you? Dammit . . . ! Why have you changed? I liked you the way you were!"

I grew angry. "What I wear is my own business. And for whom. What right have you—"

"None," he said. "No right at all. I apologize." His tone was very stiff, cold. "I might have known you would not come. It was too much to expect."

Then he turned and strode back along the gallery to the hall. I heard him say something to Dougal, and soon there was the tinkle of crystal against crystal. Then silence. I sat there in the darkness of that far corner of the gallery until I heard voices from the salon—Andrew's loud burr, Maria's laugh, Duncan's excited shrillness. Then I made sure to enter from the hall, as if I had just come down.

Andrew turned to me with an air of triumph. "Miss Fiona—my son Fergus has given us his company tonight. I'm sure you can't have forgotten him, although we see him so seldom. Fergus's manners always make such an impression."

"Good evening, Mr. Maxwell." It was as coolly said as if I had never seen him before. And I had the wry satisfaction of seeing the blackness of the look Fergus directed toward Alister as he went to take from Dougal the wine he knew I preferred. As Alister bent over me with the glass Fergus deliberately turned his back and gave his whole attention to Maria.

* * * * *

Dinner was livelier that evening. For the first time I saw Alister provoked to some passion by the taunts that Fergus threw to him.

"Wilberforce is old—spent. The English know that slavery has to survive or the West Indies is dead."

"Then the West Indies is dead, my friend—Cousin."

"It will never happen. What about the Americans?"

"The slave states in America will come to it in their own time—it will be a dreadful time. But as soon as sugar and cotton and tobacco cease to be so profitable, you will see the moralists taking over. The moral attitude will prevail when the commercial has ceased to have force."

"You are a cynic, Alister." Maria's smooth voice, unbelieving.

A slight bow toward her. "A realist, Cousin Maria. Moral fervor flourishes when a man's pocket can't be hurt any more than it has been."

Maria shrugged. "Words!—I do not believe it!" I was listening to her voice, but mostly I was looking at her. Had she ever been more beautiful?—was it just the dress, one of her more elaborate ones, or was it the company of three men, none of whom could possibly ignore her, which added the essential spark to her beauty, gave it purpose, the sometimes missing radiance.

"It will happen," Alister said, unshakable.

"Then times have changed. But I do not believe it. The whole of the Indies are founded on this institution. Can a whole region be left to die because of some old Englishman mouthing in the English Parliament? We all know it must go on. After all, it comes from antiquity. We did not begin it. We did not invent it. My family had known it from the beginning in this island."

Were any of them aware, I wondered, of the slaves who stood about? —did they imagine them deaf, or too ignorant to understand? What was behind the blankness of those faces, the features themselves lost in the dimness behind the candles. They were not quite children, no matter how much Maria wanted to believe it.

"Then your family," Fergus said, "were among the Spaniards who worked the Arawaks to death."

"They had never worked!" Maria retorted. "They did not know what it meant. So they died. So others were brought from Africa."

Suddenly Fergus spoke to Duncan. "Spanish gold!" It was almost a shout. "Duncan, never believe other than that. It was gold the Spaniards came for, not land, not work, not sugar and rum. Gold and silver. They were bad colonists. The worst! A land must be cherished, not for what it will give by force, but what can be coaxed from it. Never believe in gold and silver, Duncan—never, never!" It was as if he had known that the time would be short. The words tumbled out, nearly incoherent, oddly at variance with the way Fergus himself lived.

He had known he must be quick. Already Maria had given a signal, and Duncan's chair was being drawn back from the table. A black hand reached to take his.

"Mama . . . you promised!"

"It is late, Duncan. Long past time you were in bed. This was a favor, remember? Not a promise."

He offered no further protest. But when his mother moved her chair sideways so that he might come to kiss her good-night, he still clung fast to the black hand that led him. He deliberately turned his head.

"Duncan!" Maria's tone was sharp, furious. He kept on walking. I almost saw, as well as sensed, the pressure tighten on the hand that held his. The message was plain; she had delivered him into these hands, expelled him from this company; he would stay where he had been assigned. I could have cheered his action, and yet I knew I would have trouble with him in the next few days. He had heard the rights of slavery disputed, and yet he was entrusted to the hands of a slave. The confusion created in his mind would appear in sullen imperiousness. I would be caught halfway; both the servant, and yet white.

When the doors had closed on Duncan, Maria wheeled back to Fergus. "And where would England be in the Indies without Spain? Was it not Spain—Isabella and Ferdinand—who sent Columbus? Who paid good Spanish gold for his venture? And what did the English do? They waited until the stream of gold and silver was coming back from Mexico and Peru to send their pirates into the Spanish Main. We were plundered and robbed and wrecked. Talk to me of your Drake and Hawkins! Pirates—all of them! And your English soldiers who came to take San Cristóbal when they knew it was vital to protect the treasure routes—when they knew we had done the work of colonization, of bringing the Christian faith—"

"Of bringing the African slaves when you had exhausted the Arawaks in the search for gold."

Instead of the explosive retort I expected, the cool smile returned to Maria's lips. She was in control again. "Need is always filled from whatever source available." She nodded slightly toward Alister. "Of all men, a merchant banker must appreciate this. And the search for gold— or silver—or the riches of the earth will continue, as long as man is on earth. We Spaniards did not begin it, we will not end it. We are all its servants." She looked around the table. "Who here can claim to be free of it? I shall challenge that one, and call him—or her—a liar."

The meal broke up then. There was no formal end. The men did not stay for port. We just stood, and each went his way, to the hall, the salon, the gallery. But not one of us cared to deny what Maria had said. Greed or lust was in the very bones of all of us. Only she had had the strength to call and name it for what it was.

*   *   *   *   *

I sat on the gallery for a while alone, hoping, I suppose, that Fergus would come to me there, but he seemed to have gone. I could see Maria sitting over embroidery in the salon. Alister went to the office, and I heard him asking for lamps to be brought. After a time Maria joined him; then began one of those continuing dialogues of commerce they seemed to hold—rum, molasses, sugar, yards of cloth, sacks of corn—on and on it went. I should have gone upstairs, but I was too restless yet. I moved to go down into the garden, and as I neared the dining room I was surprised to see Andrew still at the table. I had to pass where the light must strike me, and he saw me, and called.

"Well, girl!—had a good evening?" And then laughed raucously at his bad joke. The port decanter had been pushed aside, and a jug of rum stood beside his hand. Dougal had his patient, endless position near his master, waiting, I suppose, for him to be ready for the ascent of the stairs.

I just stood there, not trying to reply. He scowled at me. "Well, evenings at Landfall have never been noted for their gaiety. Not even after I married Maria. Too late . . ." He raised his head and surveyed the whole lofty room. "Don't know why I built up the place. Better to have stayed at Winterslo." He was very drunk, I thought. It would need more than Dougal to get him to bed.

"But there's Duncan," he added suddenly. "There's Duncan. He'll make things right. Pity is, I'll not see him a grown man. Pity . . ." He had forgotten my presence. He bowed down now over the table.

"Good-night, Mr. Maxwell," I said softly, and moved on. He was not aware of my going.

After the house, the garden seemed friendly; even the night creatures that scurried and scuttled were less hostile than the humans. I walked toward the back of the house, drawn by the dying fires at the doors of the slave quarters, and the soft cadence of their voices. I stayed within the shadow of the great baobab that grew there, and none saw me. They soon would sleep, perhaps a less-troubled sleep, for all their wretchedness, than the inhabitants of the greathouse. I turned at last to go back to that lighted splendor.

"Fiona!" Fergus's voice was low; he came along the path from the stables.

"I thought you'd gone."

"Wished me gone?"

"I didn't say that! Why must you twist and invent things . . . ?"

"Well—I'll tell you the truth. I was halfway to Winterslo. But I had to come back to see you."

"I usually go to my room after dinner."

"I would have sent Charity for you. I would have gone myself."

"Perhaps you wouldn't have been welcome. After the things you said to me . . ."

"Oh, for God's sake, Fiona!" He gave a low, almost a moaning sound. "Must we go on this way? I'm no good at playing this game. Never have been. Like my father, I've got no drawing-room manners." He reached and took both my arms. "Fiona, I came back just to tell you I didn't mean those things I said—and yet I did mean them. I'm jealous—I admit it. You didn't come to Winterslo, and I've never spent such long days in my life. I have never waited like that before. Do you understand?"

"I'm not sure."

"Of course you're sure! A woman always knows when she has a man in torment. I didn't think you were the sort who teases."

"I never prom—" I couldn't finish; he had suddenly taken me in close to him as if he meant to make me part of him; I had never been kissed like this, as if I were being dragged across the threshold of some place of passion I had never known existed. But I found, once the entrance was made, that I might be there forever. This was the reply to the longing I had felt for him as we had sat together on the gallery at Winterslo. This was drawing close to something I had sensed in the second I had first seen him, seen the splendor of his beauty and strength, felt the stirring in me that had not been entirely stilled since that moment. I was helpless to prevent the response that surged through me; I could no more have left my lips cold and closed against his than I could have physically wrenched myself from his arms. Our bodies seemed to mold together, and then, knowing that the complete fulfillment was denied us now, stiffened and hardened and finally suffered the agony of withdrawal. I was weak, and almost sobbed as we drew apart.

"Tomorrow. Tomorrow I'll come for you," he said. "I have something to show you. No—we won't go to Winterslo. You have to see something else—something that may make you bear with Landfall until . . . until . . . Oh, God knows what will happen to us. I have nothing to offer you, but yet I can't let you go in peace. But tomorrow I'll come, and you'll be waiting."

I stood for a long time beneath the shadow of the great tree after he left me, until my senses had cleared, until the shaking and weakness had nearly gone. I was wild with joy, and yet bereft. I had told myself I would suffer the pain for the pleasure; well, now it was mine, and it was scarcely to be borne. I saw that the lights in the house had begun to be extinguished, and so I began to make my way back. I went straight in by the kitchen. I think I stumbled on the steps, because the noise caused both Maria and Alister to look around from the desk where they sat.

I must have been a sight to disturb them, because Alister stood quickly and came to the door of the office. Behind him, Maria's face, for one unguarded moment, lost its cool control; was it rage I saw there?—hatred for the first time plain and unmixed with contempt. She wasn't amused by me any more.

"Fiona?—are you all right?" Alister said.

I suppose my hair was disheveled, probably there were deep creases in the silk gown, and it was stained with sweat. Probably the wildness of my emotion showed as if I had spoken it. I lied, very badly.

"Perfectly all right, thank you. Good-night." I imagine my walk must have looked a little drunken as I went in toward the hall; I remember trying to hold myself very erect, and think that it must have looked strange, because things seemed to be spinning about me. I was sure of it when Maria, jolted out of character, suddenly called after me.

"Fergus—has he gone?"

I didn't look back at her. "I expect so," I answered, and floated on as if I dwelt in some magic place of secret access. I knew that she guessed it had been Fergus who had caused this disarray, this indifference to what they thought. I couldn't help it. I couldn't help it. If I lost everything I could not lose whatever there was of Fergus for me to have. I took my candle and made the slow ascent of the stairs. At the top I looked down again. Alister had come to the hall and was staring up after me. And I thought that he also knew. But his expression, inscrutable, calm, unlike Maria's, told me nothing. I felt a faint regret that I might have earned his disapproval; he had been my friend at Landfall, and for that he was precious; but I could not weigh this beside my need for Fergus.

I went softly into Duncan's room. He lay asleep, hot and tumbled in the big bed, his face in the candlelight so like the little half-brother who had always wrapped the blankets cocoon-like about him against the chill of that unheated Scottish manse. I put the candle on the table and bent lower; it was then I saw the tear stains on his cheeks, the aftermath, of course, of his being dismissed so abruptly from the dinner table. I was shamed by the sight; it was here I should have come directly myself, to comfort, to help him. But I had thought only of myself, and Fergus. I brushed the sweat-soaked hair back from his forehead; the touch half-wakened him. His eyelids fluttered open. "Miss Fiona . . . ?" Suddenly his arms came up and clutched me, clung about my neck.

"Hush, now. Sleep . . . ssh . . ."

"You'll stay?"

I put my lips, bruised and warm from Fergus's, to his forehead.

"I'll stay."

I sat with him, lightly holding his hand, long past the time when he slept again. It was strangely calming, to sit with this sleeping child, to feel the life of Landfall go quiet about me, the last closing of the other bedroom doors, the dusty shuffle of the slaves' bare feet, the extinguishing of the gallery lamps. Only the unceasing cry of the cicadas kept up. The whole house was still as I went to my room; I pulled myself quickly out of my clothes, and fell into bed. I slept at once, waking only when Charity brought the water next morning. The sun was already sliding past the edge of the gallery, the sounds were of the household well on the move. Despite the turmoil of my whole being, it was the best night's sleep I had had since coming to Landfall.

V

Fergus was waiting when I went to the stable yard. A horse also was waiting, saddled; not the drooping-headed Rosa, but a small, light-footed animal who regarded me with some suspicion as Samuel led him to the mounting block. "This is Fidelito," Fergus said. "He'll carry you better than Rosa, and I'm certain you can manage him."

Samuel's smile now was open as he helped me mount. "He will go well for you, mistress. I have spoken with him."

I regarded the slave seriously. "You can make horses understand you, Samuel?"

"Of course."

I did not doubt him, and somehow I felt more secure on this animal because of what he had told me. We made good headway through the forest path that led from Landfall. At the point where the foliage thinned and we had taken the trail to Winterslo a week ago, Fergus pointed us on a road that led, it seemed to me, through cane fields that must yet be on the Landfall plantation.

"Push him on," Fergus said, slapping his hand down on Fidelito's rump. "This is Landfall territory, and I've no wish to meet Maria and Duncan. At least, not yet. On the way back, it doesn't matter."

I had to put all my wits and strength to holding Fidelito in those first moments when we broke into a canter. It was a long time since I had ridden a horse at this pace, a horse remotely as lively as this one. But the magic of Samuel's words persisted. "He will carry you well," Fergus had said, and he did, accepting me, knowing my limitations, but not despising me for them. Fergus kept just perceptibly ahead of me, his right hand free to reach for the bridle if Fidelito should get beyond my control. But it wasn't necessary; Samuel had spoken well to him. As we settled into a steady pace I grew confident enough to relax a little and call to Fergus.

"Where are we going? Why does it matter about meeting Maria now?"

"Because if she met us now she would guess where we were going. She'd try to stop us—or insist on going with us."

"Then where are we going?"

"To visit Duncan's grandmother."

It was a second before it sank home. "Maria's mother!"

"Yes—now we'll get on. Maria may possibly see the dust we're kicking up. She has eyes for things like that."

* * * * *

It was neither Landfall nor Winterslo. San Francisco announced itself in the ruin of stone pillars that fronted a road which would eventually join the main one to Santa Marta. Pieces of rusted metal lay about the pillars, the remnants of lamp standards, or of gates—it was now impossible to tell. The butchered stumps of a once-magnificent double row of trees exposed the rutted avenue to the merciless beating of the sun. At the gate Fergus checked. "We may go easier now." I wondered if he was giving the old woman time to recognize him, and hold her fire.

He halted and wheeled his horse sideways, looking back over the cane fields we had ridden. "It all once belonged to San Francisco. Landfall—Winterslo, this land all about us, and much farther on toward Santa Marta than you can see. You once could have ridden half a day and still be on San Francisco land. But at the time when the islands were first settled, when San Cristóbal was a way-station for treasure ships from Mexico and the Isthmus, land that didn't yield silver or gold was hardly worth bothering about—or so the Spaniards thought. The Medinas didn't bother—in those days it gave them sugar effortlessly, and the supply of slaves was cheap and easy. They took it all for granted, and sent their children, as long as they could afford it, to be educated in Spain. But they were fools, or weakened by indulgence. Bit by bit it all went. The place can't sustain itself any longer. They have only a few slaves, and just the acres down to the bay there. Yields just about enough rum for the old woman, it seems to me—rum and the patch of Indian hemp she grows. They live off the few bits of vegetables and fruit they can grow—and handouts from Landfall's kitchen. There aren't any men left, you see. Just Donna Isabella, and Maria's two sisters, older than she, who will never marry."

His voice broke harshly. "Sometimes I suspect that Maria would like to cut off even the little she gives them—really starve them out. Then what remains of San Francisco would be hers, as well as Landfall."

We were riding slowly up the avenue as he talked. Already I could see the figure seated on the gallery of the greathouse. The land about us was desolate, unhoed, and therefore baked hard. Trees and shrubs struggled for their own life about the house, but no hand had tended them for many years, and the stronger had taken over. It had not the feeling of Winterslo—that simplicity which might, with care, show dignity; it had been built on a far grander scale than Landfall, but the grandeur was fallen to ruins. As we drew nearer I began to wonder if the house itself could stand the vibration of the horses hoofs; the massive columns were crumbling, remnants of their carved capitals lay among the vines and weeds. To give it added height and scale once a balustraded parapet had topped the building; now the gaps were stark and bare to the hard blue sky. An arched cloister had once joined greathouse and outbuildings; a few columns still remained in their broken beauty, the line of arches was smothered in the rampant growth.

The figure on the gallery had watched our approach intently, but without moving. No warning shots had greeted us, as with Alister. She knew Fergus, and possibly respected his anger. As we came to the foot of the steps the figure stirred to action; the thump of a massive fist upon the table seemed to echo through the emptiness of a dead house. It brought no immediate response. I knew that the figure was that of a woman, but she seemed barely that. She was grotesquely fat, clad in a soiled white gown that hung loosely from her shoulders, of no particular style, simply a garment to cover her body. Except for the pendulous breasts it might have been hard to tell that she was a woman; she wore her hair pulled severely back, greased into place, screwed into a thin knot that was not visible as one faced her. The features themselves were sexless, lost in fat, the eyes black slits, the fingers thickened stumps of wrinkled olive skin.

Eventually a slave appeared in one of the doorways in answer to her shout. It took a long time then for someone to come to take our horses; I had difficulty holding Fidelito quiet, and I somehow had the impression that the great hulking figure in the chair enjoyed my discomfort. But at last a man came, and Fergus bade him simply to hold the horses within the shade of one of the trees. Then he led me up the steps to the woman in the chair.

"Donna Isabella—may I present Miss Fiona McIntyre. No doubt you know that Miss McIntyre has come to Landfall to—"

She cut him short. "I know—I know. My grandson, the little blond boy who can't even speak Spanish, is being schooled by one from Scotland. One of the Maxwells." She gave a fierce, horrible laugh. "Old Maxwell. He keeps his own to his own."

She seemed to scowl at me through the dark slits. "Well, sit down." She waved to a dilapidated chair. It was placed so that I had my back to the view and the sea, but it also faced directly into the main salon of San Francisco. In proportion it was far more splendid than any of Landfall's rooms, but it was a scene of almost unbelievable decay and squalor. Every piece of furniture—there seemed not many of them— appeared to be broken, perhaps by the weight of this enormous creature. Upholstery was torn, and looked as if it housed mice, or even worse; empty glasses and cups stood about, smeared, flies swarming for the dregs of sugar in them. A torn mattress lay near the foot of the stairs, perhaps bedding for a slave, perhaps for the old woman who could no longer mount them. There was a central fireplace to this huge room; ashes lay thick in it, and even a fire-blackened pot hung there, as if this were a crofter's hut in Scotland. From the back regions came the heavy smell of something cooking; but the whole place also bore the smell of a thousand greasy, burned meals; the very walls seemed saturated with dust and neglect and despair.

The old woman thumped her fist again. "Katarina!—Joanna! Come! We have guests." Her manner was somehow triumphant over the filth and decay; thus she might have bidden her daughters to welcome guests to the most splendid mansion in the Indies. And while she called to them I studied her more closely, the stained, sack-like gown, the grime caked beneath the long fingernails; I smelled the odors of an unwashed body, of rum and the same pervasive smell of the hemp that Andrew smoked. Somehow I knew then that Maria had introduced the weed to Andrew, and with the purpose that it would reduce him to the same kind of hulk that faced me now.

The sisters came at last, at once reluctant and yet eager, as if they hated this public display of their poverty, and yet were starved for the sight of a different face, to hear another tongue. They had probably watched us ride up the avenue. One of them came bearing a tray with hastily washed glasses on it, still wet and smeared.

It didn't matter which was which—they were both the same. They were Maria's sisters, with her features which somehow had gone wrong, the nose hooked, the jaw too pointed, the brows too black and heavy—her body again, but thin to the point of emaciation, flat-breasted, long, dark, sinewy necks. They wore cotton gowns, faded and limp, but clean enough. Their hair was greased back like their mother's, the same tight knot. It was almost impossible to believe that the beauty of Maria had flowered from this stock.

But their manners still carried the mark of the generations of stiff Spanish ladies who had been schooled in Spain though I knew Maria was the only one who had ever been there. Tonelessly, but politely, they welcomed me to San Francisco and San Cristóbal; in the same manner I was asked about the voyage out, how I liked Landfall and the climate. Had I ever visited Spain? Did I speak any Spanish? When I answered no to this last, the old woman suddenly shrieked with hard laughter.

"I would have thought that the English spent so much time trying to chase Napoleon's soldiers from Spain that by now Spanish was their mother tongue."

"That was a long time ago, Donna Isabella. And the English are notoriously resistant to foreign innovation—so foolish of them, don't you think, to have refused Phillip's Armada the chance to teach them a few civilizing things."

The old woman scowled; I didn't feel repentant, but I had made more of an enemy than I need have done. "Phillip was once England's king through his wife, Mary Tudor."

"I think the English, and even the Scots, would dispute that England ever had a Spanish king. But I will endeavour to tell both sides to my pupil, so that in time Duncan will judge that question for himself."

"In time, when the old one is gone, my grandson—his real name is Ferdinand—will go himself to Spain to be educated. There he will learn the true story, as well as the true faith. Now he is being brought up in this heretic religion . . ." The words were final, and chilling, and I said no more. I suddenly realized that only Andrew's unsteady health and age stood between Duncan and the total influence of his mother, and of this family from which she sprang. I understood now many things that had not been clear before—Maria's taste for show, her care for business, what Fergus and Alister called her greed. She only of these four had escaped the island heritage of indolence in women. But she had escaped more than that. These pathetic women, her sisters, were the last relics of the workings of the tragedy of a long decline. I thought of Maria, only eight years removed from this, and I understood at once her cruelty and the coldness. The stiff pride she displayed was still evident in these dried-out women; it seemed all that was left to them.

Some sickly drink was finally brought, though not to Donna Isabella, who had a jug beside her, just as Andrew did. The talk drifted on. Donna Isabella—I wondered if it were a courtesy title only—demanded gossip of Santa Marta from Fergus, and when he shrugged and said he had none, she seemed to grow annoyed.

"What? You never go? You don't try to tell me that? We all know how Fergus Maxwell keeps the tongues wagging with his fights, and his gaming and that whisky they bring from Scotland . . ."

He sighed wearily. "That was some time ago, Donna Isabella. May a man never live down the foolishness of his youth? Winterslo occupies every minute of my time. I have no money for gaming and Scotch whisky."

"So you live like a monk?" she demanded scornfully. "Ah—*that* I do not believe." Her tone was rising. She had refilled her glass from the jug a number of times, and she did so once more before she spoke again. She turned fiercely in my direction. "Well, there is a reason now for him to stay nearer home—more reason than to be near my daughter, Maria. Oh, I hear about it—I hear it all. I hear how old Maxwell goes and dresses you like some doll at Rodriguiz. For what reason? He's not capable of crawling into a woman's bed any longer. It wasn't for himself, for his own pleasure all those things bought from Rodriguiz—the silks and laces and all the rest. Look at you now, in a finer blouse than my daughters possess between them, wearing boots that would clothe them for a year! Why does he do this? You—some sort of servant brought from Scotland! Because you are Maxwell, and he sees a way—"

Fergus had seized me by the arm and pulled me to my feet. "Come, Fiona. I brought you for a purpose. Now it's been accomplished. There's no need to stay for the abuse of a drunken old woman."

He was pulling me along the gallery to the steps. The two younger woman were on their feet, outraged. But the rage of the old woman was much fiercer, her tongue looser from the rum. A stream of vilifications in Spanish followed us; Fergus thrust me into the saddle, and shouted at the slave to hold his horse while he mounted; but the man was slow and muddled, and perhaps understood better than we did what his mistress shouted. By this time Donna Isabella had managed to haul herself from her chair. Struggling to hold Fidelito, I was suddenly confronted with the unforgettable sight of her vast bulk at the top of the steps, one arm clinging to a pillar, the other raised with clenched fist at us.

"I'll tell you, you Scotch slave, why the old man does these things. He thinks to marry you to his son, Fergus, and get Fergus away from my daughter's skirts. I know—I know! I hear everything and I know. There was to be another Maxwell girl to come—younger and prettier than you. She was to be for Fergus. But you came, but you are Maxwell too, so you will do as well. I hear it all—how much money Andrew has promised Fergus to make the marriage to the other one. Money for Winterslo. Money to be a gentleman again. All he had to do was to marry and keep away from Maria. Because everyone knows that Fergus is crazy for Maria. The whole island knows that he is crazy for Maria—even before she married the father. And he will keep on being crazy in love with Maria, even if the old man has tricked you out like a—"

Fergus yelled at her. "For God's sake, shut your mouth, you indecent old bitch! Fiona, don't listen! It's not the truth. *Not* the truth, you hear!"

But the anguish in his face was there to be read; guilt, shame, anger. There was some truth in the obscene ravings of the old woman, and all of us knew it. In a kind of madness of distress I suddenly brought the crop down on Fidelito's flank, and he leapt forward from the limp hand of the slave. Down the rutted avenue he plunged, beyond my control now, but the thunder of his hoofs was like the breaking of something within me. I hardly tried to check him, just sat there, not even gripping hard with my knees. If I fell, there might be the saving grace of a broken neck, and it seemed easier than having to accept the pain of the old woman's revelations. So I let Fidelito have his head, to go like the wind of fury. I didn't care. In those moments I wanted to die.

I could hear Fergus coming after me, hear his cries. But Fidelito was swift and had the start of him. We pounded on down through the cane breaks, and at last the straggling trees that marked the beginning of the Kronberg forest appeared. I had lost my hat, my hair streamed behind me, the wind blew cold through my sweat-soaked blouse; but Fidelito's sweat was working through my skirt and he was beginning to slow. I knew the danger of the approaching trees, but still I did not try to halt him. Let it be. But he also knew the danger, and he had had his wild dash. As we entered the area of the scattered trees the gallop dropped to a canter, and then as the forest loomed he slowed almost entirely. I still had no control of him; it was his own will. The wonder was that I had remained in the saddle.

Almost at once Fergus was beside me; he reached for the bridle to check Fidelito completely, and the horse accepted it.

"Fiona—what on earth possessed you to do that? You know how easily you could have been killed?"

I swung in the saddle, furious, trembling. "Would it have mattered? Yes—I suppose it might have mattered. I would not have been here for you to marry, and there would have been no money from your father. And still you would have lusted for Maria!"

"Fiona—"

I couldn't stand the pain any longer. I had to act, to make him feel something of what I had suffered. I raised my crop and hit him directly across the cheek.

Before the crop fell I knew what I had done. He sat as if he were frozen in the saddle, and small beads of blood oozed from the welt. For a moment I closed my eyes at the sight of it, wondering by what devil I was possessed that had caused me to take an action I would have despised and condemned in another. It was added humiliation to know that I was no better, no different from the shrieking Donna Isabella, no less savage than Maria with her slaves.

I pressed the crop, and the hand that had wielded it, to my mouth. "Forgive me," I said, and choked on the words. "Forgive me."

"Perhaps it is as well," he said. He seemed tired, almost resigned. "They say that punishment releases guilt. It is easier for me if you strike me than if you wept."

"But I do weep inside."

"All courage weeps inside. Yes—you know there was some truth in what the old woman ranted. But it was not all the truth. I would have told you, but without those drunken obscenities she shouted. Can you bear to hear it? You know I took you there this morning for Duncan's sake, knowing what you would learn of what he faced in the future, to help you prepare him. But I didn't believe the old devil capable of such infamy. But she is further gone than I believed. She drinks—all the time, constantly—and smokes that wretched stuff that Maria brings to my father. She is mad—mad!"

"But how much truth is there in madness?" I demanded. More blood seeped from the cut, and some had started to trickle down his face. The sight of it unnerved me.

"We have to talk, Fiona. We *must*. You'll have the truth. All of it!"

The blood flowed more freely, and I was helpless before the evidence of what I had done. He got down from his own horse, tethered it, and came to help me dismount. I was weak with fatigue and emotion, and I clung to the pommel for a moment. Then he led me to a place beneath a tree festooned with vines. The deep shade engulfed us. The wind touched the branches high above our heads, but did not reach us. The tethered horses stretched for the greenery within reach.

The final thing was the way Fergus laid his hand on mine. I tried to make myself snatch it away, but I could not. I was his, held faster than the horses.

* * * * *

"I saw her first," he said, "when she was about nineteen—a little older than I was. You can't imagine what she was like then—hush, Fiona!— I don't say this to hurt you, but to try to make you see it as a boy would see it. Life wasn't good at Landfall. I was lonely. I still missed my grandmother, and I had grown too old for the friends I had had among the slaves. Of course, there were the female slaves, but they were always there, and mine for the having. They never could be companions.

"Even with a house like Landfall, we didn't entertain—well, you know that. It seemed to amuse my father to let the rumors of its splendor spread about the island, then invite no one to visit. We rarely went to Santa Marta, and then only for short times. My father worked like a slave himself. The only companion I had was the young fellow who kept the books. He was also supposed to be my tutor. It isn't much wonder I grew up ignorant and unmannerly—but that's all past, and one can't go back. Andrew is trying not to make the same mistake with Duncan."

"But Maria," I urged, impatient. Without thinking, I put up my handkerchief to wipe the blood from his cheek. He smiled, and held my hand there for a second.

"I'm coming to Maria. I had never seen her before. Of course I knew about San Francisco—but there had been a falling out between Andrew and Donna Isabella. Not surprising. Both of them, at one time or another, have probably quarreled with everyone on the island. So we didn't visit, even though they were the closest plantation. I knew about the three sisters—the youngest a beauty, everyone said, and sent to Spain to get a husband when she was seventeen. But then she was back—desperate, probably to make good the failure in Spain. She came to Landfall uninvited. She said she never meant to present herself at the house at all, but just to walk through the garden to see it. She had walked from San Francisco. Her horse was lame, she said, but I don't think she had a horse. Of course she meant to be discovered. In any case, it was I who found her in the garden, just standing and staring at the house. I'm sorry, Fiona—I have to say it. She was so lovely then . . . fresh, with a kind of innocent beauty. Knowing her now, and what kind of hell she grew up in at San Francisco, she never could have been the guileless child I thought her. But it was as if my wish for friend and lover and wife were suddenly there in one person. I suppose I fell in love with her from the first moment I saw her.

"My father was in the fields, so I asked her into the house. It was the first time I had ever shown Landfall to anyone. I could see she was impressed, but not admitting it. That damnable pride they have—but then, at one time, San Francisco had been far grander than Landfall. But she seemed sweet then—gentle, smiling, and more beautiful in dresses that were cast-offs from her sisters than she is now in her silks. Do you understand this, Fiona?—how it was possible? How it seemed to me then?"

I nodded. I knew very well how it was possible.

"For some reason I sensed that I should keep her away from Landfall. I was afraid, I think. We used to meet at Winterslo, which was closed up—except that I got the key. For the first few weeks it seemed a sort of paradise. I had her all to myself. I was madly in love with her, and yet I didn't lay a finger on her. We talked for hours—she was very amusing, and she was much better educated than I was."

He was silent then for a while. "It seems impossible now to believe that I could have been so innocent that I thought she was too. I didn't dare to touch her. I meant to marry her, but I wanted her for just that little time to have for myself. I knew as soon as I spoke to my father and Donna Isabella, it would all be finished. From then on we would be in the middle of people—forever, probably. We would never have a time like that, all to ourselves, again.

"But of course my father got to hear of it—in time, the slaves tell everything. I think he was rather glad I wanted to marry and settle with someone, but he wished it wasn't with one of the Medinas. 'Degenerate' he called them. 'Worn out.' But in any case he told me to bring her to Landfall one afternoon, and he would made a point of staying in from the fields to meet her.

"Well—it was the end. I should have known it, but my senses just didn't take it in at the time. All I knew was that my own father was as blinded by her as I was. I sat there, dumb, between the two of them, and listened to them talk, and it was like listening to two people I had never met before. She had all the tricks—you'd think she'd been in a London salon all her life, and that she was forty years old, at least. And yet still this shining, wonderful young beauty. He was captivated—worse, infatuated. And at an age dangerous in a man. I never felt so miserable as on that ride back to San Francisco. I remember she talked all the way, about nothing—to stop *me* from talking, I suppose. She made excuses about meeting me the next day at Winterslo. It was only when I accused her of not caring for me that she gave in. I suppose at that time she wasn't sure of my father, and she was afraid of losing me.

"Well, she came the next afternoon to Winterslo, but the spell was broken. I still wanted her more than I had ever wanted anything in my life, but she was no longer untouchable. She was no better than I was—no better than my father, since she could match him so well. I took her that afternoon, Fiona—no, I'll never believe that it was force, although she might say so. I think she already had made up her mind what she was going to do, but she wasn't going to miss the taste of me, if she could help it. She is capable of all the passion that you sense under that controlled surface, even now, and when she was aroused, she wanted it as much as I did. At times, when I can hardly credit now that that afternoon happened at all, I make myself remember her hands, those passionate, greedy hands ripping at my shirt. She is like that—she was. I make myself remember, Fiona. And I hate her the more . . ."

"But you didn't marry her."

"I wasn't given the chance. Perhaps what happened that afternoon frightened her—when some sanity had returned to us both. Perhaps I was to blame. But whatever happened, I think I would have lost her, and it's just as well I did."

"*What* happened?"

"To this day I don't know exactly—I never stayed to hear the details. I left Landfall the morning I found out, and I spent a month between the taverns and brothels of Santa Marta. Finally my father came and pulled me back to Landfall. I should never have gone back—but I was a lot younger then, and my father had always told me what to do."

"Fergus—*what* happened?"

"Slut!—she came to Landfall alone one night and went up to his room. Don't ask me how—I never wanted to know. I was too sickened by it. Perhaps she made her own way up while we were at dinner. You know how easy it would be to come in by the back stairs. Perhaps it was all arranged between them. Whether she came by invitation to my father's bed, or just presented herself, in those days he wasn't a man to refuse. There she was, and the first inkling I had of it was her presence there in the house the next morning. The slaves were told that they had married—but I knew they went to Santa Marta to be married that very day. It is on some registry somewhere, but I have never wanted to find it."

I knew there was no lie here; I felt the cold horror of it; I knew she was capable of it. "But *why?*—you were young, her own age, already her lover, wanting to be her husband. A . . . a beautiful young man." I could not stop those words coming. "And he was already beginning to be old. You would have inherited Landfall . . ."

"That was it, I think. Perhaps I would not have inherited Landfall. I am called Maxwell, but my father has never attempted to legitimize my birth, to make me legally his son. I've always thought he blamed me for my mother's death, and sometimes he couldn't stand the sight of me. You heard him say it, Fiona . . . 'I got my son, but it was the mother I wanted.' Who knows what was in Maria's greedy mind. Perhaps she thought the claim could be disputed by other Maxwells. That was a risk she was willing to take—anything was better than San Francisco, and she had no dowry to attract other planters' sons. All she had was her beauty and her wits. But when she saw that my father was infatuated, she took the supreme risk. She must have known—how could she not—that no man would resist the sight of her naked in his bed. Perhaps she even made him believe she was still a virgin. In any case, she won. He was still infatuated with her when she bore her son, his first legitimate child. She knew she was secure then. Rights were established. She would be his widow, and her son would have Landfall."

The words were like a cold breath in the warm, tropic dampness of the forest. I listened to the birds, to the wind above us, to the gentle tearing sounds the horses made as they grazed. These were the beautiful things of the forest; there was also the scorpion, with the deadly lash of its tail. I was suddenly suffused with the wretched knowledge that under the beauty of the island was the evil that greed had cost. I was aware, in a way I had never been before, that each acre under cane was at the price of blood, and that when people were hardened to suffering, they did not notice how it was inflicted, nor count the cost. I was moved one stage forward in this story of Maria's greed, of Andrew's passion to pass on what he had acquired, of the whole tormented cycle of love and hate.

I had to ask the question; we had gone too far now to let me have peace until it was asked and answered. "Is it possible . . . ?" I turned and faced him fully. "Is it possible, then, that Duncan is your son?"

The question was answered in his face; the misery had been lived with for a long time. "No one can be sure—not even Maria—that Duncan is not my son. My father has never spoken of it—not to me. But he had to wonder, as I do. Once he learned what she was, he had to wonder." His hand gripped mine as if he sought strength. "That is what is at the heart of the rot at Landfall."

* * * * *

We remounted and rode back toward Landfall. I was surprised to find the sun only a little past its noon position. Too much had happened; a very long time must have passed. Only as we neared the stable yard did Fergus turn to me again.

"Fiona—believe in me a while. It's been a long, lonely passage, these years, and at times I haven't wanted to live through any more of them. But now I do—I want very much to live. Don't refuse to see me again. Don't leave Landfall."

I couldn't reply; there was a blur of tears before my eyes, making hazy the bright noonday. I half-nodded, and we moved on.

Maria waited in the center of the blazing square of the stable yard, erect, her face deeply shadowed by the Cordoban hat, the symmetry of her figure heightened by the way she held her crop with a hand at each end. Slightly behind her stood Samuel. They looked as if they had been standing there, still as statues, for a long time.

She waited until we were close, then her words, low, furious, were directed at me.

"*You*—who gave you permission to ride my horse? You are a servant in this house, not its mistress!"

I would not say I was sorry. "I didn't know Fidelito was your particular horse, Mrs. Maxwell."

"I arranged for Fiona to ride Fidelito, Maria," Fergus said. "I take the responsibility."

"You *have* no responsibility at Landfall! Nothing here belongs to you." Until now her wrath and her attention had been focused on me, but now she looked directly at Fergus, and saw the wound across his face. Suddenly a bitter, harsh laugh rang out, reminding me of the drunken old woman on the gallery at San Francisco shouting her obscenities.

"So you—you have had it! What did you try? Did you make an attempt on the virtue of the little Scottish governess? And did she give in, after an honorable struggle? You—you both are like rutting peasants!"

I could take no more of it; I tried, without assistance to dismount, and Maria, seeing that, was abruptly moved to action by her fury. I felt her clawing hands upon my legs, reaching for my arms to pull me down, as if she must actually see me in the dust at her feet before she would be satisfied.

Then an extraordinary thing happened. Suddenly, from behind, those raised arms were pinioned by Samuel's dark ones. Shock froze Maria; she did not struggle or attempt escape.

"Master Fergus help you dismount, mistress," he said.

I half fell into Fergus's arms. "Go!" he said. "Go inside, quickly!"

I knew better than to disobey. I ran. But I could not outrun Maria's scream of rage. The enormity of what had happened had finally broken on her.

"You have put your hands on a white woman!"

*   *   *   *   *

The slaves were called early from the fields that evening to witness Samuel's flogging. Alister and I had both gone to Andrew where he sat on the front gallery, and asked him to forbid it.

"It's my fault," I said. "I should not have ridden Fidelito without your wife's permission."

"Be quiet, girl," he grunted. "You don't know what you're getting mixed into. It is nothing to do with you. No slave may strike or interfere in any way with a white man. And should he dare to touch a woman . . ." He shrugged. "Samuel is lucky to have his life. Maria doesn't flog for no reason—good slaves are hard to come by, but our lives wouldn't be worth tuppence if we let anything like this go. So leave it be, and keep out of what's not your business."

I walked away; Alister stayed—perhaps to reason further. I was sickened and desolate, and thought of going to Winterslo to see if Fergus might not be able to stop it, and knew it was useless. He would have already tried to excuse Samuel, and it was already plain that Maria's fury was more against Fergus and myself than against the man who had tried to intervene. She was punishing us through him. When the bell tolled to call in the fieldhands I took Duncan and hustled him from the house lest Maria might send for him. We took the walk to the cove near the Serpents; I had a feeling that Samuel would bear what he had to without outcry, but I could not let Duncan hear the sounds of the whip. And then I told myself I was a fool; it was something to which Maria daily exposed him during the morning rides. But we sat on the rock above the cove, and I told him about the way the sea swept at the wall at Silkirk, and he told me about the great winds that flattened the crops, and shredded all but the best-built of the greathouses. He talked from hearsay; he had himself never known a hurricane.

"But we're safe now. It's too late in the year," and he repeated the jingle:

> "June too soon,
> July stand by,
> August you must
> Remember September,
> October all over."

I thought as he talked he forgot about Samuel, but he had not. As it grew dark, and I judged the terrible ritual would be over, we started back toward the house. It was saddening, then, the way he sought to comfort me. His hand went into mine.

"You know, slaves don't feel like you and I do, Miss Fiona. You have to be hard because they don't feel the pain so much."

I jerked him to a halt. "They are men and women, just like you and I. They feel the same way." Suddenly I reached and as hard as I could I pinched the tender skin of his arm.

"Ouch!" It was a howl of outrage.

"Did you feel that, Duncan?"

"Yes." He was stunned with shock.

"Then Samuel feels what the whip does to him. He *feels* it, Duncan."

He was silent all the way back to the house; not sulking, just quiet. As we parted, he to his supper, and I to prepare for dinner, he lifted a puzzled face to me. "You mean he really feels it the same way?"

"He feels it. I promise you that. When you say your prayers tonight, pray for him. And pray you never have to feel such pain."

* * * * *

I wished I could have avoided dinner downstairs that evening, but it had to be faced. So I dressed in the most flamboyant of the gowns

Andrew had provided, and even sent Charity for the camellia that I had not dared to wear before. There was open war now between Maria and myself, and if I had to be dismissed from Landfall, I would go leaving with them a remembrance of some spirit. For none of them would I ever again be "the little Scottish governess"—I who was not even small in build. I would not creep about any longer and pretend I was not there. Before I left Landfall Maria would have cause to remember that I had existed.

Charity was approving. "You look like great lady," she said. And then as she studied my shadowed face in the glass she bent forward and said softly, "Do not grieve, mistress. Samuel suffer for other things beside what he did today. He has shown pride to her before this, and he would not see you pulled to the ground at her feet. We are not fools— we know what is."

Then she straightened. "I have child by Samuel—a boy of ten years who will be as strong as his father, and bear pain as he does. So go down, now, mistress, and hold your head high. You have done no wrong at Landfall."

*   *   *   *   *

I deliberately delayed going downstairs until I thought they would all be assembled. Never again would I hurry to hide in the shadows of the farthest end of the salon. All three turned at my entrance. Alister was on his feet at once, pouring the wine even before Dougal had reached the decanter. He brought it to me.

"Will you sit here?"

"No," Maria said. "We will go into dinner."

"Dinner isn't ready," Andrew interrupted. "Let her sit."

I had taken only the first sip of the wine when Fergus appeared in the doorway. He was neatly dressed, brushed, combed; his face wore the wound of my despair as an ugly swelling all about the welt, which he made no attempt to conceal. His expression was sober, colder, more contained than I had ever seen it.

"Good evening," he said, and his bow was more toward me than Maria. "May I dine with you?"

Without hesitation Maria answered him. "Get out! Get out and stay away from Landfall!"

Andrew said nothing to his wife. He simply lifted his hand and signaled to Dougal. "Lay a place for my son."

And then in a few minutes, "Come, Miss Fiona. May I have your arm? I believe we are ready to dine now . . ." This time there was no lascivious squeeze at the waist as we went in, but a solemn, almost stately procession. It was all ruined by Fergus's harsh chuckle as he brought up the rear.

"You'd almost think we were society here at Landfall."

* * * * *

The meal went badly, as it was bound to. But the teaming-up was different this time. Alister and Fergus talked together, and somehow managed to exclude Maria; it was the first time I had seen them co-operate to the same end, whatever their feelings were about each other. And the snub to Maria was painfully evident. Andrew seemed to enjoy it.

As Maria rose, and I followed her example, the men drew together for port. It was then I asked my question, loudly, before Maria could leave the room.

"Fergus, you have been most recently through the slave quarters. How does it go with Samuel?"

"He's hurt—but he'll recover. Maria would never do away with a good slave."

A kind of hissing sound came from her; at times she seemed very much Donna Isabella's daughter. Fergus turned his head with slow insolence and looked at her. "But a very unfortunate accident has occurred. Fidelito is dead—poisoned, they are saying, by berries he must have eaten in the forest."

Maria's scream of rage echoed through the house. And for a moment, watching, I saw the faintest flicker of emotion, of satisfaction race across the faces of the slaves who stood about to attend us. They had their own weapons against the whip, it seemed.

Chapter 5.

All pretense of peace was gone from Landfall. It was not merely that the hostility between Maria and myself was now plain and open for everyone to see, but that all the tensions that had lain half-buried were stripped naked. Each time I looked at Duncan the question of which man had fathered him rose again, and was unanswered, and I thought of the nearly eight years that it had festered in the hearts of the three people who made this triangle of love and hate. Even with the memory of Fergus's kiss, his arms about me, his plea of his need for me to stay, I still could hear the obscene shouts of the old woman on the gallery at San Francisco. "He think to marry you to his son, Fergus, and get Fergus away from my daughter's skirts." I could still remember how Fergus's eyes had devoured Maria that first evening he had appeared at Landfall, the time when I had sat silent and unnoticed. The question I had not asked Fergus kept coming, and at last I asked Andrew if I might sometime ride Rosa, and he answered, "Ride any horse in the stable. They are all still mine—whatever she says."

So I asked Samuel, whose wounds were healing—though still breaking open if he strained too much, and the blood would ooze through his shirt—if he would have Rosa saddled; and I rode to Winterslo. Fergus was there. A slave must have seen me coming and had run to tell him, because he was waiting to help me dismount.

"Finally—you've come."

"I haven't come to stay. No, I won't get down. I just have one question to ask you. I want the answer—plain and honest. Don't lie to me, and don't talk around it."

"What is the question, Fiona?"

"Has your father offered you money to marry me?—money for Winterslo, as that old woman said? *Am* I to be your part of the bargain to keep away from Maria?"

His face was wracked with a kind of agony, but it was anger as well as shame. "How can you expect me to answer such a question in a situation like this? I have things to explain. You *must* come into the house."

From the advantage Rosa's height gave me I looked down at him coldly. "The truth will be no different out here or in there. Well, is it so?"

"Oh, God—you're so much the Scotswoman, Fiona. So blunt!"

"If you mean I'm not full of Spanish wiles, then *that's* the truth. I *am* plain and blunt. That's the way I was brought up to be. And the lack of truth is what is wrong with Landfall. If . . . *if* I should marry with you—if I should marry with you, Fergus Maxwell, I would want to know exactly what that marriage meant. I would want to know where love lay, and where truth lay. I would want to know where loyalty lay."

He stared up at me, his eyes squinting narrowly against the glare of the sky. "I have not asked you to marry me, Fiona."

"And well I'm aware of it," I said. "But that old woman shouted something, and my ears heard it. I want to know if there is truth in it."

It took a long time; I thought he might walk away. But finally he nodded. "You could say there is some truth in it."

"I don't want *some* truth. I want all of it!"

Now he himself was cool. "That, my dear Fiona, you will never have this side of paradise, if such a place exists. You must be content with what part of the truth I possess. We are all humans, Fiona. Why do you set yourself above sin, and greed, and loving in the wrong place?"

"Do I?" I was taken aback, as if one of my father's congregation had suddenly stood in the kirk and called into account my father's own life. More thoughtfully I answered him, "Perhaps I do. Then tell me—and let me think."

"Then think hard. You know my father—you know Maria. My father gave me Winterslo when I was barely twenty, and nothing to run it on. He told me to ask Maria for what slaves she could spare. She could spare only her sick and her old. So Winterslo stands today

almost as it did then. And then Andrew thought to have me married—
oh, yes, there was the thought to get me away from Maria. A man can
hate, and lust, after the same woman. Perhaps I should say that for
both of us. So, he thought to have me married, but there was no woman
on the island—no suitable woman—who would have me. After all—
what do I have to offer? A rundown plantation, and no claim on my
father's estate. After some years, and some highly colored tales of the
kind of women I was associating with, he began to think of a Maxwell
—a little miss, fresh from Scotland, too innocent to know what she
would be caught in. First a governess for Duncan, and then, if things
went well, a wife for Fergus. The problem solved. What to do with Fergus. Oh, yes, Fiona—there was money mentioned. But do you believe
for one moment that Maria would let slip any money from her hands—
to give to *me?* Even if there is money. I begin to doubt it. My father
talks money, but he hasn't opened a ledger there for years. Why do you
think Alister is staying on so long, if not to find out where the money
has gone? *I* don't know if there is money to spare from Landfall, all
I know is that I'll see none of it. And as for the other . . . What the
hell did I care for what they sent out from Scotland—Maxwell or not?
They could do what they liked. But I would make my choice. And all
there would be to offer would be Winterslo, nothing more."

"That is the truth."

"That is the truth, Fiona."

"Well enough, then," I answered.

We gazed at each other a long moment as if the will and the passion
and the desire must find its match. We were as near equal in those
seconds as man and woman would ever be, sizing up, weighing; it was
the final hesitation before every commodity—life, trust, hope, love—was
thrown into the scale. It was the moment before committal; we were
hard with each other, like two merchants across a counter. I might have
been saying to him, "For my love—what will you give me? For my
loyalty, my faith, my children, what will you offer?" Without a word, I
could almost believe he answered silently, "My love." But I wasn't sure.

"Well enough, then," I said, again.

And then I turned and rode away.

*   *   *   *   *

But it was not only within the household itself, but also beyond it
that the tension gathered. Maria's flogging of Samuel had seemed to

mark a point. The slaves on Landfall had been well-treated, they were not so ignorant as not to know that healthy slaves were more in the interest of the owner than those half-starved and worked to death. But Samuel had been Maria's special slave, said to be her guardian. And now the muttering was that he had only guarded her from herself, and the ignominy of his punishment was worse than the pain. So no smiles, even forced and feigned ones, greeted us in the house. The blank, impassive faces now took on the expression of real sullenness. Small difficulties arose. Meals were late, or overcooked. New sheets were torn in the wash, dishes were broken. Harnesses snapped, horseshoes were cast, the windmills were clogged with debris. A hundred small troubles plagued Landfall, but Maria could not order a hundred slaves flogged. The faults were never pinpointed; no one in particular would be blamed. The lash began to fall indiscriminately, but a flick on the shoulder was not a flogging at the post. Two expected babies were still-born. But when Maria went in the morning to see the tiny bodies, there were none.

"Buried, mistress, buried, where the spirits cannot find them." I did not believe it. But I felt that those proud mothers might have sent their children beyond even their own sight rather than deliver them to Maria's ownership. God only knew where they were, but they did not belong to Maria.

"Wilberforce is dead," Alister announced one morning. He had ridden early to Santa Marta on business, and back immediately to Landfall with the news.

"Good!—let's drink to it," Andrew shouted. "Now perhaps all this stupid agitation—this nonsense they talk of emancipation—will die with him."

"It will not die," Alister answered. "Prepare yourself for it." His face was terribly drawn, pale under the suntan he was beginning to acquire. I thought he trembled as he stood, and he had come back to Landfall, unwelcoming as it was, as his only place of privacy in which to bear a grief. Contrary to his rule of never taking spirits in the heat of the day, he went, uninvited, to Andrew's jug of rum and poured for himself.

"Alister?" I went to his side. "It grieves you—this news."

"I knew him," he said. "I met him several times. I could not call him my friend. He was too old, and too many people claimed friendship with him. But he was a voice of conscience. I admired him."

We sat together on the gallery, in silence, until Maria returned with

Duncan, and I went with him upstairs. It was the first time I had ever observed a period of mourning for someone I had never met.

*　*　*　*　*

But there was other news that disturbed the household, and every other household through the island. The news drifted in from Santa Marta; it was talked of in the clubs and shops, and no one could say if it was the truth. The tale grew. It was that a Negro—said to be a former slave in the Indies and taken to England and freed by his master—some even said bought by Wilberforce or Tom Clarkeson and trained just for this purpose—had come to San Cristóbal, and was making the rounds of the plantations in secret, coming to the slave huts at the dead hours of the night and telling them of what was going forward in the English Parliament, and that one day they would be set free by law, and must prepare. Such a man was never seen—no one ever claimed that; but the rumor spread. There was more than one man, some planters maintained. And the ships docking at Santa Marta carried tales of the same man being active on all the British islands. It became an apocryphal story—within the space of a few weeks a legend.

"But Wilberforce is dead," Andrew kept saying. "And all that nonsense goes with him."

But the tale of this nameless, formless man, secreted from slave hut to slave hut persisted, and loomed like a shadow.

*　*　*　*　*

Whatever ailed Andrew grew worse; a doctor now came regularly from Santa Marta; I noticed the pupils of his eyes were huge and dilated; the drugs prescribed must have been very strong. He did not sleep unless the strongest drug was administered, and that was not always. In my own periods of sleeplessness, I would hear him grunting and cursing—the sounds carried through the open louvers of the shutters. Then he would sit, bad-tempered all through the day on the gallery—not often now with the energy even to lift the spyglass on the ships that rounded the Serpent Rocks toward the harbor of Santa Marta. Often he would fall into a doze of exhaustion, and then awake, as if stabbed by pain, and reach irritably for his rum.

"Can nothing be done?" I asked Alister. "He's dying, isn't he?"

"Yes—by slow degrees. Maria always seems to prevent me from talking to the doctor. From the look of him I would say some disease of the liver—and the breathlessness. His heart is not strong. The doctor is a reputable man—I've made inquiries."

As if spurred by the thought of Andrew's death, Alister began to spend more and more time in the estate office. Sometimes his tone with Fellowes or Maria grew loud and impatient with frustration. Snatches of talk would reach me. "But *why* did it cost so much? I know the price at that time from our other plantations—why pay these prices?"

There would be some murmured explanation, but sometimes Maria's own voice rose in angry defense. "What did you expect? I was very young at the time—very inexperienced. My husband—well, you know how he drinks. He began to drink heavily about that time, and I had to take over. One does what one must, and I had no experience . . ."

"But you have gone on paying these prices."

"Prices rise. Haven't you noticed? And one gets less and less for sugar."

"Landfall is living beyond its purse according to these books. Our other plantations do better, even with the price of sugar as it is."

"Then they are fortunate in having a competent man to run them. What can one woman do . . . ?"

He would persist. "And here—this huge item for the replacement of the entire machinery of the factory—the crushers, new vats, all these things . . . I have looked at the machinery of the sugar mill myself, and none of it is new."

"That was very unfortunate. We built the new mill—for greater production, you know, and to be ready when the present machinery wore out. I bought more slaves to run it; we cleared more land for the extra harvest. The mill burned down. I didn't need the slaves, and couldn't afford to feed them, so I sold them. I had to let them go at a loss. There was a drought at the time, and an oversupply of slaves to be fed. No one wanted more slaves."

"The books show the purchase of slaves, but not their sale."

"Well"—the tone sulky—"I have never been trained as a bookkeeper. Our overseers come and go. Some of them stole from us. No one can keep overseers. *You* must know that. Ask!—on every plantation it is the same. 'Rich as a Creole' is an expression that has no meaning any more, Alister. The only ones who grow rich from the Indies are people like the London Maxwells—those with money to lend, and interest to collect."

The arguments between Alister and Maria were now becoming part of the general tension at Landfall; dinner in the evening becoming intolerable because there was no longer a pretense that had been maintained of cordial relations. I wondered how long it would be before Alister made stronger accusations than just those of bad management. How long could he himself stay at Landfall? He had said a month more, but that time was almost gone. And yet everything bore on the person of the dying old man; how much longer had he, and how much would he defend his wife? Any accusation in law had to be made against him, and I knew that Andrew would not live to be held to a final accounting.

Every day I expected my own dismissal from Landfall by Maria, but it did not come. Perhaps in that matter, also, Andrew was the key. But I knew I would be gone as soon as he ceased to live. My anxiety was for Duncan; one could not grieve for the old man, too far gone in indifferent cruelty to those about him, his whole nature warped by the death of a girl twenty-six years ago, and the birth of an unwanted son.

I did not go again to Winterslo, although my heart and soul yearned for it. It was a testing time; I waited, and three times Fergus presented himself for dinner at Landfall, and only made the tension more intolerable. We had no private conversation, and each time that Maria spoke and Fergus looked in her direction, I would think again of what had once been between them, and if a man ever recovered from such a love. I knew I could not share a particle of Fergus with another woman —not a thought, not a look. It was my first knowledge of jealousy. I often saw Alister's eyes upon me during these times, and I wondered how much he guessed of my feelings. Probably he had himself been part of the plan to bring out the "little Scottish governess," but that was to have been my stepsister, and a more biddable, perhaps a more easily won wife for Fergus. Of me, not even Alister, with his cool, knowing temperament, was sure. Least of all was I sure of myself.

Once, as I took my candle to go upstairs after dinner—I had never changed my habit of avoiding the salon once the meal was ended— Fergus actually left the dining table to come to the stairs as I started up.

"Fiona—won't you stay a while? It's cooler outside—won't you walk a little." And then, in a much lower tone, "I have waited at Winterslo for you. I've gone to the cove at Serpent Rocks. I've waited, Fiona—I've waited."

"Then wait longer, and learn, if you can, how a woman must be wooed. Pride is a foolish thing, Fergus, but I have it. Only when I am sure . . ."

"You fool," he hissed in anger. "As if there is any such thing as being sure. You either trust or you don't. Being sure is for those willing to take no risks. If you are that kind—I know you are *not* that kind—best forget me."

"Perhaps better to. Perhaps you misjudge me—it may be that risks aren't in my nature." I added, "Wait—wait a little longer. Something will happen soon at Landfall, and we will all know what we have to do."

He turned away, furious, humiliated, perhaps, because although our words had not been heard by the onlookers, the tones, my rebuff to Fergus, must have been plain. Instead of returning to the two men and the port, he simply stalked out of the hall. Even before he had passed the kitchen quarters, I heard him calling loudly for his horse.

It was one more night I sat for hours on the darkened upstairs gallery cursing myself for a fool that I was alone when I might have been with Fergus.

Andrew himself cornered me the next evening when I went to the salon before dinner. We were alone, and he beckoned me sharply.

"Come here, girl. Sit where I can see you." I did as I was told, and he leaned forward from the red sofa to peer closely at me.

"Well, are you going to marry my son?"

"That's a very odd question to ask, Mr. Maxwell—when he hasn't asked it himself."

"Then blast his God-rotting soul! What's he about? And what are you about? You think I'm so blind I can't see—couldn't see what happened last night. You sent him away."

"I didn't send him away. He went."

"You didn't encourage him to stay."

"Should I? Is that why I'm here? I thought it was to be governess to Duncan."

"You know damn well why you're here. So blast you too—but all women are cheats and teasers. Greedy, soulless teasers. Or are you looking somewhere else? Is it Alister you're after? Well, don't look there. Take my son. He may be the last one who offers."

"In that case, I may do without. And he hasn't offered."

"Well Goddammit, what do you want? A written declaration. My son isn't like that."

"And I, Mr. Maxwell, am not part of any bargain not of my own making. In time—*if* Fergus asks me—I will make up my own mind."

"Then be sure you don't run out of time!"

I got up and left him. The dinner hour seemed more unendurable than I had ever known it.

And so the leaden days of heat dragged on at Landfall; the trade winds some days were entirely stilled, and the heat sat on one like a tangible weight. Clothes were soaked with sweat; tempers were short.

"Hurricane weather," Andrew would mutter as he woke from one of his dozes on the gallery. "Too still. Hurricane weather."

II

The nights had never been easy at Landfall; with the trade winds still, the heat seemed trapped even in these lofty rooms, and I tossed and lay wakeful on a sweat-soaked pillow. I dreaded the night, and yet dreaded more the coming of the day which had to be met with the exhaustion of drooping eyelids. I went back to the practice of walking, barefooted for quiet, on the gallery, trying to tire myself to the point where sleep would defeat the heat. It seldom worked. I often considered going down into the garden to walk when sleep eluded me in this way, not with much hope that it would be cooler there, but I would have greater space to walk, and could do it with less care. Finally the night came when I did go down. Things had now reached the stage at Landfall where any further transgression of the normal rules—even if it should be known that I left the house at night—could make no difference. It lacked a few hours to dawn, the moon was still high, when I threw a cotton wrapper about my nightgown and went downstairs. I went by the front door, to avoid the back regions where Dougal and two other house slaves slept. Landfall was a well-maintained house—the catch slipped back silently; I propped a doorstop against it in the unlikely event that a breeze would spring up strong enough to slam it. In seconds I was down and among the sheltering darkness of the trees.

The sense of escape from the house was relief, even though here it was hardly cooler. In the time at Landfall the garden had become a friend, the garden and all the beauty beyond it, even the dusty, rolling cane fields. I trod the garden paths now with confidence, and even the wilder areas beyond it. The trees began to break, and I was on the edge of the rich Landfall cane fields. The moon made it hardly less bright than day, but there was the absence of the burning heat. It was so still not even the tall ripening cane stalks moved; they shone silver now, not green. It was a land transformed. It was strange how the fear of such things as spiders and scorpions did not disturb me as did the tension lying entrapped within the walls of Landfall. I walked on and on, those dusty cane breaks seeming now as familiar to me as the hills I had walked behind Silkirk. I walked on, like one spellbound, wondering how I could have gone all this time without daring to come at night beyond the region of the house. This was a different land I saw, moon-haunted, star-struck. There was only the brilliant sky, and the tall cane, and I walked like a sleeper in a dream, and there came to me catharsis, release, and the final, blessed soothing of the spirit.

I could not tell at what point I became aware of different sounds—not the sounds of the night, the cicadas, the rustle of the lizards disturbed by my passage, the occasional call of the night birds back in the forest. There were human sounds, indistinct, muffled, but definitely human. Without much thought I had headed for the first of the coves on the lee shore, already now glimpsing from the top of each rise, its silvered-mirror surface. But these sounds came from over on the right—several bays along from the first. Standing on the highest point of a cart track among the cane I took my bearings from the gaunt outline of the crumbled balustrade that surmounted the greathouse of San Francisco. Farther off I could see the dim speck that was Winterslo. I stood very still, and listened. The sounds were hardly there, but they were there. The ridges of these small valleys that led inevitably to each sandy cove had the effect of an amphitheatre; sounds were magnified beyond their normal strength. It is odd how memory flashes back irrelevantly but I remembered suddenly my stepmother once saying I had the ears of a fox. I knew now that something was taking place in the bay below San Francisco. I stood rooted, one fear only holding me—that I might inadvertently stumble on some ritual of the slaves, some place where they practised the ancient rites of Africa forbidden to them now. The old fortifications at San Francisco might be that place. And then another thought took me. Perhaps this was one of the meetings arranged for the black man of legend who traveled from plantation to plantation, giving the news of freedom to come. Did I dare to face that? Did I dare to try to know what the plans were when that time, dreaded by the whites, longed for by the blacks, arrived? But I had seen a vision of terror at Landfall; perhaps this night I had been sent to know its time and place.

I licked my suddenly dry lips, and thought of going back for Alister, but it was too far, and it would take too long. Long before dawn whoever moved in that cove down there would be gone.

So I went on, thankful that I had chosen a fairly dark-printed wrapper to throw over my nightgown, but the thin slippers which served well enough for the garden walks and the tracks, would be treacherous on the loose lava-rock of the fortifications. The night whose brilliance I had delighted in, was now, all at once, a menace and a curse.

I moved steadily toward the San Francisco bay, and the doubt was growing that this could be any planned meeting of slaves, or a landing place for the mysterious black leader. Even though it was sheltered from view of the sea by its jutting headland, from San Francisco itself, any vessel, however small, could be seen entering, and the noises would rise to the greathouse, just as they did to me.

I had reached the end of San Francisco's poor cane fields, and come into the stretch of territory too sandy for cultivation. Again I hesitated, knowing I could turn back at this point but perhaps not later. There was the dull sound of movement—human movement. Though I could hear them, the voices were hushed and low toned; but I heard a command, a smothered threat, and, just once, the unmistakable crack of a whip. Then I knew beyond doubt that this was no meeting organized to greet the nameless black man of legend. Wherever the whip cracked, there were white men, and I was going to see.

The path led directly to the cove and the beach, but I could not take that way. I lost track of time, almost lost direction as I pushed and squirmed through the underbrush toward the fortifications, cursing the slippers that kept falling off, and the long clinging wrapper that seemed to clasp each thorny bush. Once, in a hollow of darkness, I was stabbed in the arm by the point of some plant; I wondered if, ironically, I had fallen victim to the point of the formidable plant that could take out a man's eye, or worse—known locally as Spanish bayonet. But finally I was there, at the first outcrop of the crumbling walls, and now the light was welcome—I was remembering those roofless dungeons yawning ready for the plunging fall. I lay along the edge of one of these walls, and let the scrubby growth shelter me; then I watched and concentrated on what was happening in the bay.

It was bigger and deeper than I had supposed—with nothing to give it perspective before, I had thought it only a little larger than the others. But the vessel that rode out there, sheltered well within the hook of the headland, was no island schooner, but something as big, bigger perhaps, than the *Clyde Queen,* something that could ride the rough seas of the Atlantic. As I watched, a longboat moved from the shadow of its hull, coming to shore, catching the glint of moonlight on wet oars, giving out the dull sound of muffled rowlocks. Several figures—black or white I couldn't tell—stood waiting for its arrival at the water's edge. I watched it for a moment, and then another sound broke on me, a dreadful sound, a sort of keening, moaning cry that was an African's expression of despair and fear and pain. I remembered the room with the barred windows, and the lock on the stout new wooden door. I knew then what this whole business was about. Slaves were being brought ashore. The vessel out there, so beautiful in the calm brilliance of the bay, was an illegal slaver, probably at the end of its voyage from Africa. Illegal, I knew, because any normal transfer of slaves from island to island would dock and do its business openly in Santa Marta harbor. The closer human sounds I heard were most likely of those already brought ashore, and locked in the dungeon room.

I kept still, and waited. The longboat finally touched the beach, and all but one of the figures went to drag it ashore. And then I heard the sound that one need hear only once, and may never forget—the sound of chains being dragged by a human body. Sharp cries went up as men and woman were hauled bodily from the boat and set on their feet, lined up, and forced to begin the march up toward the fortifications. They were chained by the ankles, a long row of perhaps twenty. Once again came the crack of the whip as one of that dreadful line stumbled and fell, and was dragged by the weight of the others.

I began to put the pieces of the pattern together. Maria was using this bay, with the knowledge of Donna Isabella, if not of Andrew, as the off-loading point for the illicit ships that still plied the slave trade from Africa. I couldn't be sure where all of them went from here, but the *Savannah Trader* would have been carrying a cargo to no other place than the southern states of America. It was possible other, smaller, island vessels came here also, picking up their illegal cargo and slipping off down-island with it. Perhaps slaves from other islands were themselves brought here. For the American captains it would make good sense. They were spared the long voyage to Africa and back —the infamous Middle Passage—with the wait on the fever-ridden coast at the old slaving forts for enough bodies to fill their holds. They were spared the disease, death, the threat of insurrection of the voyage itself. Here they would have only those who landed alive, and if others were sent from different islands to this gathering point, they could be reasonably sure of fit, healthy slaves, used to plantation life, perhaps already bred for generations to the ways of the white man, inured to the life, and knowing what was expected of them.

With a kind of horror I saw that several of the females in the line carried babies, and other, older children, clung desperately to the rags of their mothers' skirts. I remembered then Maria's care for her pregnant slaves, the better feeding and rest given them to encourage them to bear more children. The result of this policy should have been that Landfall would teem and swarm with children—but it did not. There were a dozen or so about the slave huts and garden, too young yet for the fields; were the others gone, sold, like this lot here? Did Maria really sell small children away from their mothers? I suddenly remembered the two stillborn babies of these recent weeks, and the failure to produce their bodies for Maria's inspection. Had the certain knowledge that they, once they were old enough, would be sold away from Landfall caused the mothers to hide them, even risking death for it? They must believe that the day of freedom was very close at hand to have dared such a thing—to cling to their children, hidden, with the desperate hope that one day they would live to see freedom. All at once I, too, began to believe in the legend of the messianic Negro, traveling with his message of faith in freedom to come.

This seemed to have been the last shipment of slaves from the vessel. The longboat returned and was taken aboard; I heard the rattle of the anchor chain, and watched the raising of the sails, in readiness for the slightest breeze that would blow from the land. I heard more of the dreadful sound of the chains, the orders, the hiss and crack of the whip, but I could see nothing of what was taking place. All of this was on the beach below the line of the fortifications, and I would have had to go too near to see any of it. Instead I began to squirm and wriggle my way back toward the path they must take if they were bound for San Francisco; it didn't seem possible that the new line of slaves just landed could be packed into that barred room with those already there.

I stayed back from the path, in the underbrush, and I heard the chains long before the column drew level. I thought it was a white man who led them—I could see boots, highly polished, in the light of the lantern he carried. One or two more booted figures passed with the column, whips trailing; sometimes the moonlight reflected palely on a white face. I could also, from my low level, see the bare, sometimes bloodied feet with the manacles about the ankles. I did not dare risk raising my head more than a few times, knowing that my own face would show as theirs did, that my hair in the moonlight could look nearly blond. I stayed crouched and still until the procession was well past me. I did not hear the whip again; the slaves were now accustomed to the rhythm of the march and were moving with the terrible resignation of their kind.

I began to ease myself to a nearly upright position, my cramped limbs trembling after the effort of staying so still. But I had misjudged the end of the procession; I had not heard the footfalls on the sandy trail. What reached me first was the whisper—low but sharp. Maria's voice.

"Wait!—did something move there? Did you see?"

There came the murmured answer saying something I couldn't understand.

"Go and look—here, fool, take the lantern."

I had not seen the light because the door that masked its side had been closed down to a slit. Now it was opened back and the tall figure of a man began to thrust his way through the undergrowth. I flung myself face downward, but he must have heard the movement, for he came steadily in my direction; I could see the light of the lamp swinging on the ground as he came close. Very close to me he stood, and I could see his broad black feet. I knew the scrubby brush could never give me enough concealment, that the lamp shone directly on me. I turned my head sideways and looked up.

The light did not reach his own face; all I knew was that he was black—no features showed themselves in the moonlight. I moved to a squatting position, unwilling, until it was absolutely inevitable, to give my identity to Maria. The man must have realized that I did not recognize him, but he could see the fear and apprehension in my face. So with a single quick swinging movement he raised the lantern high, and I saw that it was Samuel. He gave the faintest shake of his head, and one of his hands made the gesture for me to keep down. At once he turned and plunged on through the brush, as if following some further sound he heard. He went on and on, and finally Maria's voice called urgently to him.

"Stop wasting time. If there is nothing, come."

Obediently he returned to her, passing the place where I crouched with the lantern well-shielded on my side.

"Nothing, mistress. Maybe some cat—many cats from the stables go wild over here. They go quick—you never catch them."

"Well, then, come on . . ."

I risked raising myself up to watch them go, and wondered how I had failed to recognize that slender figure, in the tight Spanish trousers and jacket, with the Cordoban hat, among the group on the beach. But she would be there, of course; nothing with which Maria concerned herself would be left to the direction of others. I thought of the white men who had accompanied the column; one of them, or the man who paid him, had scribbled that note that had come mistakenly into my hands that day at Rodriguiz's. And Rodriguiz himself would be part of it, because he had known what that note contained. But only his money or his organization would have aided tonight's operation; not for him the long ride to Landfall, the wait for the vessel, the chivying of the captives to wherever they were put to wait the next ship. He would do none of these things while someone as competent and ruthless as Maria was here to command. And I had no doubt that she did command, and I knew also, where the money from Landfall filtered, the reason for the deliberate chaos of the books that Alister argued over. Maria had made an investment that she dared not show on paper; where the profits lay probably only she knew.

And with this knowledge a shiver of fear possessed my body like a fever. If Maria knew I had witnessed her in this criminal act I was in much greater danger than merely being dismissed from Landfall. It was too easy to imagine the ways she could find to make sure I would be silent forever. What did I do now?—how did I go. Did Andrew know?—if he did, then I had no protection. I had no place to turn, no one but Alister—or Fergus. Or should I just pack my trunk tomorrow and go? Should I take the life-saving chance that Samuel's silence had offered me. But I had come, I thought, because of the vision of Duncan running toward me, needing my help. If the vision had been a true one, then I still had a role to play at Landfall. And by going, I must also leave Fergus. Would I take the swift, easy path away from danger and trouble, and spend the rest of my life, a Scottish spinster growing old teaching children that were not my own?—or did I live for my own supreme moment, and take the chances that must accompany it?

Chances?—I never seemed to make a choice. Somehow the safe and sensible way never opened itself before me; I seemed to have been born to live in turmoil. As much as I didn't want it, it was my natural place. Unless Maria forced me to, I knew I would not pack my trunk that day and leave Landfall.

It was at that moment that I remembered that I had left the door propped open. Maria would find it so on her return, and the hunt would be on. She would know at once that only Alister or myself would be gone, and it would be a simple matter to find out which. I forgot what might be coming on that day, and the next day. The thing now was somehow to get as far away from this cove as I could, and to invent some excuse for being away from the house.

The dawn was almost upon the land, and it comes as swiftly as the night in the tropics. Already, over toward Winterslo, I heard the first cock crow; I wanted desperately to go toward the house, and to Fergus, but it was too far away, and San Francisco lay between us. It would be nonsense to try to say to Maria that I had walked as far as Winterslo alone at night. So I turned my back on it, and the trail that led to San Francisco. What I must do was push my way through the scrub and over the little headlands to the first cove past the Serpents, the one they knew I had visited before. I ran, as much as that rough terrain would let me, and I blessed the lifelong habit of tramping the Scottish hills, the good strong legs that now had to carry me past the point where I thought I could go no farther. I had to be in that cove before sunrise, and I was, the breath tearing in my chest like a knife, my knees trembling under me. I was there—this, the most beautiful, the calmest cove, where the shallows were most lucid, the sand whitest. I raced down to the water's edge, shed my ruined slippers, my wrapper and nightgown, and ran on straight into the water.

Oh, God, what heaven it was; its warm soothing balm, its salty buoyance which bore my tired body like gentle, uplifting hands. For long minutes I forgot the danger, the fear, the horror of the night. I could not swim, but the calm shallows let me lie, and turn and twist in a kind of ecstasy of sensual delight; the sand was fine powder beneath me when I touched it, like a great easing down bed beneath my whole body when I came and lay at the edge, where the tiny wavelets lapped against me. My hair streamed all about me, gritty with sand, my face and limbs that were above the lap of the water already beginning to dry with a film of salt upon them. I lay there, my face on my folded arms, feeling the sun gently warm on my skin, letting the fear and fatigue slip away from me. My dawn swim would explain my absence, my excuse would be the heat and my inability to sleep; it would explain the open door. Let Maria, if she could, prove that I had been anywhere else. For the moment I was safe here, and reluctant to go, my strength and courage restored by the blissful ease of the water and sun. Perhaps for a few moments I even slept as I lay there, my senses unconsciously girding me for what I knew must greet me back at Landfall.

I shook myself awake, and the sun seemed hotter, and there was a sound in the cove. Not the sound of someone coming along the path, the crashing sound of the undergrowth, but the sound of water—the thrashing of the water that a swimmer makes.

I turned on my side and half-sat up. The swimmer came toward me, long powerful arms beating through the water, cutting diagonally across the bay, as if he had dived from the rocks at the point. I remained quite still, making no foolish, coy movement toward my wrapper. He reached the shallows, and stood up, as naked as I, and I saw the splendor of him, with the morning sun shining on his body and the wet blond-red hair. There are moments in life that make the pain of the rest of it worth the living; this one I was to hold forever. Some things are as natural in their time and place as breathing is to our every second; our coupling now was as if it had been intended from all time. There was no fumbling, no undue haste. We loved each other. There was to be no stain of virginal blood on a bedsheet to remind me of the exquisite pain of his entry; the gentle wavelets washed it away, and the sand was clean and white.

* * * * *

Fergus had his horse tethered on the other side of the cove, and I rode before him on the saddle, his arm circling my waist to hold me. My wet hair streamed about me; from time to time he would nuzzle it back across my shoulder and lean and kiss my cheek. "You are a disgrace!" he laughed. "You are wonderful! You never have been so beautiful!" And I laughed too, because it was suddenly funny and joyous that I looked so terrible. He had finally noticed my torn wrapper, and the ruined slippers, and once, as I raised my arm, and the sleeve feel back, he saw the cut from the cactus.

"What happened?"

I shrugged. "I ran into something in the dark. It doesn't hurt. The salt water washed it clean—see, it doesn't even bleed."

"Have Charity put something on it. Some of the slave remedies are better than anything our doctors have thought up." Then his arm tightened about me. "I have to keep you safe, don't I? I think you must be a little bit mad, Fiona—the way you ride horses and go walking about the island at night dressed like that. Weren't you afraid? Do you never think about things like snakes and spiders?"

"Your father told me all the snakes were gone—they imported the mongoose to get rid of the eggs."

"*Most* of them are gone, but you can get an unpleasant surprise once in a while. Oh, my mad, wild girl—if only I'd known you went to that cove to swim early in the mornings . . ."

"I never have before. But last night the heat—well, I don't think I had any sleep at all. I just meant to walk a little in the garden, but I kept on going. I know the way there—but I don't swim. Can't! The most daring thing I've done so far is to take off my boots and stockings and wade."

"Well, it's the best cove," he conceded. "I don't often get so far myself, but last night, as you say, the heat was fierce. Winterslo's too close in under Kronberg for comfort. Most mornings I swim in the bay closest to the house. But I was awake half the night, too, and with the moon so bright I just saddled up and timed it to be at that cove just at sunrise. It's one of the places I like best—I used to go over there when I lived at Landfall . . ."

He had ridden, and yet not crossed the path of the chained column of slaves heading away from the San Francisco cove? He had heard nothing? Had not seen the vessel stand out to sea from the San Francisco bay? All of it was possible—there were a dozen different ways he could have come to the cove, and the time that had lapsed between my encounter with Samuel and that final waking on the edge of the water with the sun already warm on my body had been considerable. I remembered the booted white men who had moved with the procession, but it had never occurred to me until this moment that Fergus might have been among them. Would he do such a thing? Would he join forces with Maria if money was involved? I did not believe it. I believed all the other stories of him—gambling, drinking, the women he had had, but I did not think him capable of the kind of deviousness that this morning's action would need. Fergus couldn't lie that well. I didn't think he could lie with his body; could I, myself, be so gullible and so savagely deceived? Had Maria sent him to find me when she found the open door?—had he been ordered to find out if indeed I had seen any of the happenings at San Francisco cove? Would I not have poured out the tale to the man who had just made love to me? Every woman would, so reasoning said; and was that why I had said nothing? Because the doubt was there—had always been there about Fergus. He had demanded answers of me, and I had given him none. But this morning I had made an answer with my own body. Once again I was aware of the cruel capriciousness of the gift that would let me see certain things that were to come, to sense some things that were buried in the past, but could not be summoned at will to tell me what I needed most in my life to know with certainty.

So I leaned back against Fergus, and closed my eyes and willed with all my strength to believe in him, to banish the doubts. Because now I was committed to him. For good or ill. I had loved with instinct, not reason. We came close to the house, and as if he sensed my thoughts, he checked his horse and leaned and kissed me on the mouth, a very gentle kiss, without passion, as if he sought to soothe and reassure.

"Leave everything to me," he said.

Why did I doubt? These were the words of a man assuming a responsibility, beginning to pay in love and support for what he had taken. I slid down off the horse, and he dismounted at the entrance to the stable yard. Although the path led to the kitchen entry, he led me round the building so that we might enter in the sight of everyone by the front steps. How could I doubt?—this was the action of a man proud of what was his.

They were all three in the hall—Maria dressed in a long wrapper, looking as fresh as if she had slept the night through. Andrew must have been told I was missing from the house, because he had dragged himself downstairs in his robe, and sat with his jug beside him, barefooted. Alister was dressed, impeccable and correct as always; he made it a habit to breakfast downstairs.

The doubt faded as I watched Maria's face. She had not expected this. The faces of all three registered, for brief seconds, their private emotions. The faint look of shock that Alister permitted himself was immediately tightened out of existence. As Andrew took in my appearance, a sly, knowing smile appeared; he almost chuckled in triumph.

"We were getting a little anxious," Alister said. Maria said nothing, but that fact spoke most. Her features twisted as she looked from me to Fergus, and I saw a kind of fear come into her eyes that already held hatred. But I thought the fear had nothing to do with the thought that I might have witnessed the events in San Francisco cove. She stood rock-still, gripping the edge of the long hall table. Then I saw that her eyes left me, and seemed to devour Fergus.

Fergus led me to his father.

"I want you to know that Fiona and I will be married—quite soon."

It was done. He never had asked me. I had told him to wait, and still he had not asked me. But no asking had been done this morning, either. And I had made no condition of acceptance, either. We had not discussed, nor bargained nor planned. In those few words, spoken now before them all, the questioning in my mind was stilled.

It was as if in assuming responsibility for me, Fergus had also gained authority in his father's house. He did not even glance toward Maria. "Go upstairs now, Fiona, and rest. You've had no sleep. Duncan can do without you this morning. I will come back. There will be things to discuss."

III

I bathed, and Charity's hands had never seemed so gentle. She seemed to chuckle several times while she tended me, a kind of half-suggestive laugh. "You and Master Fergus—you all fixed now." How quickly the news went among them. "And that other one—the mistress —she want to kill you for jealousy."

I roused myself from the kind of half-daze I was in. "Mistress Maxwell has nothing to be jealous of. She has her husband and her plantation."

"Those things not enough for a woman like her, mistress. You watch and take care. She not give up Master Fergus so easy—"

"Give up?" I grabbed at her arm and jerked her about to face me. "*Give up!* What is there to give up?"

"She never let go, that one. Not all these years. Why you think he never marry until now? She hold him, and make him wait. And her old husband, he drinks, and she help him to drink, and soon he be alive no longer, and then she have Master Fergus."

"That isn't true, Charity! Why would Master Fergus wait so long. He's free . . ." My voice trailed off.

"That one use Obeah woman. Her woman, Juanita, what she bring from San Francisco with her, she very skilled with magic. Mistress make her use spells to keep Master Fergus alone there, waiting, at Winterslo."

"But she didn't keep him." I was triumphant, sure. "That's wrong. Now he's mine!"

Charity shrugged. "But Mistress Fiona has magic of her own. Obeah woman see it and know it. A different kind. She tell Mistress Maria about you. So you take Master Fergus quickly, and you marry. And then it too late for the mistress."

I sank back on the pillows. "You're wrong, Charity—very wrong. There's no such thing as magic. White people don't have magic."

There was a kind of contemptuous rumble in her throat. "That what white people always say, but if they find Obeah, they punish those who make talk with the gods. So if there is no magic, why they afraid of it? I see white people die of black man's magic. I see their hearts dry up, and no white doctor able to save them. Maybe Mistress Maria already use it against her old husband since you come. She afraid now, because of you. But I think maybe your magic very strong too. You have not sickened. I watch. I see no signs."

"I have no magic, Charity."

"You *see* things, mistress. And because you see things you are strong against them. Now sleep and be rested, because there will be much trouble with the mistress."

I closed my eyes, not able to argue, and she turned the louvers against the light, leaving the room on tiptoe. But she left no peace behind. It was nonsense—everything was nonsense that she spoke. One heard, of course, the tales of the dark powers that had come from Africa with the slaves, the secret knowledge passed on to the gifted. But one never believed them. And yet—and yet somehow they had known of my own wretched glimpses of the future. How had they known that? The happiness of the morning was destroyed. Not just this warning troubled me, but the terrible, knowing words, "She not give up Master Fergus so easy . . ." But it had all happened so long ago, and he was past the fever of his young, first love. He had said he hated Maria. But did he still belong to her? I turned my face on the pillow, and tried to shut out the thought. But a thousand doubts now repossessed me, and I was reminded, horribly, of the first time I had seen Fergus, of that strong young shining beauty, laughing up at me, and the nameless, formless shadow I had seemed to glimpse in the deep shade of the tree behind him, the black rider of violence. There was no peace or rest.

* * * * *

I dozed fitfully, and when I rose again in time to meet Duncan when he returned from his morning ride, it was not Charity who came to the room to attend me, but instead a young woman, Flora, Juanita's daughter. She had always been Maria's second attendant, a faithful obeyer of her mother's instructions. I had never had any conversation with her. She was the kind who hung her head and pressed against the wall whenever a white person passed her. I had never cared much for the look of her, either—very thin, with a sharp face, and claw-like hands.

"Where is Charity?"

She shook her head. "Charity sick. Mistress say I look after you."

"Nonsense!—Charity can't be sick! She was perfectly well a few hours ago."

The girl hung her head and would not meet my gaze; I saw the faint shrug which suggested it wasn't her business to question orders. "Mistress say Charity sick, and I to look after you," she insisted.

I submitted. There was nothing I could do about it at this moment, but I hated the touch of those thin hands; even in the heat they seemed cold. I dismissed her as soon as possible, but she hung about stubbornly, folding clothes, tidying drawers, making clucking sounds of contemptuous disapproval that made her opinion of Charity's work clear. At last I had to go to Duncan, and leave her alone in the room. I hated leaving her there to poke and pry among the few very personal things I had brought from Scotland, the cherished mementoes, those last presents pressed into my hand—the little book of my half-brother's drawings of the world of Silkirk as he saw it, the worn Bible from my father, a locket of my mother which I had never worn because the gold chain seemed too thin for safety—I think it must have been hard for my father to part with this. And there was the little velvet pincushion embroidered with my name that had been Mary's gift, a sort of thank-offering for my departure from Silkirk and leaving James Killian to her. I hated the cold, claw hands touching these things, the dark eyes studying them. I began to understand better why whites kept saying that the slaves knew everything, and in time they told everything.

*　*　*　*　*

When Duncan went to his siesta I went in search of Alister; he was not in the office, nor on any of the galleries. Andrew dozed with bent head on the red sofa. I beckoned Dougal to the hall.

"Master Alister—have you seen him? Is he riding?"

The man shook his head. "Master Alister gone."

"Gone?—gone where? To Santa Marta?" I was dismayed; it was to Alister I meant to tell my story of last night's happenings. He would know what to do, how to advise me. He would take it all out of my hands, and I would not have to face the problem of telling Fergus, and wondering how he would act against his own father and Maria. I would not have to place the burden on him, because Alister would shoulder it; I didn't doubt that Fergus would be angry that I had first confided in Alister but I couldn't help that. I was shielding him; it was what one did for the man one loved.

"Yes, to Santa Marta. In big hurry. But for good."

"For good! You mean he's *left* Landfall!"

Dougal nodded. "Left. Letter come this morning, and he say he must go back to England. He say ship leaving Santa Marta on morning tide, and he still have business to finish there. So he pack and go while Mistress Fiona sleep. But he leave letter—here." He moved to the drawer of the long hall table, and took out an envelope. "He give it to me for you."

I wondered if Maria had had it first—these were the kind of thoughts that came to me at Landfall. But when I turned it over I saw that Alister had also known the same thought, and it was heavily sealed and stamped with his own personal seal. I went to the bench out under the cottonwood where we had often sat and talked, and my hand trembled a little as I broke the seal.

My dear Fiona. News has come this morning from London that I am needed as soon as I can be there. There was not opportunity for a farewell; you were sleeping, and, in any case, in this house, only the most formal words can be said without rousing the passions of those who hear them. I am sorry to leave at this stage, when perhaps my presence might make things easier for you. But my time here is up, and I have been able to accomplish little. You know I wish you happiness, always. Take your Fergus, and love and cherish him, as you know well how to. Do what you can for Duncan. There may not be much time. I have a feeling there is very little time."

And so Alister went from me. I thought of how often I had watched that elegantly clad figure limp away from me down one of the garden walks, the head slightly bent, the hands clasped behind him, and the face, when one saw it, with its thoughtful, almost melancholy cast.

He was gone; I could barely realize the fact. He had been part of Landfall since I had come, and unconsciously I had thought of him as being always here. A prop was gone from my existence. I looked back at that gleaming white house, and I knew it held no friend. For the first time I was truly frightened.

IV

After the siesta hours, all of which I had spent on the bench under the cottonwood as if the house were too hostile to enter, I went to the schoolroom to find Duncan in a perky, cheeky mood, and grinning with delight over the news that Fergus and I were to marry. He did not mention Alister, and I thought it probable that no one had bothered to tell him that Alister had gone. It would have happened during the morning ride, and perhaps Alister had never been more than a rather vague figure to Duncan, someone who had come to sit long hours in the office, and who took solitary rides and walks. He could not have known of the concern Alister felt for him, and the helplessness in the face of it. I did not speak of his going now; I had not the courage for it. For me it was supposed to be a happy day.

"Now you'll always stay?" Duncan demanded of me. "I'll always have you."

"I'll be living at Winterslo," I said quietly. "I can't be with you all the time. And then"—why be coy with him?—"Fergus and I will probably have little boys of our own—girls too."

"But I'll be *first*," he said. "I'll still be the first."

I nodded. "Yes, I suppose you always will be the first." And I conceded that indeed he might stay first in my heart, even with the always intrusive knowledge that he could be Fergus's son. "Perhaps," I said, to give him hope, "your mama will let you come to Winterslo for lessons."

He scowled, looking terribly like Fergus as he did it. "My mama says that someday I must go to Spain to be educated. That's why she always speaks Spanish to me when we ride each morning. I pretend not to understand, and that makes her angry, but it pleases my father. I know *he* won't let me go to Spain. But when he's dead mama will be able to do as she likes." The childish voice trembled; he had accepted already the thought of his father's death, but the changes it would bring were harder to imagine. "But if she tries to send me, I'll run away to Winterslo."

"I don't think we would be allowed to keep you, Duncan." Why build false hopes in him? "Try not to worry about it. You are too young to send anywhere yet, and by the time you are grown, perhaps your mama will have changed her mind. Perhaps you may even want to go—to travel off the island."

"I will *never* want to go to Spain," he answered firmly. "I think Spain is filled with ugly, dirty old women like my grandmother, Donna Isabella. My aunts aren't so bad—but they don't count at San Francisco. They do everything Donna Isabella says."

"She is an old lady, Duncan. Often old people don't understand young boys—they've forgotten what it was like when they were young."

"She was cruel to me," he said bitterly. "One time my mother took me over to San Francisco, and they talked, and told me to go to play. There was nothing to do—no one to play with. I went over to the stables, but there was no one there, either. So I started exploring those ruins at the back—San Francisco is the oldest greathouse on the island, and had the most land. They had big storerooms, and slave quarters—and places like that. They've all fallen down now, but I had a good time exploring them. Then my mother and Donna Isabella came looking for me, and when they discovered where I was, Donna Isabella whipped me. Across the breeches, and on my shoulders—not the bare skin, like the slaves. But she *did* whip me, and I hadn't done anything wrong. So now when my mother takes me to San Francisco on the morning ride, I just sit out there under the big tree, and hold my pony, and I don't even take a drink when one of my aunts brings it to me. Donna Isabella would like to whip me for *that,* too, but my mother won't let her."

I felt his fear and bitterness; I also had known the whip of Donna Isabella's tongue. I did not dare say openly that his sense of grievance was justified—that would have stiffened it, and led to more trouble."

"You will soon be grown up, Duncan, and no one will whip you, ever. That is why you must never whip a slave—they feel it just as you did then. And they hate you for it. And one day the whip may turn around, and be in *their* hands."

"It couldn't be," he said, incredulous. "The law won't let them have things like that. We are their masters. We own them!"

"Oh, Duncan—Duncan, it can't always stay this way! One day it will change. You have to be ready for the day the law says you must drop the whip, and the black man will be free."

"If that ever happens I will come running to Winterslo. Winterslo will be safer. Fergus never beats his slaves, so you see, they will go on letting Fergus be their master."

It was a childish, simplistic solution to the woes that might be to come; and yet it seemed to represent about the only answer the white man in the Indies had so far prepared for himself against the day when the whole structure for his world would tumble about him.

* * * * *

The shock of Alister's going had driven the thought of Charity from my mind; I was struck then with a strong sense of guilt and annoyance to find that Flora was once again waiting to help me dress for dinner. She stood there, sullen, with her eyes on the ground, waiting with the towels and the scented water.

"Charity is still ill?" I asked her. "What is it—a fever?"

She shook her white-turbaned head. "Don' know, mistress. I not ask about Charity. Mistress Maria jus' say look after you, and I do it until she tell me stop."

There was nothing to be got from her; the whole washing and dressing ritual was an aggravation at her hands. I submitted with as good grace as I could, but I shrunk from her touch. The final assault on my nerves came when she was brushing my hair, before tying it into its knot. It was something I disliked even Charity doing, but with this woman it became intolerable. I closed my eyes for a time, trying to calm myself, knowing it would soon be over; but the cessation of her movement, and the sudden reaching past me to the dressing table roused me. I started as I saw the pair of scissors in her hand.

With a movement as sharp as Maria might have made, I struck her arm, and the fingers, nerveless with fright, released the scissors, and they went flying across the polished floor.

"What are you up to?" I turned away from the mirror to face her directly. "What are you trying to do?"

In answer, rolling frightened eyes, she held up a handful of hair from the back of my head. "It longer than the other parts, mistress. Jus' tryin' to fix it. It not go in properly with other parts."

I stood up. "I will tell you when to cut my hair. Never dare to do such a thing. Now go—go. I will manage very well by myself."

She cringed. "But mistress say I look after you. She beat me if she know I don't do it."

"Out!" I said. "I will tell the mistress I won't want any help. I will tell her I told you to go."

"Please, mistress . . . please. Mistress Maria beat me."

"The mistress will not beat you when I tell her I sent you away."

She submitted, and the smooth glide of her bare feet announced her going. She was frightened because she was stupid, I told myself; no one would beat her if I said I preferred to wait until Charity could attend me herself—as if I needed attending! With hands that trembled with rage, I bundled my hair into a clumsy knot, buttoned my own buttons as I had done all my life, and then ran, in the gathering darkness, down through the house and out by the back way toward the stables and the slave quarters.

I wasn't welcome there, as I had known. The slaves were gathered about their fires and their cooking pots, the only time of day they were free of their master, the only time to gossip and sing the songs that had not the melancholy rhythm of the cane fields, the only time to revert to the African life that was for most of them, not even a vague memory, but only a tradition.

"Charity?" I demanded of the first group. "Where is Charity?"

They shook their heads dumbly.

"Is she sick? Does she have a fever?"

Again no reply. "Which is her hut?" They pointed, several pointed, but no one would speak a word. I went to it and looked inside. It was dark; there was no fire before its door. Even in the darkness I knew its emptiness; there was the sound of emptiness about it. I knew that not a thing remained there.

"Where's Samuel?"

Someone pointed toward the stables; I raced back there, leaving behind me a deathly silence at each of the cooking fires. They would not be at ease again, they would not sing again, tonight, I thought.

Samuel was at his last task of rubbing down a horse. He halted as I came to him.

"Samuel—where's Charity?"

He didn't attempt the policy of silence the others had given me. He had saved me the night before; a bond existed and we both recognized it. Mutual trust existed; it had been forged by this black man; it was no gift of mine, from whom it should first have come.

"Charity is gone," he said.

"Gone! What do you mean? Run away?"

"Not run away. Nowhere to run away to all alone. No—Charity sold. Sold to a man on the other side of the island. Very sudden. Mistress say she to be house slave to a man who is getting married, and have no other house slave yet." His voice jerked, but his clever, gentle, strong hands on the animal were still.

"Sold!" I couldn't believe it. "Sold!—but she belongs at Landfall."

"Charity was born at Landfall—same as I was. But she sold away from it. Her son—he go with her. But he *my* son, Mistress Fiona. Charity have two other children—but they sold away long ago. But this one *my* son. I have to find out where he gone. I have to get him back. I think I know, and if I know, I get them both back."

"But if they are just the other side of the island . . . ?"

He shook his head, and the dark face was suddenly twisted with rage. "Mistress Fiona saw las' night. She know what happen. Slaves come—slaves go. I think Charity and my son be sold off the island. I have to stop it, mistress—I don' know how I do it, but somehow I do it."

"Why should she be sold now?—*now?*"

He shook his head. "How I know what goes on in Mistress Maria's mind?" For a moment he went back to brushing the horse, as if to calm himself, to gain control. At last he spoke, hesitantly. A slave was not used to offering opinions to his masters, or to being asked for them. "I think . . ."

"Yes?"

"I think maybe Charity become too close to Mistress Fiona—she grow fond of her like she belong with her. She say these things to me. And Mistress Maria don' like that. Charity not tell her things she want to know. Maybe she not do things Mistress Maria bid her about Mistress Fiona. Mistress Maria will not stand for anyone to oppose her."

I was stunned. "Because of *me!* And you think she's being sold off the island? Where to—America? How can we stop it, Samuel? What can we do?"

His despair was in his action as he leaned his dark head against the horse's neck. The deep voice was muffled; he had begun with confidence, but the confidence was false. "What is there to do? It is death to run away. But even death be sometimes better—but Charity and my son would suffer too. Maybe they can't stand the pain so well. And if we try, where to go? No boat, no money, no place for the black man to go. No place but back to Africa, and we never get back there.

No way to get back there. Even the wind blow the wrong way for any black man to get back to Africa. Only the soul of the black man get back there after the white man has squeezed all the work from his body. Only the soul can go against the wind, mistress."

I turned and ran back to the house, and I felt the tears that Samuel would not shed running down my face. What had we done?—what had we wrought on this earth, all of us?—those who knew what they did, and those, like myself, who had been guilty of never caring until it struck at our own person, our own hearts. I had spoken more truly then I knew to Duncan that afternoon—someday the whip would turn around, and be in their hands. And our own souls would know the wind that blew the wrong way.

*　*　*　*　*

I was late to dinner; they were already seated, and Fergus was there. Somehow I had not expected him to come for the meal, but he was there, and his presence comforted me. It was strange to look across at where Alister had always sat, and to miss him. I did not offer any apology or explanation to Maria; things had moved past that.

"So Alister is gone," I said.

"Yes, and good riddance! Damned nuisance," Andrew responded. "Perhaps now we'll have some peace from reforming this and changing that."

"It is a time of change," I said. "Everywhere. Alister means to be part of it. Alister is simply a man of his age."

"Oh," Fergus said, a little ruffled, "you're becoming a politician now, are you?"

I smiled at him. "Rest easy. It will be a long time before women are politicians. I have no ambitions to change things in too much of a hurry. But I just hope I recognize change when it comes. I am sorry though, I did not see Alister before he left. I might have hoped that next time he was in Scotland he would call on my father and tell him—"

Maria cut me off. "I would not let him disturb you. I assumed you needed your rest—after your morning's exertions."

I managed to smile at the barb, both the inference of what had happened between Fergus and myself, and the suspicion that I had in fact seen something of what had taken place in San Francisco cove.

"I was quite rested, thank you—but I sorely missed Charity's help. Is it true she has been sold?"

"And what if it is?" Maria challenged directly my right to question any arrangement made by the mistress of the house.

"It was sudden."

"Sudden?—no I don't think so. Charity has not given satisfaction for some time. She has grown careless. The other day she broke several crystal glasses. She was fortunate she received no more than a reprimand. On other plantations . . ." Maria shrugged.

"But she was born at Landfall."

"So, now she goes elsewhere. Perhaps to a mistress who will not be so lenient. And Landfall will do with two less slaves. Her son went with her. What a pity Alister is not here to know about the new economy rule instituted at Landfall. Two less mouths to feed, and a handsome sale entered in the books. He would have commended me for once, would Alister. But he is gone—and so is Charity." She actually smiled at me, or it seemed like a smile—gloating, perhaps, a little, that two props of my existence had been removed. I looked around the table; there were just the four of us left, dangerously cross-tangled.

* * * * *

After dinner I waited for Fergus on the gallery, and we went into the garden together. The first moments of our embrace felt to me like a return from a long journey—and yet I had waited only since that morning. It was the beloved feel of the familiar, the longed-for, the well-known, and yet I knew only what my heart and senses told me of him. If my senses were wrong now, then they had been wrong all my life, and would be for the rest of it. Our bargaining had been swift and unspoken, and we were committed. I abandoned myself to the feel and the touch and excitement of him, the pleasure of his hands, his lips. How did one live for so long without knowing such pleasure existed?

Once again I held back the information of what I had discovered that morning at San Francisco. I would not yet shatter the happiness of these first hours in which we knew we were bound to each other. Now that Alister was gone, the urgency was gone also. It occurred to me that Fergus might already know of what went on at San Francisco, and kept silent because if he were to make any accusation, his own father would be involved—Andrew Maxwell would be held responsible for his wife's actions. Perhaps he had already talked with Maria about it, and had been reminded of the public scandal it would cause, and again his father's responsibility. It was clear that Maria did not run the operation without help from others on Santa Marta—other interests too powerful for a young man like Fergus, without money or influence, to fight. It could be that he was inured to it, just the way he and all the rest of the planters accepted slavery itself. Duncan wasn't the only one who needed re-education. I wondered, with a shade of unease, what my father would think when I wrote that I was going to marry a man who owned slaves, who believed in slavery? And then I thought wryly that emancipation, if it came soon enough, might save me that problem. We would have other problems then.

I deferred also, talking to him about Charity. Samuel would find out if indeed she and his son were intended for sale off the island, and if he came to me with that news, then I would speak out. I would speak out to Fergus, to Andrew—and mostly to Maria. I would threaten in whatever way I could, even if it were the fairly impotent threat of making her activities public knowledge. This was where my own responsibility lay. If Charity were sold into the American states now, then her chance of freedom was gone, probably forever. Tomorrow I would find out from Samuel what he had discovered. If she had really been sold to a planter on the island, then she was safe. If she had not, then I would have to act. I dreaded it, and this was a moment again when I missed Alister. He would have had so much more authority and weight than I possessed.

And then I missed nothing, because Fergus had laid his head down on my shoulder, his lips against my neck. "It will have to be soon, Fiona. I'm not going to wait—I can't wait."

"There's no need to wait," I answered. "No need to wait—if you're sure."

"Sure!" He raised his head, and his strong, rough hand tilted back my chin painfully to make me look up at him. "It's been like coming out of some wilderness. Since . . . since Maria I've been drifting. She may be savage, but she is strong. God, how strong she is! You are the only thing I have found stronger than Maria, the balance that outweighs her. Some of the things that have been in my life in between haven't been pretty—things that have happened in Santa Marta. But I kept hoping for an end—a reason to end it. Oh, it hasn't all been bad. I've been slowly coming to my senses and I've worked hard at

Winterslo. But the wine of my leisure has been bitter as gall. I've had enough—I've done with it. I want only you."

"And I—" I said. "I have to have you. I want to have children with you. To work with you. Anything, anywhere—just so long as I am with you."

His grip relaxed a little; he let my chin drop. "You believe me that there's no money, don't you? All that talk about my father promising me money to settle down and marry the right sort of woman is just so much talk. My father can say what he likes, but when the time comes, it won't be there to give—and I don't look for it. You've seen Winterslo—there's just me and that."

"I know it," I said. "I told you I was prepared to work. I've never had luxuries—not until Landfall, and everything at Landfall is unreal. What will I miss? Your grandmother and your father made enough out of Winterslo. Can't we do the same?"

"Suppose . . ." he said the words grudgingly. "Suppose all this talk of emancipation comes to something? What then?"

"You'll have to pay the slaves to work, that's what. They'll be free to leave you and go elsewhere. But there'll be compensation. There'll be something, Fergus." Now it was I who gripped him hard, and tried to shake that bulk of man. "We can do *something*. So what if we're poor, and there isn't silver on the table? We will have Winterslo, and the rain will fall, and the sun will shine, and the cane will still grow. There'll be less money—but we won't starve. You've never been in Scotland, Fergus, so you don't know how we feel about land. Just own the land, and have shelter from the rain, and you're already a king."

"A king?" He smiled, and I realized then how rarely he did it, how seldom it was not the sardonic smile that attempted to conceal bitterness and hurt. "Would you make me a king, Fiona? A king of a little worn-out strip of territory where too little rain falls, and when it does the roof leaks?"

"To me, you are a king. No less—do you want more?"

He gathered me again into his arms. "You know," he said, his lips against my hair, "I almost want to weep. Me!—a grown man. I have not wept since my grandmother died. Why do you unnerve me—un-man me?"

"I did not unman you this morning."

Now he laughed, loudly, a laugh that would be heard by those within the house, a joyous laugh of triumph and pleasure and mastery. "No—nor shall you! There will be many other mornings, Fiona."

V

Counting the candles on the long table, it seemed that I was the last to go upstairs. Only one remained—an oversight, I thought, because Alister had been so long a guest in the house. The sight of it made me feel again my vulnerability, now that Fergus was not here, and the stabilizing presence of Alister gone. I wished there had been a chance to say good-bye, but then it would have been, as he said, no more than formal words uttered before the others. I looked into Duncan's room to see that he was sleeping, and then went to my own. It was an unpleasant shock to see Flora seated cross-legged on the floor by the open louver doors, her head nodding in sleep. She sprang to her feet as I entered.

"What are you doing here?" I demanded. I heard my own voice, sharp and rasping. I had had too much this day, and I did not want this woman now.

She hung her head. "I help mistress . . ."

"I told you, Flora, I don't need help. Now go, please."

"Mistress Maria say I am to help you."

I made myself take her boney shoulder and I gave her a slight shake to emphasize what I said. "Now understand, Flora. You won't be punished—but I don't care what Mistress Maria says, I prefer to take care of myself. Go now—go!"

There was no pleading from her as there had been before. Perhaps I also was growing hard in the crucible of Landfall. But I caught her last direct look at me before the head went down into the customary position; I saw the eyes, black, passive no longer, blazing momentarily as if a fire had been lighted there. And I knew for myself what most white people must sooner or later learn in these places—the absolute and unrelenting hatred of the black. I remembered something I had once heard about needing to grow up to make enemies. I had truly come of age at Landfall.

*   *   *   *   *

Sleep fell on me like a blanket that night. Even with the consciousness of both love and hate earned on this, the most momentous day of my life, I fell into a sleep that was part exhaustion. I hadn't bothered to braid my hair—even though I would not admit it consciously, I did miss Charity's ministrations. So I spread it like a fan about me on the pillow, and I slept within seconds of lying down.

I don't know why I woke from such a sleep, except that in an atmosphere such as Landfall's, one's senses are never fully deadened. I struggled out of sleep, my eyelids still weighted. I heard no movement, saw nothing. But I had the choking knowledge of danger; I felt it, as I had felt other things, not to be explained reasonably. I opened my eyes wide and let them grow accustomed to the darkness, lying quite still on my side, and trying to keep my breathing rhythmical and deep. Then abruptly I flung myself round in the bed, sitting up in the one movement. I looked then, straight into the face of Flora; even in the darkness I knew it—its shape, the glow and intensity of the eyes.

My own hand flew to my lips to suppress the scream I wanted to let out.

"You! What are you doing? What are you about?"

I flung back the sheet and dropped to the floor; she was forced to retreat before me. "What?" I demanded. "What?—*what?*" With each word a violent shake of her shoulder.

"Nothing—nothing. Jus' to see you all right. Mistress tell me—"

I slapped her face, hard. My fear and rage were undoing me; I was scarcely able to control myself. In those terrible seconds I wondered what Landfall was doing to me—to hit Fergus as I had with the riding crop, to strike this woman who dared not strike back. And yet some powerful premonition told me that I must be done with her forever.

"Go!" I said. "Go! Never come back into this room. *Never!*" I was holding up my hand and she was retreating before me all the time I spoke. "It is bad for you to come back . . ." If this primitive ritual was all she would listen to or understand, then she should have it. "I see things . . . bad things for you."

She was visibly frightened. She backed away from me to the door, and still facing me, attempted to open it with one hand. Something dropped from her other hand, and slid across the floor. The downward slanted moonlight from the louvers caught its gleam. I went and picked it up; Flora stood as if frozen. It was the scissors with which she had tried to cut my hair the evening before.

I went straight to her, brandishing them in her face; she leaned away from me, terrified. "Why do you steal this? Why?"

"Not steal, mistress. Jus' come to look after you. Come to cut the spells that gather at the full of the moon. Mistress not understand these things. I take care . . ."

"No! You do not take care!" I held them between our two faces like a talisman. "Do not come near me again. I make spells far more powerful than scissors can cut—more powerful than your gods make. So keep away!"

Her hands scrabbled at the door handle like a frightened animal; a soft click, and she was gone. Very slowly I went back and replaced the scissors on the bureau, and returned to bed. I was trembling and soaked in sweat. There was no more sleep. I was made wretched by what I had done. To strike her was bad enough, but I had done worse. By those who know it—and the unfortunate few who possess it, the gift of "the sight," or the curse of it—is never taken lightly, nor spoken of, nor invoked without truth. It cannot be called up at will. I had used the threat of it fraudulently to frighten that poor, ignorant girl. I had misused its power. In each of the few instances when I had known its presence before it had been involuntary, and I had spoken without calculation. Tonight I had felt no such compulsion, merely used the sensations I had known before to frighten, and to protect myself. I had begun to know power, and that was dangerous. I had begun to know corruption.

Chapter 6.

It was earlier than ever before when I heard Andrew's pacing on the gallery outside—before even the first glimmer of light had touched the sky. Something had changed in the sound of that pacing, too—it was not the slow shuffle of a man with nothing to do, but someone with a purpose. Up and down, up and down—a pause, as if he stopped to see or to listen, and then the pacing resumed. I got out of bed and put on my wrapper, and went and opened the long doors to the gallery.

"Fiona?" It was no greeting. I could just distinguish his bulky outline as he leaned against the railing, staring outward, as if he strove to see what was yet hidden. The moon was down, and the first light of the dawn had not yet come.

"Come here!" I joined him at the railing; he smelled of rum and tobacco and sweat; a sleepless night for him also, I thought.

"Do you hear it?"

"What?"

"The wind, girl—the wind."

"There is always the wind—except at night and these summer months."

"Not from this quarter. It's coming from the wrong quarter, the lee shore, damn it!"

"What does it mean?"

"A storm—that's what it means. Perhaps a big one. We may have a hurricane coming at us, Fiona."

" 'October all over,' " I quoted him, from Duncan's rhyme.

"I wish I could believe it. The worst hurricane I ever knew on San Cristóbal came in early October. I remember it—when I was about Duncan's age. It took two days to pass completely over the island—and there was this great calm suddenly in the middle of it, and then the wind again. We harvested no crop at Winterslo that year, I'll tell you—nor did any other plantation on the island. And we all pulled our belts tighter, whites as well as slaves."

I felt a kind of excited fear tug at me. "You think this is one of the great winds?"

"Listen to it, girl—listen to it!"

It had a low eerie moaning sound, with sudden, sharp gusts that blew my hair wildly; and it did come from the wrong quarter—it was not the northeasterly trade that blew the ships across from the African coast. Even the air smelled different, as if it were charged with some power. In the gusts I could taste the salt, driven in on it, driven right across the island from the wrong direction.

"It's dark," I said. "Why doesn't it get lighter? It's past the time—surely it's past the time."

"It may stay dark. This may be one day you don't see the sun on San Cristóbal, Fiona." He leaned farther out on the rail, his eyes fixed on the horizon, where now, just the first sullen streak of grey was beginning to show. His white hair blew about him, his beard and chin jutted forward as if he were trying to smell something, like an animal.

"It's out there—it's out there. A big one, I think. But who knows how big?—how it will turn? I've heard them coming, and then going, and then twisting back again in two days to the same place. I wish I knew—God, I wish I knew what this one was to be! We may decide it will be a big blow, and it may pass by harmlessly, and all we will get is an hour or two of heavy rain. Or it may come straight at us, and we could be flattened. Well, I'm going down to look at the barometer . . ." He shuffled off, and I was left standing at the railing, watching the ominous grey that crept into the sky, feeling the sudden slash of rain on my face, and something that clung there wetly—the shredded petal of a blossom.

I turned and went to Duncan's room to wake him. If the great wind of legend was to come, it would be the first for both of us. I knew I had to keep him close.

* * * * *

The roars of Andrew from the outer gallery below roused any in the household who might still have slept through the rising wind. "Barometer's near bottom! Everyone up!—everyone start getting ready!"

I bundled Duncan into his clothes, and rushed to my room to dress myself. The wind was increasing. I could hear the scurry of slaves all over the house. It was very strange not to be washing and dressing in the radiant, sharp beauty of the tropic dawn. Except that it was oppressively hot, it seemed more like the dark mornings when the winter storms had raged in from the Atlantic at Silkirk. The rain was almost continuous; through the house I could hear the banging of any of the louver doors that no one had yet had time to fasten. I took Duncan downstairs with me; we ate breakfast standing around the sideboard—just bread and butter, and hot tea. We stood there, because there was no time for any of the slaves to wait on us. Duncan giggled and nudged me. "No oatmeal," he said. I thought it was lucky Andrew didn't hear him laugh. He seemed in a mood to clip his ear for levity.

Andrew appeared suddenly to have come into his own; he still staggered about, still needing his cane and Dougal's arm for support, but for the first time since I had come to Landfall, no one thought to look to other than he for orders. Maria was quiet, and seemed strangely preoccupied, as if the coming storm was a threat to more than Landfall; she obeyed Andrew without question, as we all did.

The shock of those early hours was the appearance of Alister, riding alone, drenched to the skin, a bundle of clothing wrapped in tarpaulin strapped to the saddle before him. He slipped off his horse, and hitched it to the stair rails. Andrew, moving through the hall on Dougal's arm, stopped.

"What the devil are you back for?"

Alister shrugged wearily. "I had some idea I might be of more use here than sitting it out in Santa Marta. I went on board late last night, but they began to feel the swell from the wrong quarter long before dawn. The captain said he'd not take a chance on putting out into it until he saw how it blew. If it was going to be a bad one, I thought I might help you here . . ."

Andrew just grunted. "Are you able to ride farther? There's some hours before it will reach its height, if I'm any judge. Never know, though, how quickly these things are moving. Well, will you ride out again?"

Alister's head jerked back, and a flood of crimson came to his face. "I'm able, at least, to do that!"

"All right—all right! Don't start getting touchy now. We may all be cooped up here for days, and we'll need what patience we've got. Well then, here's what I want you to do. Get Samuel to saddle you up a fresh mount, and get one or two of the cane carts harnessed up. Throw in a cushion or two if you think it's necessary. Take Samuel with you. Then get over to San Francisco and get that fat old she-devil and her two daughters over here. And all the slaves . . ."

It was then Maria made her only protest. "No—no! My mother will never come. She will never leave San Francisco!"

"Well then, if the storm grows worse, San Francisco will be her burial mound. That old heap won't stand a blow like the one we had sixteen years ago. Half of Santa Marta went with that one."

"I was at San Francisco sixteen years ago. It held up. My forefathers on this island built well."

"Don't give me any damn nonsense now about your forefathers. I'm responsible for the women they left behind. I don't care what you do, Alister, but make her come."

He turned and went back down the steps and unhitched the horse to lead it around to the stables. I had just a moment to run to the edge of the gallery, the rain slashing at me. I reached a hand toward him, and for an instant only we touched. "Thank God you've come back," I said. And his weary smile was my answer.

I stopped Andrew in the hall to ask about Fergus.

"Fergus? He's the least of my worries. Fergus knows what to do."

He paid me no more attention, and I was left to worry about what he meant by those words as he set me my own tasks. Firstly I was to supervise the removal of all the furniture from both the inner and outer galleries into the center core of the house. "If it hits us directly," he said tersely, "the rain will come at us almost horizontally. The hurricane shutters will keep most of it out, but some will come under the doors, and in at the sides. Anything valuable will have to be moved out of its reach. Anything that can move—or fly—with the wind, will go. Remember that. And when that's done, go upstairs and see that every piece of furniture is moved up against the inner walls. The lighter pieces can be moved onto the landing. We will see to closing the shutters. My wife will see to the food . . ."

The kitchen quarters were on the outer gallery at the back, and therefore vulnerable to the wind. They could not be used so long as a hurricane blew; ever since the first word had been given by Andrew there had been a flurry of cooking—the ovens brought up to heat, and the sides of meat brought in from the outbuildings to be cooked and made ready, the dough pounded for bread, as if we prepared for a siege. The fires were to be put out before the wind blew too strongly. "Seen places burned down from a spark left in the kitchen when the wind blew too fierce," Andrew grumbled.

There was a convoy of slaves set to carrying water into the house, filling every receptacle that anyone could find—vases, glasses, pitchers, bowls, and buckets. "But with all this rain . . . ?" I questioned Andrew, "won't there be plenty of water?"

He glared at me. "Don't tell me you really *are* stupid, girl? Do you think you're going to stand out there with a bucket and collect it as it falls? We can't get to the cisterns—couldn't think of opening one of those shutters at the height of it if we are hit directly. Stupid . . . didn't think you were that stupid." And he went off.

Perhaps I was stupid; it seemed to me many times that morning as I went about the tasks allotted to me, that a kind of mist would come before my eyes, and I had to keep repeating to myself the instructions that Andrew had given me, and I found my tongue seemed to stick over certain words as I gave the orders. I had never seen the slaves move as quickly as they did then—or was I that much slower? The pace that preserves one against the heat was dropped. Everyone moved with speed and surprising agility; it was as if they moved to the rhythm of a new order, a new dance. Perhaps it was fear, perhaps it was simply the stimulus of change in those unchanging lives. Duncan came with me everywhere, moving his own most cherished possessions onto the gallery around the staircase, where they would be safest from the rain. I found it sometimes hard to keep up with this new pace; I was clutching doorways, and banisters as I watched the furniture lined up against the inner walls, the cane chairs piled, the rush-matting rolled and placed safely. I did it against the crushing grip of the worst headache I had ever known, the kind of headache that made it a small agony to turn my head or bend my neck. I told myself that it was the storm—wasn't there something about atmospheric pressure? But whatever it was, I had to go on. Everyone had their tasks to see to, and mine must be done. Sometimes, though, through the haze of pain, I saw Duncan looking at me with puzzlement, but he said nothing. I found as I made my rounds, that I was leaning on him. He seemed to understand, with his precocious knowledge, that I needed him. He stayed close and didn't ask questions.

As this went on Andrew himself was overseer for the more serious preparations. As the outer galleries were cleared, the shutter doors were closed, as they were every night; then, outside them, the great stout hurricane doors were closed—those that I had thought of as largely ornamental now moved on their massive black hinges. Huge cradles of metal were ready to receive the iron bars placed horizontally into them, to lock the shutters tight against the wind. It was almost like the sound of doom as each of the big doors was swung into place, and the bars came down with a crash—the feeling returned that we were closing ourselves into a medieval fortress against a siege. I could hear Andrew swearing as some of the shutters resisted, the hinges creaking. "I'll have the hide flogged off those responsible for letting these things go. Look at this—rust! One good gust, and it could go. Lazy bastards!" And then more cursing as he saw that some of the shutters had warped, and it took several slaves with hammers to pound them into place. "Fellowes!" Andrew roared. "Where's that idiot?—why isn't he here helping?"

"I sent him yesterday to Santa Marta," Maria answered. "I expect he stayed overnight."

"Hmm . . . but Alister came back, didn't he? *He* got himself here. Must say I never expected him to have the guts. Could have sat it out nicely in Lawrence's. Santa Marta would slide into the sea before *that* place would go. Well, Fellowes always was worthless . . ."

"Are any of them any different?" Maria retorted. "Alister blames me, but—"

"All right. We'll have plenty of time to argue the merits of overseers later on. How are they going in the kitchen . . . ?"

The center of the house grew darker and darker as each shutter was closed against the slashing grey rain. Within, it was like night—like no night I had ever known at Landfall. But we were permitted few candles or lamps.

"Save the candles—save the oil. It may be all we have for the next three days."

Finally, exhausted, Andrew fell back into his red sofa; Dougal hastily topped a glass with rum. "I remember the last time we did this—before you were born, Duncan. No—not before you were born. You were a year old, and didn't care what was happening. It was a day just like this. Started with this kind of wind and rain. We made all the same preparations. Cooked up everything in the house—turned the place upside down. It must have been the tail of it we caught. The wind died that same afternoon—a little rain misted over, for all the world like the sort of thing I remember from London. One of the quietest days I ever remember on the island. We waited, in case it came back at us, but finally we undid it all and put everything back in place, and ate cooked meat for two weeks. And then the ships started coming into Santa Marta—those that were in fit shape for the voyage and not on the rocks. Down island they had caught it—Martinique, St. Lucia—torn apart. Hundreds drowned. Buildings gone, plantations ruined. That's the way of the big winds. They circle and swoop, and it takes you months—if you ever do—to find out exactly where they began and where they went to. If you pray, Miss Fiona, pray that today we are doing all this for nothing, and that we'll eat cooked meat for two weeks."

It came to the time when he roared the order. "Maria!—tell them to douse the fires. I don't like the sound of the wind."

It had been rising steadily—so much so that it became difficult to hear what was said against its howl and the drumming of the rain against the roof and outside shutters; some of the gusts rose to shrieks, and seemed to claw at the house as if it would pull its bones apart. All the storm shutters save the last one leading to the kitchen quarters, and one other, on the side away from the direction of the wind— ironically the Atlantic side—were closed. I heard them closing up the kitchen one.

"How?" I said, my voice sounding to me oddly slurred as I tried to focus more clearly on the things around me. "How will Alister get in? How will anyone get in? Once that last door is closed we'll never hear them."

"We don't close the last door," Andrew answered. "We keep a tight hook on it to stop it slamming about, but it is still open a little. It's important to remember in a big wind always to leave an escape hatch on the side away from the wind. Some wind always forces itself in— you must give it somewhere to go or you could burst your own shutters. But you've got to watch it—every minute you've got to watch it. If you should get into that calm that sometimes comes in the middle of a big wind, then you have to be ready to close that side and open up on the other the second the wind starts again, because it can be coming from the other direction. At least, that is what they tell us, those who've been through the calm. Of course, from others we never get any information, because they're dead."

He chuckled grimly, and applied himself to the rum again, and it suddenly struck me, through the growing obtuseness that the headache had brought, that he had actually enjoyed the whole performance of this ritual. He had taken all precautions, but he didn't really care what happened now. He soon would die himself, and he knew it; he didn't really care if he and all this should be swept away in the wind that blew from the direction that no man could foretell.

II

At last Alister came, his clothes plastered to his frame, his hair beaten down about his cheeks. The two sisters, Katarina and Joanna, were in the same state, the clinging wet dresses only serving to emphasize the thinness of those bodies, the dark hair hanging down gave them a strangely crow-like appearance. They stood there, pools of water forming about them, with a beaten look of exhaustion and fear. Five pathetic-looking slaves had followed them. They huddled together as near to the still-open door as they could, round, frightened eyes gazing apprehensively at Andrew.

Alister only came to the edge of the gallery; the horse and the mule had still to be stabled.

"The old woman," Andrew shouted. "Where is she?"

"Wouldn't come," Alister yelled back.

"I told you to make her come, no matter what."

"You neglected to remind me to take a gun. I rounded up the slaves—all hiding in the outbuildings, with the two women doing all the work to get the place ready. I tried to get the slaves to force her into the cart —she's not a woman you can pick up in one hand, remember. She threatened to blow my head off if I came near her. I told her she was in danger—she laughed at me. 'Just leave me a good supply of San Francisco rum,' was all she said. 'I'll sit it out, as I've sat out all the others, and in no other house than the Medinas'.'"

"I told you . . . !" Maria cried. "I told you!" And then she turned on her sisters. "And you left her. Fine ones you are! Well, you will suffer for it!"

Katarina wiped back hair from her forehead with a gesture of infinite weariness. Then she spread both hands so that we could see them—scratched, bleeding, blood welling at the knuckles. "Suffer!—as if we haven't already! How long is it, my fine sister, since you have tried to hammer a storm shutter into place, with the wood cracking and splintering before your eyes? One, on an upstairs room, came off its hinges and struck me." She made a jerking motion of her head toward her left shoulder. The rain had washed all their garments so thoroughly that it wasn't until now that we were aware of the blood that was soaking the wet sleeve. Her arm dangled limp and awkwardly.

Alister had had enough of it. His horse, held by a stable boy, was restive as the boughs of the trees near it slashed and moaned. "I did what I could," he said tersely. "If the old woman wants to die there, perhaps that should be her choice. I'm off to the stable. Will there be some men staying there with the horses?"

"Yes," Andrew answered. "The best ones I have. We try to keep the horses quiet. The stables are well-built. They'll not go in the wind, unless it's worse than it's ever been."

"Samuel will stay there," Maria said. "He is best with the horses."

"Samuel isn't here. He's gone."

Shock registered even on Andrew's face. "Gone!—gone! How do you know?"

"He insisted on driving the cart over to San Francisco while I rode. I said I would need help with Donna Isabella. He waited until he knew the ladies would come, and helped me find the slaves. Then he—" Alister shrugged. "Well, he just disappeared."

"The fool! There's no use in him running. There's no safer place than here now. No ships will be leaving harbor—he couldn't take a boat out. Well, he'll come back again. They always do when they get frightened enough." He waved his hand. "All right then, get along. We'll do well enough without the old she-devil."

When Alister was gone Maria turned on her sisters with a torrent of Spanish, wild, abusive, her cheeks flaming with unaccustomed color. At the end of it Katarina merely shrugged, and answered, deliberately, I thought, in English.

"Words, sister—words! It is not you who have any longer to deal with our sainted mother. As your esteemed kinsman pointed out—if she chooses to die at San Francisco, *that* is her right. But we—Joanna and I—prefer to live, at least a little longer. So we have taken your good husband's hospitality, and left her her supply of the best San Francisco rum—and her other necessities—and she will live or not, as God wills." She gave a long, deep sigh. "And now, my dear sister, would it be too much to ask of your hospitality that we might have dry clothes? Anything will do," she added, with deep sarcasm. "No doubt there are wornout clothing of the slaves . . . nothing too splendid, you understand, lest we get notions above our pockets. And would it be too much to ask for water and salve for our hands?—and perhaps a bit of old sheet to bind my shoulder?"

Before Maria could reply there came a bellow from Andrew. "Juanita—Juanita!" After a while the old woman shuffled up from the cellars. "Don't take so long to answer my call." He jerked his head. "Attend to the señoritas. See that they have whatever they need of Mrs. Maxwell's clothes. And bring some of your ointments—the right ones, mind. None of your witch's brew. Have Flora help you . . ."

The last task Andrew gave me was to see to bringing down mattresses and bedding and laying them out wherever they would fit in the hall, and the salon and the dining room. "Safer down here," he said. "You can never tell when the roof might go. We would be safer still in the cellars, but that's where the slaves will go, and you'd never stand the stink. In any case, we have to show ourselves superior to them even when we're all in the same boat. Believe me, if that old woman at San Francisco survives, the tale will go to every slave on the island that she is a witch, and braver than the bravest man. They're frightened of her now, but that will be nothing to what she will enjoy if she lives through this. And she does enjoy it—by God, *how* that old woman enjoys them being afraid of her!"

And Andrew would also have enjoyed that, I thought, if he had possessed it. But the passion was gone, and the power had passed to his wife. In this show he had put on since early morning I had seen a faint echo of the man who must once have been. But he was fading; he still was bellowing orders but the spring was running down; I had the feeling that he would not, from now on, very often leave the red sofa.

One thing I asked again, as the last of the mattresses was laid in place. "Fergus?" I said. I was clinging to the doorframe of the salon, wondering why nothing would stay still before my eyes. "You sent to bring them from San Francisco. But you leave Fergus in that place that's falling apart. You talk of *this* roof going. That one could fly!"

He took the pipe from his mouth. "That I can leave to Fergus. He will come or not, as he decides. I don't have to give him orders or instructions."

"You might have given him an invitation."

"Invitation!" That roar of forced laughter came. "You ought to know what happens when I *invite* Fergus. It is the one way to be sure he will not come. So leave it—and stop fussing. *All* you damn women stop fussing!"

He went back to his tobacco, and his figure slumped.

Then Alister came back from the stables; he came through the dining room, his arms loaded with the bound ledgers and journals from the office. "Is there any help?" he said peremptorily. I noticed that his limp was now very pronounced, and that he was near exhaustion. "I would like every book and paper taken from the office—it is very exposed there on the outer gallery. We can't do much with water-soaked books. It's very odd that you've taken so much trouble about everything else, and neglected this."

"So . . . ?" Maria said. "So now you are master of the books at Landfall, Alister?"

"I'm master of them to the extent that I have a right to see them preserved. We also have interests at Landfall, Maria."

Andrew stirred. "The books—the books! Goddammit, why didn't you think of the books, Maria? Idiot! Why, my mother's books from Winterslo are there. Bring them all—every last one of them! Go—set them to it!"

Alister waited long enough to see the start of a chain of slaves that were set to bringing in the rows of ledgers from the office, and then he also went, slowly and with some pain, up the stairs to seek dry clothes.

* * * * *

Fergus did come; he came when it was almost too late, when the wind had reached a force that made me believe what Andrew had said—that no man could stand upright in it. He brought with him the ten slaves that Winterslo possessed, and with each of them was a bundle, wrapped in straw matting to protect it as much as could be done from the rain.

"Fergus!" I raced forward and threw myself into his arms. I felt his embrace, eager but swift, and he was looking over my shoulder to his father and Maria.

"I tied down everything that could be tied. I nailed shutters in place, and the nailing only showed me what the termites had really done to the place. There was no way to tie the roof on. I did what I could, and in the end I decided it was better to live, if one could, to go back there, even if it was ruined, than to die with it. We have brought our own food. All we ask is the shelter of your roof, my father."

Andrew gestured broadly. "Welcome once more to Landfall, my son. You see, we are now complete. Alister returned from Santa Marta and performed the service of bringing the Señoritas Medina from San Francisco. He also has his books for company. Fiona has you. The house is well-stocked with food and drink, our slaves are thankful for shelter from the storm, and are therefore docile. All we lack is the old lady of San Francisco, who refused to come, and for which we may be thankful. Make yourself at home, my son. We should be a happy, spritely little party to sit out the storm. Yes, fill your glass with rum, Fergus, and make yourself at ease. It will be as if we celebrated a great happening, instead of facing the due date of repayment that the sugar islands exact every so often from those who win her riches. So take your glass, my son, and put a good face on it. My bones tell me that this time it will be repayment in full."

It was then, still holding Fergus, that I was no longer able to control the whirling of the room about me, the gathering mist before my eyes; it was then the full blackness came.

III

There was no single part of the remainder of that day or of the night that distinguished itself from the rest in my mind; people seemed to come and go as I lay on one of the mattresses in the salon; there was talk, but I understood little of it. I sometimes felt those who bent over me, but other times I woke from the blackness of a kind of unconscious sleep to find that Fergus's hand was holding mine, that it was he who wiped the sweat from my face, but I had not known of his being there. Sometimes Flora's face was there, and I would close my eyes upon it, because she brought a strange fear; sometimes Alister was there, and I took comfort from his presence, as one does from those of good sense and purpose. Once I was aware of some greater presence, slow and heavy, over me, and it was Andrew, with Dougal holding a lamp. The sweating, but strangely expert fingers felt for my pulse.

"Some sort of fever. But I don't know—she doesn't seem the sort to go like this. Don't like the look of it. Not a bit. If we could get a doctor . . . Well, it's beyond me . . ."

All that was constant through that night, constant through the burning that seemed to consume me, and the dizzying whirl of light and dark about me whenever I opened my eyes, was the sound of the wind and the rain. Sometimes gusts came that roused me, and I would find myself sitting up, waiting for the moment of final destruction, waiting until the walls would give before its power. Nothing could stand against the wind, I thought. We would all go with the house, buried beneath its falling walls, buried down where the slaves were, in the cellars, equal, finally, in that common grave.

But the walls held, and the roof held, and all that we felt, locked in our darkness, was the drafts and eddies of wind that forced themselves through chinks in the great storm shutters. As each new gust rose, I could hear the accompanying moan of fear that came from the cellars; the slaves could give utterance to their fears, but we, the whites, could not. For us, the release came in the kind of bickering that accompanies those who are locked up together against their will. Once they had become accustomed to the fact that I was ill, and began to accept it, the hushed tone of the voices gradually became normal. They were not afraid to wake me, because it was no natural sleep I slept. Sometimes the voices came in Spanish—often Andrew's hoarse bellow would trumpet out. I heard Duncan's voice, querulous, bored, demanding. Sometimes I was aware of the activities of this ill-assorted lot. The sisters, Katarina and Joanna, brought out the gaming table, and shuffled their cards, and carried on with some game that seemed to have occupied them for years—they had won and lost vast sums to each other, all on paper. Alister sat, under Maria's frowning gaze, and kept turning the pages of the ledgers. He hardly ever spoke. Maria had little occupation—her needlework was denied her for lack of light; she seemed unable to bear either the sight of Fergus so closely beside me, or of Alister's patient scrutiny of the books. I had the impression that most of the time she paced the hall—but her footfalls, as always, were very light; there was just the suggestion of her presence. She came back and forth, a restless, hovering spirit, waiting, as we all did.

But in the end, exhaustion came to everyone. We even grew so used to the shriek of the wind that only the worst gusts would cause us now to pause and listen. One by one, because the clocks said midnight, all lay down on the mattresses spread around, and took what sleep was possible. We had worked since dawn; even the tumult could not deny

sleep finally. Quietness fell over the house itself, while the storm outside had its way. Andrew slept fitfully on his red sofa, always the rum
beside him, and the sweetish smell of the tobacco staling the rooms.
There came that moment during the night when all of us must have
believed that the climax had come, and the final end. There was a
great tearing, shrieking sound, almost as of an animal in pain, and
then a long series of crashing noises that went on and on, for minutes.
All of us there in the room were silent, until, at last, the crashing
sound stopped.

"A tree," Andrew pronounced. "One near the house—probably the
big cottonwood. Torn out by the roots. It's probably damaged the
foundations of the house. We shall all be torn out by the roots if it lasts
at this strength much longer."

All I knew then was that the pressure of Fergus's hand in mine
seemed to increase, as if he would will some strength back into me.
There was the moment, though, when the touch was relinquished. I
heard Fergus's and Alister's voices in whispers very close.

"I'll stay with her now," Alister said. "You'll have to get a few hours'
sleep."

The offer was roughly rejected. "Mind your own business! She's
mine—I'm taking care of her."

"Don't talk rubbish, man! You'll have to get some sleep or you'll be
useless when this is all over. Perhaps by morning it may be possible
for someone to ride for a doctor—or at least to bring back some medicine. If you can't keep awake, how can you do it. Besides, there is
the watch to keep. We can't afford, all of us, to fall asleep. You might
doze off. Who knows when the slaves may come up from the cellars?
Can you be sure they haven't taken knives down there with their
bundles?"

It was only then, dimly, that I comprehended our danger. Alister
sat on a cane chair beside me, occasionally leaning down to give me
water when I asked it, performing the tasks that one would not have
thought possible of that fastidious man of bathing my face, neck, and
hands with a cloth wrung in water; and all the time he faced the
entrance to the salon, watching, his gaze going from me to it constantly. When he put down the cloth he would take up again the
pistol that he had held for all these hours. It was not permitted for all
to sleep at once, for fear of the bare feet coming silently across the
floor, and the machetes that could end a life before the sleeper woke.
I was glad that, as the party sought their mattresses, Flora had been

sent to the cellars again; her presence was almost worse than the fear of the storm.

Then it was morning, though the blackness was the same. There was a stirring; voices again. There was a movement toward the dining room, where the food was laid out on the sideboard. The wind was still with us. Was the cry of it, though, a little less shrill, the gusts a little less in force? Or was it just that our ears now were so attuned to the tumult that we no longer heard it with such fear.

Flora had been permitted up from the cellars again, and with her came Juanita. Between them I staggered to that primitive arrangement in one of the store rooms where the women could use the buckets. Even after one night, the smell was noxious. They both held me, their hands seeming to crush my flesh. I broke into a sweat again, nearly fainting as they supported me back to my mattress. As I lay down again Andrew roused himself and came close, leaning over me.

"Don't like it," he said. "She should be showing signs of coming through it now if it were an ordinary fever. Wish to God we could get a doctor—not that those quacks know any more than we do about what ails a person in this climate. But at least it would be *something*. But we can't send yet. Wind's dropped a bit, but it's still too much for a man and a horse. And no doctor would come—cowards, the lot of them."

I felt Juanita's hand thrust back the damp hair from my forehead and I shrunk from her touch, pressing myself into the mattress. "White doctor no good, master. This spell come from the wind, and Mistress Fiona's spirit fly away with it. No white doctor know about these things."

"God rot you!" I heard a crack, and I thought that Andrew had struck the woman. But I was no longer sure of anything that was happening. "I'll have none of that damned nonsense here! Are you trying to frighten her to death? Mistress Fiona is strong. She will get well. Hers is no spirit to fly with the wind. She will live and bear many children for my son. To hell with your witchcraft. Go and tell your gods that she will live." He turned heavily, in fury, to his wife. "Maria, why do you let this rag-bag near Fiona? Why do you let her say these things? Are *you* trying to frighten the girl too?"

The voice answered behind me. "You know yourself, Andrew, how skillful Juanita is with her herbal remedies. How many sick slaves has she brought back to health for us? Send for the doctor, by all means. In the meantime, who better have I to offer than my own Juanita?"

"There must be *something* to do! Haven't we anything to give her, Maria?—why the hell don't you help? You and your precious sisters . . ."

It ran on, a stream of abuse against everyone, hardly distinguishable to my dulled ears; I seemed now to be listening to sounds other than those close at hand, I seemed to hear the gurgling sound of water. The scene about me faded, and I was following the tide as it ebbed on the strand at Silkirk, leaving miles of shining sand. I felt that tide, the silvery line receding, the sand left firm and hard beneath my feet. I wanted to go with it, to catch up with it; it was then I began to feel cold. I felt my body contract against the cold, but nothing could hold it out. At that moment I began not to feel Fergus's hand in mine; I knew it was there, but I could not feel it. From somewhere, from chests long stored, at Andrew's command, came blankets. They were piled upon me, but the essential body heat was gone. There was the moment when I felt Fergus's body clamped to mine to attempt to infuse warmth into it. I passed in and out of consciousness, sometimes knowing what went on about me, sometimes not. And all the time my mind followed that silver line of sea as it receded across the sands and out into the Atlantic.

I felt something else; hands that tried to appear gentle, but instead were sharp, hands that seemed to bite into me, rather than support me as they raised me to a sitting position.

"Drink—it will do you good."

"No!" Fergus's voice.

I knew nothing but that liquid splashed across my face, and some ran down between the blankets. Then Maria said, "You asked me for help. It is an old island remedy. The best we can do now."

"I wouldn't trust a glass of water from your hands to her. Now leave her to me. After all—I am the one who loses most. If she goes— oh, my God . . ."

Did I hear him sob, or was it the cry of the wind? Did a man like Fergus weep; could he care that much? I don't know; I never will. The wind went on, and the household moved about me, and I still was cold, as was the water on the strand when I finally caught up with its foaming edge, and touched it. It was icy cold.

In my clearer moments I could feel the restlessness that gripped all those there growing by the hour. Katarina and Joanna had gone back to their cards, but they muttered sourly, without interest. Alister still looked at the books, but from the impatient flick of the pages I knew that he no longer studied them with any concentration. Maria moved about—sometimes ordering Dougal to tidy the sideboard—but there was nowhere to wash dishes. I heard the buzz of flies between the gusts of wind. Maria was the most restless of them all. She paced constantly between salon and hall, a disturbing figure who moved in and out of my line of vision. Finally Andrew could stand it no longer.

"For God's sake, woman, will you be still! You know how to be quiet enough when it suits you."

She didn't answer him, but her footsteps retreated toward the dining room, and I supposed she sat there alone. I heard Andrew heave himself off the sofa and stump out into the hall.

"Duncan—where's Duncan?"

The piping voice floated down from the upper landing. "I'm here, Papa."

"What are you doing?"

"Just getting some of my soldiers, Papa."

"Well, get them, and come down. I don't trust you up there. If you open one of those doors into the bedrooms the pressure could burst open a shutter. So get your things and bring them down."

The unusually docile reply: "Yes, Papa."

I could hear his slow, careful steps as he came down. And then there was a crash, and a rolling of small objects over the floor of the hall. The tiny vibration hit into my head like blows. Maria must have left her place in the dining room.

"Duncan!"

"Well—I dropped them, Mama. I couldn't help it."

"And look!—you have taken my little rosewood chest without permission. See—look! The hinge is damaged. You are a very bad child . . ."

"I had nothing to carry them down in." He was sullen, on the defensive, awaiting his punishment.

Andrew shouted from his sofa, to which he had returned. "Leave him be, Maria. He is cooped up. He has to do *something*. The hinge can be mended, for God's sake. Leave the child alone. Bring your things in here, son . . ."

"That box came from Spain more than two hundred years ago."

"So—it's time it had a knock or two. It's not sacred. Come—bring your things here, son. You can play with your soldiers here."

It was seldom that Andrew interfered with any direction Maria gave to Duncan, but at the times he did, the boy knew he had complete license. He seemed to know now that he was the instrument of his mother's anger against her husband. He knew that he had just escaped a box on the ear, and was gleeful over it. He chattered happily to Andrew as he came in, the toy soldiers restored to Maria's damaged little chest. Maria herself now said nothing; she must have retired again to the dining room. Duncan, having been encouraged by Andrew, sought to exploit his interest, bringing the chest of soldiers close to the sofa, and beginning to play about his father's feet. But Andrew could never for long suffer Duncan's endless questionings, his demands for attention. He wanted to be left to drink his rum in peace, and the child bored and annoyed him.

"Duncan—take your things over there. And be quiet. Stop your chatter."

I saw that Duncan crept away, hurt, bewildered. He knew he was under threat of punishment from his mother, and now Andrew had dismissed him. It was part of the constant seesaw of his life, the reason why he clung to me with such tenaciousness. He glanced reproachfully toward my mattress, as if to chide me for not being able to help him; but he kept away, as he had been told to.

The hours passed, with numbing ennui settling on everyone—hours or minutes, I couldn't seem to tell. The wind appeared to die a little, and the stronger gusts were fewer. Or perhaps I no longer heard them.

I was roused, though, by Andrew's sudden great bellow of triumph.

"The glass is beginning to rise!—*the glass is rising*. We may be through the worst of it."

Now, at this moment, it was Alister's cool hand I felt on my face. "Hold on, Fiona—hold on!"

"Take your hands off her, Goddammit!" Fergus's nerves were raw, and for a moment I thought he would strike Alister. "She's my responsibility—mine! mine!" Once again I felt his whole body pressed against me, trying to will warmth into it, uncaring of those about us. But how different it was now than our time together on the sunlit beach when we had moved with each other in a radiance of joy at the edge of the water. This tide was cold, and I was in much deeper.

Fergus began to talk of being able, in an hour or two, to ride for a doctor. Andrew grunted, and wondered aloud if any doctor would consent to come to Landfall when so many in Santa Marta would need help. I heard him order Flora to bring rum from the sideboard decanter—always the best rum in the house. With his own hands Andrew mixed rum and several spices and bade Flora build a fire in the long-unused fireplace to heat it. He also ordered my mattress to be carried close to the fire. But the wind backed the smoke down the chimney, and the room was filled. Furious, Andrew threw water on the kindling, and we choked on the smoke and the acrid stench. His failure to help disturbed him; he watched critically as Fergus made me drink the rum—its warmth was only momentary. Juanita hovered, and the sight of her black, glowering face behind Andrew's frightened me. I turned away.

"Mistress Fiona die," Juanita said. "Master not let Juanita use her remedies, mistress surely die."

"Shut your foul mouth, and get out of here," Andrew shouted. "I told you to keep away." He went back to his sofa, as though discouraged; I could hear his heavy breathing across the room.

Maria's voice was next—how long after I don't know. She had come to the door of the salon. "The wind is dropping. It is passing. When can we go out?"

"Not yet," Andrew replied, "—and you won't much like what you see when you do go out. There's nothing much left out there to hurry to."

"My mother at San Francisco?—she is nothing?"

"That worn-out old hulk!" Andrew snorted. "You would do better to have a care for this young woman here among us. *She* is worth saving—"

He was cut short by a cry from Maria. "Duncan! What are you at *now*? Haven't you done enough damage? Put those back at once!"

Everyone looked to where Duncan, seated before the great cabinet that had come from San Francisco, was playing with his soldiers. But he had progressed, perhaps from boredom, from the familiar pattern of lining them up in rows and knocking them down. He had removed the two low drawers beneath the glass doors of the cabinet and had stood them on their sides, making a fort for a detachment of his troops. With the contents of the drawers—little boxes, needlework frames, a set of dominoes, a group of small framed cameos—the flotsam of a household—he had constructed outer ramparts to his fort for the storming troops to attack.

"Leave him be, Maria," Andrew said again. "He's doing no harm— he must have *something* to occupy him. If you had any thought you might read to him for a while . . ." Then his own tone changed sharply. "What do you have there, Duncan. Is that one of the dolls? You shouldn't have that."

"I didn't *take* it," Duncan answered sullenly. "It was there—in one of the drawers. I haven't *done* anything to it."

"In one of the drawers? Why was it there?" He turned to Maria. "Why would it be there? The cabinet is always locked. How would it have come there?"

I shifted my gaze painfully over to where she stood, but her features were indistinct.

"It is nothing," she answered sharply. "Nothing—just that I noticed some of the lace was ripped the other day, and took it down to mend it. Something interrupted me, and I just laid it in the drawer. Duncan had no cause to be rummaging in those drawers."

"Well, then, put it back where it was," Andrew said, exasperated. "Then the boy can't be blamed for any damage."

She seemed first to hesitate, and then she moved swiftly, as if to forestall anyone else; I could hear the jingle of the keys as she brought them out, the rattling sound as she struggled to fit the right one to the lock.

A grumbling mutter came from Joanna. "All *our* childhood we were never permitted to handle those dolls . . ."

The doors of the cabinet swung open; Maria reached down for the doll but Duncan was there before her. "Let me put it back, Mama —let me!" He moved eagerly along the crowded rack, seeking the place from which the doll had come. At the end he stopped, puzzled. "Where . . . ?"

"Give it to me, Duncan! Give it to me."

She snatched the doll from him, and attempted to thrust it into line with the others; but there was no place for it—no empty space on the rack which supported all the others. In the dimness, the eyes of everyone in the room strained to see, to watch the frantic effort Maria made to find room for it, to make it stand in line with the others. It kept falling, and in the meantime, Duncan had made a slow inspection of that whole long shelf. The shout of triumph he gave reminded me of Andrew.

"There's a new doll!—a different doll! That's why there's no place—"

Maria cut him off, her cry much more fear than annoyance. "Duncan, leave it to me! Don't touch . . ."

But he had it down off the rack and held up for us all to see. "Look a new doll!" All we could see clearly was a whitish, shapeless thing, and a flame of red. "It's not like the others, though." His tone dropped from excitement to a kind of distaste. "It's ugly."

Andrew leaned forward. "Give it here to me, boy."

Maria made a snatch at it, but Duncan slipped past her, and ran to Andrew. "It's an ugly doll, Papa—not a bit like the other ones."

Andrew sat a long moment staring at the thing that Duncan placed in his hands. "Good Christ!" he said. "A doll of Fiona! A stinking filthy voodoo doll."

There was a terrible silence in the room; even the wind for that time seemed to be still. No one moved or spoke, frozen in their attitudes by the thing that Andrew held. It was I, in the end, who finally made the first movement, spoke the first words.

I lifted my hand in the strongest gesture I was capable of, and flung a hoarse whisper into the stillness.

"Let me see it."

He was wise enough not to thwart me; he heaved himself once more from the sofa, and leaning on Duncan's shoulder, came to the edge of the mattress. All this time Maria stood, still and erect in that way she had, before the gaping doors of the cabinet.

It was Fergus who reached for it, and held it up so that I could see it. By now the others, Alister, Katarina, and Joanna had moved closer, drawn by the horrible fascination of the thing. Fergus held it where it caught the light from the lamp on the floor behind my head.

It was a white thing—a white rag doll, utterly unlike the waxen beauties in the cabinet. This had no shaped features on its round, monstrous head, but they were indicated by crude smears of red—lips, eyes, brows, nostrils. It was, as Duncan had said, ugly—dreadfully ugly, and dressed in a shoddy little garment made from one of the old print dresses I had brought to Landfall and which had fallen apart in the wash, I had been told. So bad all this was, but there was worse. Stitched to its calico head, in a terrible matted tangle, was human hair, bright red hair smeared with some dried substance.

"Fiona! Fiona's hair!" The horrified whisper came from Fergus.

But when I reached up for it he let me have it, perhaps knowing that I needed to see all of it in order to combat it. I put up an unsteady hand to grasp it, to bring it closer to my blurring vision so that I might examine its frightfulness. I touched and felt it.

"Blood," I said. "The red stuff is blood." And as I squeezed the clumsy body, I felt the sharpness prick me through the gown it wore. Then I recognized the pearly heads of the pins that pierced the rag body at about the place where the heart and liver would be in a human; I squeezed the horrible hair, and found pins there also. "Pins from my little pincushion," I said. "The pincushion Mary gave me." I let it drop.

From far back in the room, because she had retreated once again into the shadows, Joanna spoke in a whisper. "They say the spell is more powerful the more of the things they can get that belong to the person who is to die. Fiona's hair—the pins. And setting it in a place where it could look at her . . ."

"Obscenity!" It was Alister's voice. "This is an unthinkable obscenity. Burn it! Burn it at once! To think that *you* people believe these things . . ."

Joanna replied with sullen obstinacy. "I only know what I have seen before. They have spells we don't know anything about—how they work, or why. Fiona will probably die. She is too far gone now—and that thing has looked at her all night and day."

"Die!" There was a fearful howl from Duncan. "No!—No! Fiona can't die!" He was kneeling by the mattress, his arms wrapped frantically about Fergus, his head buried imploringly against him. "You won't let her die, Fergus! She promised she would stay forever."

I brought up my hand to touch him, and he pulled back from Fergus, half-afraid to look at me in case his fear should be realized. "No," I said, "I'm not going to die."

The water around me was terribly cold, but I knew I would not die. I had something yet to do; something that concerned Duncan. My befuddled brain had no precise memory of what I had to do for him, but it had to be done. I knew it because I had once seen it; so I would not die yet. "No," I said to him and to Fergus. "I'm not going to die. It isn't finished yet. I haven't done what I came to do yet."

Fergus leaned closer. "You have something to do, Fiona? You know it?"

"Yes, I saw it—once. I can't remember . . ."

His pressure on my hand was swift. "Quiet then, my love. You will not die."

From behind came Alister's voice, barely restraining his fury. "Can we be rid of it now—this unspeakable thing! Will you burn it *now?*"

"Wait." Andrew grunted as he bent over to pick it up. "Wait. You must be careful how these things are done."

"You surely don't believe in any of this nonsense?"

"I've lived here long enough not to be surprised at anything that comes out of Africa." He faced Alister. "After all, are things so much more civilized in England? Do churchmen still not struggle and pray all night against the devil as if he were an evil shape with horns and a tail? That is all these people have done—they have put horns and a tail on the devil. Do English churchmen still not preach the fire of hell that burns forever, but never consumes? Do they believe in the saving grace of the soul? Well, then, what right have we to deny some power to a belief far stronger than any of us possess? They *believe* that they can kill by the ritual murder of this stupid rag doll. The damage must be undone by the one who created it." He turned to Flora, cowering back in the shadows behind Maria, crouching down, her face buried in her hands.

"Flora—bring up your mother. Quickly!"

She scampered away, bent, as if she were a terrified animal.

"I have to protest," Alister said. "To go along with any of these beliefs is a blasphemy. Burn it, and be done with it."

"And perhaps watch Fiona's life burn up with it!" Fergus cried. "Don't be such a bloody fool! Do it as my father says. He has a lifetime of experience, and a knowledge of these things that you will never have. Leave it to him."

"It's monstrous—monstrous!" Alister protested again.

"Monstrous, I agree," Andrew answered. "And I am dealing with this monstrosity the best way I can. Ah—"

Juanita and Flora had come—Juanita standing silent, defiant, upright before Andrew. Flora's head hung, and she seemed to shiver.

"It was your doing, Juanita, wasn't it? Even though you have been forbidden to practise these things?"

"Mistress bid me," she said flatly.

"I *know* that. And Flora helped by getting Mistress Fiona's hair after Charity had been sent away?"

The older woman did not answer, but from Flora came a wailing cry. "I afraid, master. I afraid not to do as I told. Mistress say she send me someplace far away . . ."

"You'll be more afraid when you know what is going to happen to you now." Andrew raised his hand and pointed at them both, as if uttering judgment. "Burned," he said, his big voice rising to its full force and assuming a quality of power one seldom heard there now. "Burned, as you would finally have burned this doll. But before that happens I will myself drive a nail through your heart like the pins in the doll—"

Alister broke in. "For God's sake, stop this at once! You make matters worse by going along with the pagan beliefs of these people. Just get rid of that *unspeakable* thing. Get rid of it!"

"My son has said it. Be quiet, my friend, and don't meddle with what you don't understand. Juanita will die instead of Fiona—and Flora along with her, so that the gods will have two instead of the one promised them. It will be a much worse death than that Mistress Fiona would have died, I promise you that, Juanita."

From Flora the wailing became louder; Juanita still remained silent, eyes blazing with hatred and contempt, but not fear.

"Or . . ." Andrew went on. "Or there is another way, and perhaps I will be merciful. Perhaps I will not even send you to the judges at Santa Marta, who would certainly hang you. Perhaps all will yet live. But the spell must be removed."

Juanita stood for some moments longer, her arms folded, as if she thought carefully about her final submission to the white man. Then she turned and went close to Maria, and deliberately spat at her feet.

"I die for no white woman," she said. "I take away *this* spell, but the old one, the curse put on Landfall long ago by black woman, that still stay. The one who did it is gone, and never will the spell go. So you rot here forever." Then she came back to the mattress, reaching for the doll. Instinctively I shrank back from her closeness, and she looked at me with venom.

"You tell Flora your magic greater than ours, but now you know it not the truth. If doll not been found, when I should have placed more pins at the right time, you die for sure."

"Enough of that," Andrew ordered. "Now begin."

Juanita squatted down on the floor, the doll lying before her. Then she began a strange chant in her own language; it began and then broke. She looked up at Andrew. "No good," she said. "Must be done at the middle of night, when the moon will shine."

"The gods sent the great wind because you had done wrong. There will be no moon—no middle of the night. Now get on!"

She began again, the weird chant; on and on it went, like the shriek of the wind itself. Then she broke off, and the lower pin was removed. The chant started again, sonorous, rising and falling. Another pause, and the second pin, the one in the place of the heart was removed. In the same way, three pins came from the head. I wanted to turn away, to see no more of it, but I couldn't, as none could, not even Alister. She clicked her thin black fingers, and at once Flora produced the little scissors that I had brandished in her face. With great care then, totally absorbed, Juanita began to remove the rough stitches that held the strands of my hair to the body. That done, she removed with extreme care every stitch which bound together the crudely sewn body of the doll. The stuffing flowed out, as if it were my own life blood; tiny, cut-up ribbons of cloth from all the garments that I had had to discard since coming to Landfall. It all lay there in the end, an indistinguishable mass, a conglomerate of me, Fiona, shredded.

The black eyes looked at Andrew. "Now it be sent to the wind."

"Then do so."

She gathered up the heap, and I saw everyone, except Maria and Alister, move to the hall where they could watch her go to the door that was partly open and secured on the hook. It must have been Fergus who held it open; I heard him say something to Juanita. There was a moment of that strange chanting again, and then they all returned, all except Juanita and Flora, whom Andrew ordered back to the cellar.

"An abomination!" Alister said. "I never witnessed anything so barbaric in my life. To think that you subscribe to these beliefs! . . . To think you let a child stand here and watch them. You must be mad!"

"So would you be mad, or respectful, in the same way if you lived here long enough. And as for barbaric—is there not still a law in England against witchcraft? If it does not exist, why is there a law against it?" Andrew collapsed back into his sofa. "I meant Duncan to witness this. *He* will have to live with it. Better let him know how to deal with it. What matters is that the corrective be carried out according to the manner *they* believe in. Our tendency is to deal with everything our way. It doesn't always have the desired effect. But I think we may now expect Fiona to get well."

"It was a fever," I croaked. "That's all. A fever. It broke and I got cold. But I am getting warmer now. It was the wind . . ."

"It was anything you care to call it. But it was when you got cold that I feared you were going. It is not the normal course of fevers here. But I will not try to convince you. Believe as you wish. Dougal, where is the jug!"

The jug was brought and placed beside him. He looked around the room, surveying all of us, once more in command. He seemed to brood for a while, then he pointed at Duncan.

"Time for you to rest, my son. Dougal will go up on the landing with you—lie down there."

Duncan had to make his usual protest. "But it is not yet time. We have not had lunch. It is not siesta."

"The clock does not matter while the wind blows, Duncan. In a little time the wind will be down, and we will need your strength to help clear up like the strength of a grown man. So go and rest, and be ready for it."

Reluctantly Duncan turned toward Dougal, but again Andrew called him. "Come here, my son." Duncan went to his side, and Andrew leaned forward and with a rare gesture of affection he kissed the frown on that young brow. "Be at peace, my son. Remember this old man cares for your welfare."

I glimpsed Duncan's face as he went off. It shone with a kind of joy I had never seen there before. Andrew had provided in that single gesture the antidote to the horror the boy had witnessed, the reassurance that the world would soon assume its proper rhythm; he had even given him the gift least bestowed by Andrew, the evidence of love. In that moment I forgave Andrew many things.

"Well, my wife," he said at last, when Duncan and Dougal had gone. "Well, it was an attempt. You could no longer wait for the old man to die, because Fiona would have had Fergus before that would happen. To try to kill me with too much speed would have been too obvious. I know as much as you about the poisons and their spells. So it had to be Fiona."

Maria had taken her usual seat, her face quite unchanging as Andrew spoke, her eyes half-shut as if she must endure with patience the ramblings of an old drunken man. "Your talk is foolish, Andrew. You know that Juanita has lied. You know I have no belief—"

He thumped the arm of the sofa. "By God, you *do* believe, and would practise it yourself if you could! And you still lust after him— you lust after my son, Fergus, and you cannot bear the thought that he will marry and be beyond your reach when this sick old man finally dies."

"Would I then have married you—not him? I *could* have married him."

A grim smile played across Andrew's features, the acknowledgment of some pyrrhic victory gained. "Yes, indeed you could have married him, and known a life not much better than you had had at San Francisco. You knew that Winterslo was all that was really promised him, and there was always the chance that with him married to you, and you both at Winterslo, I myself might finally have taken a wife, and Landfall would be lost to both of you. Even then, your greed was stronger than your lust. But you didn't think it would take so long, did you? I wasn't so old—I'm not so old now—but you thought I had less in me, and that both Landfall and Fergus would be yours much sooner. It has been my only pleasure, these last years, to live on in spite of you."

"If you knew all this, why then *did* you marry me? I had no way to compel you."

"Only the time honored way. And I was fool enough to honor it. Mistresses I had had, but never had I taken a woman from my son, nor believed, in my madness, that she actually preferred me. Ah, what a fool I was then, and what a woman in bed you were, my wife. My madness is hardly to be wondered at. You made me feel like a boy again, and I was a man past my middle-years. I had laughed at such foolishness in other men, and didn't know it in myself . . ." Abruptly he jerked his head around. "No"—pointing at Katarina and Joanna—"no, don't you start creeping away as if all this earthy talk was too much for your maidenly ears. You are the same clay as she, and, for all I know, you knew as well as she did what was schemed. It probably all came from the old she-devil at San Francisco. After all, with me and a child, Maria could secure Landfall. With my son, Fergus, not legitimate, who knew what might happen? Who could say what Maxwell might not come forward to dispute his claim—"

"Stop!" It was a cry of anguish from Fergus. "Must you go all through this again—and now, before Fiona? Haven't we all lived in our own hells because of this business? What good does it do to rake it all over again. We all make our mistakes—"

"Mistakes we made. You are right, Fergus. And regretted them—day after bitter day. Most of all, myself. Most of all, myself. I don't want to dwell on the evil and greed she was capable of—my own are enough. But it is one thing to be greedy and ambitious—are any of us free of these kinds of things? Attempting to murder is something else. *That* is what I speak of now, and before Fiona, who nearly was the victim."

Alister broke in: "But Fiona does not believe in such things! It was, as she says, a fever, which now has broken."

"But those who made the attempt *did* believe. That makes them guilty. That girl was coming close to death, and you know it. Look at the change in her since that accursed thing was done away with! Look at the color come back to her face. Whether you believe it or not, it almost happened. It was attempted—and by my wife. Shall we pass it over as if it had never been? It is not possible, and well you know it."

"But I deny your accusations," Maria said quietly. "I deny them. You have only the word of an ignorant, frightened old slave, seeking to save her own skin, as a charge against me. You know that is not admissible in law. How can you say Fiona has not angered Juanita in some way that earned her hate? How can you *prove* all that you say?"

"Didn't you send Charity away—without a word to anyone, to replace her with that skinny wretch who was too frightened to do anything but what you and her mother bade her? Was Charity Fiona's protection? Was that why you got rid of her?"

"I have sold other slaves off this estate. You have left all that in my hand these past five years. Why should this prove anything? You make some nonsense in your head, Andrew. You are older than I thought and," she added cruelly, "sicker. You should have a care about what you say."

"No house slave ever left Landfall before Charity. And when did she leave? The very day you knew you would finally lose Fergus. The day you knew that very soon he would marry Fiona, and be lost to you, no matter how quickly after that I died. And, my wife—this most of all—who but you has the key to the cabinet? Who but you has ever put a hand inside it since you brought it to Landfall? Haven't I seen you a hundred times dust the whole contents yourself, not trusting anyone else to handle those things you treasure so? And who but you, Maria, my clever, capable wife, would have taken time and thought yesterday morning, in the midst of all our preparations, to place the voodoo doll where it would be most likely to be within sight of Fiona and yet unnoticed. Oh, no, this is not the work of an ignorant slave, as you call her."

She shrugged. "Say what you please. I may carry my keys at most times, but they are not forever in my hands. Juanita comes and goes in my room at all times. It is too easy to borrow a key—it is Juanita you should be asking all this of, not me. And," she added, "if I am guilty of attempting such things as you charge, why did I not tell Juanita to work her spells against you, Andrew?" The tone was deadly quiet, difficult to hear against the wind that still thrust against the house. "After all, you are already unwell. Easier—far easier to kill you than a strong young woman."

Now he pointed a gloating finger at her. "Because I watched you, Maria, when Fergus and Fiona came that morning and told us they would be married. You were shaken as I had never seen you before. For the first time you were not absolutely sure that Fergus would choose you, once you were free. If I had dropped dead at your feet at that moment, you couldn't have been sure that he wouldn't still have wanted Fiona above what you could offer him. It was a different Fergus you saw that morning, wasn't it, Maria? A man liberated—happy. You were frightened. You had to hurry. And so it had to be Fiona, not your husband."

"You still make nonsense. Fergus and I have quarreled for years. If I have desired him, as you say, why did I not cause your death long ago?"

"And for how long has quarreling not been used to mask desire? You quarreled with Fergus for his visits to Santa Marta, his lack of attendance on you. And for the rest of it—patience and fear. You know how to wait for what you want, I'll give you that. Just feed your husband enough rum and Indian hemp and his spirit will give up in time. And fear—one does not place oneself in the hands of a witch like Juanita without good reason. Even *you* were afraid of that. You could wait, just so long as Fergus continued his fooling about with the ladies of Santa Marta. You didn't even worry about the proposals to invite Mary Maxwell to be Duncan's governess. You knew Fergus. He likes— forgive me, Fiona—stronger stuff than the descriptions of the kind of girl Mary Maxwell seemed to be, even if she were pretty as sugar icing. If Mary Maxwell had come there was every chance that Fergus would have taken no more notice of her than a schoolgirl, which is hardly less than she is. But instead Fiona came, and with her your trouble."

Again she shrugged as if growing weary of the whole tiresome discussion. "Conjecture, Andrew—all of it conjecture. You have no proof. Nothing real that you can charge me with. No court will accept the evidence of a slave, or of ritual murder. Even the stupid rag doll does not now exist. *You* saw to that!"

He took a long, thoughtful drink from his rum. "Who said anything about charges? I'm too well aware that no court would entertain any such thing I cared to say about you, and I've no reason to give this island a scandal that would surpass anything they've had to gossip about since I provided the last great topic for them. No—it will not pass beyond this room. But there's a law that runs between man and wife— a natural justice that has nothing to do with courts or judgments. It is here that *I* am judge. I still live. I still have the strength to carry out what punishment I deem fit."

"What?" Maria's tone was fainter. "What?"

"I still live, Maria. I still may dispose of my possessions. I still may order what is to happen after I die."

"And what will happen?"

"Fergus shall have Landfall, as it should have been right from the beginning. I shall disown you—a pittance only, so that you have no complaint before the courts. You will not dare to contest because too many witnesses now sit in this room to hear what I am saying."

"And so to have vengeance on me for some imagined crime you will disinherit your own son?"

"Duncan? *Is* he my son, Maria?—or is he Fergus's son?" The wild, drunken laughter rang out, the laughter of hurt and loneliness, the laughter of ugly triumph after the years of sitting on that red sofa brooding on age and impotence.

"Neither son will be dispossessed. Fergus will inherit jointly with Duncan, and be trustee for him until he comes of age. I will indicate that I then leave it to my son, Fergus, to see to a just distribution of whatever the joint estates of Landfall and Winterslo can command. And if he *is* Fergus's son, not his half-brother—or whichever it be—I think I may safely leave a natural justice to work itself out. It has a way of doing so."

"And me?"

"Why, my widow will, of course, be entitled to remain on at her home. Though Landfall will have a new mistress. Will you like living under Fiona's direction, Maria? I fancy not, my wife. I think you will return to San Francisco—moldering there, like your wretched sisters. Eight years older than you left it, and the lines beginning to come in your perfect face, and a reputation earned across the length and breadth of San Cristóbal as a hard woman. What man will come riding to San Francisco to court a widow without an inheritance? Not a woman such as you, Maria—not from such a family."

At this came a shriek, almost more tortured than the wind, from Katarina—or Joanna—who could tell? It was Katarina who spoke,

"No!" she said. "No—it cannot be! It must not be! We have not worked all these years—"

"Katarina, be quiet! I order you!"

"Order me!" Katarina flashed back at her sister. "You order me. How can you dare—*now!* I—" And then her words choked back; she seemed to strangle on them. Her hand flew to her mouth as if to stifle a new sound of fear. We all turned to look to the doorway to the hall, where she stared. I half-raised myself on the pillows to see.

He stood with water still streaming from the wretched rags of his clothes. As I grew used to the sight of him I could see more, the pink streaks growing redder of blood that began staining the soaked shirt, the blood that trickled from his thick mat of hair, the cut over the eye that had closed it, and gave him an oddly maniacal appearance.

"I have come, master," Samuel said.

He must have found and let himself in at the storm shutter that was still on its hook; Samuel would know the preparations for hurricanes at Landfall as well as Andrew. He had come home, and had known how to make his entrance.

Andrew grunted, but it was Maria who sprang to her feet. "So—you have come back! There was no way to escape, after all, as I have always told you. So you have taken your beating out there in the storm, and come crawling back like a dog. Well, you have been punished, and will be punished further."

There was a long, painful smile twisting those thick lips. He balanced himself lightly on the soles of those bloody feet, uncaring, defiant.

"I will be more than punished, mistress. I will die. I know what happens to slaves who disobey. But I have brought back Charity and my son with me—and I ask the master, while he still is master, to spare them."

"Charity . . . ?" Maria took a few paces toward Samuel. "You will say nothing about Charity. She is my concern. You have done wrong, but you will be spared. Now go down below, with the rest."

But still he stood there, rocking back and forth, soles to heels, defiant still. "No good, mistress. No more bargains that you do not keep. You have promised me that one day there would be freedom for me if I did as you say, but when you send Charity away I know that promise never be kept. Some of my people, coming over on the slave ships, jump to the sharks rather than go on in their chains. It would have been better, I think, if my father had done that thing. But I am here, and I have disobeyed you. I know the punishment. I know what I know about the mistress. I have come only to ask that the master will spare Charity and my son—because there is talk that soon freedom will come here in these islands, and I want them here so that they have it."

"What are you talking about?" Andrew demanded. "Doesn't make sense. Charity would have had her freedom like everyone else on this island if such a foolish measure should come to pass—which it will not!"

Fergus had left my side, and was standing beside Samuel, shaking that huge shoulder, and I saw, sickeningly, that his own hands became reddened. "What does it mean, Samuel? *Where* did you find Charity and your son?"

The massive black head turned to Fergus, and even he seemed smaller. "You don't know that, Master Fergus? I always wonder . . . though I never see you there those nights the ships come. I always wonder how much help this little woman has—whether you help her. The men who come, those I do not know. I think maybe you . . ."

He looked at Andrew. "Master does not know? He not know what his woman is about? He let her roam the country at night, and dress like a man, and he not know. But I tell myself that even if master know about San Francisco, he not know that Charity and my son sent there. He would never let them go like that, I think. So I bring them back, and I ask him to protect them. Jus' keep them at Landfall, master. We have lived through the great wind, Charity, he and myself. It is a sign of life for them."

Andrew waved his hand. "Never mind that. Where did you find Charity?"

"At San Francisco, where I think they be."

"San Francisco? Why?"

"Master not know?" A mocking, wholly knowledgeable smile twisted Samuel's lips again. "I think I give the master old news. He must know all these things."

"I'll tell you when to stop answering my questions, Goddammit."

Samuel made a slight shrug. "I go to San Francisco because that is where the mistress gather slaves from other islands and from the ships that come from Africa. She sell them—to America. Ships come. Small ships from other island. Big ships from Africa. This not the only stopping place for the ships from Africa. Too many come for such a place. She gather the slaves to wait for the ships that come from America. In America, they say, there is no talk of slaves being free. Still pay good prices for slaves. I know it against the law for British to carry slaves from Africa, but still they come, master. She gather slaves at San Francisco, master. Once a ship in that bay, no ship passing see it. Safe from the Serpents, and no one see who come or go. Sometimes ships stop at night there, leave slaves, and next morning in Santa

Marta with ordinary cargo. No one ask questions. But I speak old things, master—you know this."

"Go on!" It was neither Andrew nor Fergus who spoke, but Alister. He limped toward Samuel, and now the two white men confronted the slave. In an odd way, Samuel still seemed to dominate.

"You want to know, master? Well, they all say you own Landfall, even if you don't say so yourself."

"Never mind that. Just tell me."

"They come in and go out at San Francisco bay. But between the times the ships come, the slaves are locked in the old dungeons at San Francisco—the ones away from the greathouse. I know about it for years, master, because, mistress, she say if I help her, one day she let me be free. So I do it—what it to me? Just more black men, same as me. Going to other masters. Once this side of the ocean, they never get back, so what difference it make to me whether they stay here or go someplace else. They go to America. Perhaps America different. Perhaps things better there. I not know. I jus' do what mistress tell me, because she favor me, and because of that Charity and my son get favors also. You would do the same, master. But now with the talk of freedom, I not want them sent to America . . ."

"All right—*all right!*" Alister had had enough; he turned from that bloody figure and paced the length of the room, hands behind his back in that characteristic attitude. I looked at Samuel again, and began to wonder, then, how those three had lived through yesterday and the night and the passage of this long day without shelter. Even now, with the wind and rain still slashing, they had made their way back to the only shelter they had ever known, to Landfall. Samuel had probably carried his son, and supported Charity, but still had fought his way here, willing to offer himself as victim, but to find respite, and perhaps, if the predictions were true, freedom in the end for the two he cared about. And yet we called these people uncivilized.

"Punished you will be," Maria said in a low tone. "And just to make you know what you have done, Charity and your son will suffer along with you."

Andrew turned upon her. "Quiet—be quiet! Have you forgotten what has happened this day? Have you forgotten what will be your position in the future?"

But Samuel did not know what had happened this day; he still addressed himself to Maria. "Better they suffer pain than they drown, mistress."

"What?" Alister spun around. Samuel looked between them all, Andrew, Maria, and Alister, in confusion. In the end he spoke to Alister.

"Master I went to San Francisco with you because I not believe what the mistress say about Charity and my son being sold to a man on the other side of the island. It happen too quickly. She decide too quickly. No house slaves ever sold from Landfall. I think she need Charity away from Mistress Fiona, so she send her to wait with the other slaves for the next ship that come from America. I know the place where the slaves are locked until the ship come. It the dungeon of a very old place that have no top left to it any more—only the floor of the old rooms to hold them in. But that floor is stone, master. And the place is right there beside the ghut where the water streams down from Kronberg. In the hurricane that become a great river. It rise and rise—I know it. All inside that place will drown. They will drown in their chains, master."

"What did you do, Samuel, when you left me?"

"You remember, master, that I took the great ax from the sugar factory with me when I go with you? I say it in case any trees fall across our path with the cart and the donkey. Well, when I know the old lady not go with you, I know you could walk if trees come down on the way back. So I leave you and go to the place where the slaves are. I chop and chop—it the only good piece of wood left at San Francisco because the mistress herself see to it being made new and strong. And all the time the water rising. It come about my feet already as I chop at the door. But then I am through at last, and the slaves come out. But they in chains, master. Cannot move through the hurricane in chains. One fall—all fall. In chains they have no chance. So I have to chop at the chains, and the ax break. Then I have to search through all the old things at San Francisco. I find the great hammer in the blacksmith's place. I hurt many of the slaves breaking the chains—they all so close together. But at last all of them done, and free. I say I can do no more. They must shelter for themselves. For Charity and my son and myself I find a place in the stables where it not too bad, if the roof stay on. Water come in to the stables all night, but walls hold up, and the roof, where we are. When the wind die a bit I decide to bring Charity and my son back here to Landfall. For me—I know I die. But they do no wrong. They would have drown, master. I think perhaps Master Fergus"—but more hopefully he looked toward Alister—"might give mistress the money she

would have for them. And then they stay. That is what I have come
to say."

Behind him now appeared Charity and the boy; I remembered that
I had seen him about the house; he was being trained for inside duties.
They both were cut much as Samuel was, by the slashing of the trees
as they had come through the forest, by the falls they had taken; they
looked exhausted and beaten, as if the stables had been but little shelter from the storm; they must have been famished, too, I thought. Barefooted they stood there, and around the ankle of each was the manacle,
with its short length of chain dangling; there were deep gashes in the
skin around the manacle, and the boy balanced himself on one foot,
as if he could not put the other to the floor.

"I come back, master," Charity spoke to Andrew. "We have lived
through the storm, and you not send us away again!" It was more a
statement than a plea, as if their escape and return to Landfall was
a miracle that no one could deny.

But Andrew grunted and made no direct reply. "Go below now, and
feed yourselves, and bathe those cuts. See to the boy, Charity—his
ankle looks bad."

She had her arm protectively about her son, but now her gaze was
upon me. "Mistress Fiona need me? She sick?"

"She's better again," Fergus said. "Now do as my father says. There
is plenty of food. Eat and rest. We will need you all when it is safe
to go out again."

The three began to turn away. "One moment!" Maria's voice stopped
them. "San Francisco? Donna Isabella?"

Samuel turned back reluctantly, as if he wished she had not asked.
"I don't know, mistress. Roof gone from greathouse. The rain pour in.
Some shutters banging open. It stood many winds, that ole house, but
this the last."

"Donna Isabella?"

"I don't know, mistress. Before I leave I go and I call. Some of the
roof fallen in upon the place—some fly with the wind. The wind still
great and maybe she in the cellars and not hear. They say there are
places in San Francisco that no one know about. Perhaps she gone
in one of those places . . . I not see her."

"Liar! You didn't even look! Donna Isabella is not one to hide in the
cellars. She would have stayed where you left her."

"The wind blew through that place, mistress. Everything torn about.
Soaked with rain. How can I tell where she be?"

With a wave of her hand Maria dismissed him finally, and the three limped out into the darkness of the hall again. From Joanna came a soft whimper, not a sound of grief, but of fear.

"The slaves are loose! They will have found her. She is dead, and Samuel did not have the courage to admit it. The place is torn about—the roof gone." The tone rose to a wail. "She's dead! We all will be dead with those savages roaming free. San Francisco's gone. It is an end—an end!"

"Be quiet!" Maria ordered. "You make me sick with your endless moaning. You tremble for your own miserable skin when it is our mother you should mourn. Those slaves will have broken in. She will have been killed, and the house plundered for food and rum and anything else they fancy."

"And your doing, my wife. So it's been illegal slave-running that's occupied your spare time and thoughts these last years, has it? It has been that which has taken you from this house at night when you thought I was sleeping. I've watched you go, and thought—God and Fergus forgive me—that it was to him you sneaked away. Well, you have done what you did alone, and you have brought this, and possibly your mother's death, upon your own head. What *are* the penalties for importing and exporting slaves illegally, Alister? You know all that kind of thing . . ."

Alister gave a shrug of deep disgust. "Why didn't you inquire about that before you let your wife carry on with her activities?"

"Dear Cousin, I didn't *know*. What have I to do with San Francisco? She comes and she goes as she pleases, my wife, and no one can say her nay."

"And yet you've just confessed that you knew she went somewhere—and believed it was to the arms of your own son? What kind of rottenness is this? Believing that of Fergus, you still could push Fiona at him—or Mary Maxwell, or whoever had come to Landfall?"

"Yes, whoever had come. I made my wife write for Mary Maxwell because your father, Jeremy, put forward her name in a letter. But I had little hope about the kind of girl he described. When I saw Fiona, though, I knew at once that she would be the instrument of my vengeance against this scheming little wretch I married. Yes, I thrust Fiona at Fergus, just to see my wife burn in a torment of jealousy and rage. It was the old man's last joke."

"Filthy! And I don't believe it," Alister said. "I just don't believe that Andrew Maxwell—the Andrew Maxwell who once was, didn't know what his wife was about. Or that you made no effort to intervene if you believed that your son and your wife were lovers? Not even *you* could care so little! If the details of this come out—and with illegal slaves who belong to no one loose on the island it is bound to be known—will you stand up in court and say you didn't know what your wife was about? What court will believe that of Andrew Maxwell? That he couldn't keep his own wife under control? They will laugh. You would make me laugh now—except that you make me sick! This whole stinking business makes me sick. Whether you knew the details or not, you knew she was up to something more complex than arranging lover's illicit meetings. What was it—you just took the profits and never asked where they came from? You *never* asked where the extra money came from, the money that was never entered in any of the ledgers? I'm not the only one who will not believe you, Andrew Maxwell!"

Andrew reached for the jug of rum, and in pouring it, it clattered noisily against the glass, some spilling about him, onto the sofa, and down his shirt front. It made me aware that the wind was dying steadily, and that my senses were growing sharper. I struggled to get another pillow under me, to raise my head, but Fergus's hand was there before me. I looked at him fully in those moments of silence. In his face was an expression I had never seen there before—tenderness, despair, hurt—a kind of a plea for understanding, and for forgiveness of the sort of world that was being unfolded before my eyes. I knew then what was the truth—a truth I had made myself believe, and yet until now had not truly believed. That he had possessed Maria only once—long ago. I had been prepared to take the half-truth from him, because I was mad with a passion for him as great as Maria's must have been. And yet his look at me was a gift of the whole truth. I could rest, and there would be no more doubting. His hand stroked my cheek gently.

"Profit—" Andrew waved his glass. "Profit, you say? I knew of no profit! Don't try to pin *that* on me. The Maxwells were repaid their debt, weren't they?—and a profit commensurate with their investment? Once that was done what came and went at Landfall was my business alone." Then he put down the glass. "No—that's not really how it was. The debt was out of the way, and I was married to Maria. After that, the money that came and went from Landfall was no longer my business. I didn't care to make it so. *She* managed, and I let her. As for not caring . . . you're quite right, my cousin. I haven't cared a damn what she has done almost since the day I married her. Not since the time when I finally saw past that look of innocence, and knew to what sort of woman I had given my name and what little remained of my honor. Yes, you're right. I don't care a damn!"

There was a terrible finality about it. It was true; he simply didn't care. No one could really touch this man, behind his rum and the fumes of the hemp. No one could imagine him being made to answer for anything from that place on the red sofa.

"You realize," Alister said, "that when the news gets about the island that the loose slaves were held at San Francisco, and shipped from there, you will be held responsible. After all—you are Maria's husband."

Andrew waved his hand contemptuously. "Let them try! See how far they get! Let us first see how many others were involved, and who will first make the charge. If my wife has been shipping slaves from this island, there were many others besides herself who were involved. If you delved you'd find, I have no doubt, some very influential names connected with this affair. No one person—a woman—could organize and capitalize such a scheme. Oh, I don't at all put it past her to have thought of it all—and the use of San Francisco was perfect. She must have been dipping into the Landfall money to put up her share. But I would wager you anything I have that there will be no inquiry. These things have a way of being hushed up. Everyone knows, and no one says anything. If there was trouble, no one would come forward to stand as Maria's protector—but then I doubt anyone will come forward to accuse her either. Self-protection, my dear cousin. We all have made our mistakes."

Alister turned to Maria. "There *were* others involved, I suppose? And the American captains came gladly, knowing that those they got here had survived the Atlantic crossing and were rested and fed up before being put on the block, or else they were slaves from other islands— healthy, strong, used to the kind of work expected of them. After all, *you* took the risk of those who died on the way—the Americans just took those who survived. They pay premiums for that kind, and are spared the expense of the whole voyage to the Gold Coast and back, and the risks that go with it. It was a nice trade for you, Maria—profitable and well organized. You could not have done it by yourself."

She shrugged. "I will admit nothing. Do what you like."

"You don't admit knowledge of the voodoo doll, either. And can you deny the manacles on Charity's ankle? Come, don't try to make a fool of me! It was profitable, and you hid the profits somewhere. You took what could be stolen from Landfall and put it into this venture, didn't you? Where are those profits, Maria?—buried under the sands somewhere down there in one of the bays? Or in one of those places Samuel says no one but Donna Isabella knows of at San Francisco?"

"Profits? You are mad!" Maria's tone woke to fury. "Do you think this miserable plantation runs itself? What do you suppose has happened to the price of sugar in these last years since the British monopoly was ended? Everything I have put back into Landfall, and you, Alister Maxwell, so pious and full of feeling for the lot of the slaves, you have had your share—"

"My share! I've never shared—"

"You have! What did you think paid you the return on the capital you Maxwells invested here. Just because it appeared as nice clean money in a London bank doesn't mean it wasn't earned out of this soil. I have paid you your money. Nothing but me and my efforts have given you your profits, and yet you come out here and rant to me about the emancipation of the slaves that have added sugar to your bank accounts! No less than any of us you are guilty. There *is* no gold buried under the sands of any of these bays—there is nothing but what you see about you. There is Landfall, and its possessions, including the slaves, and there is a ruined crop outside our doors at this moment. Make what you like of it. It is all there is!"

Alister shook his head. "If that is all there is—then you *have* run the plantation as badly as the books say." He looked at Andrew. "There's nothing here in assets, and despite all the inquiries I've made on the authority of being a shareholder in Landfall, can I find anything in any of the banks in Santa Marta. The estate is living hand-to-mouth, and there's no capital anywhere I can discover. Your wife is either a very poor manager, or an extremely clever embezzler."

Andrew just laughed. "Well, that will be *your* problem, Alister. Yours, and Fergus's. I won't be here to worry about it. I told you I don't give a damn any more. I've worked all my life for nothing, it seems. When everything should have been bringing its reward to me, it all suddenly tasted sour. Nothing has been worth the struggle. But I'll not stand up to defend myself in any court, or try to untangle this mess, because I'll not last this six-month, and we all know it. You're going to be left to fight it out alone. You'll not harvest a crop after this storm for at least eighteen months. If there is nothing here, as you say, Landfall will be done for by then. There'll be nothing . . . nothing. But I won't be here to see it, and I don't care."

"But I *do* care." The note of hysteria in Katarina's voice was ominous. "*I* care. My sister, what have you done with it? Ever since you came to Landfall you promised that one day there should be ease and plenty. You were putting everything back into Landfall—the profits from the slaves—everything. And when the old man was dead we should come to live here. Where is the money now? What have we worked for, Joanna and I? We have worked for you, kept our wretched mother alive, fed your stinking slaves in their hole, and every night trembled for our lives lest they break loose and murder us in our beds! And for what? For nothing!—this Alister says there is nothing!"

"I kept you alive, didn't I?" Maria answered. "You ate. You wore clothes. You kept what little there was left of San Francisco. I could do no more. Alister is right. There *is* nothing else."

"But *this*—Landfall—was to be everything! And now your husband is dispossessing you. And why?—because you still were greedy for the son of the man you married. And Fergus—he now gives his love to another woman, and you try to kill her. So—you have been no cleverer or wiser than we." Her face was glistening—with sweat or tears of frustration. "You!—for whom the last good things at San Francisco were sold, for whom more acres were mortgaged and lost so that you could have your two years in Madrid and capture a rich husband. Well, you were not clever enough for that, but you made us believe you had achieved something almost as good. But now, you, the clever, the beautiful Maria, the favored of our mother—you end up no better than we. And not even San Francisco still stands. Its roof is open to the skies. Will you stay here on the charity of Fergus's wife, or will you come back to share our existence? Will we, my sister, spend the rest of our lives together huddled like animals in our own stables? Is that the future you promised us?"

Maria shrugged, as if weary of it all. "You talk too much—you fear too much. The future will be what it is. There is no money—I have either managed badly, as Alister says, or this plantation costs more than anyone realizes. Have it whichever way you wish. The crops are ruined, and the coffers are empty. Fergus will take anything that is left. Now cry about it if you wish, for all the good it will do, but leave me in peace."

"Peace, is it?" It was a cry of outrage from Fergus. "Peace, she says! What peace have you given anyone these last eight years? What have you ever brought to this house but shame and rottenness? When you came it was thriving, even if it had yet to taste happiness. Now you leave it bankrupted . . ."

I made a gesture with my hand to stop them talking, to try to gather strength to say what I must; but no one took any notice. Fergus's hand was still on me, but he was looking at Maria, as was everyone else. She sat in her chair with a kind of regal stillness, an unassailable strength in her that could not be beaten down with words or threats or any stirring of regret in her own heart. One knew, looking at her, that she would accept good fortune or misery, even death, in exactly the same way. In that slight, beautiful form, for the first time, I saw the stoic determination and patience of Donna Isabella. Maria also was capable of sitting out a hurricane in solitude.

"I will go away," she said. "I will bother no one. There will be no one brought to court. There will be no scandal. You can say I have gone to Spain . . . Duncan I leave to you, Andrew—or to you, Fergus. In either case, he will be with his father."

"And us?" Katarina screamed. "What of us?"

"You?—you and Joanna will manage for yourselves, as best you might all these years if I had not kept you going from whatever Landfall could spare. Learn to work—learn to work as I will have to. But I will not do it at San Francisco. I will never go back to San Francisco except to bury my mother."

"Very impressive, Maria," Alister said. "But I don't believe you. What will you do? How will you live?"

A sudden fire came into her coolness. "Why should you trouble about that? I am not yet old—nor undesirable. There are ways a woman can live, if she must. It shall not, however, be done on San Cristóbal. I have some respect for my mother's memory and name. You, yourself, Alister, may escort me to the first ship that's fit to leave Santa Marta harbor, bound for no matter where. And I tell you there will be no chests of gold dug up from the sands to go with me. And you may spend the rest of your life setting spies to find moneys deposited with some bank, somewhere, and you will find none. Because there is none. You will see. I ask just for enough money to leave. After that . . ." She shrugged, and then paused. "So how does that seem to you, my husband, as an alternative to the fate you planned for me—living here under the rule of a Scottish governess, or grubbing out an existence at San Francisco like my two spiritless, witless sisters. Oh, no—

that is not for me! I still shall wear silk, and who knows, perhaps some day I shall at last wear diamonds . . ."

It was then my plucking hand finally caught at Fergus's sleeve.

"Diamonds . . ." I said.

He bent lower. "Diamonds," I repeated, trying to make my voice heard by them all. "What about the diamonds?"

By now the magic of the word had captured them; they all were looking and straining to hear.

"It's nothing, Fiona. Just Maria dreaming her dreams. No one must ever be sorry for Maria—don't you know that? She has no pity and she cannot accept it from anyone else. The talk of diamonds is a dream."

"It was no dream. I know it now!" My anger made me stronger. She was going; she was going and leaving her son, leaving behind a dying husband and a house, a plantation wrecked, her sisters sniveling with fear and hatred at the knowledge that they must fend for themselves.

"They *were* diamonds I saw. Jewels . . . A great fire of jewels!"

"Jewels?—where?" Katarina demanded. It was the first time she had spoken directly to me since she had come to Landfall. Then she looked at Maria. "Jewels!" Her tone rose with excitement.

I struggled to raise myself higher, and Fergus thrust another pillow behind me. I was much stronger; the ache and weakness had almost left my bones. I was sweating again, but it was the usual sweat of the tropics, not of fever.

"I thought I saw once . . ." My burst of courage and confidence was quickly running out. "Once, as I entered the salon I thought I saw Maria—" Then I shook my head. "Oh, no. It does not matter. It could not have been, because when she turned from the mirror . . ." I lay back against the pillows. I could not make myself speak. I could not reveal to them all, to their scorn and their fear and their questionings that second part of my life that I tried to keep hidden from everyone. I could not speak the vision, that I had believed to be some reconstruction of the past, and reveal it as a fantasy. "It is nothing," I said faintly. "Just something I thought I saw, but I was mistaken. Because when she turned she wore no jewels."

"Go on," Alister urged me.

I turned my head stubbornly away. "I have said all I saw. It was a mistake—some trick of the chandelier prisms reflected in the mirror. It was nothing—I tell you, it was nothing!"

A thin, tired tone came from Andrew. "Listen to her . . . Listen to her! She sees—and senses. Some of the Scots have that sight. Some see what is not there, but hidden . . ." His voice faded, as if the effort was too much.

"Jewels?" Alister had caught at the thought, but I felt Fergus's hand press mine more closely, and I knew he was remembering the day that I had checked my horse at the place where his grandfather had died. It was the thing I had not wanted, to puzzle, frighten, bewilder. I had not wanted to set myself apart. Better that she should have gone with all she could lay hands on than that I should have to live the rest of my life here having given this knowledge of me into their keeping. Never afterward would I live as a normal, ordinary woman in the sight of any of them here in this room.

"Jewels!" Alister nodded, as if something was coming clear to him. He looked at Maria. "Of course you were willing to leave by the first ship and without any chests of gold. The gold has already been translated into something much more portable, easier to hide, and with no tiresome banks to give up your secret. Clever of you, Maria. Even if I had set someone to follow you, the jewels could always have been the gifts of some admirer, couldn't they, and not the product of Landfall's robbing?"

Maria ignored him; she was looking at me, quite calmly. "You have been an ill wind in this house. Ever since you came nothing has been the same. You have stolen my child and the man I would have had as my husband. You have spied on me—here and at San Francisco. In time you would have gathered it all to yourself. It is a pity that Juanita's spell did not have time to work fully. We would have been better rid of you. But I can see that the fever is still in your brain. There are no jewels—there *never* were any. You saw nothing."

I did not answer her. She was right. I had seen nothing, nothing that was tangible. Perhaps a fever of jealousy had possessed me even from that first night. I *was* jealous of Maria. Had the gift been thwarted by an unworthy thought, a desire to pull down the one whom I feared and envied? No, there was no answer.

But Alister would not let it go. "Jewels?—but how would you know you got your money's worth? Weren't you taking a great risk? It is easy to be tricked—one must be an expert."

"As to that," Katarina spat out, "I can answer that. Maria does know the value of what she sees. There have been jewels in the family. We have not always lived like peasants at San Francisco. My mother knew jewels. She had some in her young days. Our grandmother had many more. All gone now. But what was left was looked at many times, and the knowledge comes. Maria had the names of many jewelers in Madrid when she went there with the last of our little hoard, and she bargained with them all—and learned all the time. She was patient, and she got a better price even than our mother had been offered here. In those days she was truthful enough to tell us. Today she would have told us only half as much, and kept the rest."

"But how were they come by? How does one get jewels here on San Cristóbal?" Now Alister was asking the questions of Katarina who could hardly wait to pour out what she knew. It was plain now that she cherished no further thought that Maria might have shared anything she had put away with them. She, like all of us, had heard that all Maria wanted was to be gone from San Cristóbal as quickly as ship could take her. There was no hope now to silence her. Like Samuel, she knew now that her sister's promises had been worthless, and the Spanish sense of a wrong to be avenged had been roused in her. There was to be nothing for herself and Joanna; there would be nothing for Maria, either.

I made one more attempt, but I don't think anyone but Fergus heard my words, and even he was hardly attending. "But I tell you I saw nothing that was *real* . . . When she turned, there was nothing." I ended with a kind of a sob; it was no use. They were all off following their own routes of revenge, enjoying the hounding of the woman whom, for one reason or another, they hated. They were like a pack in full cry, and I had provided the false scent.

"How does one get jewels on San Cristóbal?—how has one ever got them? Oh, yes, I know the saying now goes 'Poor as a West Indian planter,' but do not forget the days when they used to say 'Rich as a Creole.' Those were the great days of the islands, and the women vied with one another in their homes and their carriages and their dress. Jewels were part of it—part of a man's fortune. The jewelers used to come—private visits to greathouses, tempting the women. The best known was the family of Greene. English. Generations of them. Grandfather, father, son. Honest—you got your value. If times were bad—a bad harvest, he would always buy back. They came to the island once or twice a year. Less often now, because the money has gone from sugar and the estates are already mortgaged. They go now to the new rich in America, but there still are some clients left, still some who trust jewels more than gold." She gave a bitter, sobbing laugh. "Do not worry—the value will be there in whatever she has bought. She has both the knowledge and a trusted source."

Alister said, "Then where are they, Maria? Not in the safe—we've already emptied that."

She shrugged. "Since you have dreamed up these jewels you can all play the game of searching for them—after all, it will pass the time, won't it, and we're all sorely in need of some occupation." She turned to Andrew. "You know the house best. Where would you suggest they all begin? There can be no secret places here as there are supposed to be at San Francisco. You rebuilt it—you know it all. So on, my husband—play their game. What do the English call it—hunt the slipper?" Then she pointed at me. "Or better still—ask her. If she sees so much that isn't in anyone else's sight, then most certainly she will know where these jewels are that do not exist. Ask her—ask her!"

I was silent. They all looked at me, and there was nothing to say. They didn't know it was not something to be summoned at will, and I had already said too much. At last, desperately, I burst out, "I only *thought* I saw them . . ."

"Leave her be," Andrew said softly. "Leave her in peace." He sipped his rum, and the liquid moved violently in the glass; he needed both hands to set it down. His facial muscles seemed to have stiffened into a mask of indifference and pain; his lips twisted sideways. The last words seemed to have been spoken with difficulty.

Joanna, though, had no thought for Andrew; she spoke, forging ahead of her sister. "The Scottish one saw her with jewels in this room. She says she *thought* she saw them—perhaps she did. Then don't trouble yourself looking in safes and secret places in the cellars. Maria's wealth—if it exists—will be in the only thing she brought with her from San Francisco. Her only dowry. The one thing that only she may open, whose contents only she may touch. Look in the cabinet."

"The cabinet?" Katarina's face grew longer as her mouth dropped. "Of course! The place where the treasures at San Francisco were always kept."

"No!" Maria's composure was shattered at last. She sprang from the chair and toward the cabinet, but Katarina had dodged between her and Alister, as Alister had stepped to block Maria's path. The doors still stood wide, as they had done from the moment of the discovery of the doll. Feverishly now, Katarina ran her hand along the shelf that contained the vellum-bound manuscripts, the ones that were too precious to handle, that only Maria could dust. Katarina came finally to the one she sought.

"Here!" She dragged it out with shaking, clumsy hands, and hurried with it to the center table of the salon.

"Leave it be," Maria ordered. She seemed shocked and surprised to find her arm held firmly by Alister and she was unable to free herself—as if suddenly an ant had stood up and blocked her path. "Let your sister show us, Maria. You have long promised me a sight of some of the illuminated manuscripts." The mockery in his tone was heavy. "It's a pity it took a hurricane to bring that time about."

Katarina was fumbling with the heavy brass clasp of the volume, but it did not yield. Without any further words she went straight to Maria, still held by Alister, and took the ring of keys that Maria had replaced in the pocket of her gown. "Here," she said, "this small brass one. I would know it anywhere. You do not forget the things you grow up with."

"Katarina, I warn you—you are making a mistake, and you will regret it. There will be nothing more from me . . ."

"Regret?" her sister answered. "What is there to regret now? What is there to lose? Have you not told us to look to ourselves? Perhaps Joanna and I now have something to gain."

The lock yielded easily; what had seemed a volume was a vellum-covered box, with edges ridged as if they were hand-cut paper. From it, not clumsily now, but with care, Katarina brought out a folded bundle of white cloth. This in turn gave way to many layers of dark velvet. Joanna came forward to join her sister, walking almost on tiptoe. Piece by piece the jewels came out—I could not see them all; the table was above my line of vision. I hardly wanted to see them. Some were unset—single stones, green, red, the flash of many colors at the heart of whiteness. I was glad Fergus had not gone to look, nor had Alister moved. The sisters' long fingers handled those stones for a while; the wind had dropped now so that in the lulls we could hear the little gasps which were the only sounds they made. The great piece was the necklace, diamonds, I supposed. There was nothing I had ever seen to gauge it by. For a long moment Katarina held it up. She did not, as many another woman might have done, go to the mirror to try what that precious thing would do for her. Instead, after studying it for a time, she laid it back gently among its velvet folds.

"There—there is for so many nights to live with those savages so near —so many days to see that they were fed, so many times to see that their stinking place was cleaned out after the ships had gone. There is for so many years of taking care of our mother, of taking orders from our cheating sister. There is for so many hopes that withered . . ."

Was she crying?—did rage then give way to self-pity? Was it too much to see their years of subjugation to a younger sister represented by the cold fire of the gems. With dark heads bent over the contents of the box, the two long sallow faces contemplated the fruits of the struggle.

"There, also, is so much stolen from Landfall," Alister said. "It is stolen from Duncan—from Fergus."

He had released his grip on Maria; there was no further need to hold her. She rubbed her wrist where he had held her as she looked at me, but the rigid discipline of her bearing suggested the control that had returned, and that, once more, she was untouchable by the lash of fortune. There certainly was no self-pity in her tone. "You—you!" she said to me, the tone very quiet, as if she were pondering, rather than lashing out. "I should have listened to Juanita the day you arrived and sent you packing. She knew. Perhaps like recognizes like. That was my mistake—not to believe what Juanita told me about you. I don't know *how* you saw these things. I rarely permitted even myself to look on them. But you did see them. Not even Juanita knew about them, but she warned me that your magic was very strong . . . How strange I should have harbored you in this house for a single hour. If I had obeyed instinct and Juanita I would have sent you back on the *Clyde Queen*. If it had not been for my husband I should have done so—but I knew he could not last, and you would have gone then. Well, it is done . . ."

"Yes, it is done, Maria," Alister said. "But why?—why, Maria? was there need? What were you afraid of? That Andrew would turn you out? That he would change his mind and Landfall might still go to Fergus? You had to steal and squirrel away against the future you were not certain of?"

She answered him calmly. "You often are stupid and pompous, Alister—but sometimes you are shrewd and guess right. What is certain in this world? I learned to ask that question very young. I learned to ask it after enduring the snubs of those who thought themselves leaders in San Cristóbal when ours was the oldest blood on the island. I learned to ask it in Madrid when possessing beauty counted for nothing, nor even the illustrious name I bore, if there was no fortune to go with it. I learned to set no store by anything I could not hold in my hands and count. And so I began to put away against the day when anything might come to pass—if Andrew should tire of me, if Fergus would not have me, if the hurricane should come, if, even, as they kept saying, the slaves would be freed and we would have no labor for the cane fields. Against the inevitable day when I would look in the mirror and know that it was all over. The small bundle in velvet was my protection against the storm, from whichever way it blew. And now, at this moment, it is again my protection, because once more the wind has changed."

"Changed?" Fergus questioned. "It hasn't changed, Maria. It's almost spent. It hardly blows any more."

"You never were very subtle, Fergus—always taking things exactly as they are said. Perhaps, after all, I would have tired of you, when your beauty was gone, as mine would be." She paused, and then her voice rang out clearly as she pointed, not toward the box on the table that had held our attention, but to the red sofa in the shadows.

"You see, once again, the wind has changed. My husband is dead."

I felt Fergus's grip on me tighten, and heard the sucking in of his breath. It seemed a very long time before Alister made himself move to that still figure, slumped, as always, against the end of the sofa. He looked no different, except that his stillness had a terrible kind of permanence to it. I realized that Maria must have been the only one watching him in those last moments, the moments when the jewels had flashed in the fingers of her sisters. She must have watched the final twist of pain of the lips, perhaps the slightest movement, the silent cry for help. She must have watched the stillness descend, and she had stood and watched as he died as untended as if he had been all alone.

Alister was feeling for pulse, and with swift fingers unbuttoning the rum and sweat-soaked shirt and bending to listen for a heartbeat. Fergus went, with a slight reluctance, I thought, to join Alister. I wondered how, at that distance, in the dim light, Maria had been so certain that life had passed from Andrew's body in the final spasm. Why had I not felt it—I, who was supposed to feel these things? But she had spoken the truth. Fergus brought a lamp close, and for five minutes the two men bent over him; the rum was useless—probably the only time that Andrew's lips had ever rejected it. There was no pulse; the heart did not beat. Finally they closed the eyelids over the little slit of vision that had remained to him in those last minutes.

Maria spoke. "I am right? He is dead?"

Fergus answered. "He is dead. My father is dead." And then with great gentleness he swung the heavy legs up onto the sofa, and laid his arms out straight; then he took the rumpled silk handkerchief from Andrew's pocket and spread it across the still face.

"Don't let Duncan come in here," was all he said.

I fell back against my pillows, and heard the little moans from Joanna and Katarina. For a moment there was no further sound in the room, and then I heard the tap of Maria's heels, a deliberate, firm tread. First she went to the table, and wrapped again the jewels in their velvet and white cloth, and locked the vellum box. She carried it with her as she walked, but she did not approach the dead figure on the sofa. Instead she went into the hall, and I could hear her calling to some of the slaves to come from the cellars. There was the familiar slap of bare feet, and Maria's voice, low, giving some order. And then we heard it, the sound we had waited and prayed for through two days and a night —the sound as the shutters to the inner gallery were unlatched on the side away from the wind, the great hammering sound as the first of the iron bars was prized out of its place, the final crash as the first of the huge outer storm shutters was thrown open.

Light and air suddenly flooded in. A rush of wind stirred through the whole house. Only one door on the windward side was opened, but it was enough. The darkness fled. Gone with the rush of the wind were the scents of our fear and bitterness, of rum and sweat and the hemp. The sounds now were not of our voices raised in accusation, contempt and hatred; the sad cries of lives ruined and choked. What we heard now was the tossing of the trees in that high, but no longer destroying wind.

Chapter 7.

In the tropics, burials are swift. With the carnage of the cane fields, the roads washed out and trees laid across them, there was no possibility of burial for Andrew at Santa Marta.

"It doesn't matter," Fergus said. "It doesn't matter where he lies now. He would probably want to be at Landfall."

"Or Winterslo," I said.

He seized upon it. "Yes—at Winterslo. That is the place he really belongs to."

The plantation carpenter was set to work on the coffin, and then Maria summoned Fergus and Alister to her. "Now we will go to San Francisco—to my mother. We will take what is necessary to make another coffin, and the slaves to carry it."

Katarina and Joanna refused to leave Landfall. "What is there to go to? And what is there between Landfall and San Francisco but those savages that Samuel has set loose?"

"There is our mother—alive or dead."

Katarina shrugged. "She didn't care for us—dead or alive. We were her slaves as much as that wretched herd. If she is dead, then our absence will not trouble her. If she is alive then we are no better or worse than before. For me—it can wait a few hours. Until the wind has died completely. Until the way to San Francisco has been cleared. I have come through the forest once in the wind. I will not again."

Fergus carried me upstairs to my bed, and Charity, the manacle removed, and her wounds bathed, came to stay with me. In a more solemn procession, Andrew's body was carried upstairs to lie once more on his bed, and await burial. I made sure Duncan was in my room with me before this happened. There had been enough grim spectacles this day to haunt his memory. There was no reason for him to look upon the pain-twisted face of Andrew, to smell, as the last thing, the smell of rum.

I told him about his father, and he lay curled against me on the bed, clinging fiercely, with the tears only slow to come; the fears were greater. "What will happen now, Fiona? What will happen to *me* now?"

"I will take care of you," I said, holding him closely. It was a rash promise; one I had little idea how I would keep. I felt the tremble of his body, and heard the ring of the axes and the crash of the machetes as the party set out for San Francisco.

* * * * *

It moved on to the early hours of the morning, and still they had not returned. By then I was out of bed and dressed; Duncan refused to stay in bed and followed on my heels like a hound. Suddenly the house was mine, and I had to organize, and command and plan. Katarina and Joanna stayed upstairs; when I sent Charity to tell them that a hot meal had been prepared, she brought back the message that the ladies would have it on trays in their room. I was both relieved and angry, and took care to show neither to Duncan.

I took on the task of seeing that Andrew's body was washed and prepared, since Maria seemed to have left no instructions for it; while this went on, Samuel took Duncan to the stables to help feed and groom his pony. The stables had survived; the slave quarters and their vegetable gardens were wrecked. With Duncan gone and Charity's help I did what was necessary for Andrew—bound his chin until the *rigour* of death should hold it firmly, did what I could to compose his features, washed his body with scented water. Charity cleaned and dusted the room, and with Dougal to help, we laid him on clean sheets. I sent Charity to see if any blossoms remained in the garden. She came back emptyhanded, save for some ferns plucked from the base of the great trees. I slanted down the louvered shutters, and lighted a lamp at each side of the bed. These things I remembered from Silkirk, and I thought they might have pleased Andrew.

When it was all done I paused, all alone there, and just as if I had been at home in Silkirk, I found myself on my knees beside the bed. What was I to pray for—for the salvation of a soul that Andrew hardly believed existed?—for the return of honor to a name that he cared about? I tried to think of things my father would have said of him. All I could think was that life had been hard for Andrew Maxwell, and the last years had brought the worst unhappiness and pain. It was indeed better that he should be returned to Winterslo for burial; those days had been his best, when he had worked with his Bible-reading mother to make the soil yield its precious drop, when he had labored with hopefulness before the tragedy that had brought Fergus to him.

While I knelt there the door opened and Duncan came to me. He came and stood beside me in the half-darkness, staring solemnly at the figure of Andrew. "Are you praying, Miss Fiona?"

"Yes, Duncan. Do you want to pray with me?"

His answer was to kneel. Before he buried his face in the coverlet he said to me, "I don't know what to say. What shall I say?"

I hadn't known myself. "Just pray in your heart. Just bid him goodbye and ask for peace for him. Peace is all that's needed in the end, Duncan."

We stayed silent there for some time, heads bowed, the last of the great wind still tossing in the trees beyond the gallery. Then finally I touched Duncan gently, and seeing his tear-wet face I bent and kissed him. "We have done what we can. Pray for him—and never forget him. The dead still live when they are remembered."

* * * * *

To ease the waiting, I set about the task of trying to get the house in order again. The slaves were subdued, talking little and with muted voices. They did not like the presence of Andrew's body in the house, and worked swiftly so that they might be released from the place of death—even if it were only to try to construct some shelter from the tangled rubble of their huts. They would not stay in the cellars. Juanita and Flora had disappeared. I didn't even ask about them. I would have been thankful never to have set eyes on either again. I could find no slave willing to sit with Andrew's body, nor would Katarina or Joanna.

"We have prayers to say for our mother," was the reply I got. "And not by the bedside of that godless man."

So Andrew waited in the final loneliness of death even before burial.

It was dawn, and Duncan had finally given in to his weariness, and allowed me to put him to bed; I stayed beside him, holding his hand, even, despite the presence of death, singing to him the old Scottish songs that were like a foreign tongue to him. When he slept at last, I went for a few minutes onto the gallery, and the growing light revealed the wreckage of the garden below me. It was almost calm now; the wind seemed hardly more than what normally began to blow as the sun reached strength each day. I looked with a kind of horror at the scene; the great cottonwood tree uprooted, its huge spread filled the whole circle of the drive in front of the house, its highest limbs lying just feet away from the bottom of the steps. Other trees had gone also, smaller ones that we had not heard in the whole hideous tumult. Oleander and hibiscus, blossomless, lay flattened, frangipani stripped bare of leaves and branches, naked and gaunt to the sky; and as the light grew I could see on past the ruin of the garden, to the wilder parts, and to the sea, where huge swells flung foam high into the air about the Serpents. And yet it was itself, a dawn of unsurpassed beauty—the peculiar intensity of the light, the moment of coolness, almost peace. The rain and wind-battered earth seemed to be settling once more into its fertile sleep. As I quietly walked the full square of the gallery I noted the tightly closed louvers of the room where Katarina and Joanna slept—or lay awake, in fear, waiting for the attack they feared from the freed slaves; I saw too, in the dawn, the breakfast fires before the remains of the slave huts. I could hear their voices—the chanting, infinitely melancholy songs they sang. I didn't know if they offered thanks for deliverance from the storm, or a dirge for a dead master. Would I ever know these people? I wondered—in the lifetime I would spend here with Fergus would I ever know what lay behind the blank mask of even those who grew closest to me? I doubted that I ever would. Suddenly I wanted very much to be gone from Landfall, to remove to the simpler style of Winterslo, to minimize the gap between these unknowable dark people and the way we lived. But then, for the first time, came the agonizing thought that perhaps Winterslo itself no longer was habitable; that it, like San Francisco, had given up to the storm, its rotting timbers letting its roof fly, and opening it to the skies and the rain. It was ironic to think that Fergus and I, like the Medina sisters, might begin our life together in a made-over stable.

But somehow it didn't matter. I also had reason for a song of thankfulness. I also had been delivered from the storm, and had survived an attack from a force of evil I had no real knowledge to fight. I went back then, more willingly, to a chair in Andrew's room, believing that he had the right to even this small vigil. I fell asleep in the chair, thinking that I would ask no more grace or bounty than to have Fergus for myself, and, somehow, to carry out my promise to take care of Duncan.

*   *   *   *   *

Within the hour they were back. I heard the sounds below, the voices, and sprang out of the chair and ran down.

"Fiona!" Fergus cried, concern marked on his mud-splattered face. "What the devil are you doing up—and dressed! You should be abed— you should rest!"

"I'm well," I answered. "Quite well. Everything has gone now. Just be quiet and don't wake Duncan. He *would* stay up with me most of the night . . ." I stopped because Fergus was holding me, not closely or passionately, but in a kind of calm of wonder, as if he had never believed to do it again. His lips brushed my forehead.

"You're sure?" he demanded. "You seemed to travel so far from me —almost slipped beyond me. I thought I had lost you."

I heard my own laugh, and was rather shocked to hear it in this house of mourning. I answered in a broad Scottish accent. "Ye'll no find it sa easy t' lose me in the future, mon. I'm wi' ye noo, and ye'll no be shut o' me fra' this day."

Now his embrace tightened to one of joy and strength. "Go on wi' ye, woman. Ha' ye no shame?"

"I dinna know the word, Fergus Maxwell."

We broke from our embrace to find that Alister and Maria had entered the hall. Once again I was impressed, as I always had been, by the unyielding strength of the woman. Her gown was covered by the red mud of the island's earth, her hair hung in tails about her face and her hands were cut, and still bleeding. Beside her, Alister was in the same state, as was Fergus, but it seemed natural to a man, and in her a further proof of her invulnerability.

"Donna Isabella?" I was forced to ask, with lips suddenly gone dry.

Alister answered, "We found her dead where Maria said she would be. One of the slaves . . . it could have happened no other way. Probably a machete." His face was very white and strained. He had stood the ordeal less well than either Fergus or Maria. Without further question I was suddenly sickeningly aware of the fate the old woman had met, the savage reprisal of a slave gone mad with hate and terror, the kind of death that Andrew's father had known in the cane field. Maria had been right; Samuel must have seen her, and would not be the bearer of such news—or feared that he himself would be blamed.

I bowed my head slightly to Maria. "I am sorry."

She nodded wearily, and then shrugged. "She was old," was what she answered, this extraordinary woman, "and very tired. She wanted no more of life." And yet in the face of the seeming indifference I knew that a rock of Maria's existence had rolled away from her. She derived her strength and her temperament from the domineering old woman; probably many times in their lives they had done battle against each other, and enjoyed the clash of arms.

"She is at rest," Alister concluded. "Maria helped dig the grave by lamplight. We waited till dawn to come back through the forest." I thought of those two women cowering over their beads in the room above, and of this woman before me, and in spite of myself my admiration and awe of her grew. On every level she was formidable. If ever I should be able to carry out my promise to take care of Duncan, I knew that any son sprung from this woman would challenge all my strength.

I waited a moment, then I said: "There is hot food—I had them make a stew from the cooked meats. The ovens are lighted again. Your husband, Mrs. Maxwell, is upstairs. I did the best I could . . . I'm sorry I could not force any of the slaves to sit with him. They seem to be afraid . . ."

"They would be," she answered, her tone contemptuous and tired. "And of course my sisters have done nothing . . ." Her glance took in the hall and salon cleared of the mattresses and swept, the dining room cleared of the used dishes.

"They were tired and . . . afraid, also, I think. They seem to fear an attack on the house by the slaves that Samuel set free."

"They always find something to be afraid of!" Maria spat out the words. Then she half-sighed. "Well, let us eat, since there is hot food. Then we will bathe and rest an hour. We must send slaves to dig a grave—you, Fergus, must tell them where. And then, before the sun is too high, Andrew must be buried."

She might have been the conventional, though strong, grieving widow. It was difficult to remember the acts of treachery, the misery that Andrew had suffered, so great now was her dignity. I found myself in the kitchen with her, putting food onto plates and trays and carrying it to the men; it did not occur to me to disregard any direction she gave, to disobey an order. She did not summon any slaves from the quarters, and none came near the house. I poured rum for the men, and wine for Maria. The food and drink brought a little color to each face, though they did not once speak except what was necessary about the burial arrangements for Andrew. I myself took the dishes back to the kitchen, and Fergus went to the slave huts, looking for his own slaves to send them to Winterslo to make the preparations. When I came back to the hall, Maria was already on her way upstairs; she did not go to her sisters' room, and they did not emerge to question her. A terrible, deadly quality of weariness and silence had descended on the whole house. I heard a door open and close, and knew it was Andrew's room; Maria had gone to look upon him. No one would ever know if it were with hatred or remorse or indifference, for she would certainly never speak of it.

Alister stood there, half-supported by the newel post; I had never seen him look as he did now. The momentary revivant of food and drink had faded; just a weariness and despair was left.

"It was terrible," he said. "It was the worst sight I ever saw, that old woman. I wish to God . . ." Then he stopped and seemed about to turn and go upstairs.

"You wish what?"

His tone became suddenly strong. "I wish with all my powers that you were not staying here. Oh—not just at Landfall. I wish you out of these islands forever. The black people—I think their time has come, and who can blame them if they show no more pity than we have done. I think we are just starting to pay the price . . . just starting."

His limp was very pronounced as he climbed the stairs.

II

The noon sun was high before they had managed to clear the road from Landfall to Winterslo for the passage of the cane cart which carried Andrew's coffin. Fergus walked, leading the mule, and the rest of us rode, most of the Landfall slaves on foot behind us.

From somewhere, perhaps a relic of her wardrobe from Madrid all those years ago, Maria had found a black dress and mantilla; she rode regally behind the cart as if she were the consort following the bier of a king. She kept Duncan close to her, he on the pony with the silver-studded harness, which had been Andrew's last, wildly extravagant gift. The rest of us just wore the clothes that came to hand, the most comfortable for the heat and ride. Alister had borrowed a shirt from Fergus, but his trousers were still the mud-stained ones of the night's digging; he wore a ragged slave's hat to shield him from the sun. Except for the devastation about us, there was no telling of the passage of the hurricane. The same blue sky above us, the same burning sun, the same cooling wafts of the trade winds to dry the sweat as it soaked our clothes. The trades would begin to blow again, and the days would be cooler. "October, all over."

Fergus had not slept, but had gone to Winterslo with the slaves to select the site. It was on the slope below the house, in a grove of mampoo trees that somehow had survived the onslaught. As we breasted the last rise, I lifted my eyes to the house, not having dared to ask Fergus, when he had returned for his father's body, the question that had haunted me. It was like a miracle to see Winterslo still intact; the roof was there—some shutters hung off their hinges, but it still was a house, and would be a home. Alister urged his horse up beside me.

"Did it worry you—I thought of it myself. But it must have been sheltered a little by the height of Kronberg. It's not so exposed as San Francisco."

"It was good of you to think of us . . ." I murmured, "in the middle of everything else."

"I am always thinking of you," he said, and his tone was edgy. He let his horse drop back, and I rode on alone.

*   *   *   *   *

Alister held the Book before him, but he spoke the words from memory, just as my father would have done.

". . . He that believeth in me, though he were dead, yet shall he live . . ."

I knew now that this grove also contained the graves of Andrew's mother and father; it was natural he should have returned here. We had a plantation, then, Fergus and I, a true one, of toil and tragedy given to this red earth. I thought that when I came to live at Winterslo I would somehow make a garden of this bare, hen-pecked place. I would bring my children here, and Duncan, and they would cherish, not shun it.

And then the psalm. ". . . He maketh me to lie down in green pastures." The awful irony of the words that followed struck me, and made me wonder at the wisdom of the choice. "Thou preparest a table before me in the presence of mine enemies . . . Surely goodness and mercy shall follow me all the days of my life; and I will dwell in the house of the Lord forever."

We murmured, "Amen"—all except Maria and her sisters, whom she had forced to follow to the graveside and witness what they considered a heretic service. I could not help thinking, as we remounted, that a table had indeed been prepared in the presence of Andrew's enemies. We rode back now, to the pickings.

III

On the return to Landfall, Maria was fully in possession. She presided over an almost silent meal, and then the siesta was observed, though it was impossible to sleep with the ring of the axes all about the house, chopping at the fallen trees, clearing some of the debris from the garden, beginning the reconstruction of the slave quarters. Fergus had remained at Winterslo to begin the work there; I missed him desperately. Without him, without Andrew, I had no shield against Maria, and I knew that my days, even my hours, at Landfall were numbered. Very soon, also, Alister would go. The end had come with savage abruptness, and none had been prepared for it, except, possibly, Maria.

It was no surprise, then, to be summoned from lessons with Duncan as dusk began to approach, to come to the salon. "I am to stay with Master Duncan," Charity said. "And he is to go on with his books."

"How will Charity know that I'm reading?" Duncan said sullenly. He didn't like my being summoned away from him; he too felt the insecurity of Andrew's absence. "She can't read herself."

"That the truth, master. But my son learn to read."

"How?"

"I have spoken with Master Fergus. He try to buy us both for Winterslo, and Mistress Fiona teach my son to read." She had never spoken of such a thing to me, but simply took it for granted that I would not refuse. "My son not spend his life in the cane fields. I am sure of it now."

And how many others, I thought, as I went downstairs, believed the same thing. We had taken them from the simpler ways of Africa, and they had learned that books and writing were the keys to the prosperity of the white man. Not all of them would forever be tillers of the soil. If emancipation should come, money, however little, would have to pass from the hands of the white into the black, and with it would be the beginning of the turn-about. By slow degrees, one or two would creep up and onward from his fellows. So very likely Charity was right; I would teach her son to read.

They were assembled in the salon—Maria, Alister, Katarina, and Joanna. I missed the figure on the red sofa. Fergus had also been sent for, and he came last, protesting. "Look, Maria, there's fully as much work to do at Winterslo as here, and I haven't anything like your number of slaves . . . I've no time for social gatherings."

He had not changed his clothes, and they were mud-stained from the still-wet earth, the old clothes he habitually wore on the plantation. It was strange to see Alister similarly dressed; only the perfect fit of the mud-caked boots were a reminder of his usual elegance. But he still bore the scratches on his face and hands, as did Fergus, as reminders of the wreckage and the journeys to San Francisco.

"It is of some importance, I think, Fergus," Maria replied. "I intend to say these things only once. All of us might as well know them at the same time. I do not want days and weeks of argument, or secondhand reports of what I said. Let us be finished with it now. We all have work to do."

Alister crossed his legs and leaned back in his chair. "Well, Maria?" I drew confidence from his tone. Alister would not be stampeded by Maria. And yet I was wondering, without Andrew, what he could do to change what was now the order of things at Landfall.

"First of all," Maria said, "the will that my late husband made is still valid. Whatever he said in this room before he died does not matter. What matters is what is written in the will that lies in the safe of the solicitor in Santa Marta, and I *know* that has not been recently changed. And that gives Landfall, its contents, its assets as well as its liabilities, to me as trustee for Duncan until he is twenty-one. From that point on, I still retain a one-third share of the estate. Is that clear to you all?"

"Is *that* what you dragged me over here to listen to?" Fergus burst out. "I knew what was to be! I expect nothing of Landfall, as I expected nothing of my father once you had twisted your way into his life. I want nothing. I want nothing but Fiona . . ."

"Take her then!" Maria flashed back at him. "Take her! I see you are mad to saddle yourself with a dowerless wife, and soon you will have a brood of children under your feet. Take her, then—and look back to this time, and regret it all the days of your life."

"Regret?—regret what? That I wanted Fiona and not you? The difference is like smelling honeysuckle—if you ever took time to do such a thing—and taking a scorpion to your bed. Thanks—if that is all I came to hear, I'll be off. Fiona, you must pack and we'll find you somewhere to stay until we can be married. They'll be dispensing with quite a lot of the formalities in Santa Marta just now. I imagine we can arrange it very quickly."

"Duncan?" I said faintly. I was haunted by my promise, by the knowledge that what I had come to do was still not yet done, and things were slipping past our control; without Andrew there was no appeal.

"And why should you concern yourself with my son?" Maria demanded. "He is no one's business but my own. He will probably go to Spain when he is older, and learn what he never could learn here. Whatever happens, my son is finished with the Maxwells."

I watched Fergus's face as this was said, and it worked strangely, anger, the flash of self-accusation again, and the half-closing of his eyes in a kind of despair were there for me to see. He was unable to do what his father had done in his time; he was unable to claim a child who might be his son. He looked at me as if begging forgiveness; I nodded, just slightly, but I could give him no hope. Maria had everything now.

"And us?" Katarina said, with her sardonic, twisted smile. "What disposition have you made for us, my sister. Are we to be allowed the crumbs from the table?"

Maria shrugged, as if their fate were of little concern to her. "You will live, I expect—but not here at Landfall. Do you think I want to spend my days cooped up with two quarreling spinsters? We shall see what can be made habitable for you at San Francisco . . ."

"Ah, good of you, I'm sure," Joanna cried. "After all, it is still our home!"

"You are wrong, Joanna. It is now *mine*—solely. You do not think that our mother was so improvident as to leave it among the three of us to have what little remains wasted and torn apart? She made her will, and showed it to me, and it also waits in Santa Marta. You will live there at my discretion, and I shall work the two estates together—thus the small acreage of San Francisco will be added to Landfall and brought back to fertility. Its cane will come to the factory here, and we shall have a more economic usage."

"You are suddenly businesslike, Maria," Alister observed dryly. "Showing more sense for proper management than you have professed all these years. But the Maxwells aren't finished at Landfall, even if you take your son from their sphere of influence. Before you start bringing San Francisco sugar to the Landfall mill, and sharing its slaves, remember that the Maxwells still own a share of Landfall—does that also mean you are willing for them to have part of San Francisco?"

"Never—*never!* No more of San Francisco goes into strangers' hands, least of all to Maxwells'. The loan was paid off—it was my husband's life work to do that."

"Not in full—remember that! Not in full. We still retain our interest for forgiveness of the last part of the loan. That is why I came here. To look into all of this. But this is not new to you. You know this very well."

"Yes—well I know it. A seemingly magnanimous gesture that had only Maxwell interests to prompt it. Why give up part of a good estate? But that same document also gave my husband or his heirs the right to buy outright from the Maxwells at the sum stated then, plus the interest on the money, that would have accumulated in these five or six years."

"And you are willing to meet that price?"

She nodded, and her tongue flicked eagerly over her lips. "Yes, I will meet that price. Jewels are good for more than wearing by frivolous women."

"Those jewels were bought with money taken from Landfall in order to finance your part in illegal slave-trading."

She sighed. "Alister—you are not stupid. Do not act this way. You heard what my husband said. There are those on this island who would never stand to see the charge of illegal slave-trading brought against me. They will unite against the outsider, and there are powerful people involved. We know how to take care of our own on this island. We can get any number to swear that they were merely selling off the natural increase of their own slave population. Why dwell on this?—

you know, as well as Andrew knew—that it is useless. After all, he himself, many years ago, when Fergus was the subject of a great quarrel, was protected by the island courts against the might of a great and powerful English family."

She rapped her nails against the arm of her chair as she considered the rest of the matter. "And as to taking the money from Landfall, you yourself have sat night after night over the books trying to find some way I have been cheating, and you have not succeeded."

"I could go on. I have not the time or the will to pursue it myself, but I could send men from London with all the time in the world. The least we could charge you with was gross mismanagement."

"You will charge *me* with nothing! Legally a husband is responsible for the financial matters of a household. It is only twenty-four hours since my husband died, and that responsibility ceased."

"*You* personally may not be held responsible, but the estate may be made to pay more. I will have a court order made to secure the books—"

"Then you will be lucky, my friend. Much vanished in the hurricane. The books no longer exist."

Alister stiffened in his chair, looking about the room that I had ordered cleaned after they had set out for San Francisco. I was certain the books had not been here when I had come down, which could only mean that Maria had made her own disposition of them before she had left the house. She had remembered them, as she had remembered the jewels and every other thing that was important to her future. Were there no weaknesses in this woman?

She was completely triumphant, but the iron discipline still was maintained; she did not permit herself to swagger. She reminded me then of the man in Silkirk who sometimes came to play chess with my father. My father, emotional and excitable, had never been able to restrain his pleasure when he had a move building up to trap his opponent, and thus had always alerted him. My father had anticipated triumph, and usually given way to defeat. With Maria it was the opposite; she showed no joys or triumphs, no sorrows or griefs. There seemed no point at which she was vulnerable. Fergus would not try to find that point; he wanted away and out and to be done with it; he would cut his losses, even the loss of his own son, if Duncan were indeed his son. Alister might try to fight, but he faced a battle of almost impossible odds. If the books were gone, Maria would make certain that they were never seen again. Alister would have to go to a hostile court with no evidence in hand. I doubted that he would; he was not the kind to make a fool of himself, nor to waste time and money on a hopeless cause. He would know it to be hopeless; and he would also know to the last penny the sum agreed upon in the document which gave the Maxwells their continuing interest in Landfall. He would calculate the interest due. He would get what he could, or send someone else to get it. Then the Maxwells would be gone—except for Fergus and myself. Suddenly the brood of children that Maria had predicted became a promise. The Maxwells would flourish again; Duncan would have cousins—they would be called cousins. There would be meetings. The Maxwell influence would not give way entirely before that of long-ago Spain.

It seemed to be over. If Alister was going to fight, he was not wasting his energy now on argument. It was Katarina who spoke for us all. "If we might prevail upon your hospitality, my sister, for just one more night . . . It is difficult to set out for Santa Marta at this hour."

"Santa Marta? Why would you want to go to Santa Marta?"

"And where else have we to go? There are still a few old friends there who will give us shelter out of regard for our mother—until there is a roof over our heads at San Francisco. Until it seems safe to return there. Of course they will wonder at us not staying on at Landfall, but then, my sister, you must accept conjecture and gossip as the price of our removal."

Maria showed a rare impatience. "Oh—stay then! Stay. Just keep out of my sight. I've more to think of than your worries."

Fergus rose. "Fiona, I shall come for you in the morning. You will be ready?"

"Yes, I'll be ready."

Did the last flicker of hope die then in Maria?—there was no telling. She showed nothing. Alister sipped his wine. "I also shall be returning to Santa Marta in the morning, Maria. I shall inform the authorities that slaves are loose in this area. I'm sure they will send what assistance they can."

"It isn't needed. I have never been afraid of a few ignorant blacks."

"Nor was Donna Isabella."

A frightened whimper came from Joanna, but a gesture from Maria silenced her. "No doubt," she said, "I shall have communications from you as regards the transfer of the rest of the property?"

"No doubt," was all he answered.

I could not believe that it was all ending; the Landfall adventure was done and over with. Fergus came and kissed me briefly on the forehead. "Tomorrow," he said, and then he was gone. Katarina and Joanna made their exit, asking for trays to be sent to their room. They were clearly going to be troublesome guests. I wondered if Maria, Alister, and myself would sit to a silent meal, the whole fabric of Landfall having been rent since last we sat to dinner by candlelight at that long polished table. This was the last time.

Chapter 8.

But it was not a silent meal to which we gathered that evening. There was a tumult all about Landfall that was nothing like the shriek of the storm, but in its way it seemed no less menacing—perhaps it was even more so, since we did not know or understand its meaning. From the slave quarters, where usually the silence of weariness brought an early quiet, the voices came loud; sudden laughter when there seemed no cause for it, and sudden bursts of song that were wild and careless— nothing like the songs of the cane fields. The cooking fires were not allowed to die, but were heaped high. I walked with Duncan around to the back of the upstairs gallery before I took him down to dinner, and we saw the dark figures silhouetted against the flames, and one or two actually leaped in the air as if in some ritual dance of joy or exaltation.

Duncan had come down to dinner because Juanita and Flora still were missing since the storm had died, and there was no one to stay with him, and put him to bed. I myself had suggested it; it seemed a heartless thing to leave him alone so soon after he had seen the man he had called his father buried. Maria had simply shrugged her assent. Her attention was more on the missing slaves.

But it was Duncan who voiced all our misgivings at the table. "Mama—why are the slaves so excited tonight? I've never heard them like this. And after a hurricane—with all their huts smashed and the gardens lost. Is it—is it because of my father?"

"Not for your father, Duncan. But we will find out why. I think they may have found some of the rum in the San Francisco cellars. It is nothing—they will exhaust themselves soon, and go to sleep. I will go myself and see later. It is nothing . . ."

The food itself was the strangest I had ever eaten at Landfall—scraps of the cooked meats that had served us through the storm tossed together in a dish that lacked the subtle flavor of the spices we were used to, watery and tasteless. It was served by Dougal alone, without the assistance of the two other slaves who usually helped him. There was nothing to accompany the dish except the stale bread baked before the storm, and some almost raw yams.

Maria thrust her plate away in disgust. "Dougal—what does this mean? Why are we given this filth to eat?"

He only half-turned from his task at the sideboard, his head low. "Cook not here, mistress. No girls to help. I try to make this myself, but I not cook."

"And Pitt and Randolph?"

"The same, mistress. Gone. Not come in to help with the table. I cannot go to look for them—I have not time. And the mistresses upstairs not been served yet. I call Charity to take a tray, but she not come. I think she gone off to find Samuel."

Maria half-rose from her chair, and then dropped back. "It has to be rum they have got hold of. Well, we shall see about that. Dougal, serve the cheese and some more wine, and take away this mess. And bring some fruit."

He shook his head. "All fruit eaten during the storm. Bananas not ripe—and what was coming in the garden all destroyed."

"There are crocks of mango and papaya laid down. Why did you not bring them?"

"I look, mistress. All gone. Shelves in the cellar all bare . . ."

I saw Maria's face tighten, and an expression that might have been the beginning of apprehension came upon it. She controlled it, as always, but her reaction was not as it had been in more secure moments, a cry of anger. She asked no more questions of Dougal. "Very well, then. You may go. And when you go to those thieving savages by the fires let it be known that the mistress is very angry, and that she will punish the offenders. No slave is to stay within the house tonight. Before you go, take wine and bread and cheese to the señoritas. And leave the keys . . ."

He was gone before the pounding of the drums began—from somewhere far off, beyond Winterslo, it seemed to be. When they first started, they were greeted with silence from the noisy fires in the slave quarters. Then, after some minutes, during which none of us spoke, either, the drums were suddenly answered by a wild shout—more of a howl than a shout that broke from the throats of those about the fires. But no drum came from Landfall to answer the one over the mountain.

"The drums!" Maria was frowning. "It has been a long time since they were heard. It is forbidden—something they brought with them from Africa, but they have gradually lost the art. It was their way to talk to each other from one estate to another. But not many now know how to read them. Juanita can . . ."

"It means something more than rum and deliverance from the hurricane," Alister said. Suddenly all of us were looking at the blackness beyond the open louver doors, and wishing, I think, as I was, that the storm shutters were still closed against the din and whatever it signified.

"We will lock up securely tonight," Maria said. "You and I will do it, Alister. In the morning they will hardly be able to stir. It will need a whip to get those dull heads awake tomorrow."

"Listen!—do you hear it, Mama?" Duncan paused with bread and cheese half-crammed into his mouth.

"What?—hear what?"

"Bells—do you hear bells?" Faintly, between breaks in the drumming, even farther off, the sound of bells, the great estate bells that were heard morning and night to call the slaves. But never this wild, unrhythmical crash, as if several men swung together on the rope, and would not let go.

Alister thrust back his chair and went onto the outer gallery. "Something is wrong! They are never rung after sunset, Maria?"

Her face was pale, more strained than I had seen it at any time during the hours of inquisition she had endured during the storm. "Never —except for an emergency! That is the bell of Harford Hall—I know its sound. And there, that thinner one, that is Drake's Bay." She had gone to join Alister, her voice drifting back to Duncan and me. "Why did they not ring directly after the storm? Why now? There is no more danger now?"

Alister jerked his head toward the back of the house, and the howls and shouts, the thud of bare feet slapping the hard-packed earth of the yards. "There is a danger we don't understand yet."

"Then we soon will." Maria strode back into the room. "I am going to find out what this nonsense is about. Duncan, fetch Mama the whip from the office."

"Stay where you are, Duncan . . ." Alister rapped out the order. "You also, Maria. Fiona—quickly run up and bring the pistol from the drawer in my bedside table. No, Maria—stay! I forbid you to move. Quickly, Fiona—and bring the shot."

As I sped up the stairs I could hear the argument begin—Maria claiming a proprietor's right to decide what should be done, Alister calmly stating a man's responsibility to a household of women. As I rushed down from Alister's room, which was lighted only by the glare from the slave's leaping fires, I was joined on the landing by Katarina and Joanna.

"What is it?" they demanded, clutching hands reaching to detain me.

I shrugged them off. "Better come down and find out." They huddled over the candle, heads together like black crows.

"We have not yet been offered anything to eat . . ." were the last wailing words I caught. I left them to their own concerns.

They were all still in the dining room, but Alister was moving very quietly around, closing and bolting the louver doors. "Can you handle a pistol, Maria?" he said, almost casually, as I returned.

"Yes—I once was taught. I think I still have some skill."

"I guessed you might. Well, then—load it, and release the safety catch. Now come with me and cover me while I close the doors. First snuff the candles so that I am not outlined for them . . . We will do the inner ones first. Leave only the hall one open, and be ready to run if I tell you. That means all of you—the señoritas also." They had slowly crept down the stairs and joined us. "Where are the bars stored that secure the storm shutters?"

"Inside—Andrew always kept them inside in case . . . The place under the stairs. I myself saw to them being stacked back there before we left for San Francisco. Andrew always felt—my God, it has not come to this, Alister?" It was the first time since the storm began that she had spoken to him as a woman to a man, a woman in need, suddenly, of help. The new posture sat oddly upon her. "It cannot be that they will try something? Why now? Because Andrew is dead? Most of them have barely laid eyes on Andrew for these last two years—but it would not explain the drums and the bells from the other estates. What is it, Alister?"

"We will talk later," he said tersely. "Just come and follow me—try to keep me covered with the pistol. Where are the other guns we had here during the storm . . . ?"

They went off together, suddenly allies in this common threat that none of us understood. Katarina and Joanna were now in the dining room, standing by the sideboard, lumping wedges of cheese on bread and eating it with a haste and lack of dignity they would normally have scorned; from Joanna's hand dangled a rosary. Between bites she murmured to her sister, "God preserve us—has it come here too? Will we have the same fate as our mother?"

Katarina was more realistic. "For us it will be worse, sister. We are not sodden with rum."

"Better meet it on full bellies, then," I said. I caught Duncan's hand, as we followed, discreetly, Alister and Maria. But being a watcher fretted me, as it did Duncan. "The bars!" I said. "We could start to bring out the bars to secure the storm shutters."

It was heavy work, between a woman and a small boy; we managed only a few. As the doors were closed the ringing of the bells was gradually blotted out, the sounds of the drums fainter. But the shouts from the slave quarters seemed to grow louder. Unconsciously, we all began to hurry, working almost in rhythm to the chant outside. We made our way around the whole house, two women at each side of a bar, lifting and holding, while Alister hammered it into place with the poker from the fireplace.

As we moved from one to the other, Duncan once pulled at my arm. "Why are we doing this, Fiona? What has happened?"

"No one knows," I said. And it was true.

It was as well the messenger came in those minutes before the last shutter was secured, otherwise the hysteria of Joanna might have made Alister decide against opening up. The man must have left his horse tethered a long way down the avenue and come on foot, for we heard no sound; he simply slipped around the hall door and stood there, panting, trembling, I thought.

"Mrs. Maxwell—"

"Luiz!" She stood for a moment as if rooted; then she hurried forward. "What is it. Have they sent you?"

"Mr. Maxwell?—where is he?" The man was very tired; he swayed a little as he stood, dressed in a shirt and thin trousers unsuitable for riding. I thought I recognized him, but I could not remember from where.

"Mr. Maxwell is dead." Maria's tone was almost reassuring, as if to tell the man that he had nothing to fear; but he looked about all of us gathered in the hall as if he wished we were not there. Particularly he looked at Alister, and there was no doubt of the recognition between them.

"My sympathy, señora. Señor Rodriguiz will be grieved . . ."

"What brings you?" Alister rapped out.

"I was sent from Santa Marta, to bring the news. The town has been badly hit, half the buildings in ruins, many without roofs. Rodriguiz fared not too badly—only a little water damage, though the tide came high in the streets. I helped carry the goods from the cellars—they say there are many drowned, swept away out to sea, but as yet no way of counting . . ."

"No one sent you all this way to tell us this. We might have guessed it for ourselves," Alister said.

The man gestured with his hands, as if to wipe out the inconsequential nature of what he had been talking about. It was then, suddenly, that Duncan proved that he had recognized a need before any of his elders. While the man had stood there gasping out his words, Duncan had gone back to the sideboard and filled a large glass with wine. Now he offered it silently. The man took it in three gulps, closing his eyes, and breathing in heavily. For a moment his hand fumblingly fell on Duncan's head. *"Muchas gracias, señor."*

"Now—quickly," Maria demanded. "What is it?"

"You hear the bells—the drums?"

"Of course we hear them."

"Except for the storm and the conditions in Santa Marta and on the roads you would have had the news sooner. But I came when it was possible."

"What for?—for God's sake—why?" Alister shouted.

"The final news, señor. The news we have all waited for and refused to believe. A British vessel managed to beat her way past the Serpent Rocks and into Santa Marta harbor before the storm grew too fierce. But no one could come ashore until long after it was over and the swells had died a little. But the news was through the town in an hour, and the bells were tolling and the people were loading their guns."

Alister heaved a great sigh, and briefly a weary half-smile came to his face; there was no exuberance, just a quiet thankfulness.

"Emancipation? Is that it? The British Parliament have finally passed the bill?"

The man took the last dregs of the wine. "Emancipation—yes, señor. All slave children under six years of age are automatically freed. Those older, more gradually, according to age."

"God!" That single word from Maria—disbelief, resignation in one. And then quickly, "Compensation?"

"Twenty million pounds sterling voted by the British Parliament to slave owners in all the British colonies."

There was silence. Maria moved across the hall and sat down, as if she needed quiet, and a place to think. We might not have been there. Her words were hardly for us, but for herself. "Twenty million pounds. —to be shared among all of us. It is nothing! It is nothing when it means the end of a way of life. We cannot work the cane fields and pay for the labor—sugar and rum do not bring that sort of money any more." She continued, softly, as if musing. "These islands . . . what is to become of them? Every plantation will end like San Francisco. Can you imagine us selling to get money to pay labor? . . . and who will there be to sell to? To *that* lot of savages out there? No white man in his right mind will buy land now. Twenty million parceled out among so many . . . so little . . . so little. *They* will not work without the lash. They will work only to eat—a mango tree, a banana tree, a hen or two to scratch the ground. The bush will take back the cane fields. All our work here will disappear, and sugar mills rot and fall apart. Oh, I know them—they will lie under the trees all day, and make sport of their former masters. And no slave will work with another for their common good. A long night is coming now on these islands. They will fall into a sleep, and the world will forget about them . . ."

Her tone quickened, and she turned on Alister. "*That* is what your Wilberforce and his like have brought upon us. *All* now will be poor, not just the slaves. That is what they think to pay off with their wretched twenty million pounds. I will make you a prediction. Twenty years from now not a greathouse on this island will still be tenanted, except by the remnants of a family who can find no other place to go—as it was at San Francisco. Who simply wait for the next hurricane to take the roof, and hope for, or expect, nothing else."

She clenched and unclenched her hands on the arms of the chair, her features suddenly bearing a strong resemblance to her sisters', all at once a dark, brooding Spanish face, proud, vengeful, pessimistic. And yet it seemed to me she spoke the truth. I too was going to pay the price of the liberation of those whose lot I had sighed over; I was going to pay with more than words. I wondered if Fergus and I would be among those who waited in a plantation greathouse with no hope, and nothing to expect except the inevitable coming of the next hurricane. Would we stand, he and I, and our children, and watch the cane fields go back to brush and spindly second-growth trees. But we would stay—I had no doubt of it. I had come late to the islands, and now their economic flowering was over. But I had found Fergus and my life, and I would never have to go to sleep at night with the weight of owning another human being upon my soul. In a sense it was a relief. The worst they had expected had happened, and there would be no more time spent uselessly fearing it. It was now my task to make good to Fergus, to make him believe what the Scots, driven from their lands, believed—that he who had land, any land, to cultivate and make fruitful, no matter how poor, was still a king. If poverty was our future, then I would make it a proud one for him and our children. It was a task my father would not have thought an unworthy one.

We all were silent for a time, thinking our separate thoughts. In the last days we had lived through momentous events—almost too much now for my crowded and weary mind to recall. Death and destruction had touched us harshly, and humans had pitted themselves, one against the one, in ugly and mortal struggle. But this new happening was far beyond all these smaller events. It was the end of a way of life, the closing of an era that had lasted more than three hundred years. The long twilight since the prohibition of the slave trade from Africa had finally ended in the night.

"They knew before we did," Alister said. "That was the message of the drums and the bells, but it had reached them here even before that. They would not tell us . . ."

I had gone back to the dining room and refilled the man's glass, and brought a plate of bread and cheese. He came to eat it at the hall table with murmured words of thanks, and bolted it as if he had not eaten in many hours. I remembered him then, prompted by the name of Rodriguiz. He was a clerk in the shop, and, I believed, the man whom I had seen riding back from Landfall the day that the message had been wrongly delivered into my hands. I understood then some of the important and influential people with whom Maria had joined in her slaving activities. No wonder she, and Andrew himself, had known that no one would come forward to accuse her. I began to think that the Rodriguiz emporium was the convenient center for all their activities. And believing there still were captive slaves at San Francisco, Rodriguiz had sent one of his badly needed help to this far end of the island to warn her.

"They think they are *all* free," Maria said. "That is why they all deserted, and will obey no order . . ."

"God defend us," Joanna wailed. "What will we do? . . . what is to become of us?"

Luiz crammed the last of the bread into his mouth, and spoke urgently to Maria. "Señora—could I have a private word with you. From Señor Rodriguiz . . ."

"We don't have to be private any more, Luiz. *They* know," she said, jerking her head toward Alister and myself. "And in any case, there is nothing to be done—no precautions to be taken. My slave, Samuel—you remember, the big one—released them all before the storm. They are loose—and now think they are free! They have already murdered Donna Isabella."

"Mother of God!" Luiz crossed himself. "Two deaths, and now this! I bring bad news upon bad news."

Maria waved aside his concern. "Have you a gun?"

"A pistol."

"Then you will stay here tonight. A second man will be a help."

He shook his head. "That I cannot do, señora. Señor Rodriguiz has sent me at considerable cost to himself. There is much talk of a slave revolt in the town, and he has to guard both the shop and the warehouses. We are very thinly spread. His instructions to me were to return immediately I have given you the news and urged . . ." His voice trailed off; he did not want to admit before Alister his knowledge of the slaves who were hidden at San Francisco. "But would it not be wiser if all of you here came into Santa Marta. Those out there"—he jerked his head in the direction of the slave quarters—"could prove more than one single man and a household of women could manage. That is what you should do, señora. We should all go back to Santa Marta together."

"When I need advice, I will ask you for it," Maria said coldly, putting him back in his place. "Do you think for a moment that I would leave Landfall to the hands of those savages? Tell Señor Rodriguiz I am indebted—and that we have not faint hearts here at Landfall."

Little whimpering sounds came from Joanna. "Please, sister—would that not be the better plan? There would be more security in Santa Marta."

"If you think so—go then! You will be one less we shall have to worry about. Go out to the stables now and saddle up, and try the ride through the darkness with Luiz—he will protect you, I'm sure, past all those plantations where the bonfires burn, and the bells ring, and they beat the drums."

Joanna shrank back. "I would not dare go to the stables the way the slaves are now. Alister . . ."

"I would not risk Alister, my sister, to save your skin. He is the only man we have, and a good shot. So long as they know he is here they will keep their distance."

Joanna lowered her head, and said nothing more. Luiz took a final look around, and then bowed to Maria. "I go now, señora, and I wish you well. Señor Rodriguiz will send news again when it is possible."

Before he slipped around the half-closed shutter I plucked at his arm. "You know Winterslo?"

He nodded, impatient to be off. "I know it. Where Fergus Maxwell is."

"Go there," I said. "Please! Just give him the news you have given us. He will make ready to defend himself if he has to."

"Señorita, I cannot. There is no time."

"Please—please! It is not out of your way. Just the distance of the avenue off the road back to Santa Marta. Please—not five minutes of your time. Just to warn him."

"Much more than five minutes, since I will have to leave my horse and go up the avenue by foot if I am not to let every slave on the place know I have come. It is too much . . ." Then he shrugged. "Well, since you ask it, señorita." Then, unexpectedly, he added. "I like Fergus Maxwell. He and I once had a good fight, and neither could down the other. We made it up by getting drunk together. Yes, it was a good fight. I'll go. Good-night."

*   *   *   *   *

Luiz had been gone for more than an hour, and I had put Duncan to bed, and seen him asleep before the pounding began on the shutters that guarded the main hall door.

"Pay no attention," Maria commanded, "and they will soon tire of it. They are drunk and crazy."

But the pounding went on, and faintly, through the din from the slave quarters, I heard Fergus's voice.

"Quickly, open up," I said to Alister. "It's Fergus."

But when he squeezed through the half-opened door, he carried the blood-soaked body of Luiz in his arms. A scream, quickly stifled by her sister, came from Joanna. My hand, holding the candle, trembled violently, so that the shadows rocked across the shocking sight of the two men, one covered with the blood of the other.

"He's still alive," Fergus said. Alister had slammed the door and was bolting it into place. "I found him on the road between here and Landfall."

Maria quickly explained his visit, and the news he had brought, as Fergus carried him through and laid him, without thought, on the red sofa that had been Andrew's. "His horse was gone," Fergus said. "And there was no pistol. I suppose they thought him dead. He was thrown among the cane, but he moaned, and I heard him . . ." A lantern, held close to him, revealed a machete wound cut deep into his shoulder. A few inches higher, and his neck would have taken the blow. He bled terribly.

Maria sped to her store room and was back with a box of medicaments and bandages, strips of linen torn and rolled ready for such emergencies. I brought what was left of the hot water from the pantry —with the shutters closed, the kitchen and its fires were once more barred to us. "I heard about it," Fergus answered. "My slaves tell me more than yours do, Maria. I didn't know whether to believe it or not, but when I heard the drums and the bells . . . well, I thought you might need help. My lot are chanting around the fire, but I had a feeling that the ones Samuel let loose from San Francisco would follow him here." As he talked he bathed the wound, and started to bind it up. "If he lies quiet it may stop bleeding. If the bleeding continues he will die before the night's out."

It was said with a certain matter-of-factness. We were all growing calloused by the events of these last days, and the weariness was almost more than one could bear. And yet we faced another night of sitting and waiting, of listening. Another night to be afraid to sleep. Another man was dying—might die, on that red sofa.

Fergus straightened and stretched his limbs, cramped from carrying the weight of Luiz. "I slipped the saddle off my horse out there, and sent him home. I hope he runs down any of those black devils who come near him." And then, "Alister, I'll borrow a shirt from you."

Alister gave a weary smile of acknowledgment. "You forget—I'm already wearing *your* shirt. I took one or two of Andrew's into my room— they'll fit you like a nightshirt, but at least they're clean." While he spoke his eyes kept moving from one end of the room to the other. He crossed now into the dining room to check there.

"Fiona will show you where," he called back.

I waited there in the room with Fergus while he stripped off the blood-soaked rag and used the water in Alister's jug to wash. In the flickering glow of the candlelight I watched with fascination the ripple of the muscles in that broad, lean back; and yet I saw that his movements were slow, and strangely clumsy. I thought we all must be slower and less nimble than two days ago, fighting the desire to close eyelids on stinging eyes, the desire just to lie and be still. But outside they were not still; they leaped high before the flames, and shouted their songs of victory, songs almost forgotten, so seldom had they been heard in the lifetimes of any of these who now seemed to learn them anew as they chanted them over and over.

Fergus came to me, and his embrace had the feeling of desperation in it, as if he must try to shut out the sounds that would destroy our pleasure in each other. For the first time, in the strength of his arms, I sensed the anxiety that his words would not express; in the way he clutched at me, trying to absorb my own body in a single embrace, I knew that he wondered if we would live to finish what we had begun. He put his head down on my shoulder, in the final gesture of a weary man.

"Fiona, love—I need you. My God, how I need you! Will it ever be over, do you think? Fiona, you're wiser than I—and better. Will we ever be alone together again, and quiet, and at peace? Will we ever be able to love each other again?"

"Soon, my love—very soon." But I was not sure. I was frightened, and it sounded like the promise I had made to Duncan that I would be there to take care of him.

We went downstairs, and Fergus set about loading the guns that had been put away after the storm. Then he took his own pistol and rifle, and made his station in the dining room; Alister took his place in the hall. Maria sat with her sister, pistol in hand, near the red sofa with Luiz. To keep himself from falling asleep, Fergus taught me how to load the rifle and the pistol, making me practise the movements again and again. "Don't wait for me to tell you," he said. "You have to do it immediately I pass each one to you." This was another art I had not thought of learning for the years to come, but I supposed it would be part of it, like the baking and the sewing, and the rearing of children.

Along with things like teaching Charity's son to read. I thought it ironic that we might perish on this, the night of freedom, the night when we were no longer the masters of those outside—like the soldier killed at the instant of the cease-fire.

Chapter 9.

It came by the means we had most feared, the one from which we had no protection. Toward dawn, when the need for sleep was almost insupportable, the slaves seemed to grow quieter. "The rum has done its work," Maria said. "They will sleep soon, and the fight will be gone from them."

"I hope you are right," Alister said. But he didn't sound hopeful. "How does it go with Luiz?"

"He is unconscious still. But there does not seem to be fever. And the bleeding has stopped. When it is light—" She stopped and spun around. I had come to the doorway of the dining room to listen to their talk, and now I motioned Fergus to come too.

We all heard it now, a faint sound against the big outer storm shutters of the doors directly behind the staircase. We pressed against the louvers of the inner gallery, trying to interpret the sounds, the width of the gallery and the thickness of two doors separating us from whoever or whatever made the sound. From here it sounded feeble, like nails scratching against the wood in the vain hope of entry.

"Don't be fools! Get back and watch the other places," Fergus called from the hall. "It could be a trick . . ."

We stepped back, but the sounds went on, slow, gentle. We could hear no voices. "It is nothing," Maria decided. "Just one of the women wanting to be let in. She is tired—drunk, probably. Perhaps she has been raped by one of the strange slaves. They always come back to their masters when there is trouble, when things get beyond them . . ."

But she was wrong, and we knew it when the first faint tendrils of smoke curled under the door that we watched, and forced their way through cracks where the louvers did not close tightly. But by this time the smoke must have filled the whole of the inner gallery, because it was coming under all the doors around the whole inside core of the house. Now the sounds became real and identifiable, the ominous crackling of burning wood. Those outside must have built the heart of the fire from the remains of the slave huts, and piled brush on it. The old, well-seasoned wood of the storm shutters, dry now that the rain had not touched them for more than a day, was ripe for burning; patience, and the supply from their own bonfires had kept the brush alight until the shutters themselves caught. From then on, their victory was certain.

"Try not to panic," Fergus said quietly. "They may not mean to kill us. They are probably after more rum—or food. They know they are not owned by us any longer. Perhaps they think they will take everything that is ours. Tomorrow . . ." he added wryly, "Santa Marta will be full of rum-filled blacks trying to sell silverplate."

"We are dead," Joanna sobbed.

"We are if we stay here," Alister said. "We'll have to break out. Leave them the house, if that's what they want."

"No—no, I won't. I won't have them . . ."

"You have no choice, Maria. Don't be foolish. There's no way to fight a fire once it takes hold here—no pumps, no equipment or men to do it. You don't think *they* will help put it out!"

I heard the last as I sped up the stairs to Duncan's room. He wakened slowly, but so used he was by now to the extraordinary events of these days that he didn't question my snatching him from the bed. I thrust him into a chair, and began lacing on his boots, remembering, even in my panic, that we probably would have to run through brush, and barefooted, he would be a handicap. He was querulous as he came out of sleep. "I don't want to go—I *won't* go in my nightshirt." His outraged masculinity was another prod to my imagination; I thought of him hampered, as we women were, by skirts, and I caught up breeches and a shirt as I dragged him from the room. I half-lifted him down the stairs, fearing the nightshirt would trip him. "Now do whatever you're told, Duncan. I'll take care of you."

Alister had hammered the iron bar off the main door, the one directly opposite the staircase. Maria stood by him with a pistol ready, and a gun on the floor beside her. Katarina and Joanna crowded about them. As Duncan and I descended into the acrid pall of the smoke he began to choke.

"Are you ready, Fergus?" Alister shouted.

In answer, Fergus appeared from the salon with Luiz in his arms, his pistol thrust in his belt. Luiz's head hung limply. They joined the group by the door. Alister glanced over us all, his arm poised to pull back the shutter. "Stay together," he said. "It's the best chance we have. Remember the fallen tree is only feet from the bottom of the steps, and don't blunder into it. We can't go too far until it gets lighter. We'll never get to Winterslo in the darkness, and you can't waste shot firing at shadows. Remember"—this was mainly addressed to Joanna to calm her—"they may not hinder us at all. They may only want what's in the house."

Maria leaned toward her sister, brandishing the butt of the pistol. "And if you scream, I'll break your jaw with this."

We extinguished the last candle, and Alister eased open the door. We moved out, going cautiously, slowly, because of Fergus carrying Luiz. We felt the scrape of the branches of the cottonwood at the bottom of the steps, but there was no sound, no flash of a machete to challenge us. We eased our way gently through the tangle of brush left after the storm, going deeper and deeper into the shadow; the way was painful and slow. Luiz came briefly to consciousness and moaned. But the sound didn't matter, because the crackle of the flames was beginning to drown all else.

When we were a distance from the house, Fergus had to lay down his burden to rest; we turned back to look.

It was a fearful sight. We had heard the terrible crash of the storm shutter going down, and had known that with it, the slaves would be swarming within the house. But none of us, least of all they, had anticipated the spread of the fire. Firing the storm shutter had ignited the floor beams of the upper gallery, and the flames were already running through, on those dry, seasoned timbers, to the bedrooms and the staircase hall. They ran like liquid along to the beams. As we stared, every window and doorframe at the back of the house caught; the night sky was brilliant with the glow, the whole dark frame of the house silhouetted before us. Frustrated by the heat and flames at the back, the slaves had run to the front, the more daring among them dashing through the one open door we had left, and on into the dining room and salon to snatch what they could—silver, glass, pictures they fancied were framed in gold. But they were quickly driven back by the heat and smoke, and the loot was small. What none of us had reckoned on was the draft created by that single open door at the front of the house acting like a chimney, and pulling the flames forward inexorably to engulf the whole structure.

"It's gone," Fergus said. "There's no saving anything. We'd best try to move on farther while they're still enjoying their show." He bent again to pick up Luiz.

Alister's voice came from the darkness. "Right then—let's go."

"I can't!" A wail from Duncan. I looked down at him. "I'm getting into my breeches." In those few seconds, while Duncan and I struggled with unseen buttons, and tried to tuck in the nightshirt, Alister had time to check the pale light reflected from the faces about him.

"Maria!—where's Maria?"

"Ma—Maria . . . ?" Joanna stuttered. "I don't know. I thought she was going ahead with you. When we came to the bottom of the steps and past the tree she suddenly put this thing in my hand. I don't know how to use it." She waved the rifle Maria had carried wildly, and Alister slapped down her arm smartly, and pushed on the safety catch. "After all—she *told* me to be quiet."

"God in heaven—where is she?"

Katarina's voice might have been Maria's, so deadly cool it was. "Did anyone see her bring the jewels with her?"

There was no answer from any of us. Katarina continued. "Then you can assume that she went back for them. It was unlike her to forget about them even when the fire first began. But they never would leave her mind completely—never. Like the slaves she thought she could race the fire."

A race it was; the fire now had turned the corners of both the upper and lower galleries; through the cracks in the shutters we could see the lower rooms illuminated, as if by some gigantic candle. "She couldn't have gone back! She *couldn't* have been so mad!"

"She could—she *is!*"

We could all see her now, the slight figure on the front upper gallery, long skirt fanned by the draft of the flames. From one hand dangled a small bundle—the white cloth that had wrapped the jewels, tied and knotted to hold them. With the one hand she gripped one of the great brick pillars. She did not look outward, toward us, and a possible salvation, but down, at the slaves who swarmed and ran below her in a frenzy of excitement and hostility. Once she looked backward, and we knew the danger was equal—try the burning staircase, or jump. In either case, in the end she would face the knives and machetes below.

It was Duncan who broke the spell of inaction upon us. "Mama!" The hold she possessed on him was strong; his short lifetime had belonged only to her. He feared her danger; he feared her loss. He had lost Andrew, and he could not bear the thought of his entire world being taken in one stroke. He broke from my hands in a sudden start of terror, racing, mad, hysterical, back toward the burning house and the mob before it. "Mama!"

It was as if, in all the roar of the flames about her, she heard the cry, because she turned toward us. At that instant, the dark figure appeared on the gallery behind her, naked, shiny with sweat, one of the slaves newly shipped from Africa, crazed with rum, hunger, and the desire for revenge on these white tormentors.

As Duncan had started to run, Fergus dropped Luiz once more and plunged through the tangle of brush after him. Without thinking, without pause, I followed him.

I stumbled many times on that run, crashing into fallen trees and debris because my eyes were dragged ever upward to the scene on the gallery. Maria had backed away from the terrible figure, her hands and bundle held behind her as if to shield it. Before he reached her, though, she retreated to the doorway of the smoke-filled room from which she had come, and tossed the bundle inside. Then she braced herself against the doorway in some mad attempt to stop his entrance. But he had no interest in whatever the small insignificant bundle contained. Now beside her, he towered over her—a black giant. First he pulled her back to the railing so that no one should miss the sight. Then, in a single wrenching movement he took the neck of her gown and ripped it between his hands—bodice, petticoat, stays—almost the whole length of the gown gave before the strength of those manic hands. Then, with her arms held tightly behind her back he turned and exposed her to the eyes of the crowd below. Howls of derision and triumph greeted the sight of her gleaming white nakedness.

Then I dragged my eyes down. I had reached the edge of the crowd that milled before the house. The Landfall slaves were there, as well as the naked black captives of San Francisco. I could hear Fergus's voice— he had thrust his way through. Duncan seemed to have vanished into the maelstrom of jostling, swirling, jumping bodies. And then I saw him coming toward me, held high over the heads of the crowd, borne, not in Fergus's arms, but Samuel's. The Landfall slaves were nearest me, and they did not menace—they parted as if to give Samuel passage with his young, screaming, kicking burden. He was almost through the central mob of the African slaves when the blow—a knife, a machete, I never saw which—hit him. But he kept on coming, propelled by a great momentum, toward me. At the edge of the crowd, where the Landfall slaves hung back, he set Duncan, with infinite gentleness, on his feet. Then Samuel crumpled slowly to the ground. Duncan, seeing me, ran to me, his nightshirt trailing from his breeches. I received him then into my arms, as I had known I would. I squatted down and held his face against my breast, the halo of sweat-damp curls outlined like a young angel's against the fierce glow of the fire. With his head pressed there hard against my breast, my other arm holding him with cruel tightness so that he could not turn, I looked up and saw the part of the vision that had been denied me. As always, the sight had been incomplete.

Fergus was gone, past and through the slaves.

"Oh God—please! No—no. Fergus . . . !" I heard my own cry, but I could not stop looking. Fergus had vanished into the house, and the fire now had reached the front of the building, the beams beneath the feet of Maria and the slave were ignited, and every door and window frame behind them. The giant black figure now lifted her in his arms, and tossed her like a baby, up and down, a plaything. Nothing was visible of his features but the broad white line of his teeth as he laughed. I could not hear Maria scream, the roar of the flames was now too loud. But I saw her mouth working, the contorted agony of her face, a woman in mortal fear. In another moment, I knew, the slave would throw her down among the crowd below.

But in another moment the black shining form had toppled, and Maria fell from his arms. Through the smoke I could only dimly see Fergus; he had taken the risk of hitting Maria as well as the slave with the single shot he could fire. The risk had been small; she would have been just as dead down there among the machetes.

I saw him scoop her up, and run back through the blazing doorframe of her bedroom. That was the last sight I ever had of him, cradling Maria's limp form in his arms. A moment later came the terrible sound that tore into my being like a knife as the staircase came crashing down.

The first flames started up through the roof.

* * * * *

I knelt there, Duncan still clutched to me, and I saw it as it would be when there was no more of Landfall that fire could consume. I saw it as it would be in the future; as it had been in the past—blackened walls and chimneys skeletal to the hard blue sky, to the morning radiance, to the evening glow. I saw it as it must have been when Andrew Maxwell had first looked upon it and coveted it.

The slaves knew our presence there, but none came near us. Perhaps fear of Alister's gun kept them away; perhaps the Landfall slaves now knew the enormity of what had happened and contained the Africans. But I thought that the fire and deaths they had witnessed had been the catharsis they had sought. The first light of dawn brought the sobering memory of the white man's justice that still ruled the island, even though the black man was free.

Alister came and touched my shoulder. "Come, Fiona."

He shouldered Fergus's burden of Luiz, and we began the trek to Winterslo. No one spoke on that long march in the growing light, no one, except Katarina. "He was a fool to have entered the house. No man could have saved her."

I did not dispute it; it was perhaps something Fergus had had to do, compelled, as I had been, by an extraordinary force beyond reason. I would not try to reason it; but I could not yet accept its fact. I was dumb, not able to speak, even if there had been anything to say. I clung to Duncan, and he to me; neither was there a sound from him. We sought comfort in the touch of each other's bodies, like animals. That was all we could do.

II

By sunset two more graves had been opened at the grove of mampoos at Winterslo; Alister had brought back from Landfall two more rough boxes with the bones of Fergus and Maria. Several heavy showers during the day had cooled the still smoking ruins. He had taken the Winterslo slaves with him for the task, but those at Landfall, subdued now, hungry, bewildered by the sudden lack of authority to impose a regime and provide food, had come willingly to help with the search. The bodies—what remained of them—were in the cellars, among the charred remnants of the heaviest beams, all that had survived the fire.

For decency's sake, and to spare my suffering, I thought, Alister had provided two boxes. But for all I knew the bones of both, indistinguishable, lay in one coffin, locked in that eternal last embrace.

The light was almost gone as Alister once more recited the burial service, this time from memory—those parts of it he could remember, since a search of Winterslo had turned up no Bible or Book of Common Prayer. The lanterns were lighted before we finished. "Dust to dust, ashes . . ." The numbness still possessed me; I seemed to feel nothing. I could not weep. The only sensation I seemed fully to experience was a deep resentment that it was Maria who lay there now with Fergus. I had thought to lay my own bones there, and to possess him forever. But he was lost to me. Somehow, in the end, she had won.

We did not try to sing a hymn, nor do anything but what was barely necessary; I think all of our hearts were as dry as the bones laid there. But the slaves took up a dirge of their own as we walked back up the slope to the house. Alister, I knew, would see to it that the graves were marked in granite—he would put on the names but no one but he would know what lay in each box. Very soon the vines that twisted from tree to tree would cover that raw earth. Perhaps I was the only living creature who would hold Fergus in my heart forever. This place would live so long as I remembered it. Even for Duncan, his hand clamped wetly in mine now, the memory would grow dim. Only I would live in it as if my life had stuck fast at this spot.

*　*　*　*　*

A meal was made; we sat down at the table. I suppose we ate, but I remember none of it. Fergus's two house slaves hurried about, making up beds with patched mildewed sheets. Alister distributed some of Fergus's stores to the Landfall slaves so that they might eat. There was a sense of unreality about our movements. We did what we had to do now, but no one seemed to have any idea of how life would carry on tomorrow or the day after. No one knew how the devastated cane fields would be restored or replanted; no one knew of a way to pay the former slaves for work they had done in exchange for food. No one knew, since there was no harvest, how there would be any money to pay. The Landfall slaves seemed reluctant to go back to the plantation now that no white man was there to tell them what to do; a slow realization seemed to be breaking upon them that the freedom suddenly conferred might be the freedom to starve. I thought that in time they would come out of their trance, and some would begin to plant their gardens again, and rethatch their huts. Others would wait for a while, waiting to share what they thought was the white man's wealth; and when it did not come, they would drift toward Santa Marta, and make a living from the streets of the town in any way they could. They would become the crowd on the street corner of any town I had ever known.

It was during the meal that the future of Katarina and Joanna was decided.

Alister suddenly said, speaking only to Katarina, recognizing that it was she who would make the decisions for both. "Have you plans—for the future?"

She shrugged, the gesture one of anger at the futility of the question. "What plans could we have? We have no money. We will have to return to San Francisco and do what we can to keep body and soul together. I suppose we are no less stupid than the slaves—we can make a few things grow. But we will have to become tillers of our own soil." She laughed harshly. The Medinas have come a long way since Queen Isabella's land grant of half the island of San Cristóbal."

"Oh, sister, do not—" Joanna wailed.

"I will buy San Francisco," Alister said flatly.

There was a long silence. "Why?" Katarina asked finally, deep suspicion in her tone. "Why would you do that?"

Alister shrugged. "Perhaps I feel a responsibility to Maria's sisters—to Duncan's aunts."

"You carry family feeling far, my friend."

He glanced over at me. "The Scots always do."

"If so," Katarina said crisply, "it is one of the few things about the Scots the Spanish would understand. But this is not the answer for us. You will give us a certain sum, and within a certain number of years we will have exhausted it. What are we to do then? Beg on the streets of Santa Marta? Poverty coupled with pride demands obscurity, señor."

"You haven't heard my offer," he answered dryly. "Perhaps pride is another thing the Scots and the Spanish have in common. I would make you an outright bid—generous in the circumstances. Part of it, I suggest, would go to the purchase of a small house in Santa Marta—they will be going cheaply now, I would wager, since there will be an exodus of merchants from the British islands. The remainder I would invest for you in London. As part of the purchase agreement you and your sister would receive an annual income from that investment—enough, I estimate, to allow you modest comfort—a servant or two.

They also would be cheap once the former slaves learn that it takes money to buy bread."

"Ah . . ." Joanna gave a long sigh. "To live in Santa Marta! To hear Mass every day, sister—to entertain old friends occasionally, to pay visits. Could it be . . . ?" She looked longingly at Katarina.

"You will have the initial payment, and the agreement for an annual income before you part with the deeds of San Francisco. I will not repeat the offer. It is accepted now, or it is rejected."

Katarina's harsh laugh again. "What choice is there? As little as before. One has to trust you, and hope the trust lies more worthily than with Maria. It is accepted."

"Ah . . ." Again a long sigh from Joanna, as if a promise of a kind of earthly bliss had been held before her. Fergus's house possessed no such refinements as table napkins; she brushed tears from beneath her eyes with her fingers.

"And then," Katarina said, "there are the jewels. You must begin at once to recover the jewels. They are rightfully ours."

Alister sighed. "For that, you must have patience. They lie somewhere in the ashes of Landfall, and it will be a long time before labor can be spared to make a search. If any of the slaves know of them, you may be sure many will not be recovered at once. But they cannot eat diamonds. For a while they will bury them, and then they will take them to Santa Marta to try to sell them. Piece by piece, they may come to light, but only if the buyer is honest. I will leave instructions. I will tell the authorities. Every possible source will be informed. But always remember that Duncan is the only child of Andrew and Maria Maxwell, and their sole heir. You may make your claims before the courts, and no doubt justice will be done. But justice will also demand that the reason for your claim to share in any jewels recovered will also require that the source be revealed. You have abetted illegal slave-trading . . ."

Katarina put down her knife and rose from the table. "You are clever, señor. Yes, we will make our claims. That is the least we will do. Come, Joanna . . ."

Her sister followed limply, in mute protest against leaving the first real food she had eaten in more than a day. She trailed up the stairs after Katarina, murmuring complaints about the roof having leaked severely during the hurricane, and no doubt their beds were still damp.

Neither had inquired as to Duncan's future.

* * * * *

Charity helped me wash and put Duncan to bed; she had simply stayed on in the house at Winterslo as a matter of course. I had had the cot he would sleep on put in my own room, and now he wore one of Fergus's shirts as a nightshirt, the sleeves rolled many times. He was silent, and very tired, his face pale. He asked no questions of me, as if he dreaded answers. It almost seemed that, like myself, he wanted no part of tomorrow. As she helped with the preparations for bed, Charity's eyes pleaded mutely with me to tell her what was going to happen, what was to become of us all, but I had no answer, no more than anyone did.

I sat with Duncan, holding his hand, until he slept, and then Charity whispered to me that she would stay until I came back upstairs, lest he woke again, and was frightened. "Father and mother both he has lost—and yet he does not weep. It is not right."

"The weeping will come," I said. "It is too much. Children are wiser than we know, and will not believe more than they can bear." It was so with me. My mind still struggled against acceptance of what my heart would not bear.

"Go down, mistress, and walk, and take some air. And perhaps tears will come for you. I know. I bury a man also this day."

I went down slowly, wondering if I could walk myself to tiredness beyond this numbness I already felt, and perhaps, finally, to sleep. But the face of Duncan haunted me. It was one thing to grieve for that which was dead, and would never be mine, but now I must take up the burden of a living promise. I had told Duncan I would take care of him. Somehow the promise had to be kept. I had very little idea of how it was to be done. But an image of Silkirk was beginning to reappear, the memory of my father's kindness, his solicitude for children. Poor man, I would load him heavily, and he would take it up with a certain joy. Perhaps there would be two Duncans growing up at Silkirk. My father would take both to his heart, and somehow, in whatever way, I must earn enough to make it possible.

A single lamp now burned in the main room. The table was cleared, but the chairs were left just as we had pushed them back, and the crumbs remained; during the night cockroaches would scurry over them. I knew all these things now about the tropics. And yet beyond the doors that led to the gallery the night was beautiful, soft and sweet-scented, a few faint wisps of white cloud moved slowly before the brilliance of the stars. The cicadas sang; the whole earth seemed to hum of its fertility. No breeze stirred, but there was a coolness against hot eyelids and burning eyes. I went to the edge of the gallery, and sat on the steps, and my gaze was drawn instinctively toward the clump of mampoos, outlined darkly against the star-bright sky.

Alister's step was soft as he came to sit beside me. From the back of the house I could hear the voices of the blacks—one could call them slaves no longer. Sometimes a voice was raised in song, as was their habit, but now they had reverted to the songs of the cane fields. There were no more shouts of triumph. They feared now, like all of us, with a different kind of fear, for their future. Freedom was not gold, only the license to earn it.

I said to Alister, "You have been generous to the sisters. It was madness, that offer you made for San Francisco. Anyone can tell it is not worth a life income for those two. No one in his senses will want land here any more."

"Perhaps I am not in my senses, and perhaps my partners will tell me so plainly. In that case, I shall pay out of my own pocket. But I want those two wretched women off my mind. I don't want to wake up and wonder if they are starving. Remember . . . I saw their mother. Let them have their court tussle over the jewels, as they turn up—if they do. It will keep them occupied. It will keep them fighting and hating. Fighting keeps people alive. But I also intend to see Duncan's interests protected."

"But the land? San Francisco—Landfall—Winterslo. What is to become of it?"

"Most of it belongs to Duncan, and I will advise him never to sell. Land will go a-begging here, in a very short time. We will work a crop, if it is economically possible, but that I doubt, without slave labor. But as he grows older, I will advise him never to sell—never! Even if land here is worthless, and someone offers him the price of a good horse, he must never sell."

"Why not?"

He half-turned to me. "Do I have to tell you, a Scot, what land is? It is the only commodity that never devalues over the long term, never wears out, never ages. It may seem worthless, but it is not. It is there, and it stays. The landlords knew it as they spread out and bought from simple farmers the fields that surrounded London and Manchester and Bristol. The great English nobles knew it when they fought one another to the death for it, and some went and dispossessed the Irish for the sake of their bogs . . ."

"But here you said without slave labor the land is virtually worthless. Perhaps the price of a good horse."

"Someday, Fiona—it could be a hundred, two hundred years from now—they will find a crop that needs this sun that I have grown to hate. I haven't a notion what it will be, but these islands will wait. Something will be found that needs this sun—and perhaps machines instead of men. Whatever it is, the land will pay heavily again. So let it sit and wait. There will be more fortunes for the Maxwells from these lands. For Duncan's heirs."

I looked once more toward the mampoo grove, and my heart and eyes and lips were dry.

"And Duncan himself . . . ?"

"He will stay with us, of course."

"Us?"

"With us. With you and me, Fiona. He will come back to England with us. You are going to marry me." It was a statement, not a question.

I jerked upright, and pulled back from him. "You are mad! You are trying to set the whole world in order, and it can't be done. Oh, you are very kind—too kind, but you only hurt us both. I loved Fergus—I loved him with every shred of my being, a love that sometimes seemed unreasonable, but it was there. I still love him. You *know* it. You must not talk this nonsense of marrying me. It mocks me, and what I feel for another man."

"I never meant to mock you—or your love for Fergus. I *know* you love him still, and always will. The lover taken at the moment of love goes on living forever. I know you will never cease to love and remember him. But still, you and I will be married."

"But why? *Why?* Knowing this, why, in God's name!"

"If I ask you, isn't that enough?"

"No!" I cried. "No—it isn't enough! You pity me. You feel responsible for me, the way you do for those two greedy, pitiful wretches upstairs. You solved the problem of what to do about them. Is this your way of taking care of *me?* Spare me that! Spare yourself! Pity can go too far. Beware of its tyranny, Alister."

"Not pity, Fiona—envy!"

"You *are* mad! No one can have envied me in all my life. What do I have?—what can I give?"

"I envied what another man had won. But I can't tell you that now. You have too lately listened to his words of love. You buried him today. What can I say in face of that? I would wound and hurt you beyond forgiving. I only ask for time—but time in marriage."

"It can never be," I said, as harshly as Maria ever could. "I thank you

—and you do me great honor. But I have to tell you that Fergus and I were lovers—once. Just once. There never was a second time. Never a second chance. But I also have to tell you that we would have continued to be lovers until the marriage was performed, and forever after that. Now, can you say you still want me? You would shame yourself."

"I knew that—of course I knew it."

"You *knew* it?"

"Oh, Fiona . . . Fiona! Do you think me quite blind? Do you forget I saw you that morning as you came back from the cove with Fergus? Until that moment I never saw a woman clothed in glory. You wore love with a radiance I had never imagined could exist. It was then I envied Fergus with all my soul."

"Envied . . . ?"

"It's very simple, isn't it? And not at all extraordinary. I *wanted* you. Until that moment I didn't know the fullness of what I couldn't have, of what I'd let go unnoticed in my own heart. I don't know that I could have won you from Fergus before that, but I didn't even try, did I? Then it was too late. Fergus possessed you, body and soul, and I was closed out. Why do you think I left Landfall that same day?—why I wrote you that pompous note that said nothing. There was no particular urgency about my return to England. I just couldn't stay within the sight of you and Fergus."

"But you—Alister—there must have been many women who would gladly have married *you*. Women with names and fortunes—with beauty. You haven't waited all this time for someone like me."

"Not someone like you—for you. Fergus waited, didn't he? Fergus gave up what Maria blatantly offered—for you. And as for what I have to offer . . . I offer nothing but the kind of life I once told you I am going to try for. It won't be an easy life, though you'll have physical comforts. You will have to make friends with people you would rather not be friends with, so that others can be helped. People with influence in the right places. You will have to curb pride, and temper and independence. I will demand loyalty to my causes—absolute and uncompromising loyalty, no matter if you think they are sheer madness, and hopeless. I don't have to ask for fidelity. I *know* you. You were born with courage and fidelity in your soul. If I am patient, if I wait, perhaps once again I will see that radiance. If not . . ." He shrugged. "If not, I still will have the woman I have wanted most."

"It cannot be," I said slowly. "Even on these conditions, as incredibly generous as they are, it cannot be. You would be cheated." I looked at him fully. In the brightness of the night I could see his features very clearly, strained, weary, hollow-cheeked. I wondered if the events of these days, the lack of sleep, had not unhinged him a little so that he talked the kind of madness I had accused him of. Was he also sucked dry, as I was, and could only cling to that which was familiar, not daring to envisage the future? But no, he had the future very clear, as he always had had. He had already pointed the way—hard work, effort, endless speaking, traveling, talking, persuading. He knew what he was about. His direction and purpose had not changed in the slightest degree. He knew what I was about, too. He had seen Fergus and me together, and he knew, as fully as any man could have done.

"It cannot be," I said again. "Do you realize—have you thought, Alister—that it is possible—it is just barely possible that already I am carrying Fergus's child?"

"I have thought of it," he replied. "I have thought of it all—everything that it implies. If I waited to find out if that possibility were a fact, any offer I made then would be false, bogus. Good God, woman!—what you did, you did in good faith! Will I condemn you for that? It isn't untouched, untroubled virtue I want! It is *you!* You *are* virtue, whether you have loved out of wedlock or not. Don't you understand that?"

"You would be willing . . . ?" I said, incredulous.

"Of course I am willing. We will be married tomorrow in Santa Marta. It can be arranged. And you will suffer and indulge me for a while until the grief slackens its bonds a little. You will grow used to accepting me, because you have the courage to do it. So that if there is a child, by the time he is born in England, neither of us will know if he is my child or Fergus's."

"That is—that was how it was with Duncan," I said. "No one truly knew whose child he was. And it poisoned three lives. They lived in hell, those three."

"It is not the same. I don't try to steal you from another man. I can never take you from Fergus. You do not come to me from greed, but because I need and want you. Leave it to me, Fiona. Trust me. Leave it to me, and let peace come into your soul. Grieve for him, and never try to hide it from me. We need never suffer dishonesty between each other. We are gone long past that. I can offer you protection, love, honor . . . a place for your children in my heart, and for Duncan, whom you love. I've gambled many times in my life. This will not be the last gamble, but it is the greatest. If I bring it off, it will be the greatest prize."

"I am no prize. I never have been." But I leaned against him, and he pulled my head toward his shoulder, his hand stroking my hair. The grove of mampoos was very still in the night air, against the radiant sky.

"Weep, my love," he said. "Weep."

I did, and it was the beginning of healing.